"Abbi Waxman is both irreverent and thoughtful."

—Emily Giffin, #1 *New York Times* bestselling author of *Meant to Be*

"Move over on the settee, Jane Austen. You've met your modern-day match in Abbi Waxman. Bitingly funny, relatable, and intelligent, *The Bookish Life of Nina Hill* is a must for anyone who loves to read."

—Kristan Higgins, *New York Times* bestselling author of
A Little Ray of Sunshine

"Meet our bookish millennial heroine—a modern-day Elizabeth Bennet, if you will. . . . Waxman's wit and wry humor stand out."   —*The Washington Post*

"Abbi Waxman offers up a quirky, eccentric romance that will charm any bookworm."   —*Entertainment Weekly*

"It's a shame *The Bookish Life of Nina Hill* only lasts 350 pages, because I wanted to be friends with Nina for far longer."

—Refinery29

"[Waxman is] known for her charming and comical novels, [and her] latest book stirs up all of the signature smiles and laughs."   —*Woman's World*

"Brilliant. Simply brilliant."

—Karen White, *New York Times* bestselling author of the
Royal Street series

"Meet your new favorite wry writer."   —The Daily Beast

"Waxman's skill at characterization . . . lifts this novel far above being just another 'widow finds love' story. Clearly an observer, Waxman has mastered the fine art of dialogue as well. Characters ring true right down to Lilian's two daughters, who often steal the show."

—*Kirkus Reviews* (starred review)

"Kudos to debut author Waxman for creating an endearing and realistic cast of main and supporting characters (including the children). Her narrative and dialogue are drenched with spring showers of witty and irreverent humor."

—*Library Journal* (starred review)

"This novel is filled with characters you'll love and wish you lived next door to in real life."   —Bustle

"Waxman's voice is witty, emotional, and often profound."

—*InStyle* (UK)

"An aptly and hilariously titled novel. . . . Waxman again delivers with her signature wit and laugh-out-loud writing, offering us authentic characters who feel like people we've met and loved in our own lives—all while offering sly commentary on the roller coaster that is the college application process for parents and their college hopefuls."   —Shondaland

"Abbi Waxman's warm, quippy novels explore familial dynamics with sarcastic wit and plenty of heart. . . . Being a teenager—or parenting one—is tricky territory, but Waxman steers her characters through it with compassion, snappy dialogue, and the right dose of zany humor. Things may (or may not) get easier for the Burnstein women, but the ride, literal and otherwise, is highly enjoyable."   —Shelf Awareness

"Funny and insightful."   —Book Riot

BERKLEY TITLES BY ABBI WAXMAN

The Garden of Small Beginnings
Other People's Houses
The Bookish Life of Nina Hill
I Was Told It Would Get Easier
Adult Assembly Required
Christa Comes Out of Her Shell
One Death at a Time

ONE
DEATH
AT A
TIME

~~~~

Abbi Waxman

Berkley
New York

BERKLEY
An imprint of Penguin Random House LLC
1745 Broadway, New York, NY 10019
penguinrandomhouse.com

Book design by Alison Cnockaert

Library of Congress Cataloging-in-Publication Data

Names: Waxman, Abbi, author.
Title: One death at a time / Abbi Waxman.
Description: First edition. | New York: Berkley, 2025.
Identifiers: LCCN 2024029845 (print) | LCCN 2024029846 (ebook) |
ISBN 9780593816677 (trade paperback) | ISBN 9780593816684 (ebook)
Subjects: LCGFT: Detective and mystery fiction. | Novels.
Classification: LCC PS3623.A8936 O54 2025 (print) |
LCC PS3623.A8936 (ebook) | DDC 813/.6—dc23/eng/20240705
LC record available at https://lccn.loc.gov/2024029845
LC ebook record available at https://lccn.loc.gov/2024029846

First Edition: April 2025

Printed in the United States of America
1st Printing

The authorized representative in the EU for product safety and compliance
is Penguin Random House Ireland, Morrison Chambers, 32 Nassau Street,
Dublin D02 YH68, Ireland, https://eu-contact.penguin.ie.

Gratefully, for Bill, Bob and Lois

ONE
DEATH
AT A
TIME

Prologue

〜〜〜

THE DEAD MAN *was not a good swimmer.*

Julia Mann had been sitting on the beveled pool edge for several minutes, propped on her palms, her legs in the water. She wasn't certain how long she'd been sitting there, but the heels of her hands suddenly started to hurt in the way so many things in her life started to hurt. One minute she couldn't feel them at all and the next they were agonizing. Hands, head, heart . . . all the same. Feel nothing, feel nothing, harpoon through the chest. She felt a giggle pushing through the panic in her throat and fought it back. She lifted her hands and curled them, little pieces of dirt and tile dropping into the water, leaving tiny divots she tried to press out against her thighs. She could smell whiskey, which helped.

Something glinted at the bottom of the pool, and as she jerked forward to look more closely, one hand slipped and she nearly toppled in. The moon's reflection in the pool broke into slices, gurgling slaps and splashes counterpointing the constant hum of the pool filter.

"Whoopsy . . ." she said, realizing the glinting was one of her shoes, the other still on her foot. There was barely anything to

hold it there, just golden straps as thin as cat whiskers in a spray across her instep and a heel not much wider. A sudden impulse, a quick flex, and the second tilted and spiraled its way down to join the first. This time she let the giggle out. One high heel is basically an impediment to walking, anyway. She didn't need it. It was evening; judging by the height of the moon, it was late. She cast a sideways glance across the surface of the pool to where the man bobbed and moved gently. He was nicely dressed, though not for swimming, a dark suit setting off the silver of his hair, his tie hanging straight down as though his head was a long-stemmed tulip. Funny, he'd kept his shoes on, even though he clearly wasn't going anywhere. She looked down at herself. A dress. Dark, like his suit, elegant, like the tulip. Had they been going somewhere together? Well . . . not anymore.

The water was pinker than it had been, diffusion being the abiding principle it is. She flashed on chemistry class, Mr. Libicki so earnest as he dropped a granule of iodine into the water, the snap of someone's bubble gum behind her, the smell of chalk and slowly leaking gas from an ancient Bunsen burner . . . She wondered if Libicki was as dead as the man in the pool. He must be. That class was forty years ago and he'd been older then than she was now.

"And that's pretty fucking old," she said out loud, making a careless hand gesture that knocked what must have been her glass of whiskey into the water. She watched in dismay as the alcohol joined the diffusion party, the tumbler end-over-ending to the bottom of the pool. She felt a little nauseous, suddenly. Dammit. A skittering metallic sound made her jump, and she pulled her feet from the water and tried to sit up. Utter fail. She lay on her back for a moment and waited for her head to stop *spinning. A clear night, the sky black velvet above her, the stars scattered diamonds.*

This whole evening had sucked. It had started badly, to be fair; the middle had been confusing; and the end was plunging swiftly downhill. Luckily, it was blurry as hell and fading fast. She turned her head, trying to recall why the man had gone in the pool in the first place. Why he had even been here. Who he even was.

Big sigh. None of this made sense. Where was her drink? And wait . . . that noise. She rolled onto her hands and knees and levered herself up, telling herself if she started to fall to make sure it was away from the water . . . smart cookie, Julia, always one step ahead.

Reality was trying to tell her something, but she didn't want to hear it. She got to her feet, which was more of a performance than she normally would have tolerated, her skin clammy, her feet slipping on the tile. She looked around and spotted it, because it was an interloper here, no more welcome than a snake. Long, shiny and much better suited to poking through the shutters of a saloon door, maybe, or sitting broken over a cowboy's thigh. A rifle, the wooden butt half over the edge of the pool, the trigger guard what had stopped it from toppling in. She took three unsteady steps toward it, bent, picked it up and threw it away as far and as hard as she could. It spun end over end, just as her shoe had.

She made a satisfied noise, then felt it die in her throat.

That was a mistake. She shouldn't have done that.

She looked again at the man floating in the pool.

Had she done that, too?

Black clouds of confusion swept back across her memory,

and she looked in her empty hand for the drink she swore blind she'd been holding not two seconds ago.

No glass.

No whiskey.

She turned and looked again at the body floating in the water. Maybe he was looking for her drink. He'd been looking for a while.

Then she turned away and started to run.

1

~~~

MASON WATCHED FROM her position on the floor as the facilitator came to her defense.

"I realize you were triggered by Mason's share, Jim, but fire is never the answer," said the woman firmly, moving the large man most of the way across the room simply by wafting him with her clipboard. He would try and stand his ground every few steps, maybe even mount a counteroffensive, but she would double-time her wrist action, and apparently the breeze in his eyelashes was more than he could handle. "We respect your right to self-expression, but not in the medium of flame." She frowned and pointed to a chair in the corner of the room. "Please take a seat until you can compose yourself. I don't want to ask you to leave Group, but I will."

Mason watched Jim carefully until she was sure he wasn't going to come at her again. Then she looked at Sherri, the facilitator, reassured by her still-mellow affect. She trusted Sherri, despite the fact that she was the only nonaddict in this particular room and had her hair in one of those messy buns Mason envied. Admittedly, unlike most "normies," Sherri had seen and heard things that would make a walrus shudder, and

those are some implacable motherfuckers. Running a 12-step
facility is not a job for the fainthearted, and this evening had
tested Sherri's self-possession as well as Mason's instincts for
self-preservation. But Mason went back to stomping out em-
bers, confident Sherri had it under control. The meeting, not
the fire. The fire was her department.

Group had been going relatively normally until Jim had
pulled out his lighter and set fire to a handful of helpful (and
flammable) pamphlets, and several group participants had
had to stamp them out. Mason had been the first and the only
one with really appropriate footwear. But to Sherri's experienced eye, this was just a minor conflagration and no one's
worst Thursday night by a long shot. Still, manners matter, so
Sherri added, "And you owe Mason an apology."

Mason laughed loudly. "I'm on your tenth step every night
lately, Jim."

The large man narrowed his eyes. "No, Mason, you're not."

"I should be," she replied, reaching to take a roll of paper
towels from a guy who'd returned from the janitor's closet with
a broom and a glittering, rustling string of black trash bags.
"Thanks, Dave." Dave nodded but said nothing. He was a man
of deep thoughts but few words.

"Well, you're not," Jim said again, truculently. For a sober
person, someone in recovery, a tenth step is a daily list of
things that might have been better left unsaid, things better
left undone, and things you might want to say sorry for. Jim
wasn't a big apologizer, and his daily inventory was usually
just a list of people he wanted to punch in the ear. He'd been
lying: Mason made that list almost every day.

Natasha Mason was an unusually pretty woman of twenty-
five with extremely short hair and striking features that might

have been overwhelming had they been paired with a more elaborate hairstyle. It wasn't her looks that rubbed Jim the wrong way; it was every other thing about her. He narrowed his eyes and watched her squat down with a wad of paper towels in each hand, circle-wiping the burnt paper mess into a pile, then scoop-lifting it into the trash bag the other guy was holding open. As she got low to the ground, several people averted their gaze from the lower back tattoo her position revealed, while others fell silent and stared. Jim couldn't see it from where he was, so he dodged the bullet that was moral judgment. Each to his own.

While this was going on, the door to the room opened and a woman entered and silently absorbed the sight of a small funeral pyre surrounded by chairs. Another woman might have hesitated, maybe turned and walked away, but this woman merely raised an eyebrow and stalked a wide and elegant circle. The little people would do what the little people did, regardless of her input, so she let them get on with it. As long as they stayed at least an arm's length away, she had no fucks to give them.

As she took a seat, Mason turned and looked at her, her own eyebrows drawn in her habitual first expression: *No, thanks.* The newcomer was maybe sixty, possibly a few years in either direction, and exquisitely dressed and coiffed. She was wearing a long, flowing, brightly patterned dress (vintage Ossie Clark) and white boots that laced up the front (vintage Beth Levine), and was carrying a small, square purse (knock-off Gucci Jackie bag bought on Melrose for twenty bucks). Her body balanced on the folding chair as though it were a well-stuffed chaise lounge, her crossed legs scaffolding the fabric of her dress like the model she might once have been. She looked remarkably comfortable, but wore an expression of extreme sufferance. Mason was used to that, though she'd never seen anyone look quite so ornamental and cranky simultaneously. She became aware that the energy in the room had changed, and looked at some of the more familiar faces. They knew this woman, she could tell that much, even though she herself had never seen her before. And not only knew her, but . . . something she couldn't put her finger on. She looked back at the woman, who was now looking at her with an expression that suggested Mason was blocking her view. Of what, Mason wasn't sure; there was nothing to look at now that the fire was out.

Sherri coughed and looked at the clipboard, not that it had anything to offer. "Welcome to Group. I'm Sherri. You are . . . ?"

"Julia," the woman replied, her voice deep and clear and maple syrup smooth. "I have a court card that needs to be signed."

Again, Mason was aware of a change of energy. What. The. Actual. Fuck?

Sherri nodded. "I'll take care of it at the end"—she looked around—"for you and anyone else who needs it." A guy at the other end of the circle sheepishly half raised his hand, and she nodded to let him know she saw him. "Mason, why don't you take your seat now that you've finished saving us all from a fiery death, or at least the inconvenience of having to evacuate the room?" Then she turned back to the older woman, who was carefully looking everywhere but at her. "Julia, why don't you tell us a little about yourself and why you're here?"

Mason sat back down, but in a different chair so she could keep an eye on Jim and on this new woman. She was less certain with every moment that passed that she hadn't seen her before. It was that kind of face. Maybe she'd seen her in meetings; that was a distinct possibility.

"I'd rather not," the older woman replied. "I've been sober before. I know the drill." She waved her court card. "I went out . . . and now I have to come back." Her tone was polite but managed to convey it had a use-by date that was fast approaching. Whoever this woman was, she had the ability to express a lot by saying very little, and Mason studied her, mentally cataloging what she saw. It was traditional not to judge other people in recovery, but it was also human to do it with big fat bells on. Mason was nothing if not human.

Sherri nodded. "Alright," she said affably, turning away. "*Going out*" meant relapse, and relapse was part of being an addict; only a lucky few get sober and stay sober the rest of their lives. Most people struggle hard, going in and out of sobriety with varying degrees of commitment and success. In that way they are no different than people joining gyms in January or starting diets in March—*this time it's going to be different*. Nobody cares. Everyone's trying. And everyone in that room had the one day they were sitting in, and the wise ones were grateful for it.

Sherri had seen it all. She looked at the sheepish guy. "This is also your first time in Group. Would you like to share?"

He blushed, and nodded. "My name is Andrew, I'm an alcoholic, and I'm here because I drove into a house."

A bubble of laughter went around the room, bouncing on nodding heads and smiles of recognition. Andrew looked surprised, but then shrugged. "I wasn't aiming for the house, I was aiming for the carport, but Jim Beam was my copilot and his eye was off by about six feet." He grinned suddenly.

"Luckily, my wife and kids already dumped my sorry ass and moved out, so I just trashed the car, pissed off the cat and woke the neighbors. They called the police." He looked around the circle, seeing no judgment. "They've been waiting for their moment, ever since I peed on their dog by accident." He paused. "I thought it was their doormat." He paused again. "It's not a very bulky dog." Deep breath. "This is day thirty-four for me, and it's sucking pretty hard."

He fell silent, then added, "Thanks for letting me share."

Everyone murmured their thanks, then Sherri looked over at Jim, who'd leaned his head against the wall and closed his eyes. He wasn't fooling anyone.

"Jim, would you like to come back to the circle?"

Jim shook his head without opening his eyes.

"Oh, come on, Jim," said Mason. "Come back to the circle."

Jim pouted. "No cross talk."

She tipped her head, setting one earful of silver earrings dangling. "That wasn't cross talk. Cross talk is commenting on someone else's share, offering unsolicited advice or interrupting." She looked at the leader. "Right, Sherri?"

Sherri nodded. "Yes, and also this is a recovery support group, not specifically a recognized AA or other program meeting, so the rules are a little different." She smiled warmly. "Insofar as there are any rules, rather than just suggestions. This is a safe space, remember." She made an encompassing hand gesture. "We all bring the energy we wish to share and receive."

Jim rolled his eyes and opened his mouth to bitch further, when Julia suddenly spoke.

"Wait, this isn't a regular AA meeting?"

Sherri shook her head. "Yes and no. This is a 12-step recovery meeting, but we have members from many programs." She gestured around at the room itself. "This is a treatment facility, and AA doesn't lend its name to any related outside enterprises; it's one of the traditions."

"Well, fuck," said Julia, getting to her feet. "Then this is a waste of my time; you can't sign my card."

Sherri nodded. "No, it's fine, this meeting was on the list the court gave you, which is how you found us."

Julia started walking. "I found you because you were happening at the right time. There wasn't a lot more detail on the list. Whoever compiled it didn't have a lot of energy to either share or receive." She slowed and looked at Sherri. "So you *can* sign my card?"

Sherri nodded. "Of course. Why don't you sit back down and tell us what happened?"

Julia frowned at her, then around the circle of people, none of whom said anything. She even looked over at Jim, but he was still pretending to be asleep. The smell of burnt paper and coffee still lingered, but when Julia sat down—in a different chair this time—Mason got a hint of Chanel No. 5 and the unmistakable smell of wealth.

"Nothing happened." She shrugged and looked down at her boots, bouncing up and down as she flexed her ankle. She hadn't fully come to rest yet, and Mason, who was close enough to hear the leather squeaking, noticed the moment when she finally got comfortable and settled into a pose she was willing to hold for a while. Mason had more energy than her body could contain and admired anyone who could hold their outsides steady for longer than twenty seconds.

"Yet here you are." Sherri might look like she breathed in rainbows and breathed out unicorns, but she was nobody's fool. "It might have felt like nothing to you, but it was enough of a something to get you into the court system."

"The police made a mistake."

Laughter around the room.

Julia frowned. "No, really. I should have refused the Breathalyzer."

An observer might have thought the wave of shrugs had been choreographed and rehearsed, but they would have been wrong. The crowd had just heard this shit a hundred times before.

Jim chimed in from across the room. "You could've, but California has implied consent, so cops can ask and a refusal looks like shit. Better to blow and take the risk." His tone was weary and experienced, as was he. "Unless of course you know for sure you'll fail . . ." He looked at Julia. "Let me guess: Too drunk to drive, but sober enough to think you could get away with it."

"Now *that's* cross talk," muttered Mason. Jim looked at her and she held up her palms. "Rigorous honesty, baby."

Jim got to his feet. "Don't call me baby." He looked agitated. "Mind your boundaries." He bent two fingers and pointed to his own eyes and then to Mason. "I'm watching you."

Mason mimed a yawn.

Julia held up her hand and spoke loudly. "The machine must have been broken. I blew point three five."

Silence. Respectful silence, because in *this* room, a unique measure of success was how stupid you'd been when you were drinking. Tripped and fell? Pfft, we've all done that. Tripped and fell with a steak in each hand because you broke into the zoo to feed the kitty cat? Props.

The point at which you're legally impaired by alcohol is point oh oh eight. Point three is blackout drunk. Getting behind the wheel of a car with enough alcohol in your system to blow a point three five was stupid to the point of, well, getting behind the wheel of a four-thousand-pound speeding hunk of metal too drunk to remember your own name.

Sherri's tone was as calm as ever. "Yes, well, that explains why you're here."

"He arrested me."

"Again, not shocking."

"I got a little . . . feisty."

The people in the circle shifted again and exchanged glances. This story was shaping up and they were here for it.

Sherri merely smiled and raised her eyebrows encouragingly. Julia hesitated and then clearly reached some kind of decision. Again, this was common. The journey from "nothing to see here" to "complete revelation of private hell" often took less time than it takes to say it. Of course, some visitors to that room never took the first step. Julia had walked in ready to keep it all to herself and now found herself scrambling to get it off her chest.

Julia said, "Yes, so, the officer didn't agree with my assessment of his machine, so when I threw it into oncoming traffic he was disappointed." She paused. "Shortly after that he arrested me." Her hands twitched in her lap. "I did apologize."

"For throwing his Breathalyzer?" Sherri was polite.

"For punching him in the throat."

"Was that before or after the throwing?"

"Uh . . . just after."

Mason snorted, then turned it into a cough. Julia glanced

over at her, eyeing the younger woman like an executioner estimating weight and drop height. Mason grinned at her, shameless.

Sherri asked, "So, you blew into the Breathalyzer, over-armed it across the median, punched a cop in the throat, yet somehow *they* made a mistake?"

Mason muttered, "Clearly, not ducking was the mistake..." She looked at Jim. "Yes, that was cross talk. Get a fucking hobby, Jim."

Sherri frowned at Mason. "Please, Mason. Carry on, Julia."

"So, once he could talk again he wanted to arrest me." The woman suddenly looked ever so slightly uncomfortable. "That's when things got sticky." She looked over and saw Jim had opened his eyes, which for some reason seemed to make it easier. "I decided to retrieve the Breathalyzer."

"And what was the cop doing?"

"Lying on the ground getting his breath back."

Sherri nodded very slowly. "I'm sorry, which freeway was this?"

"The 405."

The silence deepened.

"Near the Westwood interchange."

The respect deepened . . . deeper. The 405 was ten lanes wide at that point.

"And I would have made it, too . . ."

"If it wasn't for you pesky kids?" Mason held up both her palms. "Sorry, Sherri, I couldn't help it."

"You could and you should," said the facilitator. "Poor impulse control is something you've been working on. Please continue to work on it. Carry on, Julia."

Julia frowned at Mason, who shrugged. "But that's when the other cops arrived."

"Other cops?" Sherri looked a little lost. "He'd called for backup?"

Julia shook her head. "No, the other ones were already chasing me." She had sufficient self-awareness to look at the ground as she said, "I was driving a Lamborghini. I'd gotten a good few miles ahead."

Sherri nodded slowly. "So why were those cops after you?"

"They wanted to ask some questions about . . ." She stammered to a halt. You could have heard a flea cough. She cleared her throat. "Uh . . . about a dead body in my swimming pool." She looked contrite. "That's why I was driving so fast."

"I see." Sherri wanted to fan herself with the clipboard, but as a trained recovery professional she held it. "And why didn't you stay to answer questions in the first place?"

Julia looked surprised. "Well, because they were going to arrest me."

"Why?"

"Because clearly it wasn't an accidental drowning. Why else would she have run away? She didn't want to get arrested for killing the guy, and she was too drunk to think straight." Mason was smiling like the Cheshire cat, delighted by this whole thing. Impulse control be damned. She looked at the older woman and raised her eyebrows. "Right?"

Uproar.

Sherri looked about as annoyed as she ever did. "Mason! You just essentially defined cross talk. I'm tempted to make you go sit next to Jim."

Both Jim and Mason immediately got to their feet in protest.

"It's fine," said Julia calmly. "She's quite right. They might have arrested me for the guy in the pool, and I didn't want to let them." She looked at Mason, who seemed to be following along. "I've been in jail before, you see."

Nods around the room. Jails, institutions and death. All familiar friends here, none of them except the last one a disqualifier for recovery.

"And did you?" asked Mason. "Did you kill him?" She was still on her feet, her body ready for action, one finger and thumb clicking nervously.

There was a pause as everyone in the room held their breath and waited.

Julia studied her hands and flexed her fingers, her diamond rings glittering coldly back up at her.

She shrugged. "Well, that's the million-dollar question. I have absolutely no idea." She looked around the room and sighed. "I don't remember anything at all."

2

~~~~

NATASHA MASON HAD been living in Los Angeles for a while now, but there were many areas of the canyons she'd never been to. Julia's address was way up above Sunset, an area that reminded Mason of the Berkeley hills she'd grown up in, with their narrow, twisty streets and inexplicable parking regulations. There were more trees in Northern California, of course, and fewer enormous luxury cars trying to navigate the hairpin switchbacks, but there was still something about the hills that made her cross. In AA there's a concept of *people*, *places* and *things*: situational elements that might trigger a relapse. For Mason, the hills reminded her of home, which reminded her of family, particularly her mother, which reminded her that a drink might be a good idea right about now . . .

However, she was sober, so she acknowledged her trigger, said a brief serenity prayer, then looked around for something nonalcoholic to improve her mood. Nothing wrong with asking for help, especially if it's in the form of coffee. And if it was a triple shot, so what? Like every other drunk and addict she knew, Mason always wanted more, and right now the more she wanted was caffeine. Plus, she'd been born with twice the usual allocation of energy and one quarter the allocation of self-control. The math had worked in her favor right up until it kicked her in the teeth and left her for dead. But that's another story.

As she waited for her coffee, she thought back to the meeting the night before. Once Julia had finished her story, there had been a long silence. She remembered feeling drawn to the older woman, and when Sherri had asked if Julia had an interim sponsor and had received merely a snort in response, Mason had found herself volunteering for the job. Julia had responded with the barest sketch of a shrug, but Mason had taken her address and made plans to visit the next day. Now, in fact. True, she hadn't gotten an overwhelming sense of enthusiasm from Julia, who had implied she wasn't planning on paying Mason much more heed than she might give one of the meeting room chairs, but Mason was strangely determined. She'd never been an interim sponsor before, but she was going to help this woman whether she liked it or not. Of course, after the meeting, several other sober drunks had excitedly informed her that her new sponsee was a) a famous actress, b) additionally famous for drunkenly causing chaos wherever she went, and c) probably guilty of killing the poor dead guy in the pool, but hey, nobody's perfect. Mason barely watched TV and had no idea who Julia was, so she was just as likely to be helpful as anyone else. More, maybe. Mason was optimistic, which was a nice feeling. Possibly misguidedly so, but she was willing to take the chance.

She was only in the coffee shop for a minute, but when she walked back to her car she had a ticket under her wiper. She ripped it off and was about to rip it up when she took a breath and stuffed it in her pocket instead. She hated this fucking town. They would ticket a dog turd if they thought it could pay. No wonder the pigeons never stopped moving.

Waiting to break into the steady stream of traffic on La Cienega, she drummed on the steering wheel and sang tunelessly along with the radio, her foot bopping the brake pedal in time to the music. Growing impatient, because it had been thirty seconds, she leaned out of her open window and smiled flirtatiously at the oncoming drivers, hoping one of them would take pity on her.

One man slowed a little, his eye caught by her looks, but sped up just as she nosed her car out. The traffic forced him to stop again, of course, and their windows were level. Awkward.

"What the hell, guy?" Mason was no longer surprised by how quickly her temper rose. Fortunately, in LA she was never far from a fight. Just because she no longer drank and committed arson, it didn't mean she wasn't ready to strike a match whenever the opportunity presented itself.

"Fuck you," he shot back, wittily.

"No, fuck you."

"No." He paused, for emphasis. "Fuck. You."

Mason let her face become expressionless. She narrowed her eyes and let thoughts of violence run through her head. She'd never been good at hiding her feelings. The other driver dropped his gaze first.

That's right, she thought to herself, watching as he edged ahead, her momentary and utterly symbolic triumph making her forget for a second that she was still waiting to be let out into traffic. She sighed. These tiny battles were the kinds of things she'd drank over when she drank over little things (and big things, and medium things, and imaginary things). She shook herself and finished her triple, burning her tongue in the process, which was a distraction at least.

Twenty minutes later, driving percussively up Laurel Canyon, still singing, she'd regained her good humor but could also feel the caffeine fizzing in her veins. She wondered why she felt so compelled by Julia. There was just something about the older woman that spoke to her. Even if it was saying fuck off in no uncertain terms. Mason rarely heard a direct order she didn't long to contravene, and Julia's high walls made her want to swing her grappling hook. Besides, now she was her sponsor, interim or otherwise, and she had decided to take that shit seriously. If Mason's middle name hadn't already been Elizabeth it would have been Capricious.

On the surface, Mason looked like your classic Los Angeles native: mid-twenties, smoothly muscled from CrossFit and yoga, an air of good health and probably plant-based energy. Her almost-buzzed dark hair and lack of makeup were the only things not issued by central casting. She had a face people looked at twice but weren't sure why. However, LA wasn't really her town. Raised by hippie psychiatrists in Berkeley, she went to Yale to study political science as a precursor to law school. She was going to save the disenfranchised. But her mouth was always two steps ahead of her brain, and the scotch in her daily coffee meant she rarely waited for it to catch up. Eventually, in sophomore year she sassed the wrong person and started a street brawl that resulted in two hospitalizations and the burning down of a hot dog stand. The injuries healed, but the hot dog stand had been an institution, and the dean was apologetic but firm: "You're a smart girl, Ms. Mason. Stop drinking and go be smart somewhere else. I hear Stanford's pleasant this time of year."

She vetoed more college but decided Los Angeles was a good place to hide—thousands of young people were absorbed into its biomass every month. But why, after five years, was she still here? She'd been sober three years, her parents had forgiven her, she could go home anytime she wanted. Fuck it, she could finish her degree and go to law school. But here she was, temping and driving rideshare and putting out fires in AA meetings. Her mother probably had a professional opinion about it. But Mason dodged her calls. Her sponsor told her to take it one day at a time, so that's what she tried to do. Sometimes restless discontentment boiled in her spine, urging her to burn shit down and get fucked-up (slipping that suggestion in at the end, an assassin hiding his blade in a shrug), but not every day. Today, for example. Today was OK so far. She had a sponsee; she was working it.

Her GPS sent her right, then left, up a street that seemed almost vertical. Her car struggled a little, but eventually the road flattened out and started to wind lazily.

"Jesus, where is this place, Nevada?" She reached for another piece of gum, wishing she'd gotten something to eat at the coffee place.

At some point, she passed through a gate, then after a sharp right, the road cleared the trees and revealed an outstanding view of Los Angeles. They were at the tippy top of a steep canyon, its sides striped in layers of red and peach rock, apparently held together by love and tenacious bushes. Built across the top of the canyon, literally straddling it, was the kind of house the villain owns in James Bond movies. Two floors, with long sections extending out from a central building, like a white mid-century wing nut. Mason could see the front side was completely glass, and that a slender infinity pool ran a river between the two wings, disappearing under the house at one end and apparently spilling over into the canyon at the far edge. It didn't seem possible, yet there it was.

Mason stopped the car and stepped out. She stretched and bounced a little on her feet, cracking her knuckles and scanning the hillside. Up here there was a steady breeze, scented strongly with sagebrush and wild rosemary. Birdsong was the loudest sound apart from the pool pump and the slow ticking of the car's engine as it cooled. Yellow crime scene tape delineated the edges of the pool deck, and beyond it the city might as well have been a painted backdrop, its blurred edges and glinting sunshine stretching from downtown to the ocean.

Standing outside of the wide front doors, Mason got ready to face cranky new-sobriety energy, and when a small, dark-haired woman opened the door, she was surprised.

"Uh . . . hi, I'm Natasha Mason. I'm here to see Julia?"

The woman was elegant, dressed in a simple black dress. She could have been Middle Eastern, or Hispanic, or southern European. She was maybe fifty, with large, expressive eyes and a haughty expression. Whatever else she was, she was also entirely silent, and she gazed at Mason without comment.

"I'm from . . ." Mason paused and willed herself not to shuffle her feet. Anonymity was a foundational principle of AA, obviously; it was in the fucking name. She didn't know if this woman knew Julia was trying to get sober. "I'm a friend."

The woman raised a single eyebrow. "I doubt that," she said.

Mason raised her eyebrow in return. "And yet," she said, "I am."

"Since when?"

"Last night." The woman continued to look dubious, and

suddenly Mason's mouth engaged while her brain was still weighing its options. "Look, I don't know who you are, or why you're gatekeeping this hard, but I met Julia last night and she invited me to come over this morning, and in normal society that would be sufficient for entry, but maybe I'm missing something." She started flexing her fingers, feeling her temper begin to rise. Again.

The woman's mouth twitched. "I know that's at least partially a lie, because Julia rarely invites people over, but she did say something about a pushy kid, and that part is ringing true." She smiled so briefly Mason couldn't be sure it wasn't a tic. "I'm Claudia, Mrs. Mann's housekeeper. Are you ready to come in or do you need to run your mouth some more?"

"I'm good," replied Mason.

"I'm doubtful," responded Claudia, turning on her heel to enter the house.

The interior was dark and cool after the heat of the hill, and very simple. Everything was precisely, perfectly in place. Mason wasn't sure what she'd been expecting, but not this minimalist spread in *Architectural Digest*. Suddenly, a doorway at the far end of the hall was flung open, and a small, red-haired young woman came out, moving fast and crying hard. She ran past Mason and Claudia quickly enough to cause a breeze, her sobs barely muffled, but she neither looked at them nor said a word. Mason wasn't fazed by tears, and Claudia didn't seem to notice, so they simply walked through the door she'd left open, into the blazing sunlight of an enormous room.

The polished concrete floor was gray, the walls were bare, and nothing distracted from the view. Julia stood by the window, one hand resting lightly on the glass, wearing a tailored trouser suit (vintage Yves Saint Laurent) that looked like it had been sewn on her. She was a photograph, her poise clearly something factory installed.

Claudia spoke. "Mrs. Mann? Your . . . friend is here."

Julia turned. "The helper girl quit again," she said.

"Really?" replied Claudia, calmly. "The surprise was her coming back in the first place."

Julia frowned. "I was paying her."

"Not enough to work for you three days in a row."

"I was trying to be nice."

"Were you, though?"

"She asked me about acting."

"Perhaps she thought an ex-actress would have relevant suggestions."

"I did. I suggested she go back to Wisconsin."

"She was from Nebraska."

Julia shrugged. "Whichever flight left first."

"And she took that badly?" Claudia snorted. "Do you want me to call the agency or will you?"

Julia sighed. "You do it. I think they blocked my number."

"Are you kidding? You put that woman's kids through college."

Mason had sidled sideways during this exchange and sat on the edge of a low sofa, tucking her Doc Martens under her and watching the back-and-forth like a tennis match.

"I googled you," she said to Julia, when there was an appropriate pause. She didn't care about the girl, the job or the airplane to Wisconsin. Nebraska. Wherever.

The two women turned and looked at her.

Mason recrossed her boots under the sofa, getting them briefly tangled in the process. "Well, I googled the body in the swimming pool, to be honest. I didn't realize you were famous." This was a bit of a lie, obviously, as Jim—and most of the rest of the meeting attendees—had told her Julia was famous, but as she herself had not known, it wasn't a complete untruth.

"I'm not," said Julia. "Thus your accurate use of the past tense."

"She won an Oscar," said Claudia, providing a counterpoint.

"So did Geraldine Page," responded Julia.

"Who's that?" asked Mason.

"My point exactly," said Julia. "Every generation has its famous, all of whom end up being the next generation's *Sorry, who?*"

Mason shrugged. "Yeah, well, I don't really watch TV." She looked at Julia and smiled encouragingly. "Do you have a TikTok?"

"Jesus fucking Christ," said Julia, frowning. She looked at Claudia. "I need coffee."

Claudia nodded and left the room. Mason wasn't sure, but she might have heard her laughing as the door closed.

Julia Mann walked over to one of those iconic '60s egg-shaped chairs and sat down, crossing her legs. The minute they were set at a comfortable angle, she came to a complete stop, every line of her body elegant and still. "I realize I asked you to be my interim sponsor"—she folded her hands over her kneecaps, and Mason noticed how tightly they held on—"but I don't need anyone's help."

Mason shook her head. "We all need help. How are you feeling today?"

Julia looked at her and made a face, almost instantly

relaxing her features back into her elegant mask. "I'm fine, if fine's a term that encompasses totally terrible. I have a headache, my teeth hurt, my ankles hurt, I feel nauseous, I'm not sure this suit was the right choice and I'm having intrusive thoughts about getting a cat, which is a terrible idea. Apart from that, I'm super fantastic, thanks for asking." She held up a finger. "Oh, and a very old enemy decided to end it all by getting murdered in my swimming pool, which is both unhelpful *and* unsanitary. I have no idea why he was even there, let alone why someone decided to kill him at my place rather than, say, at their place, which would have made finding them so much easier." Her voice had risen sharply toward the end, and Mason made a face.

Nodding, she said, "That does sound like a lot, especially for this early in sobriety. How many days has it been?"

"Since I drank?" Julia shrugged. "What day is it?"

"Friday."

"Four days."

"Congratulations."

Julia snorted. "I don't have a warm, fuzzy feeling about five." She frowned at Mason. "I had ten years sober at one point, seven at another. I know how it works."

"Sure," said Mason, "but then you also know it's one day at a time." She was dying to ask a million questions, or at least a few. *Why did you start drinking again? What made you stop? Why that day and not any other day?* But these were questions she had to keep inside. There is an unspoken code of conduct in recovery. You can say anything to anyone about your own story. But you don't ask questions about someone else's unless they're already telling you and you need clarification. You don't simply come out and ask; it's not polite.

She gazed at the other woman. Close up it was still somewhat difficult to guess her age. Her beauty was all in her bones, high and angular, framing green eyes over a straight nose. Her mouth was still full, though it didn't look like it did a lot of smiling.

Mason added, "I have three years, but we both only have today, right?"

"For fuck's sake," said Julia, unclasping her hands and angling her body away in the chair. "If all you're going to do is recite slogans, you could have texted."

Mason bit her tongue. She'd sat with her own sponsor for an hour the previous evening talking over how to help Julia stay sober, but she (her sponsor) didn't cover what to do if she (Julia) was just a massive bitch. She (her sponsor) was not a massive bitch, she was a sweet and gentle angel of loveliness, and she (Mason) was having a hard time not just swinging back when she (Julia) was being difficult. Mind you, her sponsor had also beaten her abusive husband unconscious with a skillet, so she might have been less patient than Mason assumed.

Claudia came back in, carrying a tray with cookies and coffee. A silver coffeepot. A tiny coffee cup, delicately rimmed with silver. A silver dish with . . .

"Are those wedding cookies?" Mason was excited. "I love those."

Claudia hesitated, apparently not used to enthusiasm. "Yes. I made them this morning. Enjoy."

"Thanks, they look great." Mason was rewarded with a very small smile.

"Oh, get a room already." Julia's voice was sharp. She was watching Mason, who was helping herself to a cookie. Then another. Then she poured herself some coffee. Julia Mann said nothing at first, then spoke.

"Hungry?" Her voice was cool and slightly amused.

"Several times a day," replied Mason, her mouth full of cookie.

"Why did you google me?" asked Julia. "That's not a very sober thing to do."

Mason nodded. "No, but progress not perfection, and as your interim sponsor . . ."

"You don't have to keep saying it . . ."

". . . it seemed appropriate to do some homework. Besides, a dead body in a swimming pool followed by a high-speed chase is compelling content." Mason bent down and dabbed up some crumbs with a moistened fingertip. "Once I was there I couldn't help reading your name, sorry." She blushed, although very slightly, and Julia didn't know her well enough to spot it. "There was actually a lot of information about you online. One article described you as a professional thorn in the side of the establishment. A troublemaker." She shrugged. "Which tracked. It also said you and the dead guy were sworn enemies and he'd had to get a restraining order against you because you'd gone batshit crazy on him at a restaurant one time."

Julia raised her eyebrows, an expression Mason was quickly becoming familiar with. "We were not sworn enemies; there was no official oath. We used to be best friends. At one point we were lovers, before I met my husband. But yes, I did go batshit crazy on him at least once, although in my defense I was drinking at the time." She sighed and examined her fingernails. "Tony was one of those men who make you feel . . . extraordinary. As though the minute you walked through their door you changed their lives. Brought everything into sharp focus, or Technicolor. He had a way of looking at you that made you reevaluate every mean or stupid thing you'd ever said about yourself. It was a gift. Unfortunately, he did it to everyone, and meant none of it. He was a gilded shell of a man, masquerading as solid gold."

Mason gazed at her. "He was cute, too. I saw a picture."

Julia rolled her eyes and switched the position of her legs, which made Mason reflexively think of racehorses. Then she once again became utterly still.

"Like I said at the meeting, I went to jail. For killing my husband, who *was* my best friend, and someone I loved very, very much. A long time ago, probably before you were born. I was innocent, and Tony must have known it. He knew me, knew I wasn't capable of that. He could have said something at the trial, been a character witness, something. But he chose not to." She paused and issued a warning too late for Mason's very mobile face. "Don't pull that expression; I know innocence is a common claim, but in my case it was true. I was a mess walking in, but I got sober in jail, and once I could think clearly my predominant thought was *what the actual fuck?* I was furious. I got my law degree while incarcerated, which is another cliché, but it's amazing what a motivator massive unfairness can be, then I came out and discovered practicing law was a good way to exact revenge on a system run by the powerful at the expense of the . . ."

"Powerless?" asked Mason.

"Not even. At the expense of everyone. Sure, the powerless pay the highest price, but the system is broken all the way through, foundation to ridgepole." She looked at her hands. "I do as much as I can to help people like me who, for reasons as varied as they are, got screwed by the system. I take cases that interest me, I work with people I respect, and we try to unfuck the fucked." She paused. "It's more fulfilling than acting, and sometimes I get to act, as well. And what do you do, when you're not harassing the freshly sober?"

"We all need help, and I'm not harassing you," replied Mason. "I'm doing my sponsor-y job, and supporting you by providing an irritating distraction." She grinned. "It's working, though, right? You're not thinking of drinking. I temp, drive rideshare, do deliveries, personal assisting, the usual Gen Z gig economy queen, you know."

Julia shrugged. "Sounds boring and stressful, not a great combination."

"It's both of those, but better than starving."

The eyebrow went up again. "Wait, personal assisting? Come work for me. You seem energetic, you're right here, and it will save me hiring another girl from the agency."

Mason didn't hesitate. "Sure."

Julia laughed. "Want to think about it?"

"I did, that was me thinking about it," Mason said. "Here's the thing. As your interim sponsor, I can't just follow you around. It's not interim *stalker*. But as your assistant, I can keep an eye on you, make some money, keep myself busy and be ready to work the steps as and when the opportunity presents itself. It's not a normal thing, to be an employee *and* a sponsor, but if it sucks I can quit. I haven't worked for a lawyer / actress / potential murderess before."

"That you know of . . ."

"True, that I know of. I did have a client one time who had me follow her ex-boyfriend for three hours while he shopped for shoes."

"He shopped for shoes for three hours?"

"No, I *followed* him for three hours. For all I know he's still shopping for shoes. I got distracted by something and lost him. The client *might* have been planning to murder him." She shrugged. "She had a pretty short temper."

Julia snorted. "So no tasks that require sustained focus. And I mean it: I don't need your help to stay sober."

Mason shrugged. "Because you were doing such a good job on your own? We can argue about sponsorship later. Let's get started doing whatever it is you want to do." She paused. "What is it you want to do?"

Julia raised one eyebrow. "What I usually do for my clients: active defensive investigation. The police will think I killed Tony because they are creatures of habit and predictability. To be fair, I had motive and opportunity and ran away from the crime scene. Looks bad for me, good to them. However, I'm pretty sure I didn't do it, although I have no idea why Tony was even there as I would never have invited him."

"You were drunk."

"True, but even so . . . let's assume it wasn't me; we still have four million other Angelenos unaccounted for."

Mason bounced on her feet and clapped her hands like a four-year-old spotting a pony in a party hat. "Great, this is going to be awesome. Never investigated shit before, totally down."

Julia got to her feet and headed to the door. "Come on, then. Let's go."

"Where?" Mason was nearly on her heels as they reached the door. They left that room and crossed the main entranceway and down the opposite hallway. Basically the other wing of the wing nut, where there was a door identical to the one they'd just come out of. Julia paused.

"You know how Dorothy opens the door of her little house after the twister and realizes she isn't in Kansas anymore?"

Mason nodded. "Sure. I'm American. I've seen that movie a hundred times."

"Fair enough. And are you familiar with the *Narnia* books, where the children push their way through the fur coats in a wardrobe and come out into a magical land?"

Again, Mason nodded.

"And finally, are you familiar with the musical film *Brigadoon*, where every hundred years you can cross a magical bridge to a town where romance and song fill the air?"

A pause. Mason shook her head. "No, you got me there. Is it old? I'm only twenty-five. It was probably before my time."

Julia narrowed her eyes. "Well, that being as it may, this is my office, Mason. I've helped countless innocent people regain their freedom, solved mysteries that had been ignored by the authorities and generally kicked righteous butt all from this one room. It's a lot, so be prepared."

Mason snickered. "It's a room. I think I can handle it."

Julia just smiled, and swung open the door.

3

MASON—IN COMMON with many drunks and addicts— was pretty hard to surprise. If you black out a lot, you tend to swim to consciousness at random times, and literally anything could be happening. You could be on the bus. You could be in jail. You could be in Safeway with your hand on a fruit you barely recognize, about to make a purchasing choice you never would sober. But despite dozens of those experiences, Mason ground to a halt just inside Julia Mann's office and goggled.

Whatever it was she had filed under "office" in her brain was going to need revision. Architecturally, Julia's office was the same as the living room, but the similarities ended there. Yes, it was a long, rectangular room fronted by an unbroken run of glass, but these windows were covered with deep orange curtains, cooling the temperature of the room while making it feel like the kind of nightclub Mason used to get thrown out of. The walls were lined on two sides with deep bookcases, including the long back wall. Thousands of books, each marked on the spine with a catalog number. Folders of magazines and printed material. Piles of film canisters, DVDs, even video cassettes. Computers of all kinds, hard drives, laser disc players, classic turntables and other tech Mason didn't immediately recognize. Brilliantly colored rugs in shades of amber and honey were layered and piled over the polished cement floor. An enormous sectional, persimmon velvet, faced the far wall. And on that far wall? The biggest screen Mason had ever seen outside of a movie theater, surrounded by enormous speakers. It was a combination of NASA, the Smithsonian and the bedroom of a wealthy but reclusive teenage boy with hoarding issues.

Julia's tone was sharp. "Come all the way in and sit all the way down, for fuck's sake. I want you to get up to speed on what I already know." Julia faced the big screen and started working her wireless mouse like a fifteen-year-old gamer from Seoul. "One of the few things we know is that it wasn't me that killed Tony Eckenridge, tempting though it would have been to shoot him if he'd shown up at my house unannounced."

"Do you own a gun?" asked Mason, settling down on the sofa and starting to fold her legs up under her.

"No, boots off—were you raised in a barn?"

"Close, Berkeley," replied Mason, bending to undo her boots. "Was it normal for him to show up at your place?"

"Not at all. We haven't spoken since the restraining order."

"That tracks," said Mason, curling up like Alice's caterpillar. "I guess the restraining order didn't prevent him coming near you."

"Well, it literally did, but it was only a temporary restraining order. I essentially got over my temper tantrum with Tony once I started keeping other people out of jail. When I woke up and discovered the dead guy clogging my pool filter was Tony, no one was more surprised than I was."

"Well," said Mason, "you know, apart from him."

"True. I could almost see him coming over to kill himself in my pool, just for the gesture of it—directors are like that, you know, grandiose and controlling, plus he'd love the visual—but not by shooting himself in the back of the head with a rifle."

"Not that grandiose?"

"Not that flexible. Anyway, I started looking into what Tony did with his last few days on earth. The day before he ended up here, he spent the morning at the studio and had lunch with his ex-wife. Nothing exceptional." She clicked on the *Hollywood Reporter*, displaying the headline: *Eckenridge meets Eckenridge on possible* Codex *remake*, then clicked over to TMZ, a celebrity gossip site, and pointed out a photo of Tony leaving a restaurant with a vivacious-looking woman. "That's his ex-wife, Helen. She wrote much of the original *Codex*, shared writing credit with my late husband and walked home with the Oscar. Didn't do her a hell of a lot of good; an Oscar too early in your career can do that."

Another click. Coroner's report. "The day he died, Tony had a board meeting at the studio, with a catered lunch that included an ungodly amount of sushi, and then he came here and got shot in the head. Not sure what he did in between. We'll have to find out if the cops haven't already."

"Did he drown?" Mason asked.

"No, he was dead when he hit the surface, no water in his lungs at all, brains all over the place. Estimated time of death, ten p.m. And he can't have gotten here all that much earlier, because Claudia didn't leave for the evening until nearly seven."

"Pity she missed it."

"Not really. She might have gotten shot, too, and then who

would cook for me?" Julia navigated to another window. "His second-in-command at the studio, Christine Greenfield"—she clicked on a profile in *Angeleno* magazine, showing a short, dark-haired woman—"got into a fender bender that afternoon and was at Cedars-Sinai hospital with her passenger, the actress Jade Solomon." Click. *People* magazine, Most Beautiful People number 7, two years earlier. Mason wondered if Jade still made the top 50. That category had a lot of churn.

"Luckily," continued Julia, "her lovely face was unharmed, although brain damage can't be ruled out until they find an actual brain."

"Meow," muttered Mason.

"Oh, please. Tony's assistant Cody Malone was at Cedars helping Christine, and here are all three of them leaving the hospital that evening." TMZ again, Jade Solomon's smile broad, her outfit unwrinkled, Christine with her head down, Cody focused on getting them into the car.

"And of course"—Julia still wasn't done—"according to his obituary in the *LA Times*, despite a forty-year career in one of the meanest, most cutthroat businesses there is, he swam in a sea of holy water, handing out prizes to one and all. Not an enemy in the world."

Julia had pulled up the obit, and Mason didn't mention the fact that along with a large and flattering portrait of Tony, there was a smaller photo of him with Julia and his wife, on the night they'd all won Academy Awards for *The Codex*. She looked at Tony curiously. He was one of those men who had aged well, the lines fanning out from the corners of his eyes serving simply to direct attention to their sapphire sparkle, his smile confident and practiced. Charisma that came through the screen. His face wasn't familiar to her, but she realized she'd decided to like him, even though she would never meet him in person. Maybe that was what Julia had mentioned, his ability to make everyone feel special. Even from a picture. Even from beyond the grave.

Julia sat down on the other end of the sofa, curling her legs under her like a cat. "Which leaves the police with very few people to suspect, apart from yours truly. They lack imagination, that's their trouble." She threw the remote mouse across the room into a drawer, making the shot easily.

Mason pretended not to be impressed and spoke without thinking. "Yeah, not to mention you threatened his life before, fled the crime scene and already went to jail for murder once."

Silence is rarely absolute. However, at Mason's comment, a silence of inkily velvet completeness quieted the room like a quilt settling on a distant bed. There was an immeasurably subtle sense of withdrawal, and Mason realized she might just have put her foot in it. Possibly up to the thigh. She decided, as usual, to go on the defensive.

"Hey, look, everything I just said was public record. I'm sure you're innocent."

"Listen up, buttercup." Julia Mann's voice was smooth. "Here's what I know about innocence. One, it's no defense against conviction. Two, once you're convicted, it's no defense against incarceration. And three, once you're incarcerated, it's no defense against anything. I watched the innocent get eaten alive every day, and I watched the innocent turn and bloody their teeth with the rest. I am not going back to jail, and the only way to make sure of that is to catch the person who killed Tony and throw them to the wolves in my place."

Mason swallowed. "I get that. What are we going to do first?"

Julia opened her mouth to answer, but was interrupted by the office door opening and Claudia making an appearance. She closed the door quietly behind her and cleared her throat.

"Julia? The police are here."

"Oh yeah?" Julia shrugged. "What do they want?"

"I'm pretty sure," replied Claudia, "that they want to arrest you."

4

~~~

CLAUDIA WATCHED SILENTLY from the front door as Mason, Julia and two LAPD detectives—they'd introduced themselves as Wilson and Brooks—walked out of the house.

Claudia had been wrong. They hadn't arrested Julia, just politely asked her to come to the station to answer further questions. Julia had agreed, but insisted that she travel separately.

"I'll drive her," Mason said. "We'll meet you at the precinct."

"Claudia," said Julia, quietly, "call the lawyer, ask him to meet us there." They reached Mason's car, which looked, if possible, slightly more disreputable in the blinding sunshine.

"Oh hell no," said Julia. She turned to Mason. "I hope you drive stick."

The 1965 Shelby Cobra is considered by many car enthusiasts to be the most beautiful car of that decade. When Julia Mann had opened the doors of her garage, it was just one of half a dozen cars, each one under a custom cover. Even the detectives had whistled.

"They were Jonathan's," Julia had said, as she tweaked the

covers to reveal each one. "A man from the Petersen Museum comes once a month to coo over them and keep them running, but I rarely drive them. Claudia does the driving, usually." She looked at Mason. "Which one?" Mason had swallowed and pointed to the Shelby.

It is not a hard-and-fast rule that all paparazzi are men, nor is it set in stone that all men love cars. However, as the car pulled up in front of the Beverly Hills Police Department, the all-male pack of paparazzi swarmed forward and started taking pictures before anyone even got out of the car. Once she stepped out, however, they recognized Julia Mann instantly.

"Mrs. Mann, is it true you finally killed Tony Eckenridge?"

"Scared to go back to jail, Julia?"

"Is the longest-running feud in Hollywood over?"

Julia was taking the high road. "Do I look like a killer, gentlemen?"

"No," replied one, "you look like my grandmother."

Without breaking stride, Julia Mann face-palmed him as she passed, and the volley of flashes widened her smile considerably.

EVEN A HOLLYWOOD Realtor would have had a hard time selling the police station—mid-century oblongs, desecrated on the regular since the seventies, a *very* optimistic fixer-upper—and would have stuttered into silence over the interrogation room. Pale green walls, scuffed linoleum, a table that looked like a hundred heads had been slammed on it. Mason was glad she wasn't under arrest; she felt anxious enough as it was. Julia merely sat there and practiced her impersonation of granite, which really didn't need any work.

"Are you cold?" Mason asked, at one point.

"No, that's just the way I look. Be quiet," Mann had snapped back, and since then they'd sat in silence. Julia might have been thinking a mile a minute, but Mason didn't know her well enough to be sure.

Finally, the door to the interrogation room opened, and a cop poked her head around. "Your lawyer's here. Or maybe he's your agent. It wasn't very clear."

Julia was gazing at the table and didn't look up. "He's both. Jesus, Larry, it took you long enough. You know how hard it is for me to remain silent." Mason frowned; Julia had made it look easy.

"Uh . . ." A very deep voice. To go with the six foot four of masculine hotness that had stepped through the door, holding a briefcase and looking gravely concerned. Julia's head whipped around.

"Who the hell are you? Where's Larry?"

"I'm Archie Jacobson. Larry's in the hospital, I'm afraid." He started to sit at the table, but Julia put up her hand. Mason, privately, was totally comfortable with this guy, and hoped Larry was going to remain hospitalized. Archie Jacobson was wearing a charcoal gray suit over a white shirt and looked as corporate as they come, but Mason noticed a pair of *Star Trek* socks briefly appearing above his shoes and covered her smile. A secret nerd, her favorite kind.

"No." Julia was firm.

"Yes." Archie found his spine, ignored the lifted hand and sat down. "He had a heart attack yesterday."

"That was yesterday. I need him today."

"Well, the bypass surgery he's in right now makes that challenging."

Julia was still peevish. "I'm not your client. I'm Larry's client. I've been Larry's client since he booked my first commercial." She turned to Mason. "Somehow, this is your fault."

Archie flicked a glance at Mason and replied, "Larry didn't have an arterial blockage to annoy you, Mrs. Mann. I'm Larry's junior partner, which makes me temporarily your agent and your lawyer, because I, like Larry, am both." He cleared his throat. "I was briefly a criminal attorney before switching to the entertainment business."

Julia gave up. "Fine. Stay. If you suck I'll fire you later."

Mason sighed. She now had a better understanding of why Julia had gone to jail the first time, innocent or not. It was simply surprising the trial had lasted as long as it had.

"Can I ask a question?" she said, then continued without waiting. "Aren't you yourself a lawyer? Why do you even need one?"

Julia snorted. "Yes, of course I'm a lawyer—I'm a kick-ass lawyer in fact—but I can't represent myself and do a good job." She turned to Archie. "You're really a lawyer?" She explained to Mason, "Larry also happened to be a lawyer; many agents are."

Archie nodded. "I am, Mrs. Mann. Being a lawyer makes me a better agent, and sometimes I spend all day fiddling with contracts. However, I am also an agent, and Larry did ask me to ask you about Cinespia." He pulled out a notepad and pen. "Not to distract you from the business of being questioned by the police, but have you decided whether or not to do it?" He looked at Mason again, and suddenly seemed to realize he didn't know her from Eve. "By the way, who are you?"

Julia snorted. "That's Mason, my assistant. Back away."

Mason asked, "Does this conversation fall under lawyer-client privilege?"

"Yes."

"Then I'm also her interim sponsor," said Mason. "Not that she relishes that relationship."

"You surprise me," said the man, holding out his hand. "She seems generally so good-humored."

Mason shook his hand and realized she could also smell a faint hint of aftershave or something . . . lime oil, cloves, oakmoss. Sexy. *Keep your head in the game, Mason.*

"I decided no to Cinespia," replied Julia. "Big fat no."

"Larry said to tell you that's a mistake," said Archie.

Mason frowned. "How did he know she was going to say no?" She held up a hand. "Don't answer that. She always says no."

The agent/lawyer tapped his nose. "I'm starting to think so."

Julia said, "Actually, that's why I killed Tony, so I could get out of the Cinespia thing by going to jail."

"What Cinespia thing?" asked Mason. "I mean, I know that Cinespia is the outdoor movie thing, the summer thing at the cemetery, right?" All summer long, classic movies were played on Saturday evenings at the Hollywood Forever Cemetery. People brought picnics and wine and dressed up and had a blast.

Archie nodded. "Yes, and they want Julia to come and present a showing of *The Codex*, her most famous movie and the one she won an Oscar for."

"The one for which she won an Oscar," corrected Julia. "Don't end a sentence with a preposition, Mr. Jacobson. It makes you look dumber than your choice of footwear."

Mason looked under the table. Converse high-tops, nothing dumb about that, especially not with the kind of bespoke tailored suit the lawyer was wearing everywhere else. She narrowed her eyes at Julia and made a mental note to discuss

restraint of pen and tongue, another basic suggestion in recovery. Her sponsor always said, ask yourself, does it *have* to
be said, does it have to be said *by me*, and does it have to be
said by me *now*? If you've gone through that process, the moment has probably passed anyway.

Archie was leaning in. "They're going to show the movie
with or without you. They want you to wear the catsuit, of
course. The Academy Museum is going to loan it to you for the
night. You'll look amazing. It's a great idea." He turned and
gave Mason a small smile. "Don't you think?"

Mason frowned. "They want her to dress as a cat?"

There was a fractional pause. "Noooo." Archie shook his
head. "On the poster for the movie, which is almost as famous
as the movie itself, she is wearing a silver catsuit while kicking
a gun out of the bad guy's hand . . ." He had very blue eyes, Mason noticed, blue and sparkly and currently encouraging her
to search her memory banks for this image. An image she suddenly did recall.

"Wait . . . that's you?" She turned and laughed at Julia, then
immediately stopped laughing and covered her mouth. "I
didn't mean to laugh. It's just like discovering you were the
Mona Lisa or something. Everyone knows that image."

It was iconic. Like Marilyn holding her skirt down over the
subway grate, or the shark coming up below the swimmer: Mason suddenly saw the poster in her head, saw Julia in the silver
catsuit, and then . . . "Isn't it cursed? Curse of *The Codex*, I read
about it last night. Someone died on the set, lots of drama . . ."
She ground to a halt, realizing from the look on Julia's face that
she was once again putting her boot all the way down her own
throat. She kept going; might as well be hanged for a sheep as
a lamb. "Was that your husband? Was that you?"

"Me that died?" Julia raised a single eyebrow. "No, we had two deaths, a stuntwoman who died on set in an accident, and then my husband was murdered, many months after the movie was finished. Supposedly at my hand. Didn't we already cover this?" She turned to Archie. "She's got a lot of energy, but I'm not sure she has a pause button."

"Maybe that's why Tony was coming to see you? About the remake? Is that possible?" Mason thought for another second. "I'm afraid I never actually saw the movie."

Archie's eyes stopped sparkling, which was sad. Mason had only ever seen a lawyer this good-looking on a TV show about good-looking lawyers. It was a bummer to have disappointed the only one she'd ever met in real life.

Julia laughed. "Ask me if I care. Archie, can we get back to the present day? The police think I killed Tony."

"And you didn't?"

Julia shook her head. "I was blacked out. I don't remember anything. But I'm pretty certain I didn't."

"Pretty certain?"

"Almost certain."

"I'd like more certainty on that certain."

"You won't get it. I don't remember anything." She made a face. "Little flashes here and there, but nothing cohesive." She looked at her watch. "Where the hell are the cops? Do you think they're trying to make me sweat?"

The door opened again. Apparently, the cops had excellent timing.

"Sorry to keep you waiting," said Detective Brooks, whose red curls suggested a far more fun-loving personality than the one she actually possessed.

"Please stand, Mrs. Mann," Detective Wilson said. "Julia

Mann, we are hereby charging you with homicide in the second degree. This charge is in relation to the murder of Anthony Eckenridge on the evening of August the first at your home, 1440 Kestrel Way. You have the right to remain silent. Anything you say can and will be used against you in a court of law. You have the right to an attorney. If you cannot afford one, one will be appointed for you."

"I can afford one. He's sitting right there," said Julia, stretching her arms overhead. "God, this is outrageous." She shook herself and got to her feet. "I thought I was just here for questions. What changed?"

"We got forensics back on the murder weapon. Your prints, no one else's."

"It's possible I picked up the gun . . ." Julia frowned. "I vaguely remember something like that."

Archie was annoyed. "Did you have to keep her waiting so long? It's Friday. It's going to be hard to arrange bail."

Detective Wilson shrugged. "She'll survive. The guy she shot and pushed into the pool . . . not so much."

"I didn't push him into the pool," argued Julia. "The force of the bullet did that."

Detective Brooks pulled out her handcuffs. "Turn around, please."

For the first time, Mason saw a flicker of anxiety on Julia's face. "You don't need to do that." She put her hands in her pockets.

Detective Wilson nodded. "I'm sorry, but we have to transport you downtown for booking. The press is outside; the cuffs are a requirement."

"Bullshit," said Archie. "She's not a flight risk."

Julia had gone pale. Mason watched her eyes as they

scythed the handcuffs around her wrists, and she wondered what it felt like to be restrained again, after years of freedom.

Whatever she was feeling, Julia stayed calm and looked at Mason with clear eyes. "Tell Claudia to call Will and get him up to speed. I'll be back tomorrow, assuming Mr. Jacobson earns his percentage."

And with that she turned and allowed herself to be led from the room, pausing at the door to look over her shoulder.

"And, Mason, if I never see you again, it's such a pity." She waited a beat. "This could have been the beginning of a beautiful friendship."

Mason just stared at her. As the door closed behind her, she turned to Archie with her eyebrows raised.

"Actresses," he said. "They can never resist making an exit."

5

~ ~ ~

EVENINGS WERE LONG that time of year, and as Mason ran along the streets of her neighborhood, there were still plenty of people out and about. She headed for the park, passing an ice cream place with a line that stretched around the block. Later, she promised herself, a chocolate malted to undo all this effort. She increased her speed a little. She'd been a runner since her teens, trying to outpace her internal discomfort, never quite building up enough speed to do so. She still ran every day, sprints and distance. It was one of the few times her mind grew quiet.

Running through Pan Pacific Park, Mason passed people walking dogs, teenagers throwing Frisbees, people lying on the grass cuddling. She didn't really look at anyone, though, just headed for the workout equipment the city had set up in the park. Four older guys and her, pumping their muscles on a warm city evening. She ended up getting into a pull-up contest and won twenty dollars. Score.

She checked her watch and headed out of the park. Just enough time to get that malted, especially now that she had the money to pay for it. Twenty minutes later she was finding her seat in a small basement room, greeting people she knew, nodding at strangers, sipping her malted and feeling herself relax fully for the first time that day.

The woman up front smiled around and cleared her throat. "Hello, everyone, let's settle down. Welcome to the regular eight p.m. meeting of Alcoholics Anonymous."

Mason settled deeper in her chair, and for the next hour didn't think of Julia Mann or murder at all.

SHE CAME OUT of the meeting with the usual improved sense of serenity, albeit mixed with a fancy for a burger and fries.

Then her phone rang. She pulled it from her pocket and looked at the screen.

Mother of Dragons.

Shit.

She sighed and internally tested her peace and calm. She was feeling good. She answered the call.

"Hi, Mom."

"Natasha! I can't believe you answered. I'm forming a long-distance relationship with your voicemail."

"I'm a busy woman."

"No, you're an avoidant with mother issues and opposi-tional defiant disorder." Her mother's voice opened up the same bag of mixed feelings it always did. A feeling of safety, combined with an awareness that there might be a hidden switchblade somewhere.

Mason sighed. "You love the labels, Mom."

"You call them labels; I call them professional diagnoses." Her mother was a psychiatrist.

"Tom-ay-to, tom-ah-to." Mason took a breath. "What's up?"

"Just wanted to check in, see how you were doing . . . Have you thought any more about what we talked about the other day?"

"I'm not going back to law school, Mom. It's a waste of time and money. I don't want to be a lawyer."

"But you're born for it. So smart. So argumentative."

"I disagree."

"Of course you do."

"I'm a full grown-up now, Mom. Please let me live my life."

"Well, a full grown-up who's still being supported financially by her parents."

There was a silence as Mason counted to ten. It was true, and it drove her crazy. It wasn't every month, but it was often that she had to ask for a little extra help to make rent, or pay bills. The gig economy was just that, and sometimes the gigs dried up.

"I have a full-time job right now, actually, working for Julia Mann."

"The actress? The one that went to jail?"

"Yes, Mom."

"Doing what?"

"Assisting. General duties, driving, that kind of thing."

"Well, I can't imagine that lasting very long. You're not very good at taking orders, are you?"

More counting.

"It's more collaborative than that, Mom." *Hopefully.*

"We'll see, I guess. If you don't want to go back to law school then maybe you could become a teacher? Or a nurse? You've always been very practical."

"You love to tell me what I should do, Mom, but I need to work it out for myself, OK?"

"OK, Mason, but your dad and I have talked about it, and we feel like you need to make a plan for your life. Or at least the next phase. We can't keep propping you up forever."

"I know, Mom. I'm doing my best. I'm staying sober, I'm working, I have friends, it's all good."

"Are you happy?"

Mason paused. "Happy is a lot to ask, Mom. I'm busy and I'm not drinking. It's a good start."

"I just think you'd be happy if you had a real career. You need to have a purpose, Mason. Everyone needs a purpose."

"Is your purpose telling me what to do? Because you're definitely leaning into it." Mason knew she shouldn't rise to her mother's bait, but it was so fucking hard not to.

Her mom's voice sharpened. "I'm your mother, Mason. I worry."

"Well, please stop. I have to go, OK?"

"OK. Your dad sends his love."

"I send mine back. Goodbye, Mom."

"Goodbye, sweetie."

Mason hung up and immediately called her sponsor.

Goddammit, why does life have to be so fucking . . . lifey?

CURLED UP IN her pajamas later, Mason streamed *The Codex*. Sharing a bowl of butter-covered popcorn with Phil, her three-legged cat, she watched the much younger Julia Mann kicking some extensive butt. The old broad had moves, for sure, and the catsuit was definitely a high point. In one scene,

Julia kicked a rifle from someone's hand, then pulled a hidden gun from a hollow book and blew him away, all in one fluid motion. She looked it up: Jonathan had been only thirty when he made it, Julia just twenty-six. The official movie site had loads of production photos, and she found herself drawn to one of Jonathan, Julia and Tony Eckenridge, talking on set, deep in collaboration. She'd read all the rumors of love affairs on set, between Jonathan and one of the producers, between Jack Simon and the young actor David Paul (apparently the rule back then was you could only use two first names), and between Tony and all of them. David Paul was still around, in fact had gone on to a huge career, but Jack Simon she'd never heard of.

Mason finally fell asleep with her computer still open, and when she woke up, Phil was dozing on the warm keyboard, fourteen pages of C's scrolling up the screen behind him. For "cat," presumably.

6

~~~ ~~ ~

THE NEXT MORNING, Mason found the gates of the driveway closed. Possibly on account of the three or four photographers who were happy to take photos of her while the gates
creaked slowly open and then closed behind her. They did
their best to engage her in light conversation about her boss
being arrested, but she wasn't feeling chatty. Not only had
there been traffic, they'd been out of cake pops at Starbucks.

As she reached the house and got out of the car, she noticed a young man standing by the door, apparently arguing
with Claudia. Mason sighed, cracked her knuckles and prepared to eject a member of the press.

"I'm sorry," Claudia was saying, "but Mrs. Mann isn't ac-
cepting clients right now."

"Why?"

As Mason get closer, she realized she wasn't looking at a
reporter; she was looking at a college kid.

He was still pleading. "I need her help, and I have money
to pay."

"Because," Claudia was running out of patience, "she's IN

JAIL. I already told you. Leave me your name. We'll call you when she's out."

The young man suddenly heard Mason approaching and whirled around, slipping a little on the dusty ground. He was maybe twenty, if that. Pale blond hair pulled back into a ponytail, facial hair apparent but not groomed, gray eyes and long eyelashes. That much she could see right away, that and the level of anxiety ruining what would otherwise have been a sweet face.

"Who are you?" he asked, nervously.

"I'm Natasha Mason. I'm Mrs. Mann's assistant." She felt mild surprise at how easy it was to say that, after only a day. She looked at the kid with an expression she hoped conveyed a no-nonsense sympathy to his plight, mixed with an all-business intention for him to leave the premises. "I'm sure Mrs. Mann will be out of jail soon, and she'll be able to help you then. Right now, though . . ."

"But I need help right now. My sister's in trouble. My mom told me if I ever needed help, to call Julia Mann." He was literally wringing his hands.

Mason had seen plenty of people in distress. AA meetings are full of people whose lives had fallen apart or been blown up at their own hand. This kid was beside himself, and she felt a bloom of sympathy. She shot a glance at Claudia, who suddenly looked thoughtful.

"Who's your mom?" she asked.

"Jessie Sharp. I'm Ben Sharp. She said she knew Julia in prison . . ." He was so pale that instinctively Claudia took a step closer.

"Way to bury the lede, kid. Your mom did know Julia. She

knew me, too." Claudia's voice had completely changed. "Come on in, let's get you something to eat before we do anything else. You look like you're on your last calorie."

Mason stared at Claudia. She'd been in prison, too? She got the feeling she'd missed the bottom step somehow, a lurching sensation that almost made her open her mouth to ask questions, when suddenly she noticed Ben wasn't looking too hot.

Blood had rushed to his face, and his relief was palpable. "Thank God," he said, and then he went white as a sheet, pitched forward into the hallway, and Mason only just caught him before he smashed his face on the floor.

Claudia sighed. "Strong work, Mason. Bring him to the kitchen."

IT ACTUALLY TOOK nearly a full minute for Ben to come around, by which time Mason had carried him into the kitchen and laid him in one of the comfy chairs near the enormous fireplace at one end. He weighed about three ounces more than she did. She straightened and looked around at the sunshine-filled room, already swimmy with the smell of vanilla and sugared pastry. She felt her mouth start to water, cake pops be damned.

"Put his head between his knees," called Claudia from the stove, where she was melting butter in a pan. "Don't let him puke on the rug."

"Great," muttered Mason. "I haven't even had my second cup of coffee yet. And what's with the press by the gate?"

"Coffee's in the pot, grumpy, and they showed up last night

and haven't left yet. They're only doing their job. I just don't want them doing it any closer to the house. Keep your eyes peeled."

"Now I'm security?"

"It's surprising to me, too, but failing any better option, that's what it looks like."

The kid shook his head, and Mason stepped back. He sat up, slowly, and after a minute his color looked better. Mason turned and went to get coffee.

"How did I get in here?" he asked.

"I carried you, of course." She put the cream back in the fridge and leaned against the closed door, watching to see if he was going to topple again.

He was silent for a moment. Then, "Thank you. Sorry about that. I drove down from Portland last night and have been waiting in my car since five this morning. I didn't want to wake anyone." He sighed. "I guess I forgot to eat."

Claudia huffed at the stove. "Stupid boy." She slammed plates about and dished up an ocher pile of buttery eggs, putting the plate on the long table along with coffee and orange juice. "Come eat. Then we'll talk."

He got up, wavering slightly, but gathered himself and made his way over. A sip of coffee, a forkful of eggs. He opened his mouth, but Claudia raised her spatula.

"Not a word until that's all in."

He subsided and kept shoveling.

ONCE HE'D FINISHED eating, Ben looked far more on top of his game. Mason was also doing better, having joined him in packing away some more of the eggs, plus a half dozen strips of bacon. Claudia was sticking to black coffee, and now she put down her cup and spoke kindly.

"Just start at the beginning. Mason will be seeing Mrs. Mann later, and she'll tell her what you tell us, OK?"

He nodded. "I get it. I need to tell someone because I'm going nuts." He took a deep breath, folding and refolding the napkin he'd brought with him, like a two-ply security blanket. "We're twins, me and Becks. We were born a few years before Mom went to prison. My grandma raised us after that. We visited Mom when we could, and we wrote and called . . . until she died. We still had Christmas, you know? We weren't the only kids in the neighborhood missing a parent. It wasn't so bad."

"She died in jail?" Mason asked.

"Yeah. Of breast cancer. I know Julia Mann and a few other people in the jail, not prisoners, but administrators, tried to get her released in time to die at home, but the wheels didn't move quickly enough. She was only forty-one, and she died alone." His voice was flat, but his hands trembled. Mason shifted in her chair.

"She didn't," interrupted Claudia. "There were several of us with her, honey; she wasn't alone for a minute. She asked us to take care of you, and we said we would. If Julia were here she'd tell you the same." She smiled at him across the room. "Your mom loved you and your sister very much."

He was silent for a moment, his head bowed. He was thin. Mason could see the bones of his back through his T-shirt. But when he looked up, his eyes were clear and determined. "Well, now we need help. Both of us." He poured another cup of coffee and spooned sugar into it. "Becky . . ."

"Becky Sharp? Isn't that a character in a book?" Mason interrupted.

"Yeah, my mom loved to read. She was a school librarian."

"How did she end up in prison?" There was silence at the question, and Mason suddenly realized she'd broken her own unspoken rule about respecting other people's privacy. "Sorry, never mind, carry on."

"She had a boyfriend who sold pot. The police raided their place and found enough to convict him of intent to sell. Minimum mandatory sentencing put her in jail for a decade, just for being there. And maybe she should have known better, but she didn't, and he was a nice enough guy. She was lonely." Ben was defensive, even after all this time.

Claudia shrugged. "Prison is full of women who were in the wrong place at the wrong time because they loved some dumbass."

"Was he your dad?"

"No, we don't know who our dad is. It doesn't matter."

It probably did matter, to be fair, but seeing as it was history, Mason decided to stop being nosy and just let the guy tell his tale.

"Your sister . . . ?"

Ben sighed again. "My sister kind of lost her way a bit. I was always good with my hands, you know, and I wanted to be a carpenter. I'm an apprentice now. Becky was smart in school, thought maybe she'd go to college. But she's real pretty, and she met this older guy at some party, and before we even knew what was happening she was off to Los Angeles to get famous and be in movies, you know?" He looked bitter. "It all happened in the space of a week. I barely got a chance to talk to her about it. Then she texted for a while, and posted photos and stuff, and I knew where she was working, but for the last few months, nothing."

"So you came down to look for her?" Mason sighed inwardly. Finding a pretty girl who wants to be an actress in LA was a fool's errand.

"No, I know exactly where she is. She's in the hospital, because she tried to kill herself. The cops called me when they arrested her, and I got in the car right away. She'll be arraigned on Monday.

"On what charge?"

"Homicide."

Claudia went still.

"Anyone in particular?" asked Mason, her pen poised above the pad.

Ben nodded, and now his eyes filled with tears. "Yeah. She killed someone at the strip club where she was working." He wiped a clumsy hand across his face. "First she was a stripper and now she's a murderer." His voice caught in his throat. "Why didn't she just come home? None of this would have happened if she'd just stayed home." And then he put his head down on the table and wept like a child.

The two women watched him for a moment, then Claudia's phone made a noise like a cat being stepped on. She took it out and looked at it, raising her eyebrow.

"You can go. Julia's ready for you." She got up and fetched a fresh towel and ran cold water on it. She came back and handed it to Ben. "Clean yourself up, kid. Julia will be home later, and you'll want to tell her all about it." Then she turned to Mason. "I'll arrange everything else. And, Mason." She reached in a drawer and threw Mason a set of car keys. "She wants the Rolls."

7

⁀⁔⁀⁔

THE 1961 PHANTOM V is a lovely car, and when Mason carefully pulled up next to a beat-the-fuck-up Nova and three police bikes, she almost felt like apologizing to it. It was apparently a slow news day: The paparazzi were out in force. She got out of the car and leaned against the front wing, fishing a piece of bubble gum from her pocket and slowly unwrapping it. There was every possibility Julia was going to keep her waiting.

Four seconds later, Julia emerged from the police station, accompanied by Archie, who looked sternly at the press and took a position just behind his client. Julia was wearing a long, deep yellow cape with fur around the collar, a cunning little hat, and about ten thousand dollars' worth of jewelry. Mason had no idea where any of it had come from, and Julia certainly hadn't sewn it out of the jailhouse curtains. She took a more comfortable position on the car and prepared to watch Julia hold court. She also had an excellent view of Archie, not that that factored in at all.

Julia paused on the stairs. "Ladies and gentlemen, though I use those terms advisedly: Yet again the LAPD has arrested

me for a crime I didn't commit. If I'd wanted to kill Tony Eckenridge, I could have done so many times, and I wouldn't have
been so boringly obvious about it. The fact that I didn't shows
remarkable restraint, and I will apply the same restraint and
not sue the department. However, if they continue to harass
me, I may be forced to reconsider."

Mason watched Archie struggle throughout this speech.
On the one hand, the lawyer hand, it wasn't great to have your
client goading the police. On the other hand, the agent hand,
it was a great speech and an excellent tactic in the Relaunch
Julia's Career plan. In the end, he just looked uncomfortable
and at one point actually bit his lip. Not that Mason was looking at his mouth.

One of the photographers called Julia's name, and she
turned her wide smile in his direction. "Hello, Dicky, darling,
long time no see." She angled her head back and forth several
times so they could get all the shots they needed. Then she
raked the crowd for Mason, flicked her eyelids meaningfully,
and waited till Mason had opened the Phantom door before
she said, "That's it, y'all," and walked elegantly down the steps.
Archie looked perplexed for a moment, then followed her.

The photographers came, too, and several snapped photos
of Mason while shouting questions at her.

"Who are you, darling?"

"Who's your girlfriend, Julia?"

"Too old to do your own dirty work now, Mrs. Mann?"

Mason looked at Julia as she slid into the back seat of
the car. Archie hesitated, but Julia snapped her fingers and he
climbed in after her. Mason hadn't appreciated how tall
he was until she watched him fold like a deck chair to get
through the door of the old car. Julia slid along the back seat

until the photographers could see her through the window for one last shot. She smiled like the timeless movie star icon she was, then pointed at Mason to get in and drive.

The photographers turned to Mason. Fresh meat.

"Chauffeur for the day, lovely?"

"Like being told what to do? What's your name, sweetheart?"

Mason smiled and gave them all the double finger. She popped her bubble gum, and climbed behind the wheel.

"Photoshop that, bitches," she muttered, as she pulled away from the curb.

"I'm not the only one who needs to show restraint, Mason," said Julia, mildly. "Claudia texted you the address of our next destination. I have to change and get ready. This color is in-a-fucking-ppropriate for where we're going." She dug about in her bag for lotion and started rubbing it into her hands and neck. "Move over, Archie. You're taking up too much room."

Archie was already wedged into the corner, and Mason grinned at him in the driver's mirror as he compressed himself further. When they got to a red light, she looked at the address from Claudia and clicked to start navigation.

"Claudia said we had company. What is she talking about?" Julia asked.

Mason nodded. "A dude showed up at your door this morning claiming to be the son of Jessie Sharp."

Julia frowned. "Ben Sharp?"

Mason was amazed. "How do you remember that?"

"That's all Jessie ever talked about. Ben this and Becky that. I could probably tell you their immunization history if I thought about it. Did Claudia feed him? I bet she did."

Mason laughed. "She had to; he passed out in the hall. He looked like crap."

Julia shrugged. "I assume he showed up because he needed some help."

Mason nodded. "Yeah, but you've got your own troubles to deal with, so presumably he's out of luck." She looked at her boss in the rearview mirror. "We should get you to a meeting as soon as we can."

"I'm fine for now. We can do that later. Of course I'm going to help him. I made a promise. A jailhouse promise."

Mason laughed again. "I didn't realize jailhouse promises were legally binding. The appellation 'jailhouse' in front of something doesn't usually . . ."

Julia Mann snorted impolitely. "Stop speaking. In this case, it was a plain old vanilla promise, made in prison, actually, not in jail, but by people who keep their word. There were four of us in that room besides Jessie: me, Claudia, Lemon Lily and Jennifer Who Is Now Jason."

"You're fucking with me." Mason looked at Archie in the mirror and found him already looking at her. She raised her eyebrows at him and he glanced away.

Julia looked affronted. "I am not fucking with you. That's who was there. No idea where Lemon Lily is, but Jason is alive and well and living in Key West." She paused. "Or was it Key Largo?" She shook her head. "Not that it matters."

Her phone started ringing, and she made a crowing noise in Archie's direction. "Your boss . . . About fucking time . . ." She poked at the phone and a man's voice filled the car.

"Baby! The kid got you out?" It sounded like a very old New Yorker with a very sore throat.

"The kid" rolled his eyes.

Julia was smiling. "Larry! I'm mostly glad you're not dead. They fix your heart?" Mason looked in the mirror and was amazed to see an expression she'd never witnessed before on Julia's face. A sweet smile. No subtext.

"Once they found it," he cackled. "It'll take a lot more than a dicky ticker to keep this asshole down, am I right?"

"You are. The kid seems to have his brain in gear. Go rest. I'm all good."

"No! Wait! Did you kill Tony?" Larry sounded like he was asking her if she'd already ordered coffee. Apparently, any answer would be fine. "Archie said he wasn't sure."

Julia shot Archie a look. "Of course not!" Julia scoffed at the idea. "As if." She paused. "Pretty sure."

"Didn't think so. Just as well. You need to be out and about, baby. Getting calls up the wazoo over here."

"About what?"

"Everything, baby doll. Movies, TV shows, magazine profiles, it's all heating up. People are *Codex* crazy; the curse is catnip, you know that. Spielberg wants you! Christopher Nolan wants you! Oprah wants you!"

Mason flicked another glance in the mirror. Julia's smile was fading.

"I don't care, Larry. I'm done, you know that."

"Baby, don't break my brand-new heart. This is your chance for a comeback."

"I don't want to come back. I left on purpose. I'm retired from acting, Larry."

"You're killing me. I feel pain, actual pain. People are offering money, darling, real money, ten percent of which would be mine. Don't do this to me." The voice broke. "I feel the life force leaving me . . ."

"Quit it, Larry. I told Archie, no to Cinespia, no to all of it."

He roared. "No to Cinespia? Baby, it's just standing and talking for two minutes. You could do it in your sleep. Put on your silver suit, show off your incredible gams and collect the check." He paused. "You know, they'll get Jessica Lange if you don't do it."

"Great, she'll be amazing."

"Glenn Close."

"Super."

"Susan Sarandon. Any number of actresses would love to cameo in *The Codex*."

"Wait, now we're talking about a cameo? I thought we were talking about presenting a movie on a single evening this summer. What are you playing at, Larry?"

"Oh, shit, babycakes, the nurse is coming. Gotta go. I'll tell them to send the script over, yes? I'll tell the kid to give it to you."

"No, Larry, don't . . ." There was a silence. Then Julia put the phone in her bag and sighed. "Damn him, he knows I'm a soft touch for a sick old man." She leaned forward and pointed at Archie's chest. "Work on that. I'm not an actress anymore. I don't give a shit how excited people are about me, they'll have to get unexcited." She looked out of the window. "We're nearly there. It's the purple warehouse on the left. Pull over."

Mason did so, and Julia climbed out of the car. "I'll be twenty minutes. *You*"—she pointed at Mason—"bring Archie up to speed on Becky and Ben, and *you*"—she pointed at Archie—"work your contacts and get whatever information is available. I'll be right back."

Mason was confused. "Where are we? And where are we going that you need to change?"

"We're at my friend's studio. I need hair and makeup. We're going to a funeral, Mason. I can't dance on a grave in these shoes."

Mason turned in the driver's seat and looked at Archie.

"Shall I come back there, or can you handle this slightly strange dynamic of driver and passenger?"

"It gives the conversation a weird power imbalance, but I can bear it if you can. Of course, I'm the one being dri— Jesus wept, can't you use the door?"

Mason threw off the seat belt and climbed up and over the back of the driver's seat, giving Archie an excellent view of her ass as she folded against the roof and slid onto the seat next to him. Once she was there, she immediately regretted it, because now she felt like she was sixteen and they'd parked in order to make out. Or maybe that was just in her head because this man was tickling her limbic system in a way that made her want to drink and then sink her teeth into him, one right after the other. Mason had taken the suggestion not to date in the first year of sobriety very seriously, then decided to take the suggestion into her second year, then the third rolled around and she punted the whole topic. She wasn't in any way ready to entertain even fantasies, but this guy was very appealing.

She settled into a corner and started to explain. "So, this kid showed up this morning to ask for help for his sister."

"Because?"

"She'd been arrested for murdering her stripper girlfriend."

"I think they prefer the term exotic dancer. Is the fact that she's an exotic dancer relevant?"

Mason thought about it. "I guess not, although she was killed in the strip club where she worked."

"Then you don't need to mention it. Let's not be prejudiced against dancers who may or may not also be sex workers."

"You're very enlightened."

"I have three sisters and an ardent second-wave feminist for a mother."

"Congratulations. Julia wants to help. I think she's going to take on the case."

"I'm sorry, why does she care about this person?"

"Her name is Becky Sharp. Because Julia was in jail with her mother," replied Mason, as though that made everything crystal clear.

"And was her mother in jail for murder also?"

"No," said Mason. "Drugs."

He sighed. "Yesterday I was a junior agent, working at a big talent agency, shepherding contracts and negotiations. Today I'm defending a woman accused of murder who now wants to defend *another* woman accused of murder. Like a Russian nesting doll of accusation." He looked at his watch and pulled out his phone. "I don't really understand what happened."

"Julia happened," said Mason. "She has this way of saying things that makes them sound like facts when they are absolutely not. We're both conscripts in Julia's little army."

"She's not even my client—she's my boss's client," mused Archie, frowning as he waited for whoever he'd called to answer their phone. "Hello, is Charlie there? It's Archie Jacobson." He shook his head. "Having a heart attack probably felt like the easier option." He paused. "Hey, Charlie! How's it going? Long time no see." He held the phone away from his mouth for a moment. "Could you get back in the front seat, please? You're making me uncomfortable and I'm working here. You're cramping my style." Then he went back to the call. "I'm looking for information today, rather than sharing it, but I feel like you owe me . . ." He paused. "Well, that's true, but this way I'll owe you and I know you prefer it like that . . ." There was a laugh in his voice that made the edges of Mason's underpants curl, and instead of returning to the front, she started inching silently along, forcing him to move away. Just for the fun of it, of course.

Suddenly, the door flew open and Julia was back.

"Hang up," she said to Archie, and to Mason, "You, out."

"Who is this, Juju?" A very skinny blond woman wearing what appeared to be a dress made of pipe cleaners examined Mason as she climbed out of the car. "Are you a model? You have bones. Walk for me in Milan."

"Uh, no, and . . . thanks?" Mason squeezed past her and started to open the driver's door. Archie climbed out after her and stood a little ways away, still talking on the phone. He'd ignored the order to hang up, and continued to ignore Julia's pointing and clicking of fingers.

"Take this," said the woman, handing Mason a paper bag. "It is your job."

Julia was wearing a long black dress covered in pleats and folds. It looked like origami in clothing form.

"You must," said the blond woman, "steam her immediately upon arrival. Pinch each pleat to a knife edge, steam, move on, quickly, quickly, quickly." She squawked at Julia. "No! Do not sit! Recline! Lean!"

"Don't be so daft," said Julia, settling herself on the seat. "I'm not going to recline at an angle from here to the funeral. You're mad."

"That is Issey Miyake. Original. Vintage. Older than this girl of yours. I loaned it to you for love, Juju, but it better come back in one piece or we will not be speaking again."

"Calm yourself, Madrigal. It's a dress. It'll be fine."

Behind her, Archie hung up and cleared his throat. "I spoke to a journalist friend of mine. Becky Sharp has been working at Galliano's for the last six months."

"Tell me in a minute," said Julia. "First, get back in and hold my skirt."

"I'm sorry?"

Madrigal moved her pipe cleaner–clad body and pushed Archie back into the car. "Hurry, she's creasing." She arranged him on the back seat. "Protrude!" she said. "Straight out, long-legged man, straight out like a clotheshorse." Then she draped the skirt of the dress over his legs, arranging the folds and pleats carefully. "Now don't move."

There was a pause as Archie's eyes met Mason's in the driver's mirror and neither of them said a word.

"Drive slowly," said the blonde to Mason. "And try not to turn at anything greater than twenty miles an hour." She looked back at Julia. "One piece, Juju, one piece!!"

"Yes, yes," said Julia, unconcerned. "Go back to work. I'll send the dress over later by courier. Thank the girls for me." Mason looked at her properly and realized she had a full face of makeup and a complicated and shiny hairdo that she hadn't had twenty minutes earlier. She looked incredible. Elegant. Otherworldly.

Then she looked at Mason and barked, "Drive, for fuck's sake. I want to make sure Tony Eckenridge is completely dead!"

It was possible the other world she was from was Hell. Mason sighed, and pulled away.

~~~

"ALRIGHT, TALK," SAID Julia to Archie. "Tell me about Becky. How much trouble is she in?"

Archie, still sitting very carefully, replied, "Well, like I said, she was working at Galliano's."

Galliano's was Los Angeles's oldest burlesque venue, and not in any way a standard strip joint. Oak paneled and celebrity filled, it had hosted Gypsy Rose Lee and other major stars in its day. Often the women who performed there kept themselves relatively covered, but it was still considered one of the sexiest shows in town. Mason adjusted her mental picture of Becky Sharp accordingly.

"Is there actually a Mr. Galliano?"

"No, there is a Mrs. Galliano. And some financial partners, including one Tony Eckenridge, through the studio. He owned ten percent; the current Mrs. Galliano owns sixty percent; and an investment firm, Agosti Partners, owns the remaining thirty."

"Huh," said Julia. "That's news to me, and I know the current Mrs. Galliano very well."

Mason was surprised. "The club is run by a woman?"

"Yes, and always has been. This is LA history. I'm surprised you don't know this." Archie was raising his eyebrows at her. He was really very good-looking, Mason decided, but there was no point in hating him simply because he was successful and attractive. She'd have to find some other reason, and quickly.

"I'm not from here. NorCal, baby."

"San Francisco?"

"Berkeley."

"Ah, a hippie."

"Yup. Can't you tell?" As Mason was currently wearing skintight jeans and a T-shirt with Rainbow Dash from *My Little Pony* on it, he couldn't, but he just shrugged.

"Well, the original Galliano's was started by Annabel Galliano, back in the 1920s, during Prohibition. Word was the Mob was involved, too, but the Mob was involved in anything slightly illegal back then. It was a regular restaurant up front, with a burlesque and bar for those who knew the right people. After Prohibition, she simply switched things around, putting the girls front and center, and running a private restaurant in the back. Lots of power brokers used it, old Hollywood, you name it. It was quiet, the food was good, and security was tight because, like I said, Mob. Over the years, it's pretty much stayed the same. The current Mrs. Galliano, Maggie, is about your age, Julia, and the victim, Samantha Harris, was twenty-seven, according to my source. She was found in the club, and the toxicology report showed a massive overdose of fentanyl. However, the coroner found petechial hemorrhaging in her eyes. She'd been semiconscious when it happened, but someone smothered her."

Mason looked in the rearview again. "Was she naked?"

Archie raised his eyebrows again. "No. You have a vivid imagination, Miss Mason."

"True story."

"She was fully dressed and completely dead."

Julia considered this. "Why did they arrest Becky Sharp?"

"Because she was right there, unconscious, her wrists slashed. Murder-suicide. However, the wrists were really just for show. Horizontal cuts, not vertical, and shallow. The cops took her to the hospital and she's still there. Under arrest and on suicide watch. A twofer."

"What has she said? What does her lawyer say?" Mason was driving carefully, but took a corner slightly above twenty, causing Julia to roll a little and make a squeaking noise.

"Mason! Careful of the dress."

Archie Jacobson was calm. "She's said absolutely nothing, and as for her lawyer, she doesn't have one."

Julia spoke. "Yes, she does, she has me. You two can go talk to her later. It'll be sweet. You can hold hands."

Archie blushed, surprisingly. "Shouldn't you speak to her, as her lawyer?"

"You can be my legal assistant. Or cocounsel."

"I'm not really a lawyer in the sense that I can take on outside clients . . . Larry wouldn't . . ."

"Larry's in the hospital, just like Becky. You can visit him afterward and tell him for the nineteenth time I'm not a working actress anymore." She rubbed her hands together. "Alright, pull over behind these other cars, Mason, and bring the steamer." She waited until the car was stopped and ordered Archie out.

Mason climbed in the back, holding the bag.

"I've never steamed anything other than broccoli, Julia. Archie might be more qualified for this. He looks like he irons."

"Not sure why I feel mildly insulted," said Archie, through the window. "But I do."

Mason pulled out the steamer, which looked a little like a vacuum cleaner, and switched it on. "It's broken."

Julia was carefully standing as much as she could and

shaking out her dress. The pleats and folds looked perfect to Mason, but what did she know? "It's not. It takes a minute to warm up. Honestly, I can see why you might not have used a steamer yourself, but surely you've seen one before." She looked at Mason's outfit. "I mean, in someone else's hands or something."

Mason shook her head. "Oh, wait, here it goes."

Julia demonstrated, and for five minutes Mason steamed and folded and pinched. Slowly, the windows steamed up, and Julia started muttering about her hair. Eventually, she declared herself satisfied and got ready to leave the vehicle.

So it was that as the other mourners filed up to the chapel they were treated to the sight of Julia Mann, actress of some repute, emerging from a Rolls-Royce in a cloud of steam, her folded black gown making her resemble a bat straight from Hades.

"And that," said one of them, quietly to another, "is how a great actress makes an entrance."

8

MOST FUNERALS HAVE neither security nor a paparazzi line, but this was not a regular funeral. It was the hottest ticket in town and standing room only.

This being a Hollywood party, everyone was watching the door, and as Julia entered the chapel, there was a discernable shift in energy. To be fair, she did take three steps inside the room and pause, head tilted to catch the slanting light from the chapel's stained glass windows, knowing instinctively (and from decades of practice) how to hit her mark. Plus, she wasn't going to waste all that steaming.

There was an audible gasp. After all, both TMZ and the *Los Angeles Times* had reported her arrest for the murder of the dude currently reclining in a box at the front, so the word "nerve" could be clearly heard, along with "chutzpah," "cojones" and, more predictably, "balls of steel." Julia angled her head one final time, in case anyone was filming (someone almost certainly was), then started threading her way through the crowd.

"Stay with me," she muttered to Mason. "I don't think anyone's going to take a swing, but you never know."

"I'm your sponsor, not your bodyguard," Mason muttered back. "If they swing, you'd better duck lower than I do."

"Look, just pay attention. I didn't kill Tony, but I am willing to bet actual money that whoever did is in here somewhere. I want to be near the front, though, so I can make sure Tony stays in the casket."

"You've lost your fucking mind," said Mason. "The man is dead. He was dead in your swimming pool. He's been dead ever since." She turned to Archie. "You're tall. Can you see any empty seats?"

It wasn't going to be that easy, unfortunately. If you're the center of attention at a Hollywood event, it won't be long before somebody sidles up and tries to become center-adjacent. The first person to impede Julia's forward momentum was a tall, dark-haired woman who reminded Mason irresistibly of an ostrich. It was something in the head movements, she reflected, rather than, say, her inability to fly. Mason realized she was getting hungry and wondered if there were going to be snacks at this funeral. Low blood sugar is the enemy of the alcoholic: hungry, angry, lonely, tired—the four horsemen that will carry you off to a relapse if you're not watching your back. Hungry rides in front and causes a lot of damage.

"Julia, my love," said the ostrich lady, "how extraordinarily brave of you to show up today."

"Why's that, Camilla?" Julia leaned forward so the two women could air-kiss, which really cemented the ostrich-y vibe.

"Well," said Camilla, "you did get arrested for killing the man, so it's possibly a little gauche to be here. Not to mention you're the personification of the *Codex* Curse right now, and no one wants an evil fairy at a funeral."

"I think you're thinking of christenings, and maybe she's

checking her work?" said Mason, unable to stop herself. She really should have eaten.

Julia's mouth tightened. "Tony and I were old enemies. It's only polite to pay my respects."

A man appeared at Camilla's elbow. He literally had a mustache drawn on his upper lip; Mason could hardly tear her eyes away. "Julia, how lovely to see you." He lowered his voice. "Is it true you're going to remake *The Codex*?"

"No," said Julia, evenly. "I am not. I'm long retired."

"Great actresses never retire," he replied, waggishly. "They merely wait for better lighting."

Julia smiled and tried to keep moving. But the dam had been breached now, and Mason suddenly realized there was a line forming.

"Julia, I heard you're filming a sequel to The Codex*?"*

"Julia, is it true you were suing Tony to prevent him from remaking The Codex*?"*

"Darling, can you put in a word for me with the right people? I'd love to score the remake."

"I know a wonderful seamstress who can get you back into that catsuit, just say the word . . ."

Mason turned to Archie, who looked as nonplussed as she felt.

He said, "There's a seat near the front behind a row of family and power people. If we can shake Julia loose, we can put her there."

Mason sighed, watching her boss, who was still surrounded. The crowd was moving in fits and starts all around them, and it didn't seem like the funeral was going to begin anytime soon.

Archie looked sympathetic. "While we wait, want to know who's who?" he asked.

"Sure. Julia showed me a picture of his ex-wife already. She's in the front, right?"

Archie ran his eyes over the room and nodded. "Yeah, that's Helen. Next to her is Christine Greenfield, his second-in-command at the studio."

Mason nodded. "The one who had the accident . . . And Jade Solomon is sitting over there with a bird on her hat."

"Not a real bird."

"No, unless it's super well trained."

They both looked at the actress, who bounced light even better in person than she did on film. It isn't always the case. Mason knew lots of young actors who looked kind of gawky and big-featured in real life but simply amazing on-screen. Jade was wearing a tiny hat with an even tinier bird that only someone who looked like that could pull off.

"On the far side of Christine . . . that's the mayor . . ."

Mason shot Archie a look. "I recognize the mayor."

Archie shrugged. "Keep your hair on. Next to him is our lesser state congressperson, and on his other side is the guy who owns all those fancy outdoor malls and *actually* runs the city."

He kept scanning the room, and now he indicated a woman in the second row.

"The blonde behind the mayor is Patty Menninger, who heads up the Academy Museum . . . you know?"

"The one by the Tar Pits?"

Archie nodded. "Yeah, the movie museum. It's good. You should go." He pointed. "There's Tony's assistant, Cody, trying not to look like he's freaking out at all the shit he has to do now that his boss is dead."

Mason looked. It was true, the guy looked pretty unnerved. However, he was managing to text at a clip that wouldn't have embarrassed a fifteen-year-old girl, and that's saying a lot.

Archie continued. "That's Jason Reed, the director of the *Codex* remake, at least at last report. Who knows what's actually happening with that project now that Tony's dead." The guy he pointed out was one of a very few people not on their phone. He was looking around at the chapel, as if making mental notes for a re-creation later. Which of course was always possible. Archie went on to point out several studio heads, directors, producers, actors whose names Mason knew but faces she didn't, and others whose faces she knew but names she didn't. Some people were tearfully reading the order of service pamphlet, but most of the rest were texting while mourning. If you'd bombed the place, you'd have stopped production on every movie in town, Mason thought, then wondered how long it would take to fill the void and restart filming. About a week, probably.

"How is it you know everyone?" she said to Archie.

He shrugged. "It's my job. Not only to know everyone, but to know how they relate. For example," he said, pointing to a plump man a few feet to their left and dropping his voice, "that guy wrote a two-million-dollar check last week to secure the rights to *Speaking with the Moon*, the winner of last year's Booker Prize, and currently holds the lead for most popular producer in town, if you happen to be a female actor who can play twenty-two and dye your hair red. That guy"—he pointed again—"lost the bidding war for the book and is currently trying to prevent several prominent actors from reading for the winner while also trying to option the next book by *Moon*'s author, who hasn't even started writing it yet."

"Why do you care about this stuff?"

"Like I said, it's my job. Hollywood is all about secret webs of influence and power, and agents sit at the center like proverbial spiders, their many legs outstretched, trying to keep track of which fly is where."

Mason straightened up; Julia had shot her a look that meant it was time to move.

"Not sure that metaphor really made agents seem all that great, not going to lie," she said to Archie, as she moved away.

"That's OK," he replied, following. "We can take it."

Mason used her considerable strength to push through the crowd to Julia and her boots to step on enough toes to get them to the front of the chapel. By the time Mason had delivered Julia to her seat, she could tell her boss was exhausted and—and this was more serious—shaky and probably antsy as hell for a drink.

"Did you eat before they released you this morning?" she muttered. Julia shook her head. Mason noticed her own hands were shaking, and she'd actually had breakfast. She looked toward the front of the chapel. Christine Greenfield was approaching the podium, a small set of cards in her hand. She was about to deliver the eulogy.

"Do you want to get out of here?" she whispered to Julia. "We either Irish goodbye it immediately, or we're stuck here for the speeches."

"We stay," said Julia, firmly. "I'm watching for guilt. I'm fine."

"The room is filled with actors and studio executives," said Mason. "You're not going to see a real feeling anywhere. And you're not fine. We should . . ."

Julia lowered her voice, but not her vehemence. "Look, for some reason Tony was at my house, which is mystery number one, then someone followed him there and shot him in the back of the head, mystery two, and that someone is probably here, and I am going to find out who it is and send them my pool cleaning bill, if not straight to jail."

Besides, it was too late to leave. Christine was clearing her throat and gesturing for everyone to settle down.

"Go wait with Archie," Julia hissed. "I'm fine. If you don't think I spent my entire twenties hungry as hell and furious as fuck, you really don't understand the life of an actor. Go!"

Mason frowned, but beat it to the back of the room, where Archie had secured wall space for leaning against. She leaned, and watched as Christine cleared her throat again and began.

"Tony was the kind of man who continued to believe in the magic of movies," she said, looking only briefly at the cards in her hand. "He still went every week, still ate popcorn, still cried at all the endings, happy and sad. He was a true movie lover, and there are so few of those left in the business nowadays."

Mason looked over the crowd. Jade Solomon—she of the accident and the millinery bird—was staring at Julia with such intensity that Mason was amazed Julia wasn't getting a sunburn. Julia was actively ignoring Jade, but there was no way she didn't feel it.

Christine was still talking. "Tony's interest was never in rehashing the past, but in improving on it, reinterpreting it. While other studios made sequel after sequel, or shot-for-shot remakes of classic films, Tony always urged us to reinvent. Reinvigorate. The upcoming renewal of *The Codex* was to be his greatest achievement, and it will surprise no one here that he left exhaustive memos about how everything is to be done."

There was laughter around the room, and some relief. Mason wondered if being such a control freak had made Tony many friends, or just anxious colleagues. Would any of them be anxious enough to wield a rifle in the middle of the night?

"The LAPD has assured me they will not rest until his killer is in custody and justice has been served. In the meantime, the studio will move forward with the projects Tony cared so deeply about."

There was a ripple of applause as she stepped down, and then a Grammy winner sang "Rainbow Connection" and there wasn't a dry eye in the house.

Except for Julia's, of course.

AS THE FUNERAL crowd made their way en masse down the hill to where the body would be interred, a middle-aged man scurried up to where Julia, Archie and Mason were standing.

"Mrs. Mann?" he asked, even though he presumably knew exactly who she was.

Julia nodded.

"I'm Frank McClennan, of Nutter, McClennan and Fish?"

"Tony's personal lawyer," murmured Archie, proving again that he knew everyone.

"Yes," replied the lawyer. "I wanted to ask you to attend the reading of Tony's will. It's Monday morning at ten." He paused, and handed over a business card. "At our offices."

"Obviously," said Julia, "but why do I need to be there?"

"Because you're a legatee, of course. A named beneficiary."

Julia made a face that clearly expressed *what the fuck?* "You must be mistaken, Mr. McClennan. Tony wouldn't have left me anything."

The lawyer rubbed his hands together, reminding Mason of a mouse, though she wasn't sure why. "But he did, Mrs. Mann. You don't need to attend the reading if you don't want to; we can provide you with the details of the bequest another way, once the rest of the beneficiaries have heard the details."

Julia opened her mouth, then closed it again. The crowd eddied around them, and she suddenly started walking down toward the graveside.

"Actually, I'm happy to attend. Give the details to my assistant." She got a few feet away, then turned to add, "I'm sure it will be interesting to see how much trouble Tony can cause from beyond the grave. Always a director, to the end. Of course," continued Julia, raising her voice to make sure everyone could hear, "it doesn't matter what he left me. Whatever it is, I'm simply going to set fire to it." She disappeared into the crowd and Archie went after her.

Mason turned to the lawyer and grinned. "I'm the assistant," she said. "I'll be the one carrying the matches."

AFTER THEY'D DROPPED Archie at his place and returned to the house, Julia climbed out of the car and addressed Mason.

"Go home. Tomorrow morning go talk to Becky Sharp. Archie will meet you at Cedars. I'm cooked. I'm going to eat something and lie down."

Mason leaned across and studied Julia. She looked ashen, exhausted.

Mason said, "It's been a long, tough day. Let's eat together and I'll take you to a meeting. You'll feel better."

"I won't."

"You will, and you need to get your court card signed. I've never gone to a meeting and regretted it."

Julia made an incredulous face. "Then you haven't been to enough meetings. I once had a chair thrown at me in a meeting." She paused. "I don't actually regret that particular meeting; it's the boring ones I regret." She closed the door of the Rolls and leaned down to speak through the open window. "Go away, Mason. I'm fine."

Mason shook her head, stubbornly. "You're on day five of not drinking. You haven't been to a meeting. You're making it harder on yourself."

"I was sober before you were born."

"And you were drunk last week."

Julia frowned. "You're very rude." She turned to walk away, moving stiffly. "I'll go to one online."

"Text me which one. I'll see you there."

"No, stop bugging me. Go away."

Mason opened her mouth to speak. Julia didn't even turn around, but said, "Whatever you're about to say, swallow it. I'm not going to drink today. I make no promises beyond that."

She went through the door and closed it behind her.

Mason put the Rolls-Royce in gear and started a three-point turn.

"Mother. Fucker."

9

~~~

CEDARS-SINAI IS A large hospital, and the next morning it took Archie and Mason a while to find Becky Sharp. As they approached, however, the cop outside the room was a dead giveaway.

Once Archie explained who they were (Mason was temporarily appointed his paralegal), they were allowed in. The room looked like every other in the hospital. Pale beige walls, windows you couldn't open, curtains with a pattern you find calming and a variety of machines whose beeping and whirring went in and out of phase with irritating irregularity.

Becky Sharp was tiny. She looked like a child lying in bed, and even Mason—who was probably the least maternal person in the hospital—felt a pang of sympathy for her. Every line of her body expressed exhaustion and sorrow.

"Ms. Sharp?" Archie's voice was gentle.

Becky turned her head a little to look. She was, as her brother had said, very pretty.

"Yes?" Becky's voice matched the rest of her. High, gentle, young.

"I'm Archie Jacobson. Julia Mann sent me. She's taken on your case."

"Julia Mann? My mom's friend? From jail?" An expression crossed her face that was hard to read. Hope? If it was, it was only brief. Her face slipped back into despair.

Archie smiled. "Yes. Your brother came to LA and asked her for help."

"Ben's here? In Los Angeles?" Mason couldn't tell what Becky was thinking, and also realized the younger woman had either not noticed she was there or was completely ignoring her. She decided to make her presence felt.

"Yes." She stepped forward, next to Archie, so Becky couldn't fail to see her. "He came to Julia's house."

Becky said, "I don't want to see him." She turned her head away again and closed her eyes, shifting her legs restlessly. "I don't need a lawyer."

"Julia Mann's not charging you." Mason found herself a little needled by the younger woman. Maybe Becky Sharp was a really sick girl. Or maybe she was a murderer. "She's keeping a promise to your mom, and besides, you're in deep shit here and there's every chance you're going to prison for a long time."

Becky wasn't buying it. "It's not the money. I just want to die." She didn't sound like she was joking, and Mason looked at all the needles and fluid and wires and realized she was being kept alive by the hospital. At that moment, a nurse came in carrying a tray.

"Hi, Becky, time to eat something, honey." She was efficient and sweet, but firm. She pressed buttons and raised Becky to a sitting position, pulling the bed table over and lifting the lids from the dishes on the tray. "Come on now, how about something small? Jell-O? A little fruit, maybe?"

Becky shook her head. "I don't want anything."

The nurse shook her head. "Hey, listen. There are girls your age and younger dying from terrible things all over this hospital. They'd give anything to be you, even if you have gotten yourself into a little trouble. There's nothing wrong with you a good meal wouldn't fix." She held up a spoon of Jell-O. "Come on . . . it's strawberry." The Jell-O wobbled on the spoon, just like an ad. Mason started salivating. She'd gone to a meeting early and eaten breakfast on the way. Toaster Strudel. No frosting, which now felt like an error on her part. She could have used the extra calories.

Becky turned her head into the pillow. "Can you make those people go away?"

The nurse looked at them for the first time; she'd been so focused on Becky. "Would you mind . . . ?"

Archie pulled a business card from his wallet and laid it on the table. "Ms. Sharp, Julia Mann is your lawyer, and I'm helping, too. If and when you need us, just call."

"And," added Mason, trying to build on what the nurse had said, "you're being kind of an asshole. Your brother drove all the way from Portland. Julia Mann, who hasn't even met you, sent both of us to help you. Get your shit together, lady. Unless, of course, you killed that stripper, in which case I guess pulling a dying swan is better than ending up behind bars."

For the first time, Becky Sharp seemed to hear and turned her gaze to Mason. Her eyes were the same gray as her brother's, her eyelashes long and dark against her skin. The nurse and Archie, meanwhile, were staring at Mason as if she were a monster.

"She wasn't a stripper," said Becky, clearly. "She was an artist, a filmmaker, a beautiful person. She was dead when I woke up. But if Sam's dead, I want to be dead, too."

"You were friends?" Mason ignored the frowning nurse and the reproving muttering of Archie Jacobson.

"We were in love. She was everything to me."

Mason raised her voice a little. "Well then why are you letting whoever killed her get away with it? Would she just roll over if someone hurt you?"

"Look, miss, I don't know who you are, but you have to leave. My patient is very weak. I don't want her upset." The nurse was small, but apparently made of steel, because the grip on Mason's arm was bruising. Archie took her other arm, and together he and the nurse started ushering her out. Mason turned to look at Becky one last time.

"If you really give a shit about your girlfriend, help us find out who killed her. We'll help you, but not if you're going to be a dick about it."

The cop had now opened the door and was stepping into the room. Mason pushed back against the nurse, who simply tightened her grip.

"Eat the goddamned Jell-O, you tiny little chickenshit!" shouted Mason, her boot heels leaving marks on the linoleum. Then she shook off the cop, the lawyer and the nurse, like the punch line of a very bad joke, and raised her palms in surrender.

Becky stared at her, then relented. "Alright, I'll eat the Jell-O if you promise to listen to what I have to say about Sam."

The nurse smiled at Becky. "That's great. Maybe later you can try something with protein." She shot Mason a glare that made it clear Mason hadn't made a friend, then bustled out.

The cop followed her, and Archie pulled the visitor's chair closer to Becky's bed. Mason, as was her habit, leaned against the wall.

Archie voice was soft. "I'm going to ask you questions, alright? Some of them might be unpleasant, even rude, but you'll need to answer them truthfully."

Becky nodded, spooning Jell-O with increasing enthusiasm. Apparently, her appetite had returned. "I don't have any secrets."

"Everyone has secrets," said Mason.

"Not everyone," replied Becky, looking at her and shrugging. "Maybe you're hanging out with the wrong people."

Mason opened her mouth but caught Archie's eye and closed it. *Whatever.*

Archie leaned forward, his elbows on his knees. "Firstly, I'm sorry about Sam. For your loss." He smiled sadly, and Mason realized he genuinely meant it. He had an air of solidity about him she found appealing, like nothing would faze him. She thought of him in the car, tenting Julia's dress, at the funeral, dealing with the crowd . . . then she realized she needed to pay attention.

Becky nodded. "I loved her. We were going to move in together. Maybe. Once she got a better job than Galliano's. Not that there was anything wrong with working there. It was fun and Mrs. G is lovely. But Sam had dreams."

"How did you get the job at Galliano's?"

"My boyfriend took me there. He knew Mrs. G."

"And she offered you a job on the spot?"

Becky shook her head. "No, we just talked. I told her I was looking for acting opportunities, and she said to call her if I

needed work in the meantime." Becky looked at Archie carefully. "She was very nice, you know, not sleazy like everyone
else." She smoothed the hospital sheet across her lap like a
skirt at a church social.

"Everyone else?" Archie's tone was neutral.

Becky paused. "My ex-boyfriend took me all around, you
know. He knew lots of people . . . like that. He said he knew
Hollywood people, but most of his friends owned clubs, or
places where girls, you know, worked." She looked uncomfortable, suddenly.

"As sex workers, is that what you mean?" Again, that neutral tone. No judgment, just gathering facts.

Becky relaxed a little. "I don't know, but clubs and bars,
mostly. Sometimes they had rooms upstairs, you know."

"I do, but assume I don't." Archie was making her comfortable, gentling her like a horse.

Becky frowned a little. "Well, there would be a bar downstairs, and, like, a restaurant or something, maybe, and then
if you met someone who liked you, you could go upstairs and
be more private."

"And did you work at those places?"

Becky shook her head. "No. One night my ex wanted me to
'try it out,' like, just one time, with a friend of his, but I didn't
like him."

"The friend?"

"Yeah. I let him kiss me, and feel me up, you know, to be
friendly and because I didn't want my boyfriend to get mad,
but that was it. And, like, by that point I wasn't really having
any fun with my boyfriend, either; he just kept trying to make
me do stuff I didn't want to do, and he didn't know any real

modeling places, either. Just weird photographers who wanted me to take my clothes off."

"And did you?" Archie's tone and body language were making it easy for Becky to open up, and Mason wondered if it was an act, if he was actually biting his tongue to stop himself from saying *Jesus wept, kid, it's lucky you didn't end up in some serial killer's trunk* . . . and then she realized those were *her* thoughts. Whoops.

Becky was nodding. "Sure, why not. I got some nice pictures." She frowned again. "They weren't posted or anything; they were private." She paused. "And I had sex with another girl on the Internet, but that wasn't for money."

"OK," said Archie, still unflappable. "Your boyfriend asked you to do that?"

"Yeah. The other girl was really nice; we smoked a lot of pot, drank some champagne and, you know, got into each other. It was cool. But then afterward, I realized my boyfriend had been live streaming the whole thing." Suddenly, she shrugged. "I don't think he was a very nice person, actually. Sam told me you shouldn't publish content of people without their permission, but I didn't know that."

"What's your boyfriend's name?" Archie had pulled out his phone and opened the notes app.

"Rufus."

Archie looked up. "Last name?"

"I don't know."

Mason just managed to stop her jaw from dropping, then looked at Archie. Nothing. No reaction.

Becky explained. "He did tell me, but I, like, forgot, and after a week or so it was too embarrassing to ask again, you know?"

"Yes, of course, I understand."

Becky nodded, glad to have found someone sympathetic. "Anyway, he and I broke up and I went back to Galliano's. I told Mrs. G the whole story, and she was very nice and said I could work for her, no private rooms or anything like that. I started on the floor, and after a few weeks I met Sam and we started dating." She looked earnestly at Archie. "You would have liked her. Everyone did. She was really creative. She always had loads of ideas." She sniffed. "She never did drugs. Said it dulled her creativity. There is no way, *no way*, she took an overdose."

"But someone thought a drug overdose would seem plausible," Archie said.

"Someone underestimated her," replied Becky. "People did that a lot."

Archie thought for a moment. "Were drugs common at the club, generally?"

Becky shook her head. "Not at all. Mrs. G and Danny are very anti, you know? Wanted the girls to stay sharp."

"Who's Danny?" asked Mason.

"Danny Agosti, he's the money."

"Mrs. Galliano's business partner," said Archie, then asked, "Did you and Sam fight a lot?"

"No." Becky shook her head. "I mean, sometimes, but not a lot."

"Did she fight with anyone else at the club? Ever mention anything like that?"

More headshaking. "No, like I said, most everyone liked her. She was very alive, do you know what I mean? Lots of energy."

"Where was she from?"

Becky looked surprised. "Here, I guess. I never asked her."

"Did she have family?"

"She never mentioned anyone."

"What did you do when you weren't at the club?"

"How do you mean?"

"I mean did you have another job, did you go to school, did you go to the gym, anything?"

"I went to the library with Sam sometimes. They have free Internet. She worked on her stuff, you know."

Archie appeared to think for a moment. "What kind of stuff?"

Becky's face lit up. "My goodness, she always had so much stuff! Plans for this and that, ideas for businesses, projects, things she wanted to create . . ." She looked sad. "I miss her so much."

Mason, watching her, felt the first twinge of positive feeling. If she cared so much about another human being, maybe she wasn't a complete loss.

Archie nodded and reached over to pat her hand. "You're OK now." He got to his feet. "Keep eating, and I'll arrange bail when you're ready to be released from the hospital. Julia Mann wants you to come to her house, stay with her while we work on your case. Your brother's already there."

Becky nodded, the color fading from her face. She put the empty Jell-O container on the tray and lay back, turning her face to the pillow. "Thank you," she said softly. "I'm glad you're going to find Sam's killer, but it's not going to bring her back." A tear slid down her cheek and blotted itself on the pillowcase. "Nothing's going to bring her back."

~ ~ ~

OUTSIDE THE ROOM, Archie sighed. "Thanks for helping get that started, Mason," he said. "I was worried she wasn't going to talk to us."

Mason shrugged. "You're welcome," she said, airily. "Although thanks to my persuasiveness, you now have two clients who proclaim their innocence in the face of means, motive and opportunity, which means two investigations and defenses ahead of you you're not even supposed to be doing because you're an agent, not really even a lawyer."

"Hey, I am too a lawyer . . ."

"And I am so hungry right now I can barely think straight, so I'm not going to be any help at all." Suddenly, Mason was exhausted. The last thirty-six hours had been a lot. A new job, a new boss who immediately got arrested. A fainting stranger, a funeral with a fake mustache *and* a fake bird, a whiny potential murderer, a sexy lawyer . . . lots of feelings, lots of neurochemicals. It was all a bit much.

Archie looked at her and made a decision. "Look, we both got press-ganged into this a little bit, right? Julia has a way of making things happen."

Mason nodded. Her blood sugar gauge was on empty. She was about to go supercritical.

"So we're a team. Together we'll just have to do our best. And our best means we need to immediately go and eat two very large burgers, a mountain of fries and at least one chocolate milk shake each, right?"

Mason nodded again. She might be hallucinating. Had he just said "milk shake"? Milk shakes were her *jam*.

Archie took her arm. "Come on, Natasha. Let's go find some food."

"No one calls me Natasha unless they're mad at me."

"Well, something tells me I might need that in the future, so I'll go back to Mason for now."

That was the moment, Mason realized later; the moment she started getting a serious crush on Archie Jacobson. Sadly, it was also the moment things started to go downhill in every other conceivable way.

10

～～～

THE OFFICES OF Nutter, McClennan and Fish were on Wilshire Boulevard, on several floors of an eighties tower that featured colored glass mosaics and marble staircases. As Julia and Mason stepped out of the elevator, Julia suddenly clutched Mason's arm and stopped.

"Wait . . . I see Patty Menninger."

Mason frowned. "The woman who runs the Academy Museum? So what?"

"She's a fiend in human form."

Mason hadn't thought anything terrified Julia, so she peered into the lobby of the law firm with some interest. She saw a woman wearing a kicky pink pantsuit.

"That woman there? In pink?"

"She always wears pink. It's her signature color. The blush of the beast."

"You're insane. Let's go in."

Julia hung back. "No, I don't want to talk to her. Not without an exorcist. Not without a unicorn carrying an iron crossbow with silver arrows. Not without a sack of sage the size of a fucking armchair."

Mason looked at her boss. "Julia, are you drunk? Did you start the morning with a double shot?"

"No," Julia hissed, "I'm stone-cold sober, but that woman scares the shit out of me."

"Why?" Mason looked again and noticed a tiny pink dog next to the woman, who was talking on a pink cell phone. She really had committed to her signature color.

"Because she's constantly on the prowl for her museum. Or for her charities, which are numerous and random. And it's not like I don't give! I gave her some of Jonathan's stuff. Not all of it, but plenty of screenplays and papers and things like that. But the asking never stops. And she's always trying to save me from myself. It's incredibly tiresome. Eat breakfast. Go vegan. Wear crystals. Steam your vagina. Cleanse your chakras."

Mason tipped her head. "I'm sorry, back up a bit . . ."

Julia ignored her. "Stop eating dairy. Save the whales. Quit sugar. Add fiber. Do Pilates. Do yoga. Eat lunch." Other people were coming out of the elevators, and suddenly Christine Greenfield was there.

"Julia? What a pleasure to see you, even under such sad circumstances. I'm so glad you've agreed to be in the *Codex* remake. It's thrilling."

Julia took a deep breath and turned to her. "I'm not sure where you got that. I have no intention of being in the movie. You must have misunderstood."

Christine smiled but shook her head. "No, Tony left me a voicemail. He said he was sitting with you and you'd just agreed to be in it. I could hear you laughing."

"The night he was killed?"

She nodded. "Yes, I guess that's why he came to see

you." She made a sad face. "But of course if you don't want to do it . . ."

"Do you still have the voicemail?"

"Of course. It's the last time I ever heard his voice." Christine's eyes welled up, but somehow she retracted her tears and pulled it together. "Do you want to hear it?"

The doors to the lobby opened, and Mr. McClennan looked uncertainly out at the elevator bay. "Uh . . . are you ladies joining us? We're ready to begin."

Behind him, Patty Menninger spotted them and waved. "Hi there, ladies!! Aquarius is squaring Libra. It's a perfect day for this."

Christine Greenfield waved back but dropped her voice. "That woman scares the crap out of me."

"You're both nuts. She's harmless. Let's go." Mason grabbed Julia by the sleeve and pulled.

Reluctantly, the two women followed her into the office.

The conference room was large, and the long table boasted a display of breakfast pastries sufficient to feed twenty. Coffee, tea, fresh orange and grapefruit juices. A fruit platter. Cookies. It seemed like overkill, but Mason had never been to a will reading before, and maybe this was standard.

Julia had sailed into the room like a battleship under full sail, with Mason towed in her wake. She looked around and tried to identify everyone.

Patty Menninger, still on her phone, the dog on her lap now. It was a shade of pink not found in nature, but the bow on its head was pulling it together. It was more stylish than Mason was, and she felt inadequate.

Helen Eckenridge, the widow. Dry-eyed and elegant.

Mason was admiring her outfit when suddenly Helen noticed Julia.

"What's she doing here?" She stood up. "Who invited her?"

"I did," said McClennan. "She's a named beneficiary."

Helen snorted, her face becoming increasingly red. "How could she possibly benefit when she probably killed him herself? He was found dead in her swimming pool, for crying out loud." She turned to Christine. "You can't allow it."

Christine Greenfield shook her head. "Helen, she was released on bail, so presumably there's still sufficient doubt . . ."

"There's no doubt," said Julia, crisply. "I didn't kill him and I wouldn't be here if I had, would I? I realize everyone seems to think I'm shameless, but there are limits. I'm here because I thought it might be informative and interesting." She sat down, pointing to the chair next to her. "Mason, sit."

Mason sat, and looked around the table. She recognized Cody Malone, Tony's assistant. Then she looked at the selection of pastries again. With a grand total of nine people in the room, they would each have to eat a couple to make a dent. She wondered why she worried about this kind of thing, then she reached for a Danish.

Mr. McClennan coughed politely. "Good morning, everyone, thank you for coming. It was Mr. Eckenridge's wish that you all be gathered together to hear his will, and I appreciate your attendance."

"It's just like Tony to want a scene, and just like an actress to show up for it," said Helen, still clearly a little upset. Her fingernails were tapping a tattoo on the table.

Everyone pretended not to hear her. The lawyer opened a long document and coughed again.

"Mr. Eckenridge left the majority of his financial assets and various properties to his wife, Helen."

Mason raised her eyebrows. She thought they were divorced; everyone referred to her as his ex-wife.

The lawyer continued. "He also left Helen creative rights to *The Codex*, specifically, although the rest of the Repercussion catalog he left to the studio." He looked around the room. "Meaning she controls all decisions about use, distribution, reproduction and adaptation of the work, in perpetuity."

Helen's fingers stopped their tapping. She didn't look surprised, so presumably she'd known about this.

The lawyer gave another little cough. Possibly, he had a cigar habit he didn't like to talk about, or maybe he found will reading upsetting.

"His collection of Repercussion movie memorabilia he left to the Academy Museum, to be sold or displayed as they choose, for the benefit of the museum."

Patty Menninger beamed and looked around. "As he promised. It's a world-class collection." She hesitated, suddenly. "Wait . . . only the Repercussion archive? What about everything else?"

The lawyer looked quickly at the document. "It's specifically the Repercussion archive. It doesn't mention anything else."

Patty looked confused. "But he'd agreed to all of it. The Repercussion archive was the centerpiece of his collection, but for the last several decades he's been collecting all kinds of memorabilia. He was masterful." Mason was amazed to see what looked like tears in her eyes. "He agreed to give us everything. I've planned exhibits around it. His collection of famous movie footwear was going to be the centerpiece of next summer." She looked at Mason, for some reason. "I was calling it *The Sole of Hollywood.*"

Mason raised her eyebrows and nodded slowly, as you might to a small child. "That sounds . . . compelling."

Helen Eckenridge spoke. "Presumably, that means the rest of it comes to me?"

McClennan nodded. "As part of his personal effects, yes."

Helen looked at Patty. "We'll sort it out, Patty. I don't want his dusty old crap, no offense."

Patty looked like she was getting ready to take offense, but in the end she smiled a tight little smile at Helen and fell silent.

McClennan hesitated a second or two before continuing. "The studio itself he left in pieces."

"I'm sorry?" Christine sounded affronted. "The studio is in great shape."

The lawyer blushed. "You misunderstand me. I mean that he left it to several people."

Christine was definitely not understanding that. "How is that possible? He promised it would come to me, that I was going to run it after he was gone. We discussed plans in detail, right up to the week he died." She looked at Cody. "Right? You were in the room for most of it."

Cody nodded, then shrugged. "That was my understanding. You've been essentially co-running it anyway, since he got sicker."

McClennan was now pinker than Patty's poodle. "Be that as it may, the document is very clear: One third of the studio goes to you, one third to his assistant Cody Malone . . ."

Cody choked. "Wait, what? That's insane. I mean, he said

he would take care of me, but I was thinking maybe a production deal . . . or his desk . . . maybe his collection of ties . . ." He looked genuinely horrified, and turned to Christine. "I promise, I had no idea . . ."

Christine was dumbstruck. "And the remaining third to Helen?"

"No," replied the lawyer, looking like he wanted to crawl under the desk. "The final third he left to Julia Mann."

11

JULIA WAS SILENT most of the way home, but as they approached the house she finally spoke.

"Fuck my fucking life," she said. "That is the last thing I need."

Mason nodded, slowing in front of the garage. "A studio?"

Julia looked at her sharply. "No, you idiot. Additional motive." She got out of the car. "Fortunately, I already called the cavalry."

Mason followed her to the office, half skipping in order to keep up. Julia shoved the office door open with such force that it swung all the way and slammed into the wall, dislodging a few books. It was quite an entrance.

The guy sitting on the sofa must have been startled, but the only indication of it was a pause in his hand's trajectory between a plate of cookies and his mouth. Once his hair had settled back down (the door created quite a draft), he completed the journey and ate the cookie. Then he got to his feet, brushed off the crumbs and extended his hand.

"Hi, I'm Will Maier. You must be Mason." His hair was messy and his face unshaven, which, in combination with his torn jeans and faded Green Day T-shirt, made him look vaguely homeless. He smiled a smile of such innocent sweetness that unless he'd spoken, Mason would have assumed he was stoned off his gourd. But his voice had been sharp as a tack, and his eyes were sharper still.

Julia walked across the room and threw herself into one of the Eames chairs. "Will, I am about to tell you something that's going to blow your fucking mind and send you into a tailspin of research and concern. However, before we go there, because we are definitely going there, let me make a proper introduction to Mason. Mason, Will is my other assistant. My legal assistant, my king of research. We met many years ago in an AA meeting where he was able to recite the entire "More About Alcoholism" chapter of the Big Book and I realized his memory might be useful to me. I had no idea what else he was capable of, but he's become indispensable. Will can tell you anything you want to know about the California legal code, cases we're currently working on and any we've worked on in the past. Additionally, he's pretty solid on comic books, genre TV, the collected works of Rex Stout, D. H. Lawrence and Stephen Crane, and every single gun or weapon ever made. Plus, as an added but useless bonus, he's literally a world expert on the birds of California."

Will corrected her. "No, no, only the raptors. The raptors of California are a fascinating category all on their own, sufficient unto any man." He frowned. "And it hasn't been useful yet, but you never know."

Mason raised her eyebrows. "Very impressive."

The guy shook his head. "No, mildly autistic."

"And, Will, this is Mason, about whom you've heard some things. She's probably the muscle, she might be the comic relief, she's definitely the action hero. My jury isn't completely in on her, but I'm interested to see how you two gel. We also have a new agent slash lawyer. Larry apparently had a heart attack."

Will nodded, still smiling at Mason. "It's hard on the nervous system, being your agent. It's amazing Larry didn't fall off the perch completely. Who's pinch-hitting?"

"Some guy named Archie that Mason finds attractive."

"I do not," protested Mason, pointlessly. She sat on the sofa and reached for a cookie.

Will said, "No issues with nuts?"

Mason looked at him carefully and decided to take the question at face value. "In terms of allergies?"

He nodded. "Yes. The chocolate chip cookies contain finely chopped hazelnuts, so they're a little, you know, covert."

Mason bit into the cookie. "Covert nuts?"

Will's mouth twitched. "Good band name, right?"

Julia said, "Will helps me help my clients, who are usually at their wits' end and can't afford the kind of assistance we offer. The police don't care as much as they should, and their resources are stretched . . . I'm being kind. Sometimes they give up on a case if the plaintiff has no juice, but we don't." She paused. "And I like working with sober people. At least, people who are more consistently sober than I am."

Mason looked at Will, who had finished the cookies and was dusting crumbs from his fingers. "Booze?"

"Sure," he clarified, "but more seriously poker and racehorses. Five years sober, but I have a sugar habit I haven't been able to kick." He grinned. "Claudia is the biggest cookie pusher I've ever met. Thankfully, she uses her powers for good. What about you?"

Mason grinned back at him. "Everything except gambling. Booze, pot, pills, coke, speed, sex, video games . . . sober three years and grateful for it." Then she relaxed, because if there's one thing that's true about being sober, it's that other sober people make you feel better just by being there.

Julia was ready to get to work. "Now that's out of the way, here's the headline: Fucking Tony left me a third of the studio."

"Baking powder?" Will looked shocked. "Exsqueeze me? A third? Who got the rest?"

"Christine, as to be expected, and . . . wait for it . . . the assistant, Cody Malone."

"Shut the front door."

"Can't."

"Get out of town."

"Won't."

Will giggled, suddenly. "That's hilarious. Are you furious?"

"A little bit. How can I get out of it?"

Will made a face. "It's not very complicated in California to reject an inheritance. You can use something called 'disclaimer.' However, it gets complicated if you're trying to reject something from which you've already taken income. Your late husband and you both had income from the studio, and from movies produced by the studio. The law tries to stop people washing their hands of companies they've already profited from, simply because it became inconvenient when someone kicked the bucket."

Mason was watching Julia. She was curious. "I'm curious," she said. "Why don't you want the studio? Didn't your husband cofound it with Tony? Why isn't it already partially yours?"

Julia went for a casual shrug, but it wasn't super convincing, despite her being an Oscar winner. "Jonathan was an artist, a visionary. He saw money as something other people cared for . . . he was profligate. Over the last few years of his life, he got in and out of money troubles like other people catch a cold. He borrowed money everywhere, leveraged his ownership of the studio . . . Tony bought him out in sections, until there was really nothing left. Tony owned it all." She sighed. "And then Jonathan died." Years of bad behavior, recrimination and drama, reduced to a few sentences of retrospection. Such is life.

Will looked at her. "You still get considerable residuals from several movies, including *The Codex*, which shows up on the classic channels all the time, and streams pretty continuously."

Julia frowned. "Classic channels? Fuck you."

He raised his eyebrows, clearly used to Julia. "Well, it is a classic. It regularly makes 'best movies of the twentieth century' lists, Directors Guild of America recommendations, etc. Despite the curse." He shrugged. "Or maybe because of the curse."

Julia sighed. "Alright, will you look into how I can avoid inheriting it?"

"Of course. What else?"

"The police have the murder weapon. Or what they think is the murder weapon."

Will nodded. "Yeah, it is the murder weapon, and it has your fingerprints on it. According to my source it was a classic Springfield M1903. They found it in the initial search, of course, on the hillside below the pool deck, but it took a few days to process through forensics."

Julia was annoyed. "I've never owned a gun, let alone a whatever you just said."

Will shook his head. "You haven't, but Jonathan did, so did Tony, and so did loads of production companies, prop houses, etc. Long guns like rifles weren't required to be registered in the 1980s, which was probably when Jonathan got his. Interestingly, that model was used in over ninety-seven percent of all Hollywood movies made between 1965 and 1972, even though it wasn't produced after 1949. It was manufactured in Massachusetts, of course. You yourself fired one, or appeared to fire one, in three movies you made in the late seventies and early eighties." He frowned. "Still no memory of that night? No idea how your fingerprints got on it?"

Mason blew a bubble very loudly and Julia snapped at her. "Hey, shorty, no gum on the sofa."

Mason swallowed theatrically. "It's gone."

Julia laughed. "Please." She looked at Will and shook her head. "No, sorry."

"You know . . ." said Will, getting a faraway look in his eyes.

Julia's mouth twitched. "No, but I feel like I'm about to learn . . ."

". . . alcohol amnestic disorder, or blackout as we call it, is due to the effect of excessive alcohol on the hippocampus, an area largely involved in memory consolidation. Basically, you behave normally, well, hammered normal, but those memories you're making never make it into long-term storage. Thus the gaps." He paused for a moment for all three of them to reflect on chunks of drinking time none of them remembered, then continued. "Anyway, I also did a general sweep of suspects, as you asked. Do you want to hear what I found out?"

"Sure." Julia flicked a glance at Mason. "Are you getting all of this?"

Mason shook her head. "No, I was just listening. Am I supposed to also be retaining?"

"I have it written down," said Will. "The list of people who are secretly rejoicing at the death of Tony Eckenridge is longer than you think."

Mason was surprised. "I didn't think it was long at all. Everyone seems to think he was awesome."

Will shrugged. "And maybe he was, but that doesn't stop his death being a good thing for people."

"Like who?" Julia was impatient. "Who's on the list?"

"His partner, Christine, for an obvious start. She doesn't just inherit the studio . . ." He paused. ". . . part of the studio; she also gets everything that's in production, plus the back catalog, which brings in a fortune in streaming fees and royalties. The fact that he split it is going to make the industry and media go berserk." He reached for the mouse and pointed it at the screen. Front pages of several websites, all agog at the news that a major studio was now owned by a woman, a Gen Z former assistant and a suspected murderer. It was catnip; they were having a field day. "As I suspected."

"Great, nothing I like better than being in the public eye for something that has nothing to do with me."

"As opposed to being in the public eye for things you actually did?" asked Mason. "Didn't you used to be a famous actress? And then an infamous drunk?"

Julia narrowed her eyes at Mason. "Yes, but I sort of grew out of the first and am working on the second, remember?"

Mason nodded. "Yes, sorry." She looked over. "Carry on, Will. Ignore the interruption."

Will continued. "His wife, Helen, also stands to benefit, in that she inherited the rights to *The Codex*, which is getting remade as we all know. Plus a load of money and several properties, as they were still married."

"I had a question about that." Mason frowned. "I thought they were divorced?"

"Not according to state and city records. Still very much married, although they've lived apart for over ten years. It seems as if their separation was highly amicable: They dined together frequently, and they never made the divorce official. Under California law, that means she gets everything he doesn't explicitly leave to someone else."

"That's two. Who else?" Julia was suddenly looking pale, and Mason put up her hand.

"Is this going on for much longer? Julia, you haven't eaten very much, and as far as I know you haven't made a meeting yet today. Shall we . . ."

"Keep going, Will. Ignore her. I made her my sponsor and it was a huge mistake."

Will laughed out loud. "For which of you?"

"Me," they both said, simultaneously.

"Then let's go see if Claudia is making lunch yet." Will got to his feet and smiled at Mason. "Pro tip—don't ask Julia if she's hungry, or tired, or angry, or really anything. Just assume she is and act accordingly." He grinned. "Five imaginary bucks says I can beat you to the kitchen."

Two seconds later, as the door slammed against the wall again and Mason could already be heard rounding the corner of the hallway, he turned to Julia and smiled his gentle smile.

"Oh, I like her."

Julia snorted. "I thought you might."

12

~~~

CLAUDIA HAD MADE cheese straws and kept bringing more of them to the table, along with little pastry-wrapped figs stuffed with prosciutto. Her idea of lunch seemed to be a continuous stream of small deliciousnesses, and Mason was a hundred percent behind this approach.

Will had a cheese straw in each hand, and used them to punctuate his continued report. "If what you said about the museum is true, then Patty Menninger is pissed. It was openly known his collection was going to the museum: Everyone who gives a shit—not that there are many of those—will be highly surprised he reneged on that. There was also a director he was bickering with, Jason Reed, who now wins the dispute by default."

"What was the dispute about?"

Will chewed thoughtfully. "He wanted Jade Solomon released from a Repercussion movie she'd committed to so she could be in a film he was shooting. Jason was losing money every day."

Mason asked, "And who benefits from Julia going to jail for

killing Tony?" She shrugged. "I mean, someone tried to frame you, right?"

Will turned up his palms. "Apart from the media, social and otherwise, no one." He grinned. "You and I would be out of a job, though Claudia would maybe stay on."

Claudia laughed. "And who would I cook for, the roaches?"

Mason was surprised. "You haven't annoyed anyone enough for them to want you behind bars? You've irritated the crap out of me already, and I only met you day before yesterday."

Julia was calm. "Of course, dozens of people would love to see a bird shit on my head, but hate me enough to kill someone else so I would go to prison? Pretty long-winded. Why not just shoot me?" She thought for a moment. "Old cases? How about Giles Clarke? He was pretty pissed."

Will said, "Still in jail. Not out till 2027."

"Sarah DiSalva?"

"2030. Unless she gets early parole."

"That guy with the rabbits. He never went to jail."

Will had his eyes closed. "He moved to Canada, and the last time I checked was running a rehabilitation facility for rabbits cast aside by the magical profession. It's called Out of the Hat." He opened his eyes and found all three women looking at him. "What?"

Julia moved on. "What do we know about the accident that Christine and Jade Solomon were in?"

Will shrugged. "I looked into it. It happened on Robertson, in front of the Ivy. We couldn't have more witnesses if it had been live streamed. Christine swerved, hit another car coming in the other direction. The other driver was fine; she and Jade both had minor lacerations. Apparently, the top of Jade

Solomon's dress was also torn in the accident, so, clearly, a moment of enormous journalistic importance. There are photos."

"A setup?" Julia said.

He shrugged again.

Julia sighed. "Mason, we'll go talk to Cody and, if we have time, Helen. Let's find out what's going on at the studio and what happened in the board meeting Tony attended the day he died. Maybe Helen will have an insight into why Tony was here that night; maybe it was to do with *The Codex*—it's plausible. I want to hear the voicemail message Christine mentioned. I'll call her myself. Will, dig some more on Jason Reed. I'll make some calls and see if someone can get a look at his money situation. I'll also set New Larry on the will."

"Is that what we're calling Archie? I don't think he'll love it. Why would anyone talk to me?" Mason was fully confident interviewing wasn't her top skill.

"Because you're going to be charming and persuasive. Contrary action, you can do it. Your natural lack of inhibition or respect for other people's boundaries is going to be very helpful." She considered for a moment, then added, "Don't worry, it'll be a lot easier than you think. People close to a crime want to talk about it. It's often the most interesting thing that ever happened to them." She looked tired. "I want you to move into the house. Well, into one of the guesthouses. They're out back."

Mason shook her head definitively. "No."

"Yes. I'll pay you the entire time. Even while you're asleep."

"No. I have a cat. I have a life. I've known you for less than a week, and volatile doesn't even touch the edges of it. I have a rent-stabilized apartment with northern light. It's not going to happen, Julia."

"Double time at night. Sublet the apartment. Bring the cat."

Mason hesitated. She had debt; she could use the money. She did worry that the cat got bored during the day. "No, stop bugging me. I'll be here by eight every morning and work until we're done. That's enough."

Julia narrowed her eyes, then suddenly remembered something.

"Wait! Will, I completely forgot, there's a whole other case." She frowned. "Honestly, what is the matter with me?" She quickly outlined the Becky Sharp situation.

Will was intrigued. "I've been meaning to do a deep dive into the history of burlesque in Los Angeles. This is a perfect opportunity."

Julia raised her eyebrows. "Not sure history is going to solve the crime, but you never know. Reach out to Casper—he knows a lot about that kind of thing. And maybe tonight we'll all take a little field trip."

"Casper the journalist?"

"Do we know another Casper?"

Will lifted one shoulder. "Julia, you know everyone. Don't get ratty. I think your sponsor is right: You need a meeting."

Mason added, "Humor me, Julia. I need a meeting, and you need me to stay sober as your employee, and I need you to stay sober as my employer, and it only works if you work it."

"Your obsession with the slogans of the program makes me angry. Like, unreasonably angry."

Mason said, "I don't really care if it's reasonable or not."

Julia muttered, "I don't want to go to a meeting."

Mason looked at her. "Perfect time to do so, then. When you want to go to a meeting, you should go, and when you don't want to go to a meeting, you should go."

"Again, do you ever have an original thought or is it all AA?"

Mason shrugged. "My original thoughts got me in nothing but trouble. The only thoughts I have that are in any way reliable are things I've heard in the rooms. You know it. I know it."

Julia made a face. Then she sighed. Then she opened her mouth and closed it again. "Let's do it."

Will and Mason stared at her. Claudia suddenly started throwing cheese straws into a Ziploc.

"Go quick, before she changes her mind. I'll make you some coffee to take, too. Let me fire up the espresso machine. Just make sure you're back in time for dinner, all of you. It's roast beef and potatoes Dauphinoise tonight."

Mason grinned and started to wonder if moving in might not be a good idea after all.

13

~~~~~

JULIA AND MASON stood in the doorway of the garage and gazed.

"Pick your poison," said Julia. "You've already driven the Shelby and the Rolls. What else appeals?"

Mason swallowed and pointed.

"Really?" asked Julia, a little disappointed. "Fair enough."

So it was that the two of them rolled out of the driveway in a classic Volvo 960 wagon with Mason giggling like a schoolgirl.

"We had this car when I was a kid," she said as they headed down the hill. "My dad let me sit on his lap and steer. You know, Paul Newman drove one of these with a Mustang V8 swapped in and really burned rubber."

"You don't say," said Julia, gazing out of the window. "I thought you weren't interested in movies or movie stars."

"I'm not. That's a story about a Volvo, not a movie star." She took one of the tighter curves at an ill-advised speed. "The cars are a definite plus of this job, not going to lie."

Julia yawned. "I don't really drive, but I'm glad they amuse you." She looked over at the young woman grinning behind the wheel. "It's been a strange first week, right? Your boss gets arrested, inherits a studio . . ."

". . . is on day seven of early sobriety." Mason shot her a look. "How do you feel?"

Julia shrugged. "Confused. Anxious. Annoyed." She paused. "Which is how I feel most of the time, early sobriety or not."

Mason nodded. "Sounds about right. My first year of sobriety was a shit show. I kept losing my temper at everything and nothing, cried every time I opened my mouth in a meeting, refused to get a sponsor until it was almost too late . . ."

"Too late because you nearly picked up?"

"Yeah. But I got one. She's great."

Julia nodded, but said nothing. Then, "What do your parents think about all this?"

"My sobriety, or me working for you?"

"Either."

Mason shrugged. "Not sure. I spoke to my mother the other day, and all she talked about was me going back to law school. I told her I was working for you, but she didn't express an opinion. Believe me, if she had one, she'd have expressed it."

"You don't want to go back to law school?"

Mason was silent for a moment, navigating traffic. Then she sighed and said, "I'm not the girl I was when I dropped out. That girl was very angry, very focused on having a good time and very, very out of it. Now that I'm sober I don't know what I want to do when I grow up. Not entirely sure I even want to grow up. But this is good, working for you. You're kind of mean, but it's been interesting as hell so far."

Julia laughed. "I'm not mean. I'm just blunt."

"You can frame it that way if you like." Mason pulled into a parking space. "Look at that, Doris Day parking."

Julia raised an eyebrow.

"You know, how in old movies the people would just swoop into parking spaces right in front of where they needed to go. There was no long circling of the block, cursing the gods of parking." Mason looked at Julia. "I watched a lot of movies when I was a kid. I just grew out of it."

"You grew out of a lot of things, it seems. It'll be interesting to see what you grow into." Julia paused before getting out of the car. "I don't think you should go back to law school, for what it's worth. We have enough lawyers already. I want you to get your private investigator's license, much more useful to me."

Mason stared at her. "And that's the only criteria?"

"No, but it's a big one. For some reason I like you. You're fearless, if a little impulsive. Being a PI would keep your brain in gear while also enabling you to perform useful tasks for me." She reached for the door handle. "I'll pay for it. It'll be a taxable business expense." She got out and leaned down to look at Mason, who was still staring. "Think about it."

And with that, she turned and walked away.

AFTER THE MEETING, Julia suggested they go over to Repercussion and talk to Cody. Or Christine, whichever one presented themselves.

"Let's just see how the dust is settling," Julia said.

Cody Malone, the handsome young man who'd just inherited a third of a Hollywood studio, opened the door to his office and grinned at Julia and Mason as though they'd known each other for years rather than never having met before. This was something Mason had previously encountered with people in the movie business. A sort of instant rapport that reminded her that "glamour" originally referred to the magic that fairies used to blind humans to the truth. She assumed Julia was immune, or at least able to give as good as she got.

Cody flattered Julia extensively while preparing highly complicated coffee, revealing that he knew every movie she'd ever made, every case she'd worked on in the last few years and every award (movie and/or humanitarian) that she'd won for all of it. It turned out Julia wasn't completely immune, because Mason got to hear a completely novel sound: Julia giggling. Admittedly, Julia Mann giggling was not your girlish trill of laughter, but the kind of giggle an extremely sexy courtesan might issue after the king said something hilarious. Low-pitched, husky, that kind of giggle. Mason rolled her eyes and moved a stack of papers so she could perch on the corner of a desk.

Having caffeinated everyone, Cody was ready to be helpful. "So, Ms. Mann . . ."

"You can call me Julia."

"So . . . Julia . . . Christine and I were intending to contact you tomorrow to ask you how you would like to be brought up to speed . . . Right now we have four movies in preproduction, two in production and three more in postproduction. We also have about fifty more possibles, conversations we're having with other studios, projects we're trying to option, etc." He stopped, because Julia had raised her hand in the universal symbol for "stop."

"Slow your roll there. I have zero intention of being brought up to speed. You're charming, so you're welcome to tell me what you're up to, but I am in no way going to get involved in running the studio. My third will become part of your half as soon as my lawyer can work out how to make it happen."

"Really?" Cody sounded surprised, which in turn surprised Mason, who thought it had been pretty obvious at the will reading that Julia was not interested in the studio. "It's always been my dream to help run Repercussion; I just didn't expect it to happen so soon. Tony had asked me to make him an appointment with his lawyer the day before he died, but it didn't seem super urgent so I hadn't done it yet. I had no idea he was planning to leave me part of the studio."

He sighed and gestured around at what looked like normal office chaos to Mason. "We're a little bit of a mess right now. After Tony died, Christine just assumed she was taking over, and she's totally different than he is, stylistically. He kept everything in his head or on paper, he filed by piles, he hoarded everything, didn't trust email or the Internet. She's all digital, all organized, planned and executed with ruthless precision. She's having me go through everything, and I'm at the 'worse than when I started' stage of the process." He grinned. "Tony had been sorting his papers for the museum, and those are all the red file boxes you can see. Scripts, production notes, correspondence . . . he kept it all, and Patty Menninger at the Academy Museum is ready to take it. Christine says ship it as fast as possible, so that's what I'm doing."

Mason looked around at the papers. Bold, distinctive writing covered a lot of them. Even Eckenridge's handwriting had charisma.

"How did you and Tony meet?" asked Julia. "He used to have a habit of collecting an eclectic cast of assistants. What's your story?"

Cody grinned wider. "I delivered him a sandwich."

Julia laughed. "That tracks. Tell me the story." She settled herself on the small leather sofa she'd chosen, and crossed her long legs. Mason inched a little farther back on the desk, knocking over a pot of pencils.

Once those had been regathered, Cody began his story.

"So, like everyone else in Los Angeles, I always wanted to be in the movie business."

"I don't," said Mason, but then waved him on. She really needed to work on not interrupting people.

"But also like everyone else, I was doing regular jobs while I waited for my big break. I was working at Canter's Deli, waiting tables and doing random stuff, when an order came in from Repercussion. I bribed the delivery guy to let me take it instead, and when I walked into the office I walked into an argument." He grinned at the memory.

"Christine and Tony were bickering over whether Billy Wilder or Steven Spielberg was a better director for emotion. Christine was arguing that Spielberg tugged the heartstrings harder and deeper than any other, citing *E.T.*, *Schindler's List*, etc. Tony came back with *Irma La Douce* and even *Some Like It Hot*, which he said contained Marilyn Monroe's greatest performance. I walked in carrying their lunch, and Tony immediately turned to me and asked for my vote. Classic Tony, he always assumed everyone else cared as much about movies as he did. Lucky for me, I was apparently ready, because I said David Lean."

Julia nodded. "*Doctor Zhivago*, *Brief Encounter* . . . sure."

"I even suggested Nora Ephron, as the radio call-in scene in *Sleepless in Seattle* makes me cry every time. The conversation kept going, Tony invited me to split his sandwich, and the rest, as people still actually say, was history." Cody's face was glowing. It was clear this had been a very special day for him. Mason couldn't think of anything she'd experienced professionally that made her even a fraction as happy as that, and for a moment she was jealous.

Cody continued. "I never went to college. There was no money for it, you know? But Tony didn't care. He just gave me as much work as I could handle and taught me as we went along."

Julia shrugged. "That is indeed classic Tony. You know he started out in the motor pool himself, driving executives and actors. People used to joke there were many self-made men in Hollywood, but only one self-driven." She paused. "I wasn't a Tony fan, as you know. No offense, but your boss was an asshole. He made promises all over the place, and rarely kept them."

Cody turned up his hands. "He was only ever lovely to me, but I appreciate you had a different experience."

"I still didn't kill him," said Julia, calmly. "We're planning to find out who did. We'd appreciate your help."

"I want to find out more than you do, probably. He was my friend as well as my boss. He didn't have to leave me anything at all, but he left me my dream, literally." He turned to Mason, suddenly. "What's your dream, Ms. . . . ?"

"You can call me Mason. I don't have a dream, I have a plan, but thanks for asking. My plan is to keep my brand-new boss out of jail." She made a face. "Beyond that it's all misty . . ."

He deepened his smile. "Fair enough."

"So, you didn't expect him to leave you part of the studio?" Julia asked, keeping things on track.

"Not exactly, no. He always said he would take care of me,

but I wasn't really clear on what that meant. He was sick. You know that, right? I don't know how sick . . . he didn't like to talk about it. Early on he laughed and told me it was butt cancer, from people blowing smoke up his ass all the time. He wasn't scared of anything, that man, not even death." He looked at Mason. "I should have been with him that night, instead of babysitting Jade Solomon at the hospital. What a waste of time." He picked up a pen and tossed it on the desk, where it spun for a moment. "Seriously, all she did was complain about not having access to social media. Meanwhile, Christine was in the same accident she was, not that Jade seemed to notice that." He made a rueful face. "She's all up in my beak now, of course." He reached for the pen and put it back in a pot on the desk. Tidy. "Wants to nail down her part in *The Codex* remake."

Julia was watching his face. "So that's definitely happening? With Helen directing?"

It was subtle, but a change flickered across his features. Mason couldn't quite read it. "Unlikely. Helen's been carrying a script around for nearly a decade, trying to make it happen. Tony's will was explicit: She keeps the rights, so she has veto over who directs. I wondered if the rights issue was what Tony wanted to discuss with the lawyer, but that meeting could have been about anything. Helen can put her foot down and insist on doing it herself, but without the backing of the studio, she doesn't have the money to get it done. It's a delicate dance, and Helen is good at dancing . . ." He tailed off, took the pen back out of the pot and started doodling.

"But?" Mason wondered what he wasn't saying.

His mouth twisted. "But the script needs a total overhaul, and I think maybe someone else for filmmaker . . ." A small movement of his hands. "Someone younger, maybe, with a different sensibility. More current. Helen had that one flop. She's . . ." A bigger gesture; Mason was starting to realize the stuff he wasn't saying, he was saying with his hands.

Mason nodded. "I see. That's your call?"

"No, or at least not just mine." He looked mildly uncomfortable. "I mean, Christine has effectively been running the studio since Tony died, and although I'm theoretically a part owner"—he looked over at Julia—"and so are you, I'm not really ready to run anything. I've got a lot to learn and I'm in no hurry to flex my muscle."

Mason asked, "Is Christine going to fire Helen?"

He shook his head. "No, she isn't actually hired. Christine was already working with her before Tony died, trying to navigate what has now become an even more difficult situation. But Christine just got handed a mini-major to run and she's at DEFCON 1 around the clock right now."

"Mini-major? I thought Repercussion was a big studio?" Mason looked around at the other movie posters, all of them huge hits.

Cody raised his eyebrows. "Well, it's not a major, obviously, and it's not small enough to be a true independent, and it distributes its own films, ergo, mini-major." He looked at her. "It's more complicated than that, but I doubt you'd find it interesting."

"So, Christine is essentially flying solo?" Julia asked.

He nodded. "Yes, but it's fine. She's incredibly competent. She'll sort out *The Codex*. I'll miss Tony, though. He was one of the few truly nice guys in town, even if he was a little OCD. If he was here he'd tell me to use the opportunity to learn more about how a business survives a challenge. He was like that, always saw the angles. Loved to have fun with even the shittiest situations." He leaned back in his chair. "Mind you, I'll be glad to off-load all his crap. He was a pack rat, but the most anal, organized pack rat ever. He kept everything from all the movies, all in storage. Some on the lot, some at his place. Every piece of paperwork, of course, but also every prop, every costume, everything. There are dozens of boxes here. I can't ship them out fast enough." He sighed. "Not sure how it fell out of the will, but he really did intend everything to go to the museum. Christine handed that mess to me. It was like the third thing out of her mouth when we got back to the office after the will reading."

Mason said, "What were the first two?"

He laughed. "Fuck and fuck. She wasn't expecting to share ownership of the studio. She was surprised, but she pivoted fast; she always does. And putting me in charge of clearing and organizing all the documents Tony left everywhere gives me something to do while she works out a plan of action."

Julia had a question. "And on his last day Tony had a board meeting? Any idea what got discussed there?"

"The minutes will be distributed soon, I imagine. I can look. I was still assisting then. I was running around looking for fish supplies for Christine that morning. We're setting up a film about a free diver who discovers the entrance to another dimension. Christine watched some background footage and now she wants a lot of fish in the office, to make it more, you know, marine. Reefy." He paused. "Sometimes she's a little weird, I'll admit that, but who isn't? Tony spent that afternoon on the phone FaceTiming old friends. I think he was starting to tie up loose ends. The oncologists had given him a matter of months, and he had a lot going on he wanted to square away. I've got his call list, if you want it."

"We do," said Julia.

Cody went to his laptop and pulled something up, sending it to the printer. Handing the paper to Mason, he said, "And then in the late afternoon there was the accident, so I was dealing with that and didn't lay eyes on Tony after four." He rolled his eyes. "I think I set a new land speed record getting from here to Cedars. For once the traffic gods were kind and I was there while they were still in triage."

Mason looked at the list. Most names she didn't recognize, but Jack Simon was there, as were Maggie Galliano and Patty Menninger. She folded the paper and put it in her pocket.

Julia said, "Where was Tony?"

"Still FaceTiming someone when I left, but after that, no idea. They made us turn off our phones in the hospital. It was a total mindfuck. I had no idea where either of my bosses was for like six hours. Thank God one of them was also somewhere in the hospital or I would have lost my mind. Jade and I ended up playing cards to take our minds off our lack of Internet connection—she hadn't been off social media that long since she was twelve, and I hadn't been out of sight of my bosses for more than an hour or two in half a decade. I felt . . . adrift." He frowned. "And of course the next thing I knew the police were calling me and Tony was dead and I never got to say goodbye."

And then he did the most surprising thing of all, and started crying.

14

~~~~

JULIA DECIDED THERE wasn't time to interview Helen, and had Mason drive her home before giving her an hour or two to feed Phil and run a few personal errands. She'd insisted on Mason returning for dinner and further instructions, and as the young woman headed back up the hill, she realized that she was bad-tempered, low blood sugared and emotionally hungover from all the peopling she'd had to do. She was deeply displeased to be hailed as she passed through the hall. Sighing, she went into the office and saw Julia had company.

"Casper, this is Mason." Julia waved her hand in an all-encompassing gesture. "Right?"

He nodded. "Oh yes, I totally see it." Casper was at least eighty and looked like a cartoon turtle in a hat. He rose and bowed low to Mason, an abasement that wasn't really necessary as he barely reached her sternum standing on his tippy-toes.

"See what?" Mason raised one eyebrow and looked over at Will, who was sitting quietly with a pad on his knee. He grinned at her.

"Your natural charm and surfeit of 'fuck you' energy," replied Casper. "Julia had a lot of good things to say about you, and that is a rare enough event that I absolutely had to meet you." He beamed up at her. "I understand you've been running around all day. You're probably overtired and hungry right now."

Julia looked at Mason. "Go to the kitchen and grab something to eat. But hurry. Casper was about to tell us who killed Tony."

"I think it was you." The turtle sat back down and folded his hands like napkins in his lap. "I think this whole investigative lawyer thing is simply a very long plan to kill Tony and take over the studio."

Mason closed the door on Julia and Will's laughter.

"CASPER?" CLAUDIA NODDED. "One of Julia's oldest friends. Since before jail, before Jonathan even, I think. They came up together, helped each other out. He was the entertainment editor for the *LA Times*, back in the day, and then at *Variety*. There isn't much that gets past him, even these days." She was making Mason a sandwich, with the efficient movements and flashing implements of a short-order cook. Couldn't have been more than two minutes before a grilled cheese hit the plate. "He lived in one of the guesthouses for a while in the nineties, too. Once you've lived here, the door never really closes." She put the sandwich on a tray along with a plate of small yellow cakes, a classic silver moka coffeepot of espresso and a half-pint of . . .

Mason stared. "Are those Twinkies? And is that scotch?"

Claudia snorted. "They're *like* Twinkies, but I make them from scratch. They're Casper's favorite. And yes, that's scotch, to go in his coffee. Is that OK?" She frowned at Mason. "Casper is a creature of habit, but I can tell him we're out."

"No, it's fine. I'm good." She looked over at Ben Sharp, who was sitting by the kitchen fireplace, reading a book. "Hi there—did you go see Becky today?"

The young man nodded. "She was better than I expected." He smiled. "She said a pushy girl came and yelled at her. I assume that was you?"

Mason nodded. "Julia's going to help her. When does she get out?"

"Tomorrow morning." He smiled, somewhat confusedly. "Julia Mann is letting us stay here, totally for free."

Mason made a face. "Well, she's not likely to charge you, is she? It's not a hotel."

"No, but it's very nice of her."

Mason picked up the tray and turned to go back to the office. "I know. She's a weird one. A combination of mother hen and some kind of prehistoric murder bird with giant claws."

"Don't let her hear you say that," said Claudia. "'Weird' is one of those words she doesn't like. She'd much rather you called her a bitch."

"Well, that also fits." Mason headed out. She was painfully aware that the bottle of scotch was inches from her hand. She was bent out of shape, tired and hungry, but she put a lot of faith in the grilled cheese. Hopefully, Casper would drink fast.

She put the tray down, took her sandwich to a distant corner of the sofa and settled down. Then she got up to get a pad and pen. Then she went back to the kitchen to get herself a cold Coke. Then she returned and sat down again.

Julia regarded her quizzically. "You good, Mason?"

Mason nodded, her mouth full of sandwich. *Come on, blood sugar.*

Casper opened the scotch and poured it into the espresso. The crunching sound of the cap twisting free and open made the hair on the back of Mason's neck stand up. She chewed her sandwich and looked at her shoes. Casper poured half the bottle into his coffee and added some heavy cream. The smell of the Irish coffee drifted across the room, molecules of whiskey hitting Mason's nose like tiny elbows.

Casper lifted one of the Twinkies and took a bite. He sighed and clicked his heels together three times.

"There's no place like home . . ."

Then he swallowed, smiled and turned to face Julia. His little black eyes glinted like a sparrow evaluating the earliness of the worm.

"So, if you didn't kill Tony, who did?"

She shrugged. "Beats me, Casper." Mason noticed she still looked relaxed, but her eyes were as sharp as her friend's. "Not that I need an excuse to see you, but that's why I called. What am I missing?"

"I doubt you're missing much, but let's review. Are we thinking about who *could* have, or who *wanted* to?"

"Either is fine. Just tell me your thoughts."

The old man curled up, looking even more like a turtle, but also like the caterpillar in *Alice in Wonderland*. "Substantiated, or not?"

"Jesus, quit the caveats, won't you? Spill it."

Casper leaned forward and helped himself to another pseudo-Twinkie. After a moment of blissful chewing, he leaned back on the sofa and gazed at the ceiling. "Starting way back. There was the Jack Simon and David Paul thing: David almost getting Jack thrown off *The Codex* set and blackballing him around town. I mean, actors are temperamental at the best of times, but those two really got into it."

Julia frowned. "Really? That's the second time Jack's name has come up this week. Will, didn't you have something about that?"

Will flipped back through his notes. "Yes, bank records show that Tony was paying Jack Simon a moderate sum of money every month, ever since *The Codex*. We're looking into it."

Julia made a face. "Well, I can't imagine Jack or David actually care about what happened thirty-plus years ago, although I'd like to know what the money is all about."

"Jack might care. David certainly doesn't; he might not even remember. I do know he got married in 1972 and divorced in 1973, and when he met his ex-wife five years later he didn't remember her at all."

"He'd forgotten her name?" Mason was eating her sandwich and still smelling the scotch. *Three years of continuous sobriety and counting.*

"He'd forgotten her *existence.* He didn't even know he'd been married; he only discovered it when he asked his accountant why he was paying Jessica Paul three grand a month, and the guy told him she was his ex-wife, and he was paying her so she wouldn't tell the press that he hadn't been able to get an erection the entire time they were married." Casper chuckled. "Cheap at the price, considering his image."

Mason shook her head. "So what happened with him and Jack Simon?" She turned to Julia. "This was during filming of *The Codex*, right?"

Casper nodded. "They got into it over some girl on set, and David wanted Jack fired, and would have succeeded if Tony hadn't stepped in to protect him. Tony and Jack had always been thick as thieves, had known each other long before either became successful. As it was, Jack never really worked again, in large part because the David camp started a whispering campaign that he was an unreliable diva."

"Which he wasn't." Julia was clearly not buying this argument. "Move on, Casper. This is all ancient history, and I can't see how either of these men would wish Tony harm."

The journalist took a long swallow of his coffee and settled more deeply into the sofa. "You forget, Julia, wars are fought over ancient history." She snorted at him. "Let's think. Tony got into a legal dispute with Paramount in the eighties, and a dozen people lost their jobs. What about that?"

Julia shook her head. "No. Executives are venal and shallow, but they can't be bothered to kill people. They might *hire* someone to kill someone, but they wouldn't do it themselves. Besides, getting fired from one studio and hired by another is simply a warm-up exercise in this town."

"How do we know this wasn't a hired killer?" Mason was trying to keep up, but she kept writing down suspects and then having to cross them off.

Julia said, "The dumped gun. Too sloppy. Too obvious. Professionals bring their own kit and take it with them."

"And why kill Tony here?" Mason continued. "Why not at the studio or at his own house?"

"Maybe they were after Julia the whole time," said Casper. "Maybe you were the intended victim and they just got Tony by accident."

Julia snorted. "Then why am I still here? I was hammered;

it wouldn't have been that hard to shoot me. They could have walked up and pressed the bullet in with their fingers."

Casper giggled, and finished the first cup of coffee. He poured a second and went to add in the rest of the scotch when he noticed Mason watching him. "Sorry, did you want some?"

She shook her head. "I'm good, thanks." She could feel the food starting to work, her mood slowly stabilizing. She knew exactly how much scotch was in the bottle and how it would feel on her tongue, but she could handle it.

"There was talk that Tony borrowed money from organized crime to start the studio. Maybe there's something there?" He paused, made a face. "Mind you, everybody did, and Tony got along fine with everyone, regardless of their background. He didn't make that many enemies, which is surprising for someone with so much power." He continued eating the second Twinkie. "How about his first wife?"

"Delia? Delia's alive and well and living in Arizona."

"No, his first wife."

Julia frowned at him. "Casper, you're losing it. Delia *was* Tony's first wife. I was at their wedding."

Casper laughed. "Sure, the first wife he publicly married. But he was married way earlier than that, darling; married and divorced and all hushed up."

Mason and Julia waited, but the old man just smiled a pussycat smile at them. Julia snapped first. "Casper, for fuck's sake, spit it out."

With great glee, Casper leaned forward. "And here's me thinking there was nothing you didn't know, Julia. For three months in 1976, Tony was married to Maggie Galliano."

15

WHEN JULIA CAME down the stairs after dinner, Mason's jaw dropped: She looked amazing. She always looked great, but tonight she was wearing a deep green 1950s evening gown, with long gloves and an elegantly coiled and braided chignon. She looked like Holly Golightly's ass-kicking aunt, and Mason was suddenly very underdressed. Will was wearing a dark suit, and stepped forward to offer his arm. Julia took it and actually smiled at him.

Mason said, "Are we going clubbing? Or just to the store?"

"Just to the store," replied Julia. "I wanted to match the apples in the grocery section."

Mason made a face at her. "So . . . Galliano's, then?"

Julia nodded. "I've been friends with Maggie for twenty years, more. I want to know why she never told me she was married to Tony. If Casper hadn't told me, I never would have believed it." She raised her eyebrows. "I knew she was a crafty cat, but I'm impressed with her commitment to secrecy. Plus we need to talk to her about Becky, a topic on which we need to tread carefully."

The front door opened and Archie walked in. Mason swallowed. He was wearing one of his beautifully cut suits and looked like a million sexy bucks.

"Oh," said Julia, lightly, "Archie's joining us, too."

Great.

Julia looked at Mason, somewhat pityingly. "Do you own any grown-up clothes?"

"I am a grown-up, and these are my clothes. Ergo, they are grown-up clothes."

Julia sighed. "Come upstairs. There must be something more appropriate in my closet."

"We're not the same size." This was not a conversation she wanted to have in front of Archie, strangely.

Julia laughed. "I'm taller than you, but as a regular human woman, I've been several sizes over the course of my life, and I hoard couture, so let's just see, shall we?"

"No," said Mason, starting to frown. "I'm comfortable."

"You look like you just came from the arcade where you played *Pac-Man* for three hours then drank two liters of Mountain Dew."

Mason opened her mouth, then closed it again. Pointless. "I'm not changing. Not for you, not for anyone."

"Fine. You'll stick out like a sore thumb at the club, but I imagine you're used to that."

Archie spoke. "It's a burlesque club; people will be wearing all kinds of things. She looks fine." He paused. "She looks like herself."

Julia looked at him and raised her eyebrows. "Fair enough, counselor for the defense." She smoothed out her gloves against the dark fabric of Will's suit. "Let's take the Citroën. It looks so cool that the valet will leave it parked outside the club and we'll be able to get right in when we leave."

Will bent his arm, and she slid her hand through his crooked elbow.

"Come along, milady," he said. "Your chariot awaits."

Archie bent his arm and offered it to Mason. She grinned at him, suddenly, and bent her own in response. Smiling, he slid his arm through hers and they followed the others out.

MASON HADN'T BEEN to Galliano's before, and she looked around with interest. The front of the club was discreet, apart from the yellow neon of the sign, but inside there was no attempt at discretion. Red velvet booths, golden tables, ornate chandeliers and some of the most beautiful girls Los Angeles could provide, and that's a deep pool. The curtained stage was quiet for now, although a small sign promised "Mimi's Manhattan Moments" would be along later. In the meantime, there were a dozen women walking around who weren't exactly dressed for winter. But they weren't your usual fake boobs, spray tan, college to pay for, but instead women in their late twenties, each of them perfection without being homogenous. They didn't dance; they just walked and posed and stood and were happy to join you at your table, for a price. Once there, they merely flirted and engaged in conversation, and although Mason doubted any of them were explaining the basics of string theory, they were all able to put a sentence together. It was far, far sexier than a strip joint. Looking around, she saw several actors, a couple of actresses and a large number of men wearing expensive suits and even more expensive watches. She was the only person in the place in jeans, and she was one hundred percent confident she wouldn't have gotten in without Julia Mann.

Julia's arrival had caused a minor sensation, and once they had run the gauntlet of old friends and older enemies, they'd arrived at a well-located velvet booth. Mason noted how well Julia's dress went with the color, and doubted it was a coincidence. Thirty seconds later, Mrs. Galliano herself appeared, along with a man who looked like he broke noses for a living. Or maybe just for a hobby. He was darkly good-looking, but his expression was guarded.

Maggie Galliano herself was a surprise. She was heavy, and not classically attractive. She wore no makeup, and only the vaguest attempt had been made with her hair or clothing. There was something supremely unconcerned about the lady, a rarity in Los Angeles, and the minute she sat down, Mason realized she effortlessly oozed sex appeal.

"Julia, what an incredible pleasure." Maggie hugged Julia tightly. Then she looked at Mason with a not-insulting level of evaluation. "New friend, Julia? I saw her picture in the paper the other day. Very nice." She leaned across the table and sparkled at Mason. "I love a young woman who isn't afraid to use her middle fingers." She grinned deliciously and leaned back again. "After years of eating through men, you've decided to change the menu?"

"Don't be daft, Maggie, though you'd be the first to know, I'm sure." Julia was relaxed. "This is Natasha Mason, my assistant. She has very poor impulse control, so watch out."

Maggie smiled at Mason. "I'm not scared of pretty girls, Julia. You know that."

"And this is Archie Jacobson, who works for Larry and therefore also for me, and Will Maier, my good friend."

Maggie smiled around and raised her hand for a waiter, one of whom instantaneously materialized at her elbow. "Bring us something yummy, Frank, and something nice to drink. Wine for me and Danny, virgin something for Julia." She shot Julia a glance. "Or are you drinking again?"

"Not today," replied Julia, evenly.

The waiter nodded, took everyone's orders and turned to leave. Maggie gave him a quick pat on the bum as he left, but he didn't seem bothered, just threw her a quick grin. Maggie saw Mason looking and winked at her before turning back to Julia. "Are you here to ask me about the murder?"

The man with her murmured dissent, and Maggie looked at him sharply.

"Danny, there's no point pretending it didn't happen. Sam was murdered here, and it's not like she was the first. In the hundred years we've been in business, five people have died here, four of them violently. You know that."

The man made a face. "I know, but that was in the old days."

"Apparently, times don't change that much."

Julia looked at the man. "I assume you're Danny Agosti? I'm not sure how we haven't met before, but I don't think we have, have we?"

He shook his head, and then reached across the table and shook her hand. "I've only recently started spending more time here, so I guess our paths haven't crossed." He looked at Mason, Archie and Will. "I'm a partner here, but my role is mostly passive."

"Danny and his family have been investors in the club

since we opened in the nineteen twenties," said Maggie. "His great-grandfather, grandfather and father before him." She smiled at Julia. "You probably remember Mikey, his dad. He was an investor in Repercussion, too; you must have run into him all the time."

Julia shrugged. "Not that I remember. Tony handled the business side, and I didn't have as much interest in how everything worked back then." She pulled an expression that sharpened her next comment. "I was only interested in *the art*, not the money. Maybe I should have been paying more attention."

"Casper said organized crime played a fairly big role at the studio, financially," said Mason, looking at Danny Agosti. "Care to comment?"

"Are you assuming because my last name is Italian and I'm a financier that I'm also a mobster?" His tone was cool but nobody was fooled.

"If the cap fits," replied Mason. "But I'm just asking a question." There was something about Danny Agosti that caught her attention, and she realized it was a level of suppressed energy she sometimes came across in AA meetings, too. A little danger. An awareness that although these people were staying clean now, they hadn't cared to in the past.

Danny paused. "It's possible that my forebears were involved in some aspects of business that were less than . . . totally aboveboard . . . but these days, my company is entirely clean. We invest in clubs, real estate, the movie business, some Internet start-ups . . . I work hard to maintain our reputation. It's a valuable asset."

Maggie laughed. "Don't get your feathers ruffled, Danny. I expect everyone at this table has parts of their history they'd rather not air in public, and what your father and grandfather did before you were born hardly reflects on you."

Danny looked at Mason. "And yet some people love to throw stones."

Mason said nothing. She knew her glass house could only take so much, and Julia's face suggested it was time to move on.

Julia said, "I do want to talk about the murder, yes, but not just that. I'm sorry, it must have been shocking."

Maggie nodded. "It was. You know what it's like here—we're a family, and when they said it was drugs it was bad enough. She was a nice kid, talented, sharp as a tack, maybe too sharp, but she hadn't been a user as far as I knew, nor was Becky. She turned up on time, did her set, had a few drinks, went home. No trouble at all until her girlfriend killed her. And, like I said, this place has seen more than its fair share of drama and excitement of course, especially during Prohibition, but still . . . murder is murder." She looked at Julia intently. "You're Becky Sharp's lawyer, I hear."

So much for treading carefully. Mason watched Julia, ready to make a run for it if her boss seemed concerned. She wasn't.

"Yes. Her mother was a friend of mine."

"Was? Did I know her?"

"No, she was a friend from another . . . sphere."

Mrs. Galliano nodded. "I see. Well, I'm not totally convinced that little girl killed Sam anyway. They seemed pretty happy together, and not so intense they'd kill over it, you know? People do kill people they love, of course, all the time. The police seem convinced, but they're easily fooled." She lowered her voice again. "And several senior people over there don't like Galliano's looked into too deeply, if you follow me. They're keen to close the case."

Mason looked at Danny Agosti who, it turned out, was looking at her. "Not because of any bribery or corruption, Ms. Mason. Just mutual respect."

Mason shrugged. She was young, but not green enough to forget the interplay of law enforcement, organized crime and the gray world that was strip clubs, after-hours bars and the like. Whatever Agosti might claim, she doubted he'd been able to completely whitewash his business dealings.

The waiter came back with a tray of small dishes, two glasses of red wine and a bevy of icy Mexican Cokes. Mason looked over the food: bacon-wrapped dates, goat cheese–stuffed figs, Marcona almonds, anchovy olives. A better class of bar snack than she was used to, for sure.

Maggie sipped her wine and smiled over the rim at Mason. Then she looked around the table. "What else did you want to talk about, Julia?" She popped a bacon-wrapped date into her mouth. "Why don't you get on with whatever you came for, because the show's going to start soon and I'll have to focus."

Julia nodded. "Fair enough. Maggie, how come I never knew you were married to Tony Eckenridge?"

Maggie Galliano nearly choked on her date. She swigged some wine and recovered herself. The waiter came rushing over to help, but she waved him away. "I'm alright . . . Jesus, Julia, did someone take out an ad or something? I married Tony when we were both seventeen, had just discovered sex, and thought we were Romeo and Juliet. It lasted three months, which is how long it took our parents to find out, and was annulled faster than you would have thought possible. We stayed friends—actually, we stayed lovers—on and off for the next thirty years, but that was it. It was a total and complete secret until this morning, apparently, because the police also know." She looked genuinely interested. "How did you find out?"

"Casper Waggoner."

Maggie laughed. "Oh Lord, of course. He signed a pact with the devil, that man." She turned to Mason. "He used to be really quite tall, you know, and then he started reporting on entertainment and lost half an inch a year. I seriously believe he traded inches for info, to some evil spirit or other." She didn't look that upset, Mason thought, and apparently Julia agreed.

"So tell me, how come you weren't at Tony's funeral?" She snagged a stuffed fig, reached for a Coke, changed her mind, called over a waiter, and said, "Can I get a glass of seltzer with an obscene number of lime slices and plenty of ice?"

Maggie sobered a little. "I don't do funerals. If I did I'd be at one a week, and during the early eighties I would have done nothing else. That's when I stopped going. Too many good friends dying too young. I decided to pretend they'd all just gone off to the Bahamas instead, and were having a fantastic time." She sighed. "Fuck AIDS. And, now that we're all a little older, fuck heart disease and cancer, too."

"I'll drink to that." Julia raised a glass. "So who do you think killed Tony?"

Maggie shrugged. "No clue. Most people loved him, but it's hard to live that long in this town, and have that much power, without irritating the crap out of folks."

"You saw him a lot?"

Maggie nodded. "Yes, maybe once or twice a month, sometimes more, sometimes less, if he was busy on a project or out of town. He would come by here really late, once he was done with his evening stuff, and just kick back and relax. For both of us it was a pretty special friendship. We'd met in high school, right? Long before either of us became successful. We could really just be ourselves." She looked sad for a moment. "I'll miss him every day, the poor fucker. Everyone here will."

"Did you know he was sick?" Mason looked over at Julia, but she didn't seem annoyed by Mason asking questions. Doubtless she'd kick her under the table if she wanted her to stop. Or punch her in the nose.

"Sure. I was probably the first to know. Maybe after Helen; they've always been pretty close."

Julia raised her eyebrows. "She wrote a lovely obituary."

Maggie shrugged, and chewed another date before she answered. "She's a writer; of course she did. They argued from time to time, but I was never sure if they weren't about to get back together. It was a strange relationship. She'd been a writer's assistant on *The Codex*, very young." She looked over at Julia. "She ended up writing most of the script and took the Oscar for it. You must have known her."

Julia gave a wry smile. "I should have, but somehow I didn't, not really. I was . . . intoxicated quite a lot of the time, and absent a fair amount." She paused, drew a circle in the condensation on the table. "I don't have many memories of that time that aren't colored by Jonathan's death. I know she hates me."

Maggie said, "She was a total fanatic about movies. One of those that knows the smallest detail about everything, who the production designer was, gossip from the set, details of the script, everything. She fangirled all over Tony and Jonathan in pretty equal measure, but Tony was the one who returned the favor."

Julia turned up her palms. "He always loved a fan."

"Yeah, he always did. Often literally. So many women, I can't remember them all." Maggie laughed suddenly. "I forget a lot these days. I'm always so surprised when I look in the mirror and this old lady gazes back at me." She grinned at Julia. "Aren't you?"

Julia shook her head. "No. But then again, I rarely let old ladies into my house."

Maggie looked thoughtful. "It's not a good basis for a marriage, in my opinion."

"Old ladies? Or a shared love of movies?" Will was confused.

"No, fandom. It's a basic imbalance, right? One person worships the other; it's hard for that to shift into equality. It's not unusual, especially in LA, where fans can find the object of their obsession and make personal contact. There were rumors Helen had had to fight for script credit back then. Jonathan wrote the first version of the script, and had no issue sharing credit with Helen, but I guess Tony felt differently."

"He would," said Julia, sourly.

"And she was certainly obsessed with remaking *The Codex*. He told me she'd rewritten the script a dozen times, lost sleep over it, cried over it." She turned up her palms. "I can't imagine caring that much about anything." She grinned at Mason. "Too lazy."

Archie asked, "That's why he left her the rights?"

Maggie shrugged. "I guess. At one point she was broke as hell and he didn't want to give her the rights because he thought she needed money and would partner with the highest bidder. I didn't think she would have, and told him so. She loved it too hard. At that time, he wanted Repercussion to have it, end of story. Always the studio first; you know that as well as I do." She looked at Julia. "The studio, then you . . . the two great loves of his life."

There was a pause. Mason looked at Julia, who was frowning. "Don't be stupid, Maggie. His two great loves were the studio and himself."

The other woman shrugged. "Think what you like, Julia. Tony loved you from the first moment he met you, and never wavered." She turned to Mason. "Julia met Tony first, and he was a smitten kitten. A month or two of total bliss, to hear him tell it. But then he introduced her to Jonathan and it was all over in about five minutes. Not sure he ever really forgave Jonathan for stealing you."

"He didn't own me. I could hardly be stolen." Julia's tone was very dry.

"When Jonathan died and Julia went to jail, he was here every night for months, crying like a little girl. He was never the same."

Long silence. For an actress famed for her emotional range, Julia certainly could keep a stone face. Fortunately, the curtain went up at that moment, revealing an exquisitely naked girl in a giant martini glass, and the evening went downhill from there.

16

~~~~~

JULIA WAS WHINING in the elevator.

"I didn't start it," she said. "I was just having a good time. It was the guy with the toupee causing the problem."

Mason said, "Only because you took his toupee and threw it into the chandelier. He was planning a quiet evening celebrating his retirement looking at boobies, and you accused him of being a CIA agent."

"He was." Julia was tugging her gloves off, one finger at a time.

Archie chimed in. "He was not. He was a school principal from Yucaipa."

"So he said. But under that toupee he was a CIA agent." Mason watched Julia pull her gloves back on, smoothing them over her wrists. Then the finger-by-finger tugging again. Mason wondered if she'd found being at a bar a challenge; she was still only seven days in.

Will said, from the corner of the elevator, "Yucaipa has the oldest house in San Bernadino County."

They ignored him.

Julia said, "It was fine. Maggie cooled things down."

Mason snorted. "Actually, Danny Agosti cooled things down. Maggie's contribution was four new girls and a jeroboam of champagne."

Will said, "A jeroboam contains three liters of champagne, and is quite a rarity."

They ignored him again.

Julia said, "It distracted the agent, didn't it?"

"You mean the principal? Yes, but only because then he decided to get up on the chandelier and retrieve his hair himself."

"I rest my case. Would a school principal know how to vault from a bar to a chandelier?"

"No. And neither did he. Thus the need to call an ambulance and Danny's quiet suggestion that we leave." Mason thought again about Mr. Agosti and the powerful energy he exuded, and shivered.

The elevator reached the street and they stepped out. Mason realized there was a bigger crowd on the sidewalk than she'd anticipated.

"You wait here," she said to Julia. "I'll go get the keys from the valet."

Julia shrugged. "If you insist." She turned to Will and Archie. "She gets so cranky when she's tired. She's like me when I'm hungry. Mind you, she's cranky when she's hungry, too."

Mason rolled her eyes and went to fetch the car.

She started pushing through the people, fishing in her pocket for the claim ticket. Mason hadn't enjoyed crowds when she was drinking, and sober she found them almost unbearable. When the yelling behind her started, Mason was fifty feet away and wedged between two guys who were having a conversation over her head.

But still she heard it. Archie . . . yelling her name. Hard.

She turned. She could see his face above the crowd, furious and concerned and headed toward her. She turned and started pushing back through. When she was halfway, he started pointing and shouting at someone else, someone between them, someone heading toward the street.

"What?" She was pretty sure he couldn't hear her, but surely he could read lips enough to get that.

"Catch him! Stop him!" She could read lips, too. She angled toward the street, struggling to get past three drunken girls who were screaming at something on a phone. They wouldn't move, so she moved one of them. Forcibly. Gravity being the cruel taskmistress it was, the girl went down, and dragged a friend with her.

Mason stepped over them and kept pushing.

Archie got close enough for her to hear his shout. Damn, he was pissed. "A guy just attacked Julia. Shoved her over, yelled in her face and took off. Will is chasing him, but I lost them both in the crowd . . ." He looked around, and spotted an eddy in the people. "There!"

"What am I looking for?" Mason felt adrenaline flood her muscles.

"Gray hoodie, short guy."

Mason nodded and tacked left, planning to flank the guy. Archie went straight ahead, and Will was presumably somewhere to their right.

Then the guy broke loose of the crowd and Mason spotted him running like a hare, east on Sunset. He stuck to the bike lane, dodging the drunks and tourists who stepped on and off the sidewalk like tightrope walkers just starting out. A couple went down, but the guy kept moving. The spilling neon from the clubs and bars painted him yellow and white, red and blue, as he ran through puddles of light. His speed made him an easy spot.

Mason hit the street running, yelling at everyone to clear a path. She had an extra gear she hadn't used in a while, and nearly took Archie down as he stepped into the street just ahead of her.

"Heading east . . ." she yelled as she passed him, and seconds later saw the back of his shirt as he easily outpaced her. She frowned. *It's not a race . . .* then remembered it was. Mason couldn't see Will anywhere, and hoped he was somehow ahead of their quarry. She kept yelling as she went, trying to clear the way, but still took out a couple of Midwesterners who had the misfortune to pick that moment to step into the street to take a photo. Oh well, she thought to herself; it'll give them something to talk about back in Des Moines.

She could still see the guy ahead, desperation giving him wings. On and off the sidewalk, in and out of the crowds, nimble as fuck. She had him, she lost him, she had him . . .

Archie slowed to let her catch up, and panted, "I'm cutting across. Get on the inside, OK?"

She nodded, not wanting to waste effort on speech. A motorbike grazed her elbow as it passed too close, horns blaring, people yelling, but Mason kept running. She still hadn't spotted Will, but shouting and cursing to her right suggested Archie was making progress.

Then the guy was suddenly just ahead, and she nearly had him. She reached, grabbed his hoodie, and toppled as he wrenched free and sped up.

"Fuuuuck . . ." She hit the tarmac and sprawled, feeling her wrist twisting under her. Then she was up and going again, ignoring the heat and pain in her arm. Time for that later.

Hoodie Guy turned and dodged into the crowd, spotting a gap and cutting across the sidewalk.

She was right behind.

"Out of the way! Move!" She unleashed a yell she hadn't used in a while, gratified at the speed with which people scattered. Then a siren, short and staccato, somewhere behind her.

Dammit.

She caught sight of Archie away to her right, slowed by the crowd.

The man ran through a doorway, bright lights, noise. The smell of beer. Spirits.

She screeched to a halt. *We got you now, motherfucker.*

Then Archie was there, looking up at the sign.

"He's in here," panted Mason. "I'll go around the back. Where's Will?"

Archie bent double, trying to catch his breath. "Lost him. He was right behind you." He looked up at Mason. "You go in. I'll go around the back."

"No," said Mason. "I try not to go into bars. You go in."

"Mason"—Archie shook his head—"you're not drinking, you're apprehending."

Mason shrugged. "I'll stop him if he comes out."

Archie was just opening his mouth to argue further when Will showed up. Sweaty, red-faced, but very much there.

"What's going on?" he said. "What are we waiting for?"

"The guy went in the bar and Mason won't go in."

Will shrugged. "I get it. People, places and things." The triad you're supposed to avoid when you're sober.

"Told you," said Mason, "but I will go around the back."

Will shrugged. "I'm a gambler. I'll go in. Unlikely to get caught up in a random blackjack game . . . Gray hoodie, right?" And with that he plunged in.

Archie was still frowning at Mason, but he pointed. "The alley's half a block that way. Run, Mason, Jesus."

She took off.

The surface of the alley was loosely graveled, and Mason nearly fell as she rounded into the stretch that ran behind the bars. Some back doors were open, some closed, and she realized she should have paid attention. She wasn't sure which door went with the bar . . . the name of which she hadn't even looked at.

And then a door ahead swung open and in the trapezoid of red light she saw Hoodie Guy running full tilt, and three arm's lengths behind him, Will.

Will was not an athlete, and had neither acceleration nor control, but what he had was commitment and momentum. The guy was fast, though, and turned up the other end of the alley with Will on his heels and Mason closing quickly.

Hoodie Guy was only a few feet ahead of Will when he reached Sunset again, bursting onto the sidewalk, scattering a group of Japanese tourists like pigeons, squawking and fluttering out of the way. Will reached the street a second later, his mass carrying him across the suddenly de-touristed space like a boulder down a hill. He grabbed for the hoodie, got hold of it, Mason was half a foot behind, it was suddenly all going very well . . . when Hoodie Guy reached the street and ran in front of a Starline Tours bus doing forty in a twenty-five zone.

"And over there," the announcer on the bus was saying, "is where Leonardo DiCaprio was arrested for . . . Oh, shit . . ."

Brakes. Sirens. Screams.

Mason ran into Will as he bounced off the side of the bus himself, tossed and spun back against her, both of them hitting the sidewalk like sacks of potatoes.

Mason scrambled to her feet, expecting to see Hoodie Guy pâtéd on Sunset Boulevard.

But there was nothing to see at all. He'd gotten away clean.

17

~~~

TWO HOURS LATER, Archie, Will, Mason and Julia were sitting on a bench in the police station, waiting to be told to go home. The cops had shown up to deal with the assault on Julia, and had taken everyone to the station for statements. Now they were presumably typing up their reports, one tired finger at a time.

Mason had missed the actual assault of course, but she'd heard all about it. Hoodie Guy had pushed Julia to the ground and yelled, "The *Codex* Curse will get you. You're doomed," in a highly dramatic fashion. She'd even seen the video, because someone had been filming something else and captured the moment for posterity. The press was enjoying yet another paragraph for their already active *Codex* Curse stories, and Julia was vexed as hell.

"Bad lighting, unflattering angle; honestly, it's not fair." Now she shifted on the bench, tugging irritably at the tear in her dress. "He ambushed me. I didn't even have a chance to take a wider stance. Asshole."

Archie shrugged. "Well, he narrowly avoided getting creamed by a bus, so it was apparently his lucky night."

Julia nodded, and yawned.

The cop who'd interviewed them appeared around the corner holding a sheaf of printouts. He limped a little. He was tired. But he was the pointy end of law enforcement at two a.m. on a Tuesday morning, and he was doing his best.

"If you can sign your statements and remain available for follow-up questions, you can go home now."

They all signed and handed the papers back to him. "It's possible the detectives will have follow-up questions, especially for you, Mrs. Mann. While it's highly likely this was just a random crazy, they'll let you know if they think it's connected to the homicide you're already"—the cop paused, realizing he had dug himself a little hole—"connected to."

Julia was gracious. "Thank you, Officer. If they need me, they know where to find me."

There was a small crowd of reporters outside, and Julia took a minute to give them a better shot than the one they'd been running all night. This improved her mood somewhat.

Archie turned to Mason and lowered his voice. "Are you OK to drive?"

Mason nodded. "I got my second wind an hour into sitting on the bench back there. I'm good." She was actually exhausted, but she'd reached that wired stage of exhaustion that feels a lot like wakefulness. "Thanks."

"I'm sorry I busted your balls about not going into the bar. You know, back then."

Mason shrugged. "It's all good. I go into bars sometimes if I have to, and you could argue that was a time that I should have, but for some reason I balked."

"It worked out."

Archie paused. "I was worried about you. I thought you'd gone under the bus for a second."

"Actually, it was Will who got hit by the bus. I got hit by Will." She smiled up at him. "He's much softer than a bus."

Julia was done with the photographers, and called out, "Mason, Will, let's go. Archie, you with us?"

Archie shook his head. "No, I'm toast. I'm going home. I'll see you in the morning." He laughed. "Later this morning." He looked at Mason. "I'm glad you're OK. Good night, Mason."

"Good night, Archie."

She watched him walk away down the street, pulling out his phone to call an Uber. Watched the way his body moved, thought about the way he'd blown past her during the chase, his smile.

"Pull it together, dreamy," said Julia, suddenly right next to her. "Head in the game. Go get the car. We've still got work to do."

ONCE THE CITROËN was underway, Julia turned to Will. "You were in the middle of reporting earlier, when Casper arrived. I realize it's been a busy night, but did you have anything else? Now is as good a time as any. I'm wide awake and I'm going to be sore and cranky later."

Will nodded, although he was presumably going to be the sorest of them all in the morning. "You asked me to look at Jason Reed, the director who was squabbling with Tony."

Julia nodded, shaking back her hair and leaning her jaw on an elegant hand. "Yeah . . . there was an implication that Tony was thwarting Mr. Reed's hopes and dreams."

"He was." Will looked at his notes. "Jason Reed wanted

Jade Solomon to appear in his feature about a small dog who assisted in the American War of Independence."

"I beg your pardon?" Julia looked skeptical.

Will nodded, entirely serious. "It's called *The Shih Tzu Heard Around the World*."

Mason looked at him in the driver's mirror. "You're kidding."

He shook his head. "Not at all. Don't forget, someone green-lit a rom-com with tiny talking dogs and it turned into *Beverly Hills Chihuahua*. $150 million gross. Two sequels." He turned up his palms. "I'm not responsible for the moviegoing public, and numbers don't lie."

Mason frowned. "How would a shih tzu even become *involved* in the War of Independence?"

"Interestingly," said Will, his expression brightening, "it couldn't. Although the breed has been around for a very long time, they weren't known in the United States until the mid-twentieth century."

"So . . . how . . ." Mason was frowning harder. "I don't get . . ."

"Mason," said Julia, "are you forgetting he just compared it to a movie with a talking Chihuahua?"

"More than one in the sequels," added Will, conscientiously. "Anyway, he wanted Jade for it, but Tony wouldn't release her because she was still working on a movie for him."

"Which happened to *also* be about a dog who took part in the War of Independence, called *Yankee Poodle Came to Town*?" Mason started giggling and realized she was very, very overtired.

"No . . ." Will looked confused.

Mason kept going. "Or a Vietnam War remake called *Full Metal Jack Russell*?"

Will shook his head briefly and continued. "I'm ignoring you. So this was going on when Tony was killed, which means it's no longer a problem. The project Tony had Jade on is on hold now." He looked up. "What's strange is they worked together—Tony and Jason that is—on several things before, and everyone says they were friends."

Julia shrugged. "So the bottom line is that Jason and Tony had beef that was settled by Tony dying, but not really very significant beef."

"No, not really. I mean, it was money, but it was not huge money and it was only money." He hesitated. "Jade Solomon is a kind of theme I noticed running through several beefs, actually. She wants to play the lead in the *Codex* remake, Helen doesn't want her, Christine does, then she was in that accident." He paused. "She had a bird on her hat at the funeral. I saw a picture."

Mason sympathized. She'd found it hard to get over, too.

Julia nodded. "Mason, go talk to her. Anything on Christine?"

"Wait, why do I . . ." Mason was frowning, but Will rolled right over her.

"Christine seems about as clean as a Hollywood studio executive can be, bearing in mind what faint praise that is. UCLA, USC film school, assistant, development executive . . . the traditional path up through the system for a smart, driven person who lives to make movies on the studio side. She's got an eye for the new thing, for the coming attraction, you know. She has very good taste. Several majors have tried to tempt her away, but she had her eye on Tony's job and nothing was going to shift her from that. Not that she didn't have plenty of power as his second-in-command, but she wanted sole control."

"And she and Tony were tight? No issues there?"

Will shrugged. "None that I could find in a day. Give me time and maybe I can dig something up. She's been with him for over a decade."

Mason turned into the driveway and pulled up in front of the house. "Final stop. All out who are getting out. You don't have to go home, but you can't stay here." She had a sudden thought. "Will, I'm sorry, I didn't ask if you wanted to be dropped somewhere else."

"Why would I?" he asked, surprised. "I live here, in one of the guesthouses. There are three of them." He climbed out of the car. "See you in the morning, Julia. I'm on bank records, more Helen, more Christine, more everyone . . ."

"Yes, and Becky Sharp's background. Let's not drop the ball on that case because we're too busy juggling balls on this one. Good night."

He came over, and Mason watched in mild surprise as they hugged each other. Julia was so prickly, and yet Claudia and Will—and Casper—all seemed so fond of her. She wondered if she'd ever get there.

"You," said Julia, turning to her, "park the car and be back in the morning. If you took my suggestion and moved into the other guesthouse you'd already be home." Then she frowned at Mason and went inside.

Mason sighed and turned the car around. She wouldn't hold her breath.

18

~~~

AFTER MASON PARKED the car, she had a sudden, pleasing thought. *Leftovers.* That grilled cheese had been a while ago, and the snacks at the bar had been . . . just snacks. Plus there'd been all that running and then all that waiting.

The house was dark and quiet, and when the light from the fridge cut across the kitchen floor, Mason was thrilled to see she was right. Plenty of leftovers. Feeling slightly guilty, she quietly started assembling a plate. It would just take a minute or two in the microwave . . .

A noise. From the main part of the house. Fuck, Julia was going to find out she was a leftover thief. Dammit. A basic tenet of recovery is promptly admitting when you're wrong, so Mason sighed and headed out into the hallway to face the music.

Nothing. She stood in the hallway with her head cocked.

Another noise, this time clearly coming from the office. Julia had seemed so tired, but maybe she'd decided to keep working. Mason frowned, and started quietly along the hallway. Suddenly, the hairs on the back of her neck prickled, and she realized the noises she'd heard weren't Julia, but someone being stealthy. She slowed down, paused, listening. She felt herself tensing, getting ready. *Help me out, central nervous system*, she told herself. *Get that adrenaline up and running.* She could feel it moving through her body, feel it like cocaine, like a shot of scotch, like high-quality chemistry, which of course it was. Bespoke, calibrated perfectly, which is why it works so well.

She got close to the office and started hugging the wall, moving toward the door. She could feel silence now, feel someone else's stillness, the rat-brain sense of being watched. She paused again, waited.

Come on, motherfucker.

And they came.

A shadow detached from an angle she didn't expect, past the door, into the curve of the corridor. Darted faster than you would think possible, coming at her with their arms folded tight against their body. Mason had been watching the door, thinking they were in the room behind it, and as they slammed into her, she realized she hadn't been ready, not even close to ready for the full weight of an angry person determined to take her out and down. The attacker had a much more developed plan than she did, aiming solely to disable her and escape, and they nailed the execution. Glancing off her, spinning her against the wall, hard. Her body weight did the rest, and her attacker took the kinetic energy generated by the collision and rode it along the hallway like free fall. It was elegant despite its desperation, and they were halfway to the front door and freedom when the lights came on.

Mason was lying on the floor and had an excellent view of

Julia's legs as she came flying down the stairs, yelled *stop* and
was ignored. The front door slammed and a second later Julia
was pulling at Mason's arm.

"Get up! Let's go! Come on!" Mason flipped over and scrambled to her feet. She heard an engine start as they reached the
front door. Julia had it open and was through; Mason was
faster than she was and passed her. The criminal's car had
been parked up the hill behind the house, which was why they
hadn't seen it when they'd gotten home. She'd parked the
Citroën in the garage, though, and nothing blocked the car as
it came down the hill and nearly hit her before accelerating on
the driveway. There was a notable concussion when it hit the
flat area by the house, and then it was gone, dust flying, wheels
spinning, out and away.

"Shit!" Mason was literally choking on its dust, bent double and trying to get her systems online.

"Get the fuck in, Mason," Julia yelled, pulling up in front of
her. She'd ignored the escaping car and run into the garage,
driving out in something low and sleek, its engine overwhelm-
ingly loud as she leaned across and flung the door open.
"Get in!"

Mason scrambled in and barely had the door closed before
Julia took off like a rabbit, the force of acceleration momentarily pressing Mason against the seat, making it impossible to
put on her seat belt. She felt the engine directly behind her, the
sensation of being pushed by a giant hand, scooped along as
effortlessly as a thistle. Something clattered in the seat well,
but she couldn't even lower her head to look.

"We'll catch them." Julia was strangely calm now that they
were underway.

"Do I call the cops?" Mason searched herself and realized

she'd left her phone on the kitchen counter. Literally had a moment of panic at being separated from it, in the midst of all this, addiction being what it is.

"No," said Julia. "Catch first, cops later."

Mason finally looked at her properly. Julia had clearly been getting ready for bed. Her hair was down, half her makeup off, half still on. She was wearing boxer shorts and a Grateful Dead T-shirt. Mason had the random thought that if she'd made a list of the top ten things she thought Julia wore to bed, this particular ensemble would not have been on it. The older woman was sitting well back in the driver's seat, driving barefoot. Her body was completely relaxed, even as her hands gripped and spun the wheel. Her face was calm, her eyes sharp as they took the dusty curves of the hill road, the high beams cutting through the dark in fat slices, jumping from tree to bush to gaps that led to the precipitous drop Mason knew was right there. The driveway hugged the canyon wall on one side, but nothing separated it from a fall that would kill them if they went over the edge.

Mason looked at the speedometer. Ninety-eight. Fuck.

"Julia," she said, her adrenaline starting to modulate, fight ebbing away in the face of so much flight. "What's the plan here? Killing ourselves probably isn't the smartest . . ."

"Shut it," said Julia. "They broke into my house. I have questions." She took a sharp curve without hitting the brakes till the last minute, timing her hard foot to perfectly fishtail the bend and cut the most geometrically efficient corner ever seen. The lateral force pushed Mason against the door and the corresponding centripetal acceleration flung her back as Julia hit the gas out of the corner, and for the first time they saw taillights ahead of them. Again, the noise of something getting thrown around under the seat. Mason risked a look down, but couldn't see anything.

"Yesssss," hissed Julia quietly. "Momma's gonna catch your ass now, cocksucker."

Mason suddenly felt herself starting to grin, despite her healthy fear of imminent death.

"Get him, Julia," she said, "but don't kill us in the process."

Julia snorted, flying through the gateposts at the end of the drive and accelerating on the smoothly finished surface of the city street. Up here there were no parked cars, the hill road narrow and prone to catching fire. The curves and bends were sharp, and the gradient of descent severe. Some canyon roads took their time to make it from the crest of the hills that surround Los Angeles to the flats of Sunset Boulevard or some other long horizontal that ran along the foot, but not this one. This street was in a hurry to get to town and fuck things up. Julia had traveled it several times a day for nearly two decades, and she knew it like a lover of old, its curves familiar, her fingertips on the wheel completely certain, anticipating every inch.

Mason realized Julia was singing under her breath. She was happy.

"I thought you said you didn't drive," she said.

"No," replied Julia, evenly, "I said Claudia usually did the driving, but that's because I like to drive like this, and she prefers to observe the rules of the road. She drives, fewer tickets. Plus, I find it hard to remember if I currently have a license or not."

She paused as the car ahead of them bottomed out momentarily in a dip and lost a hubcap, the silver disc spinning back toward them. She effortlessly avoided it. "Like right now, no license, obviously." She rolled her eyes, leaning forward a little as they drew closer and closer to the car ahead. "Get the plate, Mason. Once we hit the city, things are going to get a little trickier." She was right behind the other car now, still doing ninety, her expression suggesting she was driving Mason to school rather than chasing someone who really didn't want to be caught.

Mason looked around. Nothing. "Do you have your phone?"

Julia shook her head. "Glove box."

Owner's manual. Mason discovered she was riding in a Lamborghini Miura, which might have meant something had she known anything about fancy cars. She wondered briefly if this was the car Julia had chosen when she was trying to get away on the night of Tony's murder, then she realized there was nothing to write with. She looked ahead and tried to read the license plate. First letter a B, maybe? She blinked, tried to see better, make it out through the clouds of dust both cars were throwing up, the speed and her adrenaline making it difficult to focus.

Julia pulled up to the much taller car in front, then oversteered a little as she started to pass on the right, nudging the nose of the car against the flank of the pursued, the momentary contact literally causing sparks. She handled the car expertly, inches separating the two vehicles as they took another downward curve, the canyon wall high at this point of the hill, dry, scrubby grass atop a striped twelve-foot wall of clay and rubble. The other car hit the wall for a second, knocking rocks and sending up a cloud of dust.

"Stop, you asshole," muttered Julia, pulling the car halfway alongside, nudging it against the other car again, still totally in control. "I will end you here and now." The car rocked and fishtailed as the other driver brought their car hard against them, the two cars now completely filling the road, side by side and still going waaaaay over the speed limit.

"Julia . . ." Mason held on tight to the door handle, bracing herself. "If anything comes up the hill, we're fucked."

"Then hope it doesn't. I want him to stop."

Mason looked at the other car. It was much, much taller than they were; from the passenger seat in the low sports car she couldn't even see the driver. The windows were tinted, anyway. She wished she knew more about cars. All she could tell about this one was that it was big, fast and had zero interest in stopping.

"Should have taken the fucking Mercedes," muttered Julia. "I went for speed when what I needed was speed plus mass . . . Note to self."

The other car definitely had mass, and Mason thought maybe the driver suddenly realized their advantage, because as they took the last long curve of the hill, the one that opened up onto Sunset in less than a quarter mile, they pushed back against the Lamborghini, steadily forcing it toward the open edge of the street.

And then, ahead, around the corner, a truck. The driver, tired from navigating the city as it was waking up, the Los Angeles drivers fucking insane—honestly, this city was the worst—saw them and hit his brakes and horn simultaneously, but it was too late. The thief's car gave them one final shove, and at the moment Mason decided this was where her life was going to end, head-on collision at eighty in a tiny sports car built before airbags, Julia hit her brakes and angled the wheels perfectly to avoid the truck, spinning out onto the dusty side of the road, coming to a rocking rest four inches from the wall.

"God fucking dammit," she said, smacking the wheel. She breathed hard and closed her eyes for a moment. Then she turned to Mason.

"Did you get the plate?"

Mason shook her head. "Sorry. First letter was a B. I think." She paused. "Not sure."

Julia said *fuck* and stared out of the windshield. A thick layer of dust was still settling on the car. The sun was coming up, the sky purpling. Mason suddenly realized the car was yellow, and wasn't sure why that surprised her.

Miraculously, the engine was still purring. Julia put the car back into gear and hit the gas.

"You need to work on your situational awareness. And your eyesight. That was fun. Let's go home and work out what they were looking for."

19

WILL WAS POLITE, but incredulous. They'd gotten him out of bed, and he was moving slowly, clearly feeling the effects of being hit by a city bus. However, his brain was working as smoothly as ever.

"How did you not get the plate? You weren't driving. You had one job."

Mason frowned at him. "Yeah, staying alive. Have you ever driven with Julia? It was terrifying." She paused. "The first letter was B." Beat. "Pretty sure."

Will shook his head. "Julia?"

Julia shrugged. "I was busy feeling alive for the first time in, like, eight days." She looked around the office. "Whatever they were looking for, they either found it exactly where they thought it would be, or they didn't look very hard. Nothing looks disturbed."

"I'm disturbed," said Mason. "You really need to install a security system."

There was a pause. She looked at their faces. "What?"

"Uh, there is a security system. She just never turns it on."

"Why not? You got attacked a few hours ago and we just

had a break-in. A security system is only as good as its on button."

Another pause.

Julia clicked her tongue. "Will's being polite. I turn it off because when I'm drinking I set it off all the time and we got tired of dealing with the cops and fire brigade showing up only to find me wandering around my own house in my underwear or whatever." Julia was pacing back and forth. "If I manage to stay sober for a while, I'll turn it back on."

"Wait," said Mason, suddenly remembering the sound she'd heard during the car chase. She ran out and was back a few moments later, clutching a small film canister. "This was in the car. Any idea why?"

Julia stared at her, the color draining from her face. "Oh my God," she whispered. "I remember . . . Tony brought that the night he died. I must have grabbed it when I was running away."

"It was under the seat," said Mason. "It was thrown about when we were driving, or I wouldn't have known it was there."

She went and pulled the curtain back. The sun was up now, the light thin but clear.

The door opened and Claudia appeared, drying her hands on a dish towel.

"Will told me about the excitement. Sorry I missed it. I made waffles. I got the guest room ready. Becky Sharp gets here today, and Ben is already in the other one." She didn't look sorry to have missed it; she looked as bored and as unruffled as she always did. She spotted the film canister. "What's that?"

Julia was still staring. "Tony brought it. I remember that, but not much else. I don't remember what it is."

"Let's watch it." Mason was ready to go. "If we can. I mean, if we have whatever you need to watch old film." She paused. "I can take it somewhere and get it digitized."

"No need," said Will. "It's Super 8. We have a projector." He coughed. "A dual, of course, 8 mm and Super 8."

Julia's color was returning, and the hesitation was gone from her voice. "Load it up, Will. Let's see what we've got."

IT TURNED OUT they not only had a projector, but a large screen that whispered down from the ceiling, and blinds that darkened the windows completely. Will was clearly at home with the equipment and seemed entertained by the process of loading up the film. All that was missing was popcorn, and Mason was pretty sure she could have had that, too, had she wanted some.

The film appeared to be simply candid footage, shot on set. There was a lot of sound, but all overlapping voices, hard to distinguish.

"*The Codex*," said Will, as soon as the film began. "There's Jack Simon, standing next to you, Julia."

Julia was leaning forward, the light from the projection playing across her features. A small smile appeared. "Oh my God, was I twelve? So young . . ." She caught her breath. "There's Jonathan." A man of average height, maybe even a little less, walked across the frame. Julia breathed deeply. "He was so handsome."

Mason didn't see it, personally. Jonathan Mann looked pretty average to her, but he was obviously charismatic, because the whole set moved around him like a fulcrum. Everyone in the frame was angled toward him as he walked over to

Julia and the actor Will had identified as Jack Simon. They
conversed, and apparently someone said something funny,
because they suddenly all laughed. Mason looked curiously at
Julia, who couldn't have been much older then than she herself was now. Beautiful, full of life, and with an air of energy
and movement she'd apparently left behind with the feathered haircut.

Whoever was filming pulled back, revealing the area
behind the main film camera, two men standing behind it,
chatting. A makeup artist darted up to Julia, puffing her face
and fixing her hair. She looked at Jack Simon, and apparently
decided he was fine as he was. Mason agreed with her: Jack
Simon had been a fox, back in the day. She wondered what he
looked like now.

Jonathan appeared again, talking briefly to the camera-
man, then walking out of frame. The photographer followed
him as he approached a small group of men, three of them,
who were sitting and standing to one side.

The men shook his hand, and for a moment things seemed
amicable. Then the man who was sitting stood up suddenly,
turning to one of the men standing behind him. He raised his
hand and abruptly the dynamic of the group changed.

"Huh," said Will. "Trouble."

It was clear. The body language became tense; Jonathan
stepped forward and then, just as quickly, back again as the
men turned to him and formed a tight circle. One of them
placed a hand on his chest and pushed, just once, but it was
enough. A threat. Jonathan put his hands up, dipped his head
in compliance, and the photographer stepped closer. The men
shook their heads, Jonathan was talking quickly, and just as
suddenly as the exchange had started, it turned again, the

three men relaxing, the one man returning to his seat. The photographer changed his focus, panning back to Julia, who was laughing and practicing a fight move with two other women, one of whom was slightly taller but with an identical hairstyle.

"Bella Horton," murmured Julia, "my stunt double. This must have been early in filming, before the accident." She grimaced. "We were friends. I still miss her. Filthiest sense of humor of anyone I've ever met, even in prison. She was a loss. And I believe that other woman is Helen Eckenridge. I forgot she started out as a Bella's assistant. She couldn't get out of it fast enough; writing was much more her speed."

The three women practiced a moment longer, Helen and Bella demonstrating a throw that Julia subsequently nailed.

"Nice moves," murmured Mason.

"Thanks," said Julia. "Bella was a good teacher."

The film ended abruptly, the projector came to a halt, and Will stepped over to it. "Want to see it again?"

Julia shook her head. "No. Digitize it, please. Why would Tony bother to bring that to me, and why now?"

"You don't remember anything he said?" asked Mason. She wasn't really expecting a positive answer—there were many days of her own life about which she remembered nothing—so when Julia shook her head, she wasn't surprised.

"No, but he presumably had a reason, both for coming over and for bringing the film." Julia turned to Will. "Recognize any of the men?"

"Nope." Will was futzing about with the projector and a laptop, presumably preparing to digitize the film.

Julia thought for a moment, then turned to Claudia. "Is Casper still here?"

Claudia nodded.

"Is he awake?"

Claudia shrugged. "Doubtful, it's not even nine a.m."

"Go wake him up. If anyone's going to recognize those men, it's him."

CASPER YAWNED WIDE enough to fit one of his homemade Twinkies in sideways, and snapped his teeth shut with an audible click.

"Mikey Agosti is the one in the chair; the other two I have no idea." He reached for the double espresso shot Claudia had placed on the side table, and drank it in two gulps. "I'll need more coffee. What time is it? Why is it so bright?"

"It's nine a.m. This is what it looks like in the mornings."

"Hideous." The journalist shuddered. "Remind me not to stay over again if this is the treatment I'll receive."

"You'll go back to sleep and remember nothing of this," said Julia. "And I needed your expertise."

Casper rolled his eyes, but stopped complaining. "Ask Maggie," he said. "She was close with Mikey Agosti: He was an investor in the club, and she's still partnered with his son, Danny. She's more likely to have known his associates than I am, and she's always been good with names." He paused. "Mind you, she can also keep a secret like nobody I've ever met, so you just have to hope she has no reason to keep quiet."

Julia nodded. "We'll go see her again soon." She looked at Mason. "You can go back to Maggie's and show her the video. You have to talk to Helen, too."

Mason frowned. "I didn't get any sleep last night. I fell in the street twice and got the wind knocked out of me. I need to eat, take a nap and make a meeting. Aren't you going to report this to the cops?"

Julia shook her head. "You continue to delight me with your conversational gambits, Mason, try as you might to bore the shit out of me with personal details. And no, why involve the police? I don't even know if the intruder took anything, and it's not necessary to tell the police about the film; it might not be relevant at all." She turned to Will. "Someone is up to something that killing Tony didn't solve. I don't think the attack last night was coincidence, and the break-in was intentional as hell. If I might quote a better detective than any of us, the plot thickens. It's time to start asking around. Lower channels, you know what I mean."

He nodded.

Mason frowned. "I don't know what you mean."

Julia waved her hand airily. "You will come to realize," she said, "that I am a deeply charming and friendly person. Due to my career in Hollywood, my time in prison and my subsequent legal career, I have friends in high places, low places and all places in between. Often that means I hear about things regular channels might not reveal. It never hurts to ask."

Mason deepened her frown. "That didn't really clear it up."

Claudia was still standing by the door. "Stop bickering and hurry up," she said. "My waffles don't deserve to be kept waiting, and nobody's doing anything until they've eaten."

20

~~~~~

MASON ATE THREE waffles, then went home and threw herself onto her bed. She had been asleep for a little over an hour when she was woken by a ping from her phone. A text, from Julia.

> Will texting you digitized film. Go show Maggie, get names, then go see Helen and ask her what she and Tony talked about at lunch the day before he was killed. Report back.

As she was reading, another text arrived, this time with the film. She watched it quickly, enjoying Bella's fighting skills and Julia's feathered haircut in equal measure, then sighed a deep sigh and dragged herself out of bed.

Another text, this time from her mother. How's the job going? Still got it?

She frowned and headed into the bathroom. Her mother's low expectations were usually only matched by Mason's low performance, but she realized she wanted to keep this job. It was entertaining. She regarded her rapidly darkening bruises in the mirror and reached to turn on the shower. The ache in her arms made her groan involuntarily. OK, she told herself, maybe only entertaining in the widest applicable sense of the word.

THE HOT SHOWER made her feel a whole lot better, and as she put her car in gear and headed to Galliano's, she wondered if anyone would be there this time of the morning.

Everyone was. Including a phalanx of reporters outside of the club, one of whom recognized her and hailed her like a long-lost sister.

"Natasha Mason! Julia Mann's new right-hand girl! Why's Julia interested in Galliano's?"

"She's not," replied Mason, pushing past.

"She's representing the woman accused of murdering the stripper, right? She filed appearance with the court yesterday. That makes her representation official."

"Did she?" Mason kept moving, wondering what else Julia had done that she didn't know anything about.

"Yes," replied the reporter, "and when Julia takes on a client, it's pretty rare they get convicted. What does she know?"

"Very little," said Mason, finally reaching the door of the club, which she prayed was open.

It was. And the club was full.

IT TURNS OUT even burlesque requires rehearsal, and that midmorning, Maggie was auditioning new acts and tweaking old ones. She looked up as Mason came through the door and started grinning.

"Please tell me you came back to pay for the chandelier?" She pointed to a guy on a ladder, repairing the chandelier that had taken the full weight of the principal from Yucaipa the night before and was clearly feeling the effects. "I realize you weren't the one dangling from it, but your boss was standing underneath shouting *jump, jump*, so I hold her responsible."

"Not going to argue with you," replied Mason, coming over and sitting down.

"I read about the attack this morning. Normally, my bouncers would have sorted out the guy. Sorry about that."

"Not your fault," replied Mason easily, although she could feel her muscles stiffening up from the previous night's many activities. Lucky she was young and limber.

Danny Agosti was there, too, eating a croissant and drinking espresso from a cup that looked like dollhouse china in his hand. On the stage, a contortionist in a transparent leotard was pretzeling in a way that managed to be both erotic and weird. Mason could barely drag her eyes away. How did she even *get* her feet up there?

Maggie looked coolly at the contortionist and then at Mason. "What brings you here, if it's not reparations?"

Mason pulled out her phone. "We found a Super 8 film canister last night, and Julia remembers Tony giving it to her. We've identified one of the people in it." She looked at Danny. "It's your father, Mikey, but Julia wondered if you knew the other two?"

She cued up the film and played it, handing over her phone.

"Oh my God, Bella," said Maggie immediately, and then,

"Oh my God, the haircuts. Those were the days." She watched for a moment in silence, and Mason imagined the film, the body language of the men. "That's Mikey, for sure, and one of the guys was called Don, I think. The other one I don't know." She tapped the screen to replay the film and handed it to Danny. "Any ideas?"

He pushed the last piece of croissant in his mouth and reached to take the phone. Watched in silence, his lips tight.

"Yeah, it's my dad. Don, sure. The other guy looks familiar but I don't remember his name. It might come back to me." He frowned at Mason. "There's nothing actionable happening there; it's just guys interacting. Nothing to see."

"Might your mother know?" Mason was slightly distracted by the arrival of three identical triplets shimmering mostly naked across the stage, but held it together.

"No idea. Not going to show her, if that's what you were about to ask. I don't want her involved in any way." He handed Mason back her phone. "What is this supposed to prove?"

Mason shrugged. "No idea. Tony gave it to Julia for a reason, and we're assuming it's to do with Jonathan's death. But no one's investigating that crime, so Julia's simply being nosy, as is her way. And she still doesn't remember anything about the evening Tony was killed, so she's looking for information that might jog her memory."

"Well, I've nothing to add, and if that winds up on the Internet I'm going to be pissed."

Mason felt her back get up. "Why? It's just an old home movie."

"Well then, let me rephrase. If that hits the Internet with any suggestion of criminal wrongdoing, *then* I'm going to be pissed."

"No one's even looking into Jonathan's death. Why are you so defensive?" Mason could hear her tone getting pretty aggressive, and tried taking a breath. Pause. Don't lose your serenity over this guy.

"Do you think triplets works?" asked Maggie suddenly. "Or does it feel like one too many?" She raised her voice. "Can just two of you do it?"

"No," called back one of the three girls. "We come as a unit."

"So to speak," said another.

"If you'll pardon the phrase," said the third.

Maggie laughed. "OK, then, run through it again. Are the feathers really necessary?"

"Yes."

"Adds atmosphere."

"And cushioning."

Maggie laughed again, then turned back to Mason and Danny. "I'm not sure why you're so cranky about this. It happened a very long time ago. As Mason says, no one's interested in Jonathan's death; they're focused on Tony's. No one's suggesting a link between your family and that, so why so stressed?"

Danny looked cross. "I don't want anything to get started."

"It won't," replied his partner. "You care too much about what other people think. Fuck them." She looked at Mason. "Sorry we can't be more helpful. If I remember the other guy's name, I'll call Julia." She paused. "Has she met with Becky Sharp yet?"

Mason shook her head.

"I've been thinking about it. I really don't think she has it in her to kill Sam. I think you need to look elsewhere."

"I believe that's the plan."

"Well, that I'd like to help with. Let me know." She waved her hand. "Now I need to get back to work." She reached over and stole what was left of Danny's coffee, then waved the cup at a waiter for more.

Mason got up to leave as the triplets exited and a miniature horse clip-clopped across the stage.

"No!" barked Maggie. "No livestock!"

Mason made her way out of the club, grinning.

HELEN ECKENRIDGE LIVED in Silver Lake, up in the hills. Silver Lake was the LA neighborhood that reminded Mason most of Berkeley, thanks to its winding narrow streets, Craftsman-style houses, prayer flags and peace signs. The air smelled of pot rather than money.

Mason squeezed past an enormous car in the driveway and rang the bell. She couldn't hear it, but clearly it rang somewhere, because a pack of dogs started barking furiously. It sounded like there were at least a dozen, but when she looked through the glass panels of the front door, she saw only four, piling through from the large courtyard that extended up the hill.

The front door swung open. "Don't worry, they're harmless..." Close up, Mason could see faint lines around Helen's eyes, occasional silver in the golden hair. She was maybe forty-five? Fifty? Still much younger than Tony. Fit and muscular in the way so many women in Los Angeles were. And beautiful, of course, but within the normal range of humanity, rather than Hollywood Outstanding. "Do you mind dogs?"

"Not at all, I love them," Mason replied, bending to pat the suddenly friendly mass of wagging tails. She straightened up and found Helen looking at her inquiringly. They'd met at the will reading, but Helen showed no signs of recognition. To be fair, no one had introduced Mason, or maybe Helen was just bad with faces.

"I'm Natasha Mason . . . I work for Julia Mann. We're investigating Tony's death, and I was hoping you could answer a few questions?"

Helen smiled tightly. "Julia and I aren't exactly friends, but if she didn't kill Tony, then I've no reason to see her go to jail for it."

"Well, I guess that would depend on how much you're not friends," replied Mason, "but I don't intend to take up a lot of your time."

Helen shrugged. "Come on in. I'm in the middle of casting for a show, so we may be interrupted a little." She turned and made a path through the dogs.

The house was decorated in the deceptively casual style Mason was familiar with. As a delivery person, she'd dropped off single boba teas to wealthy teenagers in this neighborhood, and the piles of cushions (interesting fabrics, clashing colors), eclectic artwork (three-dimensional pieces paired with obscure movie posters) and pleasingly simple (but handmade to order) mid-century furniture told her a lot about the woman walking away from her down the hallway. The French doors onto to the courtyard were open, the air smelled of jasmine and rosemary, and she could see a yoga mat unrolled on the flagstones. Nice life.

She followed Helen into the kitchen, which rivaled Julia's in size but which clearly didn't see as much action. Copper-bottomed pots hung gleaming from a rack above an industrial cooktop, but the spice jars were all immaculate and full to the brim. The bottles of expensive oil were artistically chosen and elegantly arranged but still unopened. The roll of paper towels was unused . . . Nobody cooked in this kitchen. An array of headshots, all young men, were spread out on the counter.

A housekeeper was bustling around the kitchen, but Helen ignored her and turned to Mason.

"Tea?" asked Helen, then hesitated before opening a cupboard containing many kinds of grains and beans in matching canisters, but no tea. She tried a second cupboard and struck gold. "I have Lapsang souchong, jasmine green, peppermint, chamomile . . ." She turned to look at Mason. "Or would you prefer coffee?"

They both looked at the chrome-handled espresso machine and Mason took pity on her. "Just water, thanks."

"Sparkling or filter?"

Inwardly, Mason sighed. Sometimes people were just too damn hospitable. She flashed a glance at the housekeeper, but she was busy doing something to the contents of the fridge and was ignoring Helen as hard as Helen was ignoring her.

"Tap's fine."

"Ice?"

"No, straight up, thanks."

Once that little pantomime was over, Helen led the way into the courtyard and took a seat at a weathered French café table with charmingly mismatched wrought iron chairs. The whole place felt like a set, and Mason wondered if it was a professional necessity, the curating of environment. Then she met Helen's gaze and was surprised at the intense appraisal she saw there—she wasn't the only one judging. But maybe she'd been mistaken, because the other woman smiled and her tone was completely neutral.

"How can I help?"

Mason shrugged. "I was hoping you could tell me about the last time you saw Tony, how he was, what you talked about, that kind of thing."

The front doorbell rang, and moments later the housekeeper passed by, heading to open it. Helen paid her no attention, and answered Mason's question.

"We talked about work, as usual. Exchanged notes about *The Codex*, about some other projects he had coming up, that kind of thing. I've been working on a screenplay about Palm Springs in the late sixties, and we talked about that." She described a graceful arc with her hands. "Various things, you know." She paused. "He asked after my dogs; he knows I'm always happy to talk about them." A gentle, wry smile. "He seemed normal, for him."

"You were still married but separated, is that right?"

Helen nodded. "Neither of us felt a desperate urge to divorce, no new relationships approaching that level of seriousness, you know . . ." She hesitated. "We were both married to our work."

The housekeeper appeared in the arched entrance to the courtyard, in the company of an extremely handsome, dark-haired young man. Helen looked up at him and frowned.

"No, thanks."

The young man flushed. "Can I leave a headshot?"

"Sure," said Helen, already back to looking at Mason. "You might be right for something else."

The housekeeper led the young man away. Mason raised an eyebrow and went back to interviewing.

"You're a writer?"

Helen nodded. "I'm a director, but I also write."

"You won an Academy Award for the *Codex* screenplay."

"A long time ago. I think of myself as a director first."

Mason nodded. "Are you directing *The Codex* remake?"

Helen nodded. "I intend to." Another elegant, subtle movement of her shoulders. "The final choice is up to Christine, but she and I have been talking it over for months." She looked like she was maybe going to say something else, but didn't. "Tony and I didn't discuss that, if that was your next question."

The door again. The same soft padding of the housekeeper, the same presentation of an almost identical handsome young man.

This time Helen gazed for slightly longer, but then shook her head again. "Sorry, we're looking for something different."

"I can be different," said the actor. "I could dye my hair. Wear contact lenses."

"No, thanks," said Helen, dismissively. He turned and skulked away, the housekeeper behind him.

Mason got things back on track. "I was going to ask where you were the night Tony died?"

"At home."

"Alone?"

"Unless you count the dogs, yes."

"Did you speak to anyone?"

"Yes, I had a work Zoom call in the middle of the evening. Or at least, I was supposed to. With Christine. But she had been in an accident or something, so when I logged on she told me she was too frazzled to do the call. We rescheduled."

"What was the call about?"

"Several things. The Palm Springs script, one or two other things."

"Did you discuss *The Codex*?"

Helen shook her head. "Like I said, we didn't end up discussing anything."

"One final question: You seemed surprised that Tony left the studio the way he did. Were you?"

Helen nodded. "I expected him to leave it to Christine, end of story. But that was Tony all over. He loved to make promises, especially to women. And then he'd do whatever the hell he wanted. He did it all the time."

"To you?"

"Not as much to me, but he did it. He would get carried away, promise the earth and deliver a handful of dirt. He expected his charm to carry him through, and usually it did." Helen stood up. "If you have more questions, you should feel free to email my agent, but now I need to get ready for that call. Thanks so much for coming by. Please give my regards to Julia."

A third ring on the doorbell.

"I'll get it," called Helen. "I'm just showing my guest out." She started walking and Mason followed.

She said, "I'll certainly pass on your regards, but I thought you weren't friends."

Helen laughed. "This is Hollywood, Miss Mason. Friends or enemies, everyone is cordial on the surface, otherwise we'd never get anything done."

"You're all pretending?"

Helen didn't answer, just led the way to the door. Once there she smiled another gentle smile and said, "All the world's a stage, remember."

"And all the men and women merely players?"

"Sure. We just play better than most." She held the door as Mason walked through, then took one look at the hopeful and stunningly attractive man waiting on the doorstep.

"No thanks, but thanks for your time."

Mason and the young actor both watched the door close in their faces, then turned and headed down the steps.

"Is she casting the female lead, too?" the guy asked Mason.

"I'm not an actress," she replied.

"You should be," he returned, looking at her with open appreciation. "You have a definite look, do you know what I mean?"

"I don't think I could handle the rejection," Mason said. "How do you do it?"

He shrugged, pausing to let her go ahead at the bottom of the stairs. "You get used to it."

"Yeah," said Mason. "Well, good luck."

"Thanks," he said, beaming a million-dollar smile that in any other city would put him in the top one percent of beautiful residents and which here got him precisely zero. "Today could be the day, right?"

"More castings?"

"Two more and a callback," he replied, heading down the street to where his bicycle stood locked to a lamppost. "Living the dream."

Mason looked at her phone. A text from Julia: You're taking too long. Claudia made pizza for lunch but I ate yours. Hurry up.

"Yeah," she muttered, "living the dream."

21

~~~~

WHEN MASON GOT back to the house, she found her boss and Will in the office, along with Becky and Ben Sharp. The sofa was pretty full.

"What did I miss?" she muttered to Will, as she sat next to him. The office door opened and Claudia came through with her magical coffee tray, accompanied by Archie, who was carrying a yellow layer cake and a pile of plates.

"Very little so far. We've only been here ten minutes and she wanted to wait for you." Will watched the progression of the cake through the room, much as a cat watches a bird hop along the ground. He started to reach for the cake, then pulled back, then reached, then pulled . . .

"Have some cake," said Mason, noticing Archie's hands as he set the cake down. She frowned at herself, internally.

Will shook his head. "I'll regret it. It's not good for me. I already had a slice in the kitchen; it's only my mouth and brain that want it."

Mason raised her eyebrow at him. "Isn't that normally who wants food?"

He shook his head. "My brain is an unreliable narrator and

my mouth is a sulky toddler with no grasp of the big picture. The toddler wants more sugar and the brain wants the toddler to shut up. These are not good reasons to eat more cake. It's like any other compulsion; it'll pass."

"Hey," said Julia. "Stop muttering, you two."

Archie sat down on the sofa between Mason and Will, and Mason tried not to notice the faint scent of his aftershave, or the pressure of his thigh against hers. She wasn't doing too well at it, but she was trying.

Julia turned her attention to Becky, looking at her for several minutes in silence. Becky was wearing a simple pair of jeans and a Clippers sweatshirt and looked about fifteen. Gorgeous, but fifteen. Finally, Julia said, "You look like your mother."

"Thank you," replied the girl.

"Can you tell me about the night that Sam died?"

Becky sighed, and Mason saw tears glisten in her eyes for a moment. While this girl might have come to Hollywood hoping to become an actor, there was no doubting her emotions were genuine.

"It was a pretty standard evening. We'd done two floor shows, we'd worked a full shift, but we stayed after the club had closed, just hanging out. Sam was in one of her really good moods." Becky turned to her brother. "You would have loved her; she was like Tessa."

"Tessa from the cleaners or Tessa from the video store?"

"The cleaners. The one who was always redecorating and having big ideas."

"Wait, you still have a video store in your town?" Will was clearly surprised.

"It's a very small town," replied Ben, somewhat dryly. "No

one ever told us the twenty-first century had arrived. There are only a hundred videotapes in the place, but seeing as there are only a few hundred people in town, it works out."

"Huh," said Will, reaching for the cake again. This time he connected, cut himself a slice and sat back for the rest of the story.

Becky continued. "Anyway, she was in that mood, the one where she loves everyone and everything is going to be amazing. She was unstoppable. We were having a great time." She frowned. "Then we were having a bit too much of a good time and I got really drunk and went behind the bar to get something to eat, peanuts or something, I don't know, and when I sat down to look more closely"—she looked at Mason—"you know, how you do . . ."

Mason shrugged and nodded. "Oh, I know how you do. When you reach that level of drunk where time and motion stop cooperating and sitting down turns into lying down . . . I get it, sister."

Becky smiled uncertainly at her, as if she wasn't entirely sure Mason liked her. "Yeah, well, I lay down for a moment to think about things, right, and when I woke up a while later, Sam was dead and I had no idea what had happened."

Julia nodded. "I can identify. Similar thing happened to me only the other week . . . Do you know how much time had passed? Any idea?"

Becky shook her head. "The club closed at two. We'd been drinking at least an hour, and by the time the police arrived, it was getting light outside. At least a couple hours." She looked at her wrists and then at her brother, sadly. "I tried to wake her up, I tried really hard, but she was gone. I lost my mind a little bit, hurt myself . . ." She shook her head. "Then I sobered up, pulled it together and called 911. The police showed up, then an ambulance . . . Maybe if I'd called right away, they could have helped her."

"I doubt it," said Julia, not unkindly.

"It wouldn't have made any difference," said Will. "I read the coroner's report. The level of fentanyl . . . Maybe if you'd been there with a big shot of Narcan and a medical team."

"You're forgetting the salient point," said Mason. "Someone *was* there, smothering her, making sure she didn't ever wake up. If you'd been awake, you might have died, too, and then where would you be?"

Becky looked at her, her eyes dry and clear. "I'd be with Sam," she said.

The door opened and Claudia came in. Unusually, she looked flustered.

"The police are here again," she said.

Julia snorted. "Oh my God, they just let me go. Jesus, you would think . . ."

"No," said Claudia. "They don't only want to talk to you; they want to talk to you *and* Mason."

Everybody turned and looked at Mason, who threw up her hands. "Why?" She turned to Julia. "For showing a video at a strip club? For watching young men get rejected?" She paused. "I haven't had a chance to report. It was a full day."

"No." Claudia shook her head. "Someone broke into and trashed the Repercussion offices last night. Broke a load of fish tanks and scattered dead fish everywhere. Walloped Cody Malone on the head and left him bleeding and unconscious. I guess you were on the visitors' list yesterday?" She made a face. "I didn't ask for a full download; I just asked them to wait in the living room."

Julia clapped her hands together. "Oh, this is fantastic news."

Everyone slowly turned and looked at her. Will asked the question.

"And why is it fantastic news?"

"Because we spent a chunk of time at the police station last night, so I have an alibi for this one. It also means whoever killed Tony is apparently not done. Every new action they take makes them more vulnerable. I wonder if the same person broke into the office and then here. Busy night for somebody, right?" She looked genuinely thrilled. "Let's go talk to the nice detectives. Archie, come, too." She got up and literally capered a little bit. "This is great. Once we're done with the cops, Mason can go talk to Jade Solomon. She's benefitting from Tony's death because it ended the squabble between him and Jason Reed. She wanted to appear in Jason's movie and now she can. Actually, now she can do the movie, his streaming Netflix show AND *The Codex*. It's all coming up roses for Jade."

"Why me?" asked Mason, crossly. "Why do I have to talk to Jade?" Mason was tired and achy and worried about the police. "I hate actresses. They're spoiled and dumb and irrational. All they ever want to talk about is themselves."

There was a long pause. If a silence can grow icicles, that one did.

Mason swallowed.

"Actually, I'd love to." She got up and headed quickly for the door. "But first let's go talk to the nice police people. Come on, Archie."

22

~~~~~

THE COPS TURNED out to be the same detectives from the other day. They were waiting in the living room, one silently looking out at the glittering lights of the city, the other staring at her fingernails. Mason wondered if their day had been as long as hers. At least she'd gotten a nap. Julia swept into the room, making an entrance as she always did. Mason felt like a flower girl, or maybe a page of some sort. If Julia had been wearing a cloak, Mason would have had her hands full.

The first detective turned away from the window and regarded Julia, Mason and Archie as impassively as he had the view. "Good evening, Mrs. Mann. I'm Detective Wilson and this is Detective Brooks." Brooks was the one with the nails. "We met the other day."

"When you inaccurately arrested me, yes."

"That's right. And you are?" Brooks looked at Mason.

Claudia walked in carrying a tray. Mason realized she couldn't help herself. The Grim Reaper himself could show up and Claudia would bring cookies and offer to hang up his scythe.

"I'm Natasha Mason. You can call me Mason."

"My assistant," clarified Julia.

"Legal or investigative?"

Julia answered, "Neither, personal assistant. You know, errands, light dusting, drug purchases."

Detective Brooks seemed to be having a hard time processing this information and kept looking from Mason to Julia Mann and frowning. "*You* work for *her*?"

Mason shrugged. "I serve at the pleasure of the queen." She inclined her head. "And she's the queen."

"Been with her long?" Detective Wilson was making notes.

Mason grinned. "Five days. So far it's been pretty humdrum, but things are looking up." She assumed an eager-to-please expression that was totally misleading.

Julia was getting irritable. "Can you get to the point?"

Detective Brooks shook her head. "We're just asking questions, Mrs. Mann. It's how we find answers."

"A concise elucidation of your process, Detective, but it doesn't explain why you're being so slow about it. I don't have as much life left to waste as you do." She shifted a little in her chair. "Out with it."

Detective Brooks was not to be rushed. She looked at Archie. "You were at the station the other night. You're her lawyer."

Wilson raised an eyebrow as he looked at Mason and Mann. "What was so pressing that you needed to call your lawyer over in the evening?"

Archie said, "I was consulting with another client."

"You have two clients in the same house?"

"Yes."

"You were consulting with both at once?"

Archie shrugged. "I'm very popular and highly efficient. What can I say?"

Brooks picked up the ball. "Miss Mason, Mrs. Mann. Leaving to one side the issue of your lawyer and his multiple clients, we were hoping to ask you some questions about your visit to the Repercussion studio yesterday. You both met with Cody Malone, Tony's ex-assistant and now a partial owner of the studio."

Julia shook her head elegantly. "Yes, we talked to Cody yesterday. It was entirely friendly."

"You understand you're still very much a suspect in the death of Tony Eckenridge. While you're free on bail, you might want to steer clear of the studio and anyone else connected to the case. I'd hate to think you were tampering with witnesses."

"Then don't think it," replied Julia, calmly, "because I wasn't. I am keen to prove my innocence and plan to do so by finding the person actually responsible."

Wilson said, "You're not a licensed private investigator, Mrs. Mann. You're skating on pretty thin ice here."

Julia just shrugged.

"What did you ask him?"

"Probably very similar questions to the ones you asked him," she replied. "I wanted to know about Tony's activities in the time leading up to his taking a final swim in my pool. Uninvited."

"So you say."

Julia shrugged again. "So I say indeed. Tony Eckenridge hasn't been welcome at my house in many years. I realize he was dying . . . Perhaps he thought that gave him dispensation. It didn't."

"Maybe it made you mad."

"It might. But not enough to kill him. If irritation was sufficient motive for murder, then I'd never have gotten out of prison."

There was a pause.

Detective Wilson looked at Mason. "What were you doing last night?"

"I was at Galliano's."

"The strip club?"

Julia corrected him. "It's a burlesque show." She turned up a palm. "Entirely different."

"Do they take their clothes off for money?" asked the detective.

"Not necessarily." Julia was calm.

"But potentially?"

"Potential always exists, Detective, especially in burlesque."

Wilson turned to Mason. "Did they take their clothes off last night?"

Mason shook her head. "Not all of them."

"Not all their clothes?"

"Not all the performers."

"In fact," said Julia, "at midnight specifically we were at the police station making a statement about being attacked outside the club, which you should already know."

"Ah yes, the *Codex* Curse strikes again." Brooks looked at Archie. "You were there, too, correct?"

"I was," said Archie. "You should have all of our statements in the system. If you don't have any more specific questions for my clients, maybe we could conclude this interview? Both of them left Cody Malone yesterday intact and under entirely friendly terms. Further, both of them have a cast-iron alibi with multiple witnesses for last night."

"Wait," said Mason, "is Cody going to be OK?" She thought of what he'd said, about inheriting his dream. He'd taken quite the journey in the last week, from assistant to studio head to beating victim.

Detective Brooks folded up her notebook and put it away. "He was apparently working late in the studio office when someone entered. He may have known them; there was no sign of forced entry. They attacked him, then ransacked the office and destroyed thousands of dollars' worth of valuable fish tanks and associated fish."

Mason thought that Associated Fish was another good band name, but she didn't mention it. She was proud of her self-restraint.

Brooks was still talking. "He suffered a very severe head trauma and is in the ICU. The next twenty-four hours will be critical." She sounded deeply disappointed, and maybe she was. "While I appreciate your stated desire to clear your name, neither of you are licensed investigators. We advise you in the strongest terms to butt out and let us do our job."

"You don't appear to be doing it very hard," replied Julia.

"Appearances are deceptive," said Brooks. "As an actress, you should know that better than anyone." She regarded the older woman narrowly. "We'll show ourselves out."

And they did.

23

~~~

IT WAS A little after nine p.m. when Mason pulled up at Jade Solomon's place. Jade was almost exactly the same age as Mason, and although they'd both grown up feeling conflicted about Barney and reading *Goosebumps* under the covers, Mason was aware they might as well have been from different species. Jade was one of those rare birds with plumage sought the world over. Mason was more along the lines of a wood louse, or some other beetle too numerous to count. Jade was a billionaire's granddaughter who'd grown up with houses in Gstaad for the skiing and Saint-Tropez for the beach. Mason was a psychologist's granddaughter who'd grown up in a house filled with books and parents who kept asking her how *she* felt about that. However, Mason was surprised to find Jade easy to talk to, even if it turned out she knew very little.

Jade's apartment was a giant duplex loft downtown, and probably cost more per month than Mason made in a year, but it was casually decorated and comfortable. Jade Solomon was wearing pajamas when she came to the door and stayed in them. They were very nice pajamas, and she had the shiny coat and wet nose that only pampered good health and lack of financial insecurity can bring, but it was hardly her fault her family was rich. At least, not any more than it was Mason's fault that her family were all psychiatrists.

"When you called, you said you needed to ask me some questions? That it would be helpful to Julia Mann, who I *love*. She's an icon," Jade said, reaching for her cup of tea. "Is this about the movie? Are you press? You didn't say you were press, so I guess not."

"No, I'm not press. I work for Julia. We're investigating the death of Tony Eckenridge."

Jade's eyes grew large and moist. "Tony was such a wonderful man. It's such a loss to the world." A tear actually started sliding down her cheek, adorably, and she let it. "He was so super nice to me both times we met. I'll never, never, never forget him." She paused, sighed, counted to three, then wiped her cheek. "I thought Julia Mann killed him, but I guess not."

"Nope," Mason said. "Or, if she did, she's going to a lot of trouble to find herself."

If Jade got the semi-joke, she gave no indication. She just looked at Mason and waited to hear her name. Her posture was magnificent.

"Can you tell me what the argument was about, between Jason Reed and Tony?"

"Am I allowed to?"

Mason frowned. "Why wouldn't you be?"

"I don't know." Jade sipped her tea. "Sometimes the lawyers tell me not to talk about stuff, you know, after it happened. Or I'll read a script and they'll tell me not to talk about it. Or I'll sleep with someone and have to keep it quiet." Mason suddenly wondered if she was as guileless as she appeared; she had a successful career and presumably had her wits about her. She started silently despairing of her own generation but pressed on regardless.

"Yes, it's fine to talk about it."

"It really wasn't that big of a deal. Tony had me in a movie he was making, but I was pretty much done with my shooting, right? And Jason wanted me for something else and Tony wouldn't release me. Jason's thing was at Netflix, which is, you know, the coolest shit right now. Then Tony spoke to someone at Netflix because, you know, he knew everyone, and the streaming thing went away, like, overnight. Jason was pretty steamed. But then Tony died and Christine called Jason about directing *The Codex*, and Jason got his Netflix thing back on track and everything's fine now." She smiled. "*The Codex* is going to be fun. The remake of a classic is an excellent next step for me."

"How come?"

"Well, I'm following my ten-year plan, and I'm already two years ahead of schedule."

Mason was ready to bite. "What's your ten-year plan?"

Jade looked surprised. "Well, I started out on TV, on a Disney show. Then I did an edgy indie film where I played a drug addict, to show range. Then I did a rom-com where I played the sassy best friend, to show comedy chops and character and that I didn't need to be the lead to shine. Then I did a supernatural TV miniseries to remind people I was flexible and to pay for this apartment." She pussycat smiled. "I won an Emmy. Then I did the lead in a big-budget tragedy where I got to die at the end. And last year I did a movie where I played a gutsy but troubled lawyer who saved little children from a big corporation." She shrugged. "Action movie is next, and classic movie remake is bonus points. Two more years and I'll have my first Academy Award nomination for Best Supporting Actress, and two more after that I'll be mentioned frequently in contention for Best Actress." She tipped her head to one side. "Everyone knows this; it's a pretty standard ten-year plan."

Mason stared at her. She didn't even have a ten-day plan. Back on the beam. "Can you tell me about the accident you had, the one with Christine?"

"Oh, it was terrible." Jade showed Mason her jawline. "Look, I have a scar."

There was absolutely no scar, but Mason made sympathetic noises.

"Christine must have been high or something, I guess. She just lost control of the car and we drove right into that cranky guy in the Prius. He wasn't nice at all. And then we had to wait AGES at the hospital, and Cody was being so sweet but it was still pretty boring."

"Were you with Christine?"

"No, she was in another area. Maybe for older people?" Mason looked carefully at her, but she was not making a joke. "Cody stayed with me, of course." Jade leaned forward. "He loves me, you know."

"Oh yeah?"

"Yes. He said I was a piece of work." She smiled. "He's very shy about it, though. I asked him to rub my feet while we were waiting and he said he couldn't. Or wouldn't, I can't remember. I understood. It's like that with men, sometimes. They get flustered and need to stay away from me."

"Huh." Mason raised her eyebrows. "Just too much sex appeal to take?"

"I guess." Jade turned up her palms. "They're all super friendly at first, but after a few days they just get overwhelmed." Her glossy hair swung about her shoulders, her slender neck as elegant as the proverbial swan, or maybe a goose. Despite the ten-year plan, Mason was starting to feel a little sorry for her.

"I see." Mason looked at her notebook. "So, what time did you leave the hospital?"

"No idea. They wouldn't let us use our phones, which was nuts, but there was a photographer there. You can ask him."

"Did you recognize him?"

Jade shook her beautiful head. "He had a camera in front of his face."

"Good point. Thanks."

The actress's eyes widened; she'd had a thought. "Do you think Julia Mann would talk to me about the movie? About the character?" She looked hopeful. "I could bring gluten-free cupcakes."

Mason thought about it. It was so tempting. But in the end she shook her head.

"I think she might find it challenging to talk to the actress who's going to play the part that made her famous, you know?"

"Because she'll be worried I'll do it better?"

"Yes," said Mason. "You know what actresses are like."

"Oh yes," said Jade, nodding. "Because I am one, you mean?"

"Yes," said Mason slowly. "So, how steamed did Jason Reed get? When Tony derailed his Netflix thing?"

"Oh, really mad. He said he was going to kill Tony, and for a minute I thought he meant it, you know, because he was really red-faced and everything. But then he took a Xanax and calmed down."

"That'll do it."

"I guess." Jade suddenly giggled. "It's so funny when people get mad, don't you think? I never get mad. As Jane Austen said, '*Angry people are not always wise*.'" She stood up, her cotton pajamas looking like couture on her five foot ten of perfection. "I decided a couple of years ago to read *Time* magazine's hundred greatest novels of all time, and Jane Austen is a total banger. Have you heard of her?"

"Little bit," replied Mason, and watched the other woman walk off into the kitchen. She really needed to work on her prejudices. And maybe her pride, while she was at it.

"Hey," called the actress, "you want some Lucky Charms?"

AS SHE STEPPED out of Jade's apartment, Mason was surprised by how quiet it was. This section of the city was sparsely inhabited, and several of the streetlights were long broken and very low on the city's list for repair. She could hear music from a bar somewhere close, and smell the back-of-the-throat bite of human urine. Ah, the beauty of downtown Los Angeles, the city where even angels need to pee. Beneath her boots, broken auto glass gathered into long cracks and gullies in the sidewalk, making her think of flying into town at night, the lit streets and freeways like rivers of diamond headlights and ruby brake lights. Mason found herself smiling at the conversation she'd just concluded. She and Jade had started talking about movies they both liked, agreeing on *The Princess Bride* and agreeing to differ on *Spice World*, following which Jade had enthusiastically invited Mason to go out sometime. Literally one of the world's most famous faces, but Mason had ended up really liking her. Maybe not always the sharpest knife in the drawer, but very sweet, startlingly well-read and apparently lacking in the friends department. Befriending a movie star hadn't been on her bingo card for this year, but there you go.

Downtown was as deserted as ever, unless you count rats and roaches as big as rats. However, appearances were deceptive, because as Mason pulled out her keys to open her car, someone grabbed her from behind and held a knife to her neck. She froze, mentally inventorying the contents of her wallet. Did she have enough cash on her to make this asshole walk away before stripping her of her credit cards?

"The *Codex* Curse is going to get you all. Stop digging around in buried history . . ." The voice was low but clear, and Mason felt the knife actually pierce her skin, which really fucking hurt. She was also intensely surprised. What she'd taken for a simple robbery, to be borne as stoically as every city resident bears this kind of thing, was actually far more personal. And personal hurts.

Truth be told, Mason had a black belt in Tae Kwon Do, but it had been nearly a decade since her sulky teenage self had attained it. However, the feeling of blood trickling down your neck and the awareness that it really was your exact neck that was the target of attack has a very galvanizing effect, and suddenly it all came back.

She stepped forward to throw the attacker off-balance, slipping slightly on the miniature ice cubes of broken glass underfoot. She dropped one knee to pull out of his grip, causing him to stumble but not completely release her. Mason stepped on his instep, which isn't a traditional Tae Kwon Do move per se, but is very effective, and at the same time raised her arms, clasped her hands together and drove both elbows back into his groin. This made him let go, but also made him angrier. She realized he had a ski mask on, which was creepy, irritating and probably contributing to his bad mood.

Mason yelled, "911, fire!" as loudly as she could and kept yelling as the guy came at her again. This time she stepped forward into his run and flipped him over her back, his wrist tight in her hand, twisting. He hit the ground with a satisfying thud, and Mason waited to hear his wrist snap. Sadly, it turned out he'd also had martial arts training of some kind, and just slid his hand around to grab her wrist and throw her, too. She tried to roll with it, but her head hit the sidewalk with an audible crack, and for a moment she saw stars. Mason was starting to black out when she suddenly heard Jade Solomon's voice in the distance. Or what sounded like Jade, but with a lot more certainty and conviction.

"I see you, motherfucker. I called the police *and* I'm filming you in hi-def, and this is the latest iPhone, which has incredible resolution and three cameras, so you better fucking run, you piece of shit!" which was quite the speech for someone who wasn't a writer; a charming blend of Gen Z tech obsession and Tarantino-esque bravado. The attacker cursed and took one last blinding swing at Mason before taking off. Mason murmured a thank-you to Jade, which of course she couldn't hear, then slipped into unconsciousness.

MASON CAME TO as they were loading her into the ambulance. She was strapped in and wearing a cervical collar, but still struggled to sit up. Her jaw felt wrong and hurt like a bastard. She could smell rubbing alcohol and pee. She hoped it wasn't her own, but wasn't one hundred percent confident.

"Steady on." The EMT leaned over and shone a light in her eyes. "You got quite a knock on the head, and we need to stabilize you till we get to the hospital. Lie down." Her face was concerned but calm, as EMTs' faces always are. Mason suddenly felt enormously grateful to be alive and also incredibly nauseous.

"I'm going to be sick," she said sadly, and then was. Puking through a dislocated jaw? One star, would not recommend.

"Ew, gross," said a voice somewhere to her right. Jade Solomon was sitting in the ambulance, still in her pajamas, but with the addition of a Prada puffer jacket, a slouchy cashmere beanie and Uggs. She looked like a billion bucks. Mason looked at the EMT, who smiled.

"We couldn't stop her. She says she saved your life."

Mason closed her eyes, waves of nausea overwhelming her as a mixture of pain and spent adrenaline coursed through her body. "She did," she muttered, and blacked out again.

"See?" squealed Jade. "I told you!" She looked excited. "My agent is going to be so pleased!"

The EMT checked Mason's blood pressure and then leaned over to Jade. "I'm such a fan," she said. "Would you sign this sick bag?"

24

~~~

THE NEXT FEW hours were a little blurry. At one point, Mason became aware someone was taking her clothes off, which gave her a brief drinking flashback to evenings she'd rather not remember. But then she realized they were redressing her in a hospital gown, and although that was also a drinking memory, she calmed down and stopped swearing and swinging. They also gave her something for the pain, which made her sleepy and emotional.

After being wheeled to a room, she realized Jade Solomon was still there and told her very earnestly they were BFFs for life. Then she told the doctor, who was slightly bemused, that he and Jade should maybe date.

"She's very nice, really," mumbled Mason, tugging at his sleeve. "She is very, very, very nice." She sighed heavily. "She doesn't have very good taste in movies, though. Would that be a problem?" Her lip trembled. "Nobody's perfect, you know." She looked over at Jade, through a haze of medication. "You're pretty close."

Jade nodded, looking up from her phone. "I know. A guy

once told me my face was ninety-six percent symmetrical." She shrugged and looked back down.

Everyone gazed at her for a second, then the doctor shook himself like a wet dog and showed Mason some X-rays on his tablet. "Your jaw was dislocated but not broken, which is amazing, and you have a slight cheekbone fracture that should heal unnoticeably." He looked at her. "I'm married, but thanks for trying to fix me up with *People* magazine's Most Beautiful Woman. My wife would probably give me a pass, but you know, I'm good." He patted her arm. "Are you an actress, too?"

Mason shook her head, and then regretted it. "No, I'm a ne'er-do-well, a loser, a tough guy who isn't so tough." A tear ran down her cheek. "And I'll never get to the Olympics."

The doctor looked up at the IV hanging next to her bed, and then to the nurse waiting patiently. "Maybe turn down her meds a little?" he murmured, then spoke again to Mason. "We're keeping you in overnight for observation, but you can go home tomorrow. Is there someone there who can help you? You're going to find it hard to eat for a few days."

"I'll take care of that. I do a mean chicken soup." Claudia appeared behind the doctor's shoulder and grinned at Mason. "Glad to see you're not dead, lovely. Julia would have been so annoyed."

Mason's eyes filled with tears again; everyone was being *so kind*. "How are you even *here*?" She frowned, suddenly. "Did Julia put a tracker under my skin?"

Claudia hesitated, clearly deciding what to do with that lobbed setup, but then looked over her shoulder at Jade, who waved. "Your friend called Julia and I drew the short straw."

Mason's chin wobbled. "Jade's *the best*," she said, "and I love you, Claudia. You're so, so, so, so nice. And you make such lovely baked goods, and gravy . . ." She continued in this vein for several minutes.

Claudia turned to the nurse. "How long until the meds wear off?"

"A while, because if she wasn't high as a kite she'd be in considerable pain."

"Oh good," said Claudia, pulling out her phone. "I want to make sure I get all this. It's YouTube gold."

"I love you so much, Claudia," Mason said, the tears rolling down her cheeks. "I love your croissants. I love your mashed potatoes. I even love Julia a very little bit." She held up her hand, not very well, and made a tiny space between finger and thumb. "A teeny, tiny, itty-bitty, weeny little bit . . ." Then she fell asleep again.

Jade Solomon laughed, and introduced herself to Claudia. "I saved her life, you know," she said. "Or at least, I stopped the guy from hitting her more. Maybe Julia Mann will talk to me now?"

Claudia nodded, and smoothed her palm across Mason's forehead. "She will," she said softly. "She's very fond of this girl, you know." She sat down and pulled a novel from her bag. "Come to the house in a day or two."

Jade nodded happily and left. Claudia sighed and settled into *War and Peace* for the twentieth time. She was still there when Mason woke up the next day.

WHEN MASON WALKED carefully into the office wing later that day, Will winced at the sight of her face. He and Archie were sitting on either side of a young man Mason had never seen before, who had his head down, his giant oversized sweatshirt and baggy jeans making him look more like a pile of laundry than a guy. He also had a baseball cap pulled way down and a pair of sunglasses, making him look like a pile of laundry who was here to play poker.

On the big screen was the front page of TMZ: *Julia Mann's Assistant Attacked—The* Codex *Curse Strikes Again*.

"I made the papers," said Mason, tiredly. "My mom will be thrilled."

"Holy crap," said Will, raising his eyebrows at her face. "That is going to look even worse tomorrow."

"Did you at least get in a few knocks yourself?" asked Archie.

Mason shook her head and sat down carefully. Her whole body ached from fighting and hitting the ground, and she was starting to wonder if it had been smart to leave the hospital. The young man didn't even look up at her.

"No, that's the worst part. I landed jack shit." She settled back into the cushions. "I feel like crap."

Julia hadn't said anything, but now she came over and bent down in front of Mason. She reached out a hand and gently touched the bruised side of her face, where the first tints of blue were appearing. "I thought you had a black belt?"

"I do. His was blacker."

"Maybe next time you'll look behind you."

Mason just shrugged and regretted it. Julia's tone was still neutral. "You'll stay here for a few days, to recover and avoid trouble if you can. Archie went to get your cat. He's already in your room."

Mason turned to Archie. "You broke into my apartment? What if I had booby-trapped it?"

He made a face at her. "You? You apparently can't even fight. No, your neighbor let me in. She said to tell you she'd have taken the cat, but . . ."

"She has a dog, I know." She looked at Julia and nodded. "I guess I don't have any choice." There was a pause. "Thanks." Mason felt like it was more an order than an offer, but nonetheless, she really couldn't face going home. Julia walked toward the big screen, and when she turned back, it was business as usual.

"So, what did the shithead say to you before he beat you up? I assume it wasn't a random act of violence? Did our friends from the Detective Division come by to see you?"

Mason nodded. Claudia came in with a steaming mug with a glass straw in it. "Chicken bouillon, drink up, you'll feel better." She handed her two white tablets. "And two Vicodin."

Mason shook her head. "No, Advil is fine." She went back to Julia. "I'll tell you what I told them, which is he said the *Codex* Curse was going to get us, just like the guy that attacked you, and to stop digging around, then we tried to hurt each other for a bit, which didn't work out so well for me, and then Jade Solomon saved my life."

Julia sighed. "Yes, I heard. And now I owe her."

Mason frowned. "No, I owe her."

Julia waved her hand. "Whatever, a debt is owed, and she's apparently coming over to talk to me about *The Codex*." She shrugged. "I haven't chewed up a young actress in weeks."

"Be nice, Julia. She bravely stepped in and filmed in my defense. Which reminds me, what happened to the film?"

"The cops have it," Will answered, "but the guy was wearing a mask, so they can't get that much. He left the knife, too,

but it's just a generic box cutter, and he wore gloves of course."
He cleared his throat. "There's blood on the knife, and on the
street, but so far it's all yours."

"What did the cops say?" Julia asked.

"Not much, just that I should be more careful, and let them
know if anything else happens. They *also* suggested you back
the fuck off, although not in such colorful terms."

Julia said, "Was it definitely a guy?"

Mason thought about it. "I think so, but not sure why. He
or she was strong and fast, and knew what they were doing;
that's about all I can say for sure. They didn't even really land
a punch. I did this against the curb." She looked around.
"Where are Becky and Ben? Still here, presumably?"

"Of course. Becky can't leave Los Angeles. I think they
went to Disneyland."

"Really?" Mason almost laughed. "She's about to stand
trial for murder and she wanted to go to Disneyland?"

"What better time?" Julia shuddered. "Prison would be
such a relief."

"Not a Mouse fan?"

"I'd rather be boiled in oil. Before you got walloped, you
were talking to Jade. What did she tell you?"

Mason reported the conversation, and added, "I think we
should talk to Jason Reed, the director. He seems to have
come out of the whole thing better off. And he has a temper."

"Tomorrow. Today you rest." Julia waved her hand. "Starting right after we hear from Larissa." She turned to the pile of
laundry. "We appreciate you coming to talk to us."

"Mason, this is Larissa," Will said, and the young man re-
moved his sunglasses, revealing that he was, in fact, a young
woman.

"Wow," said Mason, "that's some disguise. I totally thought you were a guy."

There was a pause, but Larissa wasn't fazed.

"Yeah, I get that a lot. But hey, who doesn't want to challenge the patriarchal assumptions of our highly discriminatory oligarchy?" Her voice was deep, but clearly feminine.

"Larissa responded to our gentle inquiries about information surrounding the club murder, and she was kind enough to come tell us about it."

"Plus you paid me," said Larissa, "in food." She turned to Will. "What was that stuff at lunch called again?"

"Boeuf en croûte. Potatoes Dauphinoise. Lava cake."

Larissa nodded and looked wistful. "So worth it." She rubbed her hands on her thighs. "So, I didn't realize at the time that I'd seen anything important or of course I would have gone to the police." She waited a beat, and then she, Julia and Will burst out laughing. "So on the night in question, I happened to be on the roof of the club."

Will nodded. "In the course of business."

"Taking in the view," added the young woman.

"Larissa is a cat burglar," said Julia, then raised her eyebrow at Larissa's murmured disagreement. "Well, how would you characterize climbing up buildings, leaping from fire escapes, dangling from ropes and entering windows sideways, intending to remove things?"

Larissa replied, "A parkour-influenced exercise and life-improvement regime?"

Julia shrugged. "Continue."

"So," began Larissa, "I was hanging out on the club roof, which at that time of night is usually deserted."

"What time was that?" Mason could feel the bouillon

working, or maybe it was the Advil. She thought about the potatoes Dauphinoise and wondered if there was any left and if she'd be able to eat it. "The official time of death is around four a.m."

"It was a little after two. The club closes at eleven on week-nights. Before that, you sometimes run into girls and customers on the roof, and it's irritating." She turned to look at Julia. "On the one hand, I abhor the perpetuation of the consumer/product relationship inherent in the client/hooker paradigm, but on the other hand, a girl has to make a living, am I right?"

Julia's face was serious. "Big-time."

Larissa continued. "Not to mention the risibility of a moral and legal code that declares only the female half of that para-digm a criminal."

Julia nodded. "Let's agree that it's exploitative and unfair and move on."

Larissa pulled her legs up onto the sofa, appearing smaller still. "I was looking down into the street, just, you know, ab-sorbing the scene, when I saw a guy approach the door of the club and try to open it." She shrugged. "He was walking pretty steadily, but clearly he'd lost the ability to tell time; the club had been closed for hours. He stood there for a bit, and I guess he pressed a bell or called someone or something, because I suddenly heard music for a moment and he stepped into the club."

"Music?" Mason pulled out her phone to take notes. "I thought the club was closed?"

Larissa pondered, then nodded. "Yeah, but I guess there were still people there, because someone let him in. Maybe there was a private party. Who knows? To be honest, I was watching the apartment across the street to make sure it was empty, and I didn't even think about it until I heard you guys were interested in information about that night." She turned to Julia. "How do you know Carrie the Fish?"

Julia shook her head. "I don't, but I presume she knows someone who knows someone who knows someone I know. That's how it works, right?"

"Communication and shared knowledge is a wonderful thing," agreed the tiny cat burglar.

Mason looked over at Julia, who was frowning. "So now we have a new person entering the club around the time of the murder, someone who wasn't there when the police arrived. When did he leave?"

"I actually know that, too, although funnily enough, I was already in the apartment across the street." There was a pause. "Visiting."

Mason laughed. "Visiting an empty apartment?"

"It was a brief visit. Anyway, I was checking the street and saw the guy come out. Two forty-five. Totally different angle, obviously, but definitely the same guy."

"Face?" Mason asked.

Larissa shrugged. "Presumably, but I didn't see it. Blond, I think, but I couldn't even swear to that. It was just a glimpse; there were several big cars parked in front of the club."

Archie asked, "Did he get into one of the cars or walk?"

Larissa shook her head. "No clue. I literally just saw him step away from the club and the door swinging shut behind him, and that was that. For all I know he stepped into a portal to another realm."

"Was the music still loud?" Will was clearly worried about noise pollution.

"Sorry, couldn't tell you. My . . . friends . . . have excellent soundproofing, as befits an apartment overlooking the street."

"I'll ask my client if she remembers this person," said Julia.

Archie frowned. "Maybe the crime was already committed at that point and Becky was on the club floor, unconscious?"

Julia shook her head, but said, "Maybe, but then why didn't our mystery guy call the cops himself?"

Claudia came in with a tray, and Mason looked up hopefully. She put it down on the coffee table. "For Mason, and anyone else who still has room." Tiny potato latkes (literally, bite-sized), sour cream and caviar. Chocolate mousse, whipped cream. "All small and soft enough that you should be able to eat it without too much pain." She was unsmiling as she looked at Mason's darkening bruises, but all the love was on the plate.

Mason's aching mouth watered. She helped herself, then offered the plate to Larissa.

"Oh, I'm not hungry," replied the small burglar. "Plus, I'm in training for an endurance event."

"Oh, you're a runner?" Mason couldn't help herself. "I'm a runner, too. Cross-country scholarship, 1500 meters track, marathons of course . . ."

Larissa raised her eyebrows. "That's very . . . interesting. I'm not a runner. I'm planning to visit four different friends who live in the same building, and I want to be in shape." She turned to Will. "Get this: luxury fourplex, tenants all work tight schedules, and there is a one-hour window where all four are out at once." She grinned and raised her hands in prayer. "And if that isn't an invitation from God to exert myself, I don't know what is."

Will nodded. "A magical thing. It would be a crime not to."

"Actually . . ." said Archie, then tailed off. Mason realized the lawyer wasn't super comfortable with this conversation, and smiled to herself.

Larissa ignored Archie, and answered Will. "Right? The universe giveth."

Mason frowned. "Uh, and the universe also taketh away."

Larissa shrugged. "Much less frequently, though, have you noticed?"

There was a pause as the three addicts in the room thought about that. Then they all shook their heads.

"No," said Julia, "I don't think that's true for any of us. But I wish you all the best in your chosen challenge. May they all get stuck in traffic on their way home."

Larissa grinned.

"May the locks be well oiled and the hinges silent," added Will.

Larissa nodded.

"And may your blood sugar be well-balanced so you don't get a headache." Mason smiled.

Larissa frowned, then turned to Julia and Will. "Not a thief, then?"

They shook their heads sadly.

25

~~~

ONCE LARISSA LEFT, Claudia took Mason to her room, which was off the kitchen in a part of the house she'd only seen briefly when Ben had arrived. Like the other wings, the walls were white, with gray stone floors and floor-to-ceiling windows, but because it backed into the canyon side it felt cozier.

Claudia pointed to a pair of doors as they passed. "Ben and Becky are in these two, and you're at the end." She turned her head slightly and lowered her voice. "Apparently, nearly getting killed gets you the big room."

Mason hadn't seen a small room yet, but when Claudia opened the door at the end of the hall she stopped. This room had two walls of glass, one of which apparently hung out over thin air. The stone floor was covered with thick Persian rugs, and the muted colors complemented the simple furniture. An open door near the bed led into a bathroom, in which she could see a claw-foot tub.

"Holy shit, Claude, is this for visiting royalty?"

Claudia was checking bathroom supplies. "No, this was Jonathan and Julia's room when they were married. After she got out of prison, she moved to the other end, where there's

another room somewhat like this one." Apparently happy with
the choice of towels, she went to turn down the bed. "It doesn't
have as nice a bathtub, but she says she doesn't have time to
lie in her diluted filth anyway."

"Wow, I was sort of looking forward to a bath, but now, not
so much."

There was an irritated meow, and Phil appeared from under the bed.

"Hello, you." Mason sat down on the end of the bed and he
jumped up, letting her know this kind of change was exciting,
but he wasn't entirely convinced it was wise. She scritched his
ears and accepted his complaints.

"What happened to his leg?" Claudia was fluffing pillows.

"A car. Or a truck, maybe. When I found him, he was lying
in the road, and I thought he was dead because he looked like
shit. Then, as I ran past, he meowed this pathetic little meow
and I totally fell for it. Two grand in vets bills later, here he is."

"Well, he seems appreciative." Phil had curled up on Mason's lap and was purring.

"He's no fool."

Claudia was at the door. "You'll find pajamas in the dresser,
a dressing gown in the bathroom and a suitcase of your
clothes under the bed."

"Archie went through my clothes?" Mason thought about
her underwear drawer and felt vaguely green about the gills.
She was not a tidy drawer-keeper.

"No, your neighbor packed them, I think." She walked out,
pulling the door. "Go to sleep, Mason. I'll wake you up for dinner." Mason heard Claudia's sensible shoes squeaking down
the hall, then she took off her clothes and climbed into bed.
Phil went under the covers, his irritation mollified by high-

thread-count sheets, and the two of them slept the rest of the afternoon.

MASON WOKE IN the early evening, a sliver of moon sharing space with the last of the sun. She could smell dinner . . . meatballs, possibly? She got up and looked in the top drawer for pajamas. Simple cotton ones, flannel ones, silk ones: Apparently, pajamas were a thing. Then she realized all of them still had tags; they'd gotten these pajamas for her. She was touched and pulled on the flannel ones with the dog pattern. The dressing gown was more simple, smooth satin lined with thick Turkish towel, like at a fancy hotel. It was almost worth getting beaten up for.

As she hobbled down the hall, passing open doors, Becky called her name. She turned and saw the girl sitting on her bed, wearing a pair of Mickey ears.

"I heard what happened to you. I'm sorry." She didn't look all that sorry, but then again, she and Mason hadn't really had much to do with each other yet, and Mason had called her a little chickenshit when they met, so, you know, awkward.

"How was Disneyland?"

Becky smiled. "It was distracting. Ben threw up on Space Mountain."

"Good times."

Becky nodded. "Have the police made any progress? Do you know?"

"Are you coming for dinner? I'm starving." Mason turned, and Becky followed. "I don't know. I'm sorry. I only got here this afternoon, and Julia didn't mention anything about the cops. You can ask her at dinner."

But Becky never got a chance, because when they walked into the kitchen, there was a stranger sitting at the table, next to Ben. A tall, angular woman who had once been beautiful, but probably only briefly. Now she just looked worn-out, and something else . . . Mason had a second or two to realize the woman was furious, when Becky stumbled next to her.

"Grandma?" Her voice was a whisper; the thud as she hit the ground was much, much louder.

"WHAT'S WITH THIS family and the fainting?" Mason had picked up Becky and laid her on the sofa, next to the fireplace. "Seriously, you guys need to have your iron tested."

Will was there and pushed his glasses up his nose. "Actually, syncope is typically caused by a temporary lack of oxygen in the brain, largely due to hypotension."

Mason looked at him and raised her eyebrows.

"Low blood pressure," Will explained. "In this case, it was almost certainly the vasovagal response to shock. Psychologists have suggested it's a vestigial adaptation to protect us from continued attack by predators."

"She's playing possum?"

Becky had come round during this mini lecture, and as she opened her eyes and saw Mason, she whispered, "Is she still here?"

"Yes, Becky, I'm still here." The old lady's voice was dry and humorless. "Ben told me you have to stay here until the police sort this mess out, so I came to make sure you don't cause any more trouble."

Becky looked at Mason, and for a moment Mason saw

panic in her eyes. Then a shutter came down and she broke eye contact, struggling to sit up.

"I'm fine now. Sorry about that," she said contritely, standing up and opening her arms to her grandma. The old woman stepped forward for a hug, which was brief considering all that Becky had been through.

"How did you know where I was?" Becky went over to the table and sat down. Julia was watching her closely, as were Claudia and Will. Ben looked pale, and Mason got ready to catch him, too, if necessary.

"I called her," Ben admitted. "Once I knew you were OK, I thought . . ."

"In what way is she OK?" demanded Grandma. "She's accused of murder, is guilty as heck of being a stripper and probably a whore, and has been sleeping with women, which is a biblical sin, Romans 1:26." She turned to Julia. "She didn't get it from my family, you know. The bad blood comes straight from her father's side."

Julia just looked at her, then over at Mason. "Mason, this is Anna Jones, Becky and Ben's grandmother."

Mason sat down. She had been right: meatballs. Claudia put a plate of finely cut spaghetti and crumbled meatball in front of her. "I got that," Mason said to Julia. "Welcome to Los Angeles, Mrs. Jones."

"It's a crappy city, full of terrible people," replied Anna. "If Becky had never come here she would still be safe at home, and probably not doing unnatural, perverted things and dancing about in just the skin God gave her." She looked sharply at Mason, and Mason—who was impervious to most things—felt layers of her own God-given skin peeling off. "What happened to your face?"

"I buried it between my girlfriend's thighs and she got overexcited and squeezed too hard," replied Mason, helping herself to Parmesan cheese. "I lost consciousness for a moment, but hey, what a way to die." She opened her eyes wide at the old lady. "Am I right?"

Becky choked a little, down the table, and when Mason chanced a glance at Julia she saw the hint of a smile. But Grandma wasn't amused. She leaned forward and stabbed her finger at Mason.

"Maybe it's time you found Jesus," she said.

"I didn't know you'd lost him," replied Mason, around a mouthful of spaghetti. She needed more painkillers, but she was having too much fun to get up. Luckily, Claudia came over and put two Tylenol and a glass of water with a straw in front of her.

"Try not to talk too much, Mason," she said. "You'll hurt your face."

"Actually," chimed in Will, "a little exercise will reduce the swelling."

"Thanks, Will," said Julia. "I think Mason will get enough exercise from eating her dinner. She doesn't need to overexert herself." She turned to Anna Jones. "So, you just arrived this afternoon?"

The old woman nodded, straightening her shoulders and indicating a small suitcase that sat over by the door, with an umbrella and an atrocious hat on top of it. "Yes, and a colored man who couldn't speak a word of English brought me here. I was sure he was going to stop and rob me, but he didn't."

Mason had her mouth full and couldn't call her on the racial slur, but made a mental note to trip her later if she got the chance.

Grandma turned to Julia. "You look like a normal person. How do you deal with all the sin and depravity around you?"

Mason opened her mouth, but Julia cut her off. "Well, Los Angeles is a very cosmopolitan city. People from all over the world come here following their dreams, you know."

"Bringing their filthy habits and sexual perversions, no doubt."

"Sometimes," replied Julia, mildly, "but we grow plenty of our own."

Mason was starting to feel better as the food went down, and she wondered why Julia was being so nice to this bigoted old fart. She was the mother of a dead friend, true, but that wasn't reason enough.

Anna was just warming up. "The problem with this country," she said, leaning over her plate and getting spaghetti sauce on her boobs, Mason was pleased to see, "is people come and take advantage of us, feeding off the government teat. They don't work, they don't contribute anything and they steal our jobs."

Will frowned. "I thought they didn't work. How can they also be stealing our jobs?"

Anna was undeterred. "They ruin everything they touch, the filthy animals." She looked at Becky, who was trying to eat and mostly failing. "I warned you that man was trouble, but you wouldn't listen. You had your foolish head turned all the way around and couldn't be told." She sniffed. "And now here you are, in trouble up to your neck, and who knows if you'll go to jail." She looked at Mason, nastily. "I expect you'd be happy in jail, plenty of sinful women there."

Mason just grinned at her. Or at least, as much of a grin as was possible with all the bruising. Julia had had enough, suddenly.

"Well, Mrs. Jones, Becky and Ben are my guests, and I'm sorry I don't have any additional space for you. Did you arrange a hotel room?"

"They'll be coming with me." The woman turned to her grandchildren. "Finish eating, then get your things together."

"No, Grandma, we're staying here. We'll come see you tomorrow." Ben's voice was firm; he was clearly not as scared of the old witch as Becky was. "We have to stay here so Becky's lawyer can find us."

Everyone swiveled to look at Grandma, to see if she was dumb enough to fall for this. Apparently, she was, though she didn't like it.

"If you say so. Call me tomorrow. Presumably one of you has a working phone."

Then she picked up her fork and continued eating.

The silence was deafening.

LATER, WHEN THE old lady had left, grumbling, in a cab, everyone gathered around the kitchen fireplace. Becky was eating an ice cream sundae with homemade hot fudge sauce, and Mason got up to get one, too. Reaching into the freezer, she said, "Well, I can see why you wanted to work as a stripper. Better class of people." Butter pecan, excellent base layer, although the nuts might be a challenge. Mason rustled around and found chocolate.

Becky shook her head. "She wasn't always like that. When we were kids she was cool. But then Mom died, and she fell in with a bad lot."

"Church folks," explained Ben.

"She got into it in a big way, and it changed her. By the time I was a teenager she was a holy terror. All our friends were scared of her."

Mason sat down with her bowl piled high.

"Have some ice cream, Mason," said Julia, sarcastically.

Mason swallowed. "It's medicinal. The cold is helping my jaw."

Will looked serious. "Religion is the opium of the people, you know."

Becky nodded. "The sigh of the oppressed creature, yeah."

Mason paused mid-bite and watched Becky get up and take her bowl to the sink. First Jade quotes Austen and now Becky quotes Marx? What the fuck?

Becky turned to Julia and smiled a sweet smile. "I'm tired. I'm going to bed. Thank you for everything, Mrs. Mann. You're awesome."

"I have my moments," replied Julia. "Good night, Becky."

Ben got up, too, and they all watched them walk away. They heard the bedroom doors close, then Julia turned to Will. "She's going to run."

"Totally," he replied.

"Gone before dawn," said Claudia.

Mason was confused. "Wait, what? Becky's going to leave in the middle of the night? Why?"

"Because she's scared to death of her grandma, clearly. Who wouldn't be?"

"Well, apparently Ben isn't, or is he running, too?"

Julia looked at Will and raised her eyebrows. He looked at Claudia, who shrugged. "Maybe."

"Probably not," Will said. "It's not the same with him."

"But why would she run? She's safe here, right?"

Julia turned up her elegant hands. "I think so, you think so, but judging by the expression in her eyes, she doesn't. I wonder what she's so scared of."

"Shall I follow her?" Will went to get some ice cream. "I can set up at the bottom of the canyon. She won't see me."

"Maybe," said Julia. "I'm still thinking."

"You're all nuts. I don't think she's going anywhere. But I'm going to bed." Mason wandered off to her bedroom, hearing the low rumble of voices behind her. They were still talking when she dropped off to sleep, and when she woke up the next morning, Becky was gone.

26

~~~~

MASON DIDN'T WANT to admit it, but living at Julia's house
was pretty fucking rad.

The thing that blew her mind was the quiet. If the wind
was in the right direction, it carried traffic noise up the hill,
the soft billows of sound like so much surf. Right then, early
morning as she stood sleepily by the side of the pool, she heard
two or more cars getting into it, blaring back and forth. Somehow the frenetic anger of it was lost, and it sounded like birds
calling.

She sipped her coffee, the thick cream Claudia had added
carrying tiny pockets of cold against the scald of the espresso,
all of it waking her up sense by sense. She noticed little flags
of police tape flickering along the fence bordering the pool's
edge. She wandered lazily along, picking them up. No litter-
ing, people. She looked at the stretched edges of the tape, the
puckers and curls, and thought about leaves. She was just
beginning...

"Hey..."

Mason turned. Christine Greenfield was standing there,

phone in hand, hair blowing, eyebrows raised, as though she'd been waiting for Mason and Mason was showing up late.

"Yes?" It's possible her tone was a little sharp. There were few things she loved more in life than daydreaming with a cup of coffee in her hand, and this woman had just interrupted a perfectly good reverie.

"I know you."

"Not really," said Mason, putting the police tape in her dressing gown pocket and starting toward Christine. "But I'm Mason. Can I help you?"

"I want to see Julia Mann."

"Well," said Mason, "it's not even eight in the morning, and a call might have been a good idea. I'll see if she's even awake."

"I'll wait."

Mason paused. Christine hadn't said or done anything up until then that suggested she was capable of waiting, for anything or anyone. But after three years of sobriety in Alcoholics Anonymous, Mason had grown open to miracles.

She led the way inside and put Christine in the living room.

Then she went to the kitchen, told Claudia what was going on and went upstairs to get dressed. She was confident in her ability to be badass in a dressing down . . . but the bunny slippers had definitely taken the edge off.

JULIA WASN'T UPSTAIRS in her room, and Mason eventually found her in the office, talking to Larry on the big screen.

Larry, it turned out, was working from his hospital bed as though this was an entirely reasonable thing to do. He literally had EKG cables snaking out of his pajama top, but he had his glasses on, a pen in his hand and all his faculties intact. He looked like the world's biggest cherub, with a framing halo of gray curls edging a shining head. Big blue eyes and an expression that swung between beseeching and bullying without any apparent whiplash at all. Julia was clearly used to it.

"Why are you trying to kill me, Julia?" For a second Mason saw tears in his eyes, then she blinked and they were gone. Damn, he was good.

Julia was sitting on the sofa with her legs crossed, unconcerned. "I'm not, Larry. On the contrary, you are very much alive and doing your best to kill me. We've been doing this dance for decades now; it's obviously taken its toll on you. You never had a heart attack before. Maybe you should take this as a sign from the universe."

"It is! I do! It's a sign that life is short and you should take advantage of the opportunity to start your movie career up again. Jason Reed has been on the phone to me every single day, begging me—BEGGING me—to get you to be in the new *Codex*. He says you can do anything you want. You can play a bit part or have a major role. Carte blanche, baby, carte blanche. Do you know how many actresses of your age, of any age, dammit, would kill for this opportunity?"

"Unfortunate choice of words, Larry. I didn't kill anyone for it, and I don't want it. I'm a lawyer / avenging angel now, not an actress."

"The media are going mad for the story, Julia, just insane. The lead article on the *Variety* website today was a complete redux of the *Codex* Curse—every event, every on-set disaster, the death of Bella Horton, you and Jonathan, the fire, everything. Tony's murder, your arrest, the attack on Cody Malone, the attacks on you and your assistant . . . It's all proof that the curse is alive and well. They're eating it for breakfast. The dead piranha were the icing on the cake. The headline was *Fishy Business Resurfaces on* Codex. Gotta love it."

Mason cleared her throat. Larry looked over. "Who's the chicken?"

"That's Mason, my assistant."

"Wow, they did a number on her face, huh? Nice bones," said Larry. "Pity about the hair."

What is it with people and my bones? thought Mason to herself. "Sorry to interrupt, but Christine Greenfield is here, waiting to see you."

Larry laughed out loud. "See? The mountain is coming to Mohammed now. I bet she's here to beg you to be in the movie. Or at least promote it. Can we circle back on Cinespia? Helen Eckenridge called me this morning; she really wants you to do it."

Julia sighed. "Why Helen?"

Larry shrugged. "Apparently, she's running point on the event. She owns the rights. I guess she wants to control things. Born director, that one."

Julia shook her head. "I don't want to do it. Not going to do it."

Larry replied smoothly, "I told her you would."

"Then you lied, you hideous old fart. Call her back and tell her the truth."

"Don't want to do it. Not going to do it." He looked off to the right, obviously pretending. "Gotta go, the nurse is here." He disconnected.

Julia clicked the window closed and laughed. "He's a terrible bully, but I can't help loving him." She performed her parlor trick with the remote, lobbing it almost the length of the room and into the drawer. "Hey, I went to a Zoom meeting this morning, thought you'd be proud of me."

Mason was surprised. "I am. That's fantastic. Day ten to-day. You're doing great. Do you want to talk to Christine? She's been waiting awhile."

Julia nodded. "She should have made an appointment."

"I told her so."

"And how did she take that?"

Mason shrugged. "I didn't really wait to find out. Shall we go see together? Should I find Will?"

"Will's already out checking alibis for the night of Tony's murder and the attack on Cody. He'll be back later. We'll have to tackle the scary lady alone. Luckily, I'm a scary lady myself."

IN THE END, Christine Greenfield waited over an hour. To be fair, she was a studio executive, so in that hour she spoke to five other executives and issued four demands, three direc-tives and a lunch order. She watched Julia Mann and Mason walk through the door and finished her conversation before hanging up and fixing Julia with what she possibly hoped was a withering look.

Julia didn't wither.

"Miss Greenfield, I understand you've been waiting. My standard practice is to make appointments with people I want to talk to. I suggest you think about adopting it."

Christine nodded. "Of course. Normally, I would have, but I am so close to the end of my tether that I found myself driv-ing here at half past seven and decided to go with it. I'm sorry if I threw your morning."

Mason was feeling more on top of her game now that she had her ass-kicker boots on, but even so, she found herself wrong-footed again. Christine Greenfield had resting cross face, but then, what she actually said was entirely reasonable. It was giving Mason a stiff neck.

Julia, of course, merely crossed her legs at the ankle, turned her body to the most flattering yet comfortable angle and ceased all movement.

"That was an elegant apology," she said. "Did my house-keeper offer you coffee?"

Christine nodded. "She did, but at the time I wasn't ready for it. Now I distinctly am."

Julia looked at Mason, who rolled her eyes and turned to-ward the door. Two steps later she stopped, because Claudia was already there. It was like a magic telepathic coffee service.

And cookies. Magic telepathic cookies.

Julia kept speaking. "How may I help you, Miss Green-field?"

Christine said, "I should have come to see you earlier. We are business partners, after all."

"Not for much longer. I have no interest in the studio."

"Really?" Christine looked surprised. "Why not? Tony gave me no warning he'd changed his plans, but I see the Big Idea. An experienced executive, a young, scrappy assistant and an Oscar-winning pain in the ass. It's bizarre . . . but it might just work." Suddenly, Christine smiled a smile of such genuine amusement that Mason nearly dropped her cookie. "And if it doesn't work, it'll make a great movie."

Julia tilted her head and smiled back. Mason guessed she'd been as surprised as she was. "Or it could be three rabid minks in a cage. I doubt your board of directors is as thrilled about it as you are."

Christine shrugged. "I'll make sure to ask them at the next board meeting. When we met in the immediate aftermath of

Tony's death, you were in jail and Cody was still fetching my coffee, out of habit. Things are changing and moving so fast right now."

"Very true. So what brought you here so early?"

Christine leaned forward. "Anger. When I walked into the office yesterday, someone had nearly killed that scrappy young assistant, and I discovered I was really, really steamed about it. Someone killed Tony, messed up my office and callously threw a load of tropical fish on the floor for no reason at all. I don't feel safe, I don't like what they're saying about my studio in the media and I don't want it to continue. Seeing as you might also be on the hit list, I thought you might have a vested interest in tracking down the asshole who drew it up."

Julia shook her head. "I'm not saying no; I'm shaking my head because you're way behind. The morning after Tony died . . . well, once I sobered up enough to understand what had happened, I knew I had to find out who did it because otherwise the police would assume it was me. I would have, in their place, and so it transpired." She moved her shoulders delicately, the foreshadow of a shrug. "But this is personal for so many reasons. I don't need money to motivate me." She looked at Christine. "I'll find out who did it, I assure you."

"How can I help?"

Julia looked at Mason, who held up her notebook and pen. "I got you," she said.

"The day Tony died there was a board meeting—what was discussed?"

"Upcoming projects, an issue on a shoot in Romania, possible directors for the *Codex* remake, a lawsuit we were considering against a streaming service, quarterly earnings . . .

fairly standard stuff. Tony didn't explicitly discuss changing his will, for example."

"And did he seem normal? As normal as he ever was?"

Christine had lost the smile and gone back to her pugnacious potato expression, but the corner of her mouth twitched. "I never really understood the bad blood between you two. In all the time we worked together, and I think we were friends as well as partners, I never heard him say a single bad thing about you."

That subtle shoulder move again. "We had a fundamental disagreement a long time ago."

"About the studio?"

"About my husband. About ownership of creative work. About valuing a contribution and sharing credit. About ego and power. About money. About legacy. About love."

Christine raised an eyebrow. "Just the small stuff."

"Yeah. Little things." Julia took a breath. "Was he worried about anything lately?"

"Tony didn't worry. He thought about things a lot, obviously, and things went wrong all the time. But he was never visibly worried. He always saw another way."

"What was the issue in Romania?" Mason looked up from her notebook and raised her pen.

"It was complicated."

"Talk slowly, then," said Mason.

The other corner of Christine's mouth twitched. "The local electricians union was providing much of the day-to-day labor during filming, with the key grip and gaffer being from here, obviously. The gaffer asked for something the local guy thought was impossible, the key grip got involved and proved it *wasn't* impossible, a small altercation broke out, the best boy swung and hit the other best boy by accident and the local folks walked off set and everything stopped."

Mason's pen hovered above the page. "How can there be two best boys? Wouldn't that make one of them the second-best boy?"

Christine opened her mouth, but Julia made an impatient noise. "It doesn't matter. Write it down and think about it later, Mason." She turned back to Christine. "What's going on with the remaking of *The Codex*? And do you have that voice-mail? I want to hear it."

If Christine was surprised by the change of subject, she didn't show it. "We're in preproduction. Nothing is set. Some key things are nailed, others still loose as fuck." She smiled. "Are you certain you don't want to be in it? It would be great." She was scrolling through her phone.

"No."

"Could be a little cameo, doesn't have to even have lines; you could Hitchcock it and just carry a violin case." She apparently found what she was looking for. "Here's the voice-mail."

For the first time, Mason heard Tony Eckenridge's voice. Mild, with a lot of laughter in it.

"Christine, you're going to love this." (Sound of laughter in the background.) "Julia has agreed to be in the remake!" (Indistinct chatter.) "No, you did, you definitely said yes. Ignore whatever she says in the morning. She said she'd do it . . . Talk tomorrow, baby."

They sat there quietly, each of them reacting in their own way.

"Well," said Julia, finally, "it's a week or so later and I'm still saying no. Sorry, but I really am retired."

"I'm going to keep working on you—be warned," said Christine.

Julia shook her head. "Save your energy. Jason Reed is confirmed?"

Christine nodded.

"Jade Solomon?"

Another nod.

"Screenwriter?"

Shake of the head. "Not confirmed."

"Is Helen Eckenridge on board?"

Christine's head was still. "Yes and no. She holds the creative rights and she wrote the working draft, but she still needs to collaborate with the studio in order to get the movie made." She flipped her hand over, palm uppermost. "Helen doesn't know Jason Reed super well, so that's been a problem. But Repercussion has always been a director's studio. Tony wouldn't have it any other way; it's where he came from. Even though he moved into production and then into running the studio, he was always a director at heart."

"And you?"

"No. I have no interest in creative control. I hire good people and stay out of their way. Tony taught me that." She hesitated.

"Yes?" Julia was patient.

"The funny thing about *The Codex*? There's all this fuss about the curse, all this lore, right? It gets the fans revved, the media laps it up and spreads it around. The stuntwoman getting killed."

"Bella Horton. Her name was Bella." Julia's voice held a note Mason hadn't heard before. Hard to place.

Christine heard it, too. "Bella getting killed, yes. Admittedly, Jonathan being killed and you going to prison, that's serious stuff. But the fire. The real bullets in the gun. Drama and infighting on set. It's not a curse; it's just the regular bullshit that happens on a badly run production. I said that to Tony once and he agreed. He said Jonathan was drinking and partying so hard the production fell apart all over the place..." She stopped. "Not true?"

Julia's face was white. "Not at all. You asked me before why I hated Tony. That's why. He lied so much he believed his own stories. If anyone was messed up on that set it was him. It might have been a long time ago, but he was standing right next to me when Bella hit the ground. After the thud, the first noise anyone heard was a coked-up Tony giggling his ass off."

Christine nodded thoughtfully. "Hard to imagine for me, I won't lie. He was clean many years by the time we met. Regardless, I think we should remake it as a streaming series anyway. Not a feature."

Julia's eyebrows went up. "Oh yes? Who agrees with you?"

"Jason does. Cody isn't sure. Jade doesn't care and Helen hates the idea. We'll see." She looked at her watch. "What else?"

"Did you stage the accident? On Robertson, the day of Tony's death?"

"No, it was an actual accident." Christine paused. "At least, I didn't plan it. Jade caused it, actually. She saw someone she knew and reached across to wave and knocked the wheel. You know how close traffic gets on that stretch. We just swerved a little but it was enough." She sighed. "I don't want this craziness to go on much longer," she said. "I want it to be done. Find who did it."

Julia had nodded and shrugged at the same time. "I'm trying," she said. "Breaking into the studio offices suggests to me that whatever they wanted to achieve by killing Tony they didn't actually achieve. They'll keep trying, and they'll make mistakes, and we'll catch them."

Christine nodded, then stood up.

"OK, I've said my piece. I admire your commitment, as I've always admired your talent. Please consider appearing in the movie. It would be wonderful."

"Not going to happen."

"Fair enough. The movie is going to be huge. It'll be a tribute to everything Tony cared about."

"The only thing he truly cared about was himself."

"I think you're wrong about that," said Christine. "I can see myself out."

There was a pause after Christine left, then Julia looked at Mason.

"Alright, back to work. Go see Jason Reed next, I think," she said.

"You want me to drive you?" said Mason.

Julia walked past her, a drift of chiffon and perfume. "No, I want you to drive yourself. Take your new best friend, Jade, and go find out whether Mr. Reed has enough of a temper to kill for what he wants."

27

HOWEVER, WHEN JULIA opened the living room door to leave, she revealed Claudia standing just outside.

"Why are you lurking in the hallway?" she asked, taken aback.

"I wasn't lurking," replied Claudia, testily. "I was coming to tell you that Danny Agosti is here to see you. Do you want him here, or in the office?"

Julia frowned. "What on earth does he want?"

Claudia frowned right back at her. "Beats me. I didn't quiz the man. I just offered him coffee and left him in the foyer. I'm not a mind reader." She turned and headed back to the kitchen. "I'll send him in and you can ask him. I imagine he'll know."

Danny Agosti walked into the living room wearing another beautifully cut suit, which seemed appropriate for a financier and investor in a burlesque club. Mason noticed Julia's body language as he entered the room—she doubted it was just the suit that was catching her eye, but the way she angled her body as he crossed the room suggested it had truly been caught. Mason wondered for a moment about her boss's love life, then decided to change the internal subject. On the one hand, her boss was a vibrant, beautiful, sexy older woman, and on the other hand . . . ew.

"Mr. Agosti, how nice to see you." Julia settled herself back into her favorite chair and crossed her legs, resting her hands on her knees. "How can I be of service?"

"I'd like you to stop investigating Tony Eckenridge's murder."

Julia's eyebrow went up. Just one. "What makes you think you have any right to make that request?"

Danny shrugged. "I don't, but I'm asking anyway."

"Why? What business could it possibly be of yours?"

The man sighed. "Let me be blunt. I can't help thinking Tony's murder is connected to the studio, and possibly to the death of your late husband. I further can't help thinking that that might connect it to my family, specifically my father. He died a few years ago, so it won't matter to him, but the publicity of a case, the dragging up of any hint of organized crime, will negatively affect me, my company and my mother. She's a tough old bird, but I just don't want the past to come back. My father moved away from the business dealings my grandfather put in place, and I've moved further still. But people"— and here he looked at Mason—"people love to throw mud, and it's hard enough to convince the public that we're a completely legal business now without reassociating our name with what may have happened long ago." He smiled for the first time, presumably seeing if honey would work better than vinegar on Julia. "Your involvement is ratcheting up the feverish interest of the press. We've had reporters at the club every day, disturbing the patrons and the performers. I know you know what that's like."

Julia waited a moment. Then, "I do. My past has an alarming tendency to come and hit me on the back of the head, but usually because I've done something to deserve it. Maybe you want us to stop investigating because you suspect Maggie has something to do with Tony's death."

Danny looked surprised. "No, I don't."

"Do you think she has something to do with Sam's death?"

"Absolutely not. She cares about those girls, and Maggie doesn't have a criminal bone in her body. If she wants something, she'll go for it, balls to the wall, but she's not one for hiding." He paused. "I admire her very much. I don't want to see her dragged through the mud, either."

"Mud washes off."

"Never completely." He paused. "No one is paying you to investigate Tony's murder, but I'm prepared to pay you to stop."

Mason said, "Is this all because of the video? Everyone knows your father was an investor in the studio. If he'd had something to do with Jonathan's death, the police would presumably have found out at the time."

Julia snorted. "I don't think they investigated all that hard. They had me, remember?" She paused, and Mason and Danny both saw the slight shudder that ran over her frame. "They were very . . . focused." She looked at Danny and frowned. "Offering to pay me is very insulting. I don't know you, but I'm surprised."

Danny raised his hands. "I don't mean to insult you. I'm

merely aware that you're a businesswoman among everything else." He looked at Mason. "What happened to your face?"

"Somebody else wanted us off the case and thought physical violence might be an incentive." She stared at him. "Maybe you tried that first and when it didn't work you came to offer us money."

"I didn't attack you," he said disdainfully. "I just said my business is completely aboveboard."

"Doesn't mean you don't know people for hire."

"Now who's insulting who?" His face had flushed.

"You just offered my boss money to walk away from investigating a crime she is herself accused of—"

"Children, children," interrupted Julia, "I'm too old for this bickering." She got to her feet. "Mason, you getting attacked was great. Not for your face, but for us, because it means someone thinks our investigation is getting close to the truth and needs to be derailed. I'm sorry, Mr. Agosti, but we will continue to dig into Tony's death, and Sam's, too. I don't currently think your family had anything to do with either, and I don't personally see why Jonathan's death figures into it at all, but it's early days yet. If you yourself have done nothing, then you have nothing to worry about."

"Being innocent is no protection, you know that. The media is already camped out outside the club, pestering employees. I want it stopped."

Julia made a face. "Take it up with the mayor. My best advice is to keep your head down and go about your business. If your company isn't involved, then it isn't involved, end of story."

"The club is my business."

"And murder is mine. Mason will see you out."

~~~~

ONCE DANNY AGOSTI was gone, Mason went to find Julia. She was back in the office, replaying the film of Agosti's father threatening Jonathan.

Mason threw herself down on the sofa. "He's gone. What on earth was he thinking?"

"He wasn't," said Julia, "but he made a big error in coming here, because now *I* am."

And she rewound the film again.

"You seem remarkably calm," said Mason, watching her boss's face. "We've been investigating for a week and have nothing."

Julia was watching the film. "I can tell Jonathan is scared of these guys, but not much else."

Mason tried again. "I mean, you're in danger of going to jail for something you didn't do, again."

"Not much danger, I don't think. The police are very quiet. Have you noticed?"

"Sure, today. But they're clearly still watching you."

Julia nodded. "Just doing their job."

"You're not scared?"

Julia looked at her, finally, pausing the film on a frame wherein Bella was throwing her assistant over her shoulder. "Of course I'm scared. I'd be a fool if I wasn't. But I learned a lot of patience in prison; you don't really have much choice. You have a hearing. You fail. You have to wait six months, a year, or more until the next chance. You fail again. End of story. The mills of God aren't the only things that grind exceeding small, you know what I mean? Time takes on a new meaning when it's all you've got." She wiped her palms on her legs. "But I am not going back to prison, because I'm going to find the people responsible for both of these murders and send them instead. Now go question Jason Reed, like I said. Directors love control and big gestures, and what bigger gesture is there than murder? I myself am going to go scream into a pillow." She stood and walked toward the door. "But first I'm going to go eat something. I suggest you do the same."

28

~~~~

GETTING TO JASON Reed proved to be easy. Mason simply called Jade. The actress sounded bored and was pleased to hear from her.

"Sure, I'll introduce you to Jason. I think he's on location right now, but we can take a ride. It'll be fun. Do you wanna pick me up?"

Which is why, an hour later, Mason was driving the '55 Porsche Speedster, a car capable of racing speeds, at twelve miles an hour down Beverly Boulevard. She'd picked Jade up at her hairdresser, and despite the fact that she'd just spent three hundred dollars having her hair done, Jade begged her to leave the top down.

"Then people can see me," she explained, simply. "It'll be fun."

It wasn't fun, and Mason didn't enjoy it. The first fan scream happened as they turned up Robertson, and seeing as they moved at a snail's pace, continued pretty much all the way up the four blocks they had to drive. People mobbed the car, asking Jade for selfies, autographs and kisses. Paparazzi had been quick on the uptake, and TMZ ran several shots of

Jade looking gorgeous while a "mystery woman" threatened everyone in sight. Mason managed not to kill anyone with the car, but not for lack of desire. Once they reached a stretch without screaming or flashes, she pulled over and put up the top.

"Spoilsport," pouted Jade, then grinned and settled back for the drive to Solvang.

IT TAKES AROUND two hours to get to Solvang, and Mason learned a lot on that drive. She learned that finding your "best side" for selfies was more a science than an art, that you don't actually need to sleep with anyone to get a job these days, and that Jade had originally wanted to be a kindergarten teacher when she was a kid but once she got rid of her braces and grew six inches in her thirteenth year she had to give up that dream and become a movie star and model instead. Mason also learned a lot about *The Baby-Sitters Club*, a series of books that Jade considered central to a woman's understanding of herself, and which Mason promised to read while knowing full well she'd rather cut her own throat. She also learned that Jade spent a lot of time volunteering at the same animal shelter that Helen Eckenridge did.

"Oh yeah, Helen's there quite a bit. She's more of a big-dog person, so she and I are usually in different sections, because I am, like, a small-dog *fanatic*. But we've talked, sure." Jade's eye's widened. "She's a writer, which I think is amazing. I can't write at all, seriously. I love writers; they know so many words and always say what I'm thinking, but better, right?" She laughed. "Mark Twain said writing was easy, all you have to do is cross out the wrong words, but I bet it's more than that." She paused. "Tom Sawyer was a little bastard, am I right?"

Mason nodded. She'd tried conversing at first, but realized it was more restful to just wait for a gap in the flow and nod. Sometimes she murmured, but that was about the extent of it.

Jade was still going. "Jason's a writer, too, did you know? I mean, he's a director, but he also produces and writes." She laughed. "Bossy and controlling like a director, but nervous and self-absorbed like a writer. It's a cute combination."

Mason muttered unintelligibly, but then decided she might as well gather some background.

"How did you meet Jason?"

Jade frowned. "It was a while ago. I think it was at a party." She pondered, and her face cleared, suddenly. "No! It was organized by my agent, because of the Netflix thing." Another pause. "No, it *was* a party, it was just my agent that introduced us." She turned to Mason and smiled brilliantly. "Does it matter? I'm not good with details."

Mason shook her head. It might matter, but listening to Jade plumb the shallows of her recollection was challenging her anger management. They were approaching Solvang, and Jade got on her phone to an assistant who told her how to get to the shoot.

Solvang is a pretty California town, famous for its windmill, half-timbered houses and giant red clog. The whole town was founded in the early twentieth century by Danish Americans who were presumably homesick, but not enough to go home. The weather in Southern California may have been a factor. It was adorable and cute and kind of like Danish Disneyland.

"Are you hungry?" Jade asked, pointing to a pancake restaurant. She asked it in the form of a question, but Mason knew it was more of a request.

Ten minutes later, they were sitting in a booth, waiting for
the house special, a pancake the size of a sea turtle.

"What are they filming here?" asked Mason, playing with
her cutlery.

"Are you going to do that knife thing from *Aliens*?" Jade
was semiserious; she clearly viewed Mason as a kind of super-
hero, despite the fact that she'd personally seen her get her ass
kicked. She spread her hand on the table and looked hopeful.

Mason was fine with disappointing her. "No, I was preparing to spread butter on the pancakes."

"I think they're filming a car commercial." The pancakes
arrived and Jade made a little ooh of happiness. "They usually are."

Mason poured syrup. "So Jason doesn't just do movies?"
She thought about how important work was to all these people, the way they took it all so seriously. But seriously enough
to kill for? It felt a little silly to her.

"No, of course not. He has to eat. He says even car com-
mercials can be cool." She poured precisely a teaspoon of
syrup on her pancake and spread it around. "Have to watch
the waistline, am I right?" She then sprinkled about half a
pound of confectioners' sugar over the whole thing. She looked
up and caught Mason's expression. "This doesn't count. It's
powdered."

JASON REED WAS indeed filming a car commercial, for a
cute little Fiat that made Mason think of baby shoes. He
seemed to be focused on getting a shot of the car driving past
the giant clog, because that was what was happening when

they arrived. The car would drive past; Jason would look at a monitor, then tell the driver to do it again.

"Can you be more jaunty?" Jason asked through his headset. The car drove past again, exactly the same way.

"Again, with more jauntiness, please." He was clearly getting a little frustrated.

Mason was surprised to see Jason Reed was young, probably no more than a decade older than she was. He was very attractive, with the kind of energy that Mason saw a lot in Los Angeles, a type of highly focused interest in the matter at hand, whether that matter was making a movie or taking an order for lunch.

"How is the driver supposed to be jaunty? You can't even see him." Mason was standing pretty close to Jason when she asked the question, and he jumped slightly. Turning, he saw Jade and broke into a smile.

"Hello, lovely. Did you just ask a question?"

"No, that was me," said Mason. "I was just wondering how you'll know the driver is jaunty when you can't see him?"

Jason frowned. "Firstly, it's a woman; secondly, it's not her I want to be jaunty, it's the car."

"How can a car be jaunty?"

"Let's see." He told the driver to try it again, while at the same time holding up his phone playing the music that would accompany the shot. Undeniably jaunty.

"Huh," conceded Mason, then stuck out her hand. "I'm Natasha Mason. Jade was kind enough to bring me here so I could ask you some questions about Tony Eckenridge. Any chance you're going to take a break soon?"

Jason looked surprised, which was impossible because

Mason had heard Jade tell him essentially the same thing on the phone, and then concerned.

"Of course. What a terrible loss Tony was to the whole city. The whole world, really; his movies transcended national boundaries."

"If you say so," replied Mason. "So, a break?"

"Sure," the director replied. "Once I get a few more shots done. Why don't you ladies go wait by craft services, and I'll come find you when we stop for lunch."

Then he turned back to the monitor and the five people who had been waiting to speak to him, and that was the last Mason saw of Jason Reed for another four hours.

EVENTUALLY, MASON GOT annoyed and called Julia.

"He's dicking me around," she said.

"He's also dicking Jade around. Let her go cause trouble. She's an actress; it's expected."

Mason rolled her eyes. "Are you joking? After thirty minutes she left to go shopping. Then she texted me that she found a spa and was having a massage, a manicure, a pedicure and a blowout of her hair which she just had done five hours ago."

Julia chuckled. "A true professional. I might like her after all."

Mason shook her head, not that Julia could see her. "Can I just come back? I can see him when he's back in town."

"No, stay there. Will found out he's mortgaged to the hilt, which isn't rare, but could increase his rage at having his project shut down. Get back to waiting, and get used to it. A lot of basic detective work involves long periods of waiting for something to happen."

"Thanks for the advice. I'll get it embroidered on a pillow. Did Becky show up yet?" Mason watched as a girl in a headset tried to prevent pedestrians from crossing the road, something they seemed pretty intent on doing.

"No. She's not missing. I put her somewhere safe."

"You did? Where?"

"Somewhere useful to me, and safe for her. It's not important that you know the details. Just stay there, Mason, and call me once something interesting has happened." She hung up, and Mason sighed and reached for another bear claw. Her new job was so rewarding. At least craft services was well stocked, with pastries, burritos and soft-serve ice cream. She might die of impatience, but not hunger. She noticed that the girl with the headset had resorted to handing out twenty-dollar bills to the pedestrians; once, that is, they had signed a piece of paper. Mason idly wondered how much she could make if she just attempted to cross the street repeatedly but talked herself out of it. She reached for a banana; she must be growing up.

Several times over the course of the next few hours, people came up to Mason and asked her questions, assuming she was part of the production. She started off saying she didn't know, but after the fourth or fifth time she began making stuff up. She told one frantic girl the last time she'd seen the production designer he'd been heading to the nearest bar, which sent her off in a panic; she told another guy that a dingo had taken the second grip, whatever that was; and just as she was about to defy Julia and get up to leave, she had the pleasure of telling a guy that Jason Reed had last been seen calling an impotence clinic in tears.

"I've got plenty of issues," came a voice from behind her, "but keeping it up isn't one of them."

Mason briefly closed her eyes, then stood and got ready to brazen it out. But fortunately, Mr. Reed appeared to have a sense of humor, because he was laughing.

"I'm sorry I kept you waiting so long, but it seems like you found ways to amuse yourself."

She nodded and shrugged. "The devil makes work for idle hands. What can I say?"

He just smiled and took her arm. "The bruises make more sense, that's for sure. Let's go find some coffee and privacy, and we'll find a way to keep your hands busy." His hand was warm on her skin, and as he guided her across the street, she could smell a faint but clearly expensive aftershave. There was something about him, something . . . seductive. Mason frowned at herself and stepped slightly away from him. He said nothing, just pushed open the door of a large trailer and gestured her to precede him up the steps.

Inside the trailer was a mess, but clearly a working mess, and more importantly there was a small espresso machine. Jason Reed made them both a coffee and sat down and grinned at her.

"I am ready for the third degree. Shoot."

Mason crossed her legs and tried to look serious. "What was your show for Netflix about?"

He didn't flicker. "It's about Galliano's, the burlesque club. I have Maggie Galliano ready to cooperate fully; I have access to all their historical documents, which are extensive; and I have the beginnings of an A-list cast lined up. It's going to be a great show."

"Going to be? I thought Tony shut you down?"

He nodded. "He did, but I can go back to it now, while pre-production on *The Codex* is happening. I've always got several projects on the go. You have to, in this business." His face got serious. "They had a murder recently, so the place is trending."

"Lucky for you," Mason said, dryly.

"Yup." He looked at her. "Don't judge, Miss Mason. The victim was actually a girl I was thinking of hiring for the show. She was smart, talented. This business is all about publicity, about what the public is interested in. You have to move quickly and watch for the right moment. The idea that *The Codex* is cursed generates inches and inches of coverage every time it comes up. Coverage drives business, and business means more movies being made."

"I'm not judging you. I'm just being generally sarcastic. Did you and Tony ever have a conversation about it?"

He nodded. "Yeah, but only over the phone. He was as charming and evasive as ever. He didn't deny he'd had a hand in shutting me down, but he suggested I'd be better off working on a different project anyway, like directing *The Codex*. Galliano's isn't as interesting as you think, he said, which I seriously doubt." He turned up his palms. "I was pretty mad, but you can't stay mad in this business. You make a little note in your brain for payback later and move on." He looked suddenly somber. "And payback came for Tony without any effort on my part, so there you go."

"Divine intervention?"

He shook his head. "Probably just bad luck, wouldn't you say?" He looked at her and tipped his head slightly. "You have a great look, despite the bruising. Have you thought about acting?"

She ignored him. "And now you're directing *The Codex*?"

"Yes, Christine called me the day after the funeral and sent over Helen's old script. It's a placeholder, obviously; we'll get it rewritten. It gave us enough to start talking to people. I've been attached on and off for years; it's one of those projects that rises and falls. With all this publicity now it might actually happen." He grinned. "Which is good because I need the money. Made a few investments that didn't pay off quite the way I'd hoped, you know?"

"And Jade Solomon?"

"Signed up to play the lead, which is good for all of us." He smiled. "Jade isn't an intellectual, but put her in front of a camera and watch the magic happen. She's a real talent."

"She's not dumb." Mason found herself defending her new friend. "She's read a lot of books and has a ten-year plan."

Jason raised his eyebrows and said, "We also hope to get Julia to do a small role, and we signed up Jack Simon and are still pursuing David Paul, although I heard there was bad blood between those two. Hopefully, it was long enough ago that it won't matter. Jack Simon was a hard get, but we got him in the end. David Paul says he's considering a reality show instead, but he's just hoping for more money."

Mason finished her coffee. "So, do you have any theories about who killed Tony?"

He shook his head. "I thought it was your boss. She's a force of nature."

"She's going to a lot of trouble if it was."

"Smoke screen. She couldn't stand Tony, remember? She blamed him for the death of her husband. She accused him on the stand, though he had an alibi and she didn't. She had been sleeping with him, of course, and also—allegedly—had moved on to an affair with David Paul. Or was it Jack Simon? Both of the men were on set during the time of the murder, and she was nowhere to be seen. That's what put her away, in the end.

Well, that and the fact that she called the judge a colossal square and referred to the jury as 'the dozy dozen.'"

Mason didn't comment. Jason continued. "Don't get blinded by loyalty. Your boss killed one man. What makes you think she didn't kill another?"

"I have no idea if she killed the first one, and she has an alibi for the second one."

"*I was too drunk* is not an alibi."

Mason had to acknowledge the truth of this, but not out loud.

"Tell me about your relationship with Christine. She must like you more than Tony did."

He shook his head and stood up. "I doubt that. Tony loved me. And Christine has respect for my work. Nothing in Hollywood is personal, Miss Mason, it's all just business. Sometimes it's also pleasure, but more often it's just another day at work." He took the cups to the tiny sink and rinsed them. "Still, I suppose it could have been someone else, it being your boss is a little predictable. How about his wife? I've seen her lose her temper, and for all her quiet affect, she's as power hungry and obsessive as anyone else in the business."

"You saw Helen lose her temper with Tony?"

He shook his head. "No, working on a project. She's a successful writer, you know, works all the time, although she's always wanted to direct instead. She did one feature that was dead on release and got put in movie jail for a while."

"What's movie jail?" she asked.

"A period of time where you can't even get a meeting, let alone a job. Most people visit movie jail at some point in their career; some just stay longer than others. I wasn't sure Helen was ever going to get out."

"You know a lot about it," said Mason.

He shrugged. "We have the same agent, Helen and I."

"Everyone seems to have the same agent."

"They don't, but good agents know everyone, so it ends up much the same."

"Did Helen and Tony not get on?"

Jason shrugged. "They were separated, so presumably not. The rumor is he thought I'd be a better director for *The Codex*, and if she'd heard that she wouldn't have been pleased. But they had lunch before he died, right? He can't have disliked her; he wouldn't eat with people he didn't like, said it put him off his food. I'm the same way. I tend to want to spend more time with people I like, don't you? At least until I know them better and realize I don't like them so much anymore."

"Does that happen often?"

"Sure, I'm as fickle as the next guy." He grinned at her. "Would you like to spend more time with me? We could find out if we like each other."

Mason frowned. "Or discover we have a physical allergy and blow up like puffer fish."

He burst out laughing. "I have to go back on set now. Can I take you out to dinner when we're back in the city? I'm sure there's much more you want to know, and I'm happy to lay bare my soul." He leaned over and looked into her eyes, a crooked and charming smile taking the edge off his words. "I can be very cooperative given the right incentive."

Mason stood, too. "I'm never inclined to offer incentives, Mr. Reed."

"I doubt you ever have to." He held the trailer door open for her, and she passed very close to him as she went down the steps. Sometimes her physical reaction to people reminded her a little of her cravings for alcohol, a sense that some lower portion of her mind had wrested control of the wheel for a while. She paused at the bottom, relieved to have put some distance between them.

"Yeah, usually my sunny personality is incentive enough. Thanks for answering my questions. I'll be in touch if I need to know anything else."

"Promise?"

Mason just turned and walked away, pretty certain that making promises to Jason Reed was something one could live to regret.

ONCE SHE AND Jade were on the way home, one of them smelling of essential oils, the other of frosting, Mason asked the actress what she knew about Helen, and about Christine.

Jade shrugged. "I don't know Christine at all, really. We met last week for the first time, when Jason wanted me for *The Codex*. She didn't even really say very much, just looked me over, had me read some lines, hold a gun, make some coffee, you know, that was it."

"Coffee? Is that a pivotal part of the script?"

"I don't know. I only read my parts. I think she just wanted a cup of coffee. Cody wasn't there."

Mason shot her a look. "She couldn't make it herself? And doesn't she have a second assistant?"

Jade looked surprised. "I have no idea. I didn't see anyone else. Maybe she fired them. It happens all the time. Studio executives don't make their own coffee, and I was having one, so you know, whatev." She turned to look out of the window, watching the coast slide by. "I'll tell you one thing, though, that struck me as really weird."

"Yes?" *Finally*, thought Mason, *something useful*.

"She really likes fish. Her whole office was, like, full of tanks."

Mason briefly closed her eyes. "Thanks, Jade, that's helpful."

"You're welcome." The beautiful young woman fell silent, then made a sudden noise that almost scared Mason off the road. "Ooh, look, a dolphin!" She was quiet for a moment, then added, "I know Helen a little bit because of the animal shelter. Like I said, she's big dogs, I'm small dogs so, you know, we don't run across each other very much."

"Neither of you are cat people?"

"I like cats," said Jade cheerfully, "but sometimes they look at me funny and I get nervous."

Mason was touched and was about to launch into a description of Phil and their strange relationship, when her phone rang. It was Julia, so Mason kept it off speaker.

"Are you nearly home?"

"No," said Mason, "we just left Solvang."

"Jesus, alright, come report as soon as you get back."

"No, I'm tired. I spent all day waiting. I'm going to bed."

"You work for me, come and report."

"No, as your interim sponsor and also as an individual human being, maintaining a work-life balance is important, Julia. If I do anything other than eat and sleep it will be go to a meeting. You went to one this morning; I haven't yet. You know what they say: Everything you put before your sobriety you'll lose."

"Well, you'll certainly lose your job."

"Fine with me. I work to live, not live to work. Your generation got sold down the river; mine has handed in the paddle completely. I'll see you first thing tomorrow." She was about to hang up the call when Jade suddenly leaned over and shouted, "Julia, I love you!"

There was a pause.

"What was that?" asked Julia.

Mason sighed and handed over the phone. Jade squealed.

"Julia! I am such a huge fan! I am so excited to be playing the part you made famous. I was wondering when I could come over and talk to . . ."

She fell silent, listening.

"Yes, but . . ."

More silence. She frowned a little. Mason wondered if Julia was being mean.

"But I saved Mason's life." Jade issued this statement in much the same way a small child might say, *but you said Santa Claus was real*, and it seemed to have the desired effect. A smile broke across the beautiful actress's face and she said, "That would be wonderful. I'll bring gluten-free muffins!"

Another pause.

"Really? I didn't know that. Never mind, then." She hung up and handed Mason back her phone. "She says I can come over tomorrow. She must really like you."

"Hmm," said Mason, not willing to accept this verdict.

They drove in silence for a moment, then Jade added, "Did you know gluten-free muffins cause vaginal dryness? I had no idea."

29

~~~~

THE NEXT MORNING, Mason got up early and went to a meeting before heading back to Julia's house. Skipping a day here or there wasn't going to kill her, but the combination of not going to meetings and dealing with Julia just might.

She found Julia in the kitchen with Will, Ben and Archie. They were taste testing cinnamon rolls, while Claudia looked on and made notes on a recipe card. The smell of coffee made her mouth water; the smell of frosting over warm dough made her tummy ache. She reached out and snagged a half bun and leaned against the sink to eat it.

Will was judicious. "This one is the best. Number three. The perfect amount of cinnamon and some other . . . Is it nutmeg?"

"Mace."

Mason frowned. "You pepper sprayed the cinnamon rolls? What the hell did they do?"

Will shook his head. "Mace is the gentler version of nutmeg. It's actually the soft skin that covers the nut."

"Ground-up nut skin?" Mason wasn't sure if she was getting punked or not, but she decided life would be easier if she just went with it. "Do you want to hear my report about Jason Reed?"

"Yes," said Julia, "but first Will has something to share that has been causing him to struggle to contain himself. I told him he could tell it as soon as you got here, so if he's peed his pants, it's your fault."

"My pants are entirely dry," said Will, "but this case is starting to get really fucking weird."

Julia made a face at him. "Spit it out."

Will did. "So, you asked me to follow up on Jack Simon. He is indeed living in Palm Springs, or he was."

Julia sighed. "Was? You lost him?"

"We all lost him. He died."

"Natural causes?"

Will shook his head. "Nope. Suicide. The night of Tony's funeral."

There was a long pause, and Julia's face got a little sad, then a little angry. "Right," she said. "This *Codex* Curse is starting to piss me off." She got up and went to wash the frosting off her fingers. "If Gen Z can bring herself to work an overnight, it's time for a road trip."

"That's not a good idea." Archie was using his serious voice.

"Why not?" Julia didn't sound like she was going to give a shit about his answer.

"Because the police already warned you to keep your beak out of their business, and another death is their business."

"Not if they think it's suicide. No one's paying attention."

Julia's phone rang. She hesitated, looking at the caller ID, then answered.

"Larry, I'm not . . ."

Silence. She hit speaker and put the phone on the table, dangerously close to a slick of frosting.

". . . now Jack's dead and it's on the news and the phone's been ringing off the hook. Jason Reed, Christine . . . Oprah again. The curse claims another victim . . ." He fell silent. "You still there, baby?"

Julia leaned over the table and spoke clearly into the phone. "Larry, I'm still here. I'm not doing Cinespia, I'm not putting on that catsuit, I'm not going to be in the movie, or any other movie, I'm not going on Oprah, I'm not doing any of it."

"Baby . . ."

"You know," said Mason, leaning over a little, too, "you need to respect her boundaries. She has firmly established them, repeated them—which she shouldn't have to do—and is asking you politely to back the fuck away. You and I have never met in person, Larry, but you've edged onto my list."

He didn't miss a beat. "Which list is that?"

"My list of people who have no respect for my boss. Everyone around her wants her to say yes to things she's already said no to, and it's starting to piss me the fuck off. Not going to lie."

There was a long silence.

Then Julia spoke. "Like she said, Larry. Talk soon." She hung up. Then she turned to Mason. "I appreciate the support, Mason, but I can speak for myself."

"I understand that. Sorry. I'm not good at impulse control."

"I understand that, too." For a split second a smile deepened her dimples, then it was gone as quickly as it had arrived. "Now go get your shit together. We're hitting the road."

~ ~ ~

MASON HAD NEVER been to Palm Springs, despite the fact that it was only a two-hour drive from Los Angeles. It was the playground of another group of people: the wealthy, the famous, the sons and daughters of both. And, of course, once a year, the festival crowd. Luckily, there was no festival right now, and traffic on the freeway wasn't too bad.

Mason was happy to be driving, and as they were driving a 1968 Daimler 250 V8, she liked it even more. The car wasn't as comfy as a modern car, but it certainly wasn't a rough ride. Julia had picked it because it had a reclining front bench seat, and she was currently out like a light, emitting the occasional little soft snore. The windows were down, the GPS was making sure they didn't get lost, and as they entered the San Gorgonio Pass, Mason saw hundreds of wind turbines stretching and spinning like toys.

Mason realized she hadn't felt depressed in a while, which was a pleasant surprise. Depression was something she'd grown to accept as just part of her life. She'd have times when she couldn't even feign interest in life, where making AA meetings was more important than ever, and less appealing than anyone could imagine. Since meeting Julia she'd felt . . . useful, challenged, interested. True, she'd had her face bashed in, which sucked, but she'd also visited strip clubs, met thieves and verbally sparred with a true professional. She wondered what her mother would say if she became a private investigator. She'd be able to support herself, be able to use her skills to help people, work with Julia . . . She realized suddenly it was something she wanted. Maybe. Possibly. She smiled, then stopped smiling because it hurt like a motherfucker.

Julia woke up and stretched, winching the split bench seat back up and gazing out of the window.

"Oh, look," she said. "The Village People are playing the Morongo Casino."

Mason frowned at her. "I didn't peg you for a Village People fan."

"I'm not," Julia replied. "I was just commenting. Do you think in thirty years the musicians you listen to will be playing the Morongo? Will Taylor Swift be telling the audience not to miss the early bird special?"

"Doubt it," replied Mason. "I don't think Ms. Swift is going to be hurting for cash. Besides, why would she play the Morongo after headlining stadiums?"

"For the love of performing?"

Mason took her eyes off the road and gazed at her. "Really? Die-hard fans throwing their incontinence panties up on stage?"

Julia shrugged. "Why not? Think how many musicians end up not playing anymore at all. I'm telling you, kid, I've seen the far side of celebrity, and it's not pretty. Famous and gorgeous one day, utterly ordinary and old the next. These aren't people who've developed a lot of fallback skills, or at least not often. Nothing sadder than a matinee idol with a walker, baby."

Mason flicked the indicator and started to exit to Palm Springs. "You're a deep thinker, Julia. I had no idea."

"I'm frequently underestimated," the other woman replied. "It's part of my arsenal of sneaky tricks."

"I'll bear that in mind," Mason said, as her phone told her to take a left. "It shouldn't be much longer. Do you want to stop at the hotel first and drop our stuff, or go straight to the house?"

Julia looked at her watch. "Hotel. We're meeting a friend for some help before we start investigating how Jack Simon's death factors into everything else."

"You have friends in Palm Springs?"

"I have friends everywhere, Mason. I already told you." She pulled out her phone. "High places, low places and everyplace in between."

JULIA'S FRIEND'S NAME was Mikki, and she had a box of noses.

She'd come into the hotel room and burst out laughing at Mason's face. "Is that why I'm here? Are we covering up?"

Mason was slightly affronted. "I earned these bruises fair and square. No need to cover them up."

Mikki, who had pink hair cut in as razor-sharp a bob as any Mason had ever seen, shook her head, sending her bangs dancing. "Don't be offended, honey. I've covered up way worse. And created way worse, too." She leaned in close and looked at Mason's neck. "Nice pointy weapon scab. Hang on . . ." She pulled out her phone and took a picture. "Thanks." She turned to Julia. "Mrs. Mann, it's a pleasure to hear from you. It's been a while." She looked around the room and spotted a chair that suited her. Dragging it into the bathroom, she indicated Julia should take a seat in front of the mirror. Then she opened several cases she'd brought with her, and swirled a cape around Julia's shoulders. "What are you looking for?"

"Unrecognizability. Complete."

Mikki laughed again; amusement was clearly her default

setting. "It won't take too much. You'd be surprised. People will just think they met you somewhere before. It's how the brain works." She pulled out brushes and powders and the aforementioned box of noses. She had another one of wigs and hairpieces, earlobes and eyebrows, which looked like a little caterpillar commune.

She prepared Julia's face with creams and foundation that darkened her skin a little. Then she considered her noses and selected one with a shape very different from Julia's patrician profile. "Also, if we use a distinctive enough nose that's all people will see. Add heavier eyebrows and we are cooking with Crisco, I promise you."

When she was done, Mason could see she was as good as her word. Julia looked like someone she might have met sometime, or seen at a meeting. Slightly familiar, but at the same time, totally different. It was amazing.

Julia looked at herself in the mirror and grinned. "You unwittingly gave me my grandfather's nose. Now I look like I inherited that instead of my mother's. Weirdly, I like it."

She shook off the cape, quickly changed her clothes and crooked a finger at Mason.

"Come on, kid. Let's go investigate shit."

30

~~~~~

WHEN MASON AND Mann pulled up to the gated community where Jack Simon had lived, it turned out to be impossible to get to his house. They could see the house from the gate, but there was no going over, under or around the fence. It was hot, but not unbearably so, and Mason could see why people liked Palm Springs—it was quiet, sunny and surrounded by mountains. Apart from the average age being north of seventy, it was great. She turned to Julia.

"What now?"

Julia was on her phone and held up her finger. "Hello? Blackbird Country Club? This is Mrs. Gregory, how are you?" She'd added a very subtle quaver in her voice—nothing too crazy, but she sounded a decade or two older. That in combination with the new nose, eyebrows and gray wig was giving Mason a brain-ache of fairly epic and giggle-inducing proportion. She wasn't sure how . . . then she realized Julia had been accessing the residents list on the gate. If you had a code, you could enter it to open the gate, or you could buzz your hosts directly and they would let you in. Julia had simply scrolled until she found a name she liked.

"I'm sending over a couple of friends who are interested in joining the club. Do take care of them, won't you? Who should I tell them to ask for?" She smiled, and it came across in her voice. "Robert? Of course, I'll let them know. They'll be along shortly, for dinner. Go ahead and put it on my account, would you?" She hung up. "That was lucky. Mrs. Gregory could have been a European with a memorably stupid accent, but apparently not. Phew."

"Risky," Mason said, "but it apparently worked."

"It often does. Especially when you're talking to someone for whom all the customers are the same. It's possible Mrs. Gregory would have turned out to be a staff favorite, someone who remembers names, gives generous holiday tips and asks after the correct children, but that was a risk worth taking." She headed to the car. "The car will help, too, although it does make us memorable, which isn't great." She looked at Mason, who today was pairing her beaten face with boyfriend jeans and suspenders over a tank top that said "Do No Harm, But Take No Shit." She sighed. "Not that the car is going to make much difference."

THE BLACKBIRD COUNTRY Club was a mid-century icon, designed by distinguished architects and carefully built by experts. In its heyday it was home to celebrities with household names, and its golf course was an exquisitely green jewel in the middle of the desert. In the amber light of early evening, it was as elegant and well-preserved as its clientele.

Julia and Mason swept around the drive and pulled up in front of a stone-and-wood entryway. A valet tripped over himself getting to Julia's door and took the keys from Mason with a gleeful air.

"We're here to see Robert," Julia told the concierge, and Robert was duly called. He was a middle-aged man with a Hollywood level of suavity, but with added deference. His eyes took in both of them: Julia's simple but expensive resort-wear shift, the several strings of real pearls she'd just added in the car, the diamond studs, the cashmere shrug, the Ferragamo ballet flats, the careful makeup, and Mason's . . . bruises . . . and smiled as if these were things he saw every day. And maybe they were; maybe rich older women often bring skinny, banged-up chicks to evaluate country clubs.

"Mrs. Gregory is an old and valued member," he said to them, as he led them around the club, pointing out its various amenities. "It's a pity we don't see her very much anymore."

"Yes," replied Julia, "she's not as well as she was." She made a sorrowful face, hoping she wasn't wrong.

"Ah well," confided Robert, "age does have its infirmities." He simpered at Julia. "Although they seem to have passed you by, Mrs. Anderson."

"My granddaughter keeps me young, as you can see," Julia said, archly. "Are most of the members here of advanced age?"

Robert nodded. "Palm Springs is a wonderful place to retire. I spent many years working at the Beverly Hilton, and I don't miss anything about the city, least of all the traffic. The climate here is conducive to pulmonary health, we have world-class hospitals and facilities, and the homes are spacious and elegant."

Julia looked across the lawns of the club, over to where

long, low houses could be seen around the edges of the golf club. "I can see that. Are any on the market right now?"

They had reached the bar. Robert gestured to the barman on duty, and he shimmered over. Julia settled herself on a stool and patted the one next to her.

"Please do join us." She smiled at Robert. "I'm really very interested in becoming a member of the club." He hesitated, and she turned up the wattage. "Besides, you must see and hear such fascinating things, running a club with a history like this."

He gave in and sat on a stool. Mason took one behind Julia, so she could watch his face and the door at the same time. Her jaw was aching, and she'd forgotten to grab painkillers at the hotel. She could smell wine.

Robert leaned forward. "Actually, there will be a home on the market shortly. We just lost one of our long-term residents."

"Really?" said Julia, making a face that skillfully combined sympathy for the demise of an old person with the acquisitive gleam of a house hunter. "How sad."

"Very," Robert replied, lowering his voice. "Suicide, apparently." Hastily, he added, "Not in the house itself, as it happens, but on the golf course."

"Oh," said Julia, "I'm not superstitious about things like that."

"Of course not," he purred, "but, you know, some people are."

"How shocking," Julia said, ordering Robert a glass of wine. "Are you allowed to drink while working?"

He shook his head but winked and picked up the glass and took a sip. "It's after five, and I won't tell if you won't," he said.

She giggled and said, "Your secret is safe with me. Tell me more about the house . . . your poor resident, I mean. Have you had"—she dropped her voice—"the authorities crawling all over? What a difficult thing to manage."

He sighed, pleased to be understood. "Indeed. The other residents are most upset, and my boss is upset when the residents are upset, you understand." He paused, and lowered his voice. "There is a waiting list for homes, but you've come at a fortunate time. It isn't even really available yet."

She nodded, sympathetically, and patted his hand. He continued.

"The gentleman in question was a very quiet person and the house is lovely. He ate here every evening, but I think I've barely exchanged more than twenty words with him. He had the same thing always, a baked potato with a steak and green salad, followed by peach slices and cream, and then he would head back home in his golf cart."

Mason coughed. "They drive golf carts?"

Robert looked at her as if a chair had spoken. "Of course! It's a golf course."

Mason nodded and subsided. He regarded her narrowly for another moment, then returned to Julia. "I had no idea he was even depressed, let alone suicidal. He was an actor, though, and they are often temperamental." He paused. "Of course, I could be being gauche—are you an actress, Mrs. Anderson?"

She gave a low chuckle. "Oh, dear me, no. I was a lawyer in practice in Los Angeles, but since my husband died I've been traveling a lot." She indicated Mason. "With my niece."

Mason opened her mouth, but Richard beat her to it. "I thought she was your granddaughter?"

There was a fractional pause, then Julia reached a hand

back and placed it on Mason's knee, squeezing gently. "She keeps me young, as I said."

Richard looked at Mason, who attempted to look like a secret sexual dynamo, and apparently pulled it off, because he suddenly leaned forward to Julia and lowered his voice. "You can feel comfortable here to be as open or as private as you wish. Palm Springs is a very relaxed place."

"How very nice," she replied. "Tell me more about this house."

31

~~~~

THE TEMPERATURE DROPPED very quickly once the sun went down, this being the desert. They had joined Robert for dinner at the club, and after a surprisingly good meal, they climbed into his golf cart and headed away from the clubhouse.

"There are eighty properties on club grounds, and many of them have been in the same families since the opening of the club in 1951. It is rare these properties go onto the open market, as there are always people looking out for an opportunity to acquire one." Robert skillfully navigated the smoothly paved paths of the golf course, heading across a wooden bridge that xylophoned flatly in the cool, dark evening. The golf course itself was a dark green ocean in the moonlight, the occasional immaculately manicured sand traps like miniature islands. It was beautiful.

Robert slowed down as they approached the house the women had seen earlier from the gate. "Just want to make sure we're able to visit . . . unobserved," he said. The houses nearby were in darkness, despite there being cars parked outside. Mason looked at her watch: ten thirty p.m. She thought of her own grandma, hitting the sack at nine every night, and getting up at five. Old people were strange. Then she looked at Julia, who was calmly lying her head off in order to fight crime. Old people were strange in a variety of ways.

Jack Simon's house was insanely beautiful, and Mason made a note to ask Will how he had afforded it. One level, it curved around in a lazy S shape, fronted mostly in glass, interspersed with cream-colored rough rock walls that doubtless harbored countless scorpions. A pool gleamed out front, its lights on despite the owner no longer being home. Mason could hear a hot tub bubbling somewhere close.

Robert pulled a key from his pocket and unlocked the kitchen door. "The front door is actually on the other side," he explained, "but this is a more private entrance." The kitchen was smaller than Mason had expected, but perfectly appointed, with a large central island she managed to bang her hip into. Twice.

They turned into the main room and Mason further upgraded her opinion of Jack Simon: The room was very elegant without being cold. A large and beautiful photograph showing women sunbathing beside a home much like this one hung on the facing wall, adjacent to an enormous rough stone wall with a fireplace she could have stood in. Maple doors covered what was presumably a screen, and the low sofa formed an L around a coffee table. It was a lovely room, and Julia commented enthusiastically.

"Yes," replied Robert, "wait until you see the master bedroom." He winked at Mason. "You ladies are going to love it!"

As he and Julia headed across the room to go investigate the rest of the house, Mason hung back. Once they were out of sight, she went back to the kitchen. The living room had no drawers to speak of, but the kitchen did, and she wanted to start there.

She pulled on a pair of kitchen gloves, and began opening drawers. The top one contained the usual kitchen drawer crap: bills, crumpled receipts, pens with no caps. She smoothed out a few bills: Mr. Simon had apparently paid on time and carried no balance on his credit card. A fat lot of good that did him. Mason scanned the bill, hoping to see a charge for a vintage gun store, or purchases in Los Angeles, but no luck. Jack Simon enjoyed Netflix, supported several animal charities every month, spent a small fortune somewhere called "Eddie's," and nothing more interesting than that. She took a photo and kept rustling. She found a phone bill and pounced hopefully, but it was useless. Very few calls at all, and none to Los Angeles. Of course, it didn't list incoming calls; Tony could have been blowing up his phone every day. Who knows? She kept looking, but there was nothing more. Bank statements must be elsewhere, or on his computer, assuming he had one.

A movement outside caught her eye, and she looked up in time to see something small skirting the pool. Mason frowned—what deadly things lurked in the desert? Scorpions, but this was bigger than that, she fervently hoped. Rabbits? Maybe. Coyotes? Yes, this did look more doglike. But it was gone anyway.

She moved into the living room and through to a hallway that started behind the far wall. She opened several doors, all of which led to clean, clearly unused guest rooms. She followed the sound of voices and wound up at the end of the hall, in the master bedroom. It was roomy and reminded her of the large guest room she was sleeping in at Julia's. Julia and

Robert were sitting on the bed trading war stories about crazy people.

"Did you guys go check out the pool yet?" Mason asked, startling them.

"Ooh," said Julia. "Let's do that!" She slid open the large glass doors and stepped out, with Robert close behind. "That reminds me of a story I heard once about Esther Williams."

Mason started poking about. She didn't know how much the police would dig around in a suicide, but it was worth a look. No one was infallible.

Bookshelves lined one wall. Mr. Simon had enjoyed classic American literature, Golden Age mysteries and books about people stranded in dangerous places. Disaster porn. Spines were all facing out, the books looked well-read but taken care of, and Mason thought about the quiet life Jack Simon had enjoyed, so far from Hollywood.

She moved to the bedside table, opening the drawers. Lube, condoms, a couple of pre-rolled joints in fancy packaging. Not so quiet a life, then.

The room had a desk, with a laptop sitting on it and file drawers underneath. The laptop was dead and the file drawers were locked. Awesome. Mason took a quick peek outside; Julia and Robert were standing by the pool chatting, and seemed pretty comfortable. Mason popped into the bathroom, which did indeed have an enormous tub, and looked for something to break the drawer open. The vanity drawers offered up a nail file, which was classic, so Mason went to try that. In the movies, people just inserted the nail file above the lock and wiggled it, but sadly, that achieved precisely nothing. She pulled open the other drawers of the desk and was slightly chagrined to find what was obviously the key to the file drawer, just sitting there. Guess they didn't get a lot of burglars at the country club. She also wondered if a trained private investigator wouldn't have just looked in the drawers first, and sighed as she fitted the key in the lock.

The drawer was full, folders bulging with newspaper clippings, headshots, correspondence of all kinds.

Tony.

She fingered open the hanging file and discovered a bundle of letters, elastic banded together. On some the ink was faded and pale; on a few others it was fresh and sharp. A minor internal struggle ensued. Private letters, in a locked drawer. Probably important letters. Mason started opening the first one, ready to put her own morals about privacy to one side, but just as she was drawing the first letter out, Julia called her from outside. Mason hesitated, then quickly stuffed the bundle of letters down the back of her jeans.

Julia and Robert were standing next to the pool, pointing at something. It was the small thing Mason had seen before, and now she recognized it was a dog. Possibly the ugliest dog she'd ever seen, but a dog nonetheless.

She knelt down and put her hand out, feeling the bundle of letters rustling against her skin. The dog wagged its tail but didn't move. She looked up at Robert.

"Do you know this dog? Did it belong to Jack Simon?"

He nodded. "I thought someone had already taken it away, but apparently not." He made a face. "Its name is Lorre, after the actor."

Mason tried again. "Lorre? Come here, boy. Come on, Lorre." The dog took a few steps but was still unsure.

Julia sighed. "Oh, let me do it." She bent over and, in the sweetest voice Mason had ever heard, called the dog. The dog ran straight to her and let her pick him up. Mason gazed in surprise at Julia, who just shrugged.

"Dogs like me. I don't know why."

Up close the dog was even uglier. He had a foxy little head, but with the bulging eyes of a pug, which did give him a resemblance to Peter Lorre, and the body of a dachshund. Which would have been OK, except he also had long, skinny legs like an Italian greyhound, and an enormous plumy tail, like a golden retriever. He didn't seem to care about it, and was licking Julia's face enthusiastically.

"Are you thirsty, little man? Are you hungry?" Julia continued to murmur endearments as she carried the little dog into the kitchen. Robert and Mason followed, somewhat bemused.

"So, what do you think of the house?" Robert leaned carefully against the kitchen island as Julia fed and watered the little dog.

Julia looked at Mason, who subtly nodded. "It's lovely, Bobby, but not what we're looking for right now." She looked down at Lorre. "Are you going to take him back to the clubhouse?"

Since a sale didn't seem to be imminent, Robert lost some of his bonhomie. "The dog? No, I shall call the dogcatcher in the morning. Mr. Simon didn't have any relatives that I know of, and there's no way I'm taking that ugly hound anywhere." He made a face at it. "I am not someone who enjoys animals."

"But maybe one of Mr. Simon's friends would take him?" Mason asked.

Robert shook his head. "I doubt it. Mr. Simon kept to himself, largely. I don't think he had any close friends at all."

Mason frowned. "He lived here for decades. He must have had friends somewhere."

Robert shrugged and started moving toward the door. "Not as far as I know."

Mason looked at him. "So you're just going to leave the dog here?"

"Sure," replied Robert. "He seems quite happy. She fed him, the catcher will be here tomorrow, there's no issue." Indeed, Lorre had curled up in a basket under the kitchen table, and seemed to be already asleep. Julia frowned, hesitated and looked at Mason. Mason raised her eyebrows and herded her out. The dog was not their problem.

BACK AT THE hotel, Mason told Julia about the letters. She held out her hand for them, but Mason hesitated. "Don't you think we should give them to the police first?"

"Nope. Which police? The LAPD has no jurisdiction down here, and the Palm Springs Police Department isn't investigating Jack's death at all. Besides, you already got your mucky fingerprints all over them and took them out of the house, so their origin is hearsay." She took the letters and opened one at random. "This is from several years ago." She read, frowning. "This is insanely boring. Literally just gossip and news from LA. People they know in common, people . . ." She paused. "Huh . . . 'Julia's drinking again, it's amazing she stays as beautiful as she does . . .' That's nice, for a backhander." She folded the letter, tucked it back in the envelope and reached for another. "Yes, this one's the same. What the hell. Why keep these at all, let alone in a private place?" She yawned, suddenly.

"Right, time for bed. Tomorrow we dig a little deeper." She started piling pillows at the top of one of the beds. "Hand me a pillow. I need to sleep on my back to keep my nose intact. Ah, the challenges of deception." Then she giggled.

"You're really enjoying this, aren't you?" said Mason.

Julia thought about it for a moment. "Yes," she said. "I like to play dress-up from time to time." She paused, "Do you think that dog is OK?"

Mason nodded. "He'll be fine. Worry about your nose."

32

~-~-~

THE NEXT MORNING, Mason asked the concierge if he knew a place called Eddie's. The man stopped smiling and looked surprised.

"Eddie's is a very low-end place. I'm surprised you've even heard of it. Our clients rarely frequent that kind of establishment. It's really just for locals, to be honest."

"It's a bar?"

"Yes, but it's what you might call a dive. They've been pulled up many times for illegal gambling, there are frequently fights, that kind of thing."

"Illegal gambling? In a casino town?"

"Oh yes." The guy was clearly shocked they weren't on top of this. "You need to have a license, of course. The gambling commission takes these things very seriously." He handed them their bill. "There are very fine casinos in town, if gambling is what you're in the mood for."

"Actually"—Mason grinned at him—"Eddie's sounds right up my alley, thanks."

But when they arrived at Eddie's, even Mason wasn't sure they were at the right place. It looked as if it had been condemned many years before, and completely ignored since then. Graffiti covered the outside, the roof was patched and listing slightly, and the doors were heavily chained and padlocked.

They climbed out of the car and went closer.

"Excellent curb appeal," Julia said dryly. "It just screams hospitality, doesn't it?"

Mason held up a finger. "I can hear music."

Julia frowned, and they both stepped up to the doors. Yes, definitely music, and a low buzz of voices. Then, as they stood there, a couple of elderly lovers appeared around the corner of the building and wove off down the street. Mason and Julia walked around the building, following the music and now unmistakable smell of pot smoke and spilled alcohol.

They found the back door, which was slightly ajar. Mason paused and put her hand on Julia's arm.

"Wait, is this going to bother you, going into a bar?"

Julia shook her head. "At ten a.m.? No, I was never a morning drinker. I always woke up determined never to drink again. It wore off every single day around two p.m., but still." She paused. "Thanks, though. What about you?"

"I don't love a bar, but I'm not going in alone," replied Mason, pulling open the door. "Hopefully, we'll keep each other sober long enough to ask some questions."

Eddie's was actually exactly the kind of place Mason used to like to drink in. It was dim, which was in its favor, because it was also a complete mess. Mismatched tables and chairs, a floor that probably hadn't seen a mop since the seventies, and the kind of atmosphere that hit the sweet spot between frat house and the *Star Wars* cantina. It was completely full, which was impressive given the earliness of the hour. Looking around, Mason realized she was the youngest patron there. By about forty years.

Everyone turned around as they opened the door, and conversation stopped completely.

"This is a private party," yelled the barman. "Come back later."

Mason stood her ground. "We're looking for anyone who knew Jack Simon. He used to come here a lot."

The barman laughed. "Well, you've come to the right place." He put two more glasses on the bar and waved them over. "This is his wake."

IT TURNED OUT Jack Simon was anything but lonely. Over the course of the next two hours, Julia and Mason met three women who claimed to have been his girlfriend, two guys who said they'd been his boyfriend, and about half a dozen people who said they would have given him a kidney. Considering their age, that was a pledge that actually meant something.

"The thing about Jack was his kindness," one of the women said. "He was a very gentle soul who also loved to party hard and sleep around. But never in a mean way; in more of a hippie way, right? He was a child of the seventies, as many of us are in here, and he never sold out." She wiped her eyes. "He was a flower child with a MedicAlert bracelet, and I loved him dearly."

Another friend was more reserved. "Look, Jack had a temper, and sometimes he could be an asshole, but hey. Mostly he liked to chase fresh flesh and drink a lot and talk about the old days in the acting game. He made quite a few movies, you know." He learned forward. "He knew Julia Mann, did you know that?" Mason and Julia feigned surprise. "Yeah, and I mean knew in the biblical sense . . ." The old man chuckled. "Oh man, in her day she was quite the looker. She's probably dead now."

"At least partially," murmured Mason.

The man continued. "He was never married, but I think he had one long-term side piece. He occasionally got drunk and mentioned his 'main boo' . . . but generally he never liked anyone more than six months." He took a long drink of his beer. "He loved his dog, he loved movies, that was about it."

"This main boo . . . someone here?" Julia was interested.

"Nah," said the guy, "I think someone from the city. He never brought them here."

"Was he angry at anyone? What made him commit suicide? Was he depressed?" Julia asked.

The man shook his head and echoed what several other people had said. "There is no way Jack Simon killed himself. That man was happy to his core, you know what I mean? He lived within his means, he had a nice place, he had good friends and tail for days."

"Then you think someone killed him?" Mason asked.

The old man shrugged and called for another round. "Must have. Why, I couldn't tell you. He didn't have an enemy in the world."

"Well, apparently at least one," said Mason, and the old man nodded sadly.

THE CROWD STARTED thinning out eventually, and Mason and Julia got in the car for the drive back to Los Angeles. It was another crystal clear sunny day in Southern California, but Mason wasn't paying attention to the weather. She

couldn't shake the feeling she was missing something and
said as much to Julia.

Julia just leaned back in her seat and let the wind blow her
hair through the open window. Suddenly, she sat up in her
seat and pointed. "Holy fuck, check it out."

They were passing the golf club where Jack Simon had
lived, and as Mason turned to see what Julia was pointing at,
she saw Lorre the dog streaking along beside the street, a man
in city uniform chasing after him with a loop on a long pole.

"Wow, that dog can really go," Julia commented. "There is
no way in hell that guy is going to catch him."

Mason jammed on the brakes as Lorre suddenly swerved
in front of them, and Julia threw open her door and called the
dog, who, hearing the beloved voice of the Lady with Food of
the previous night, spun on a single rear leg and rocketed
back toward the car. Mason looked in the mirror.

"He's catching up. Hurry." The guy with the pole looked
pretty pissed off and started yelling. Mason took her foot off
the brake. "Julia, seriously, he's really close."

The dog leapt a good six feet into Julia's lap and she yanked
the door closed. "Floor it," she said, hugging Lorre. "Go, Mason. Burn rubber."

As the dogcatcher faded behind them, waving his pole in
rage, Mason looked over at Julia and the World's Ugliest and
now Luckiest Dog. "You two are nuts," she said.

Julia snuggled the dog. "We're in love. We can't help it." She
smiled at Mason. "Thanks, though, for supporting my sudden
impulse to steal a dog. I knew you were a softy, under all that
hard-ass." Lorre licked her chin, devoted for life.

Mason said nothing, but as they passed the windmills
again on their way north, noticed what a beautiful day it was.

33

~~~~~

"WHAT ON GOD'S green earth is that?" Will's tone was a mixture of incredulity and mild horror.

"It's a dog, Will." Julia was still holding Lorre as they walked back into the office, and Will hadn't failed to notice the newest member of the group. He was, after all, a trained professional.

"Are you sure?" Will's eyebrows were essentially in his hairline. "I mean," he added, judiciously, "it looks broadly like a dog but specifically like nothing on earth. Like a dog that someone made after hearing about dogs but never seeing one. Like out of spare parts. Like a child's interpretation of dogness."

"Wow," said Mason, "that's a lot of judgment."

"It's a lot of dog. Where did you find him?"

"He was Jack Simon's dog." Mason sat down heavily on the orange sofa and got up again almost immediately to go back to the kitchen to look for food. "We stole him from the crime scene."

Will opened his mouth, but Julia interrupted. "Not actually, Mason. The crime scene was a sand trap. We *rescued* him"—heavy emphasis—"from the street outside, where he was being pursued by The Man."

"A man?" Will was gamely trying to follow.

"No, The Man, you know, the establishment, the powers that be, the Law."

"He was on the run from the law? What had he done?"

Mason was nearly at the door when Claudia opened it carrying an even larger tray than usual. She was of the opinion that if she hadn't seen her people eat, they hadn't eaten, and were at death's door. She saw the dog, didn't flicker, put down the tray and went out again without comment.

Mason sat down again and reached for a fresh donut. "He hadn't done anything; he was just trying to live free. And to be fair, he has no owner, seeing as his owner is dead, so we weren't even stealing. We were rehoming."

Julia put Lorre down, and he immediately proved his intelligence by running over to Will, balancing on his back legs and bowing. Then, when Will didn't immediately capitulate to his charm, he hopped around in a circle, still on two legs. Will narrowed his eyes. Lorre was presumably about to start juggling oranges when Claudia came back in, with one bowl of cooked chicken and another of water. She clicked her tongue and Lorre shot over. He sat there, his head cocked, as she put the bowls down, then waited, watching Claudia's face intently. Claudia made a "go ahead" kind of noise, and he fell on it. Claudia was pleased.

"See, that's what I like, excellent manners and a good appetite. My new favorite."

WILL WAS ACTUALLY ready to explain one of the mysteries of the trip. "While you were there I looked up Mr. Simon's finances. He was a very comfortable man, not from the movies, but from an investment he made in a tiny computer company back in the early '80s. Apple went public at twenty-two dollars a share, somewhat lower than today." He coughed. "He also received the monthly payment from Repercussion, nothing extravagant, but consistent."

"Since when?" Julia was frowning again.

"1982."

"The year after *The Codex*." Julia looked at her feet for a moment, thinking back. "We need to work out what that was about. He never did any more work for the studio, and I'd always assumed David Paul had prevented it. Maybe Tony paid him off instead."

Will had more. "So, the amount changed over time, which was interesting of course."

"Of course," said Julia, dryly.

"So, I got a hunch, and checked it. Basically, he'd been receiving a payment equivalent to ten days' work at scale each month. As scale went up, the payments went up."

Julia laughed. "Sounds like Tony to me. It's the kind of kooky agreement that would appeal to him. Jack was able to work at other studios, so it wasn't like he was blackballed completely, and this way Tony could make it clear he would hire him if his other actor wasn't such a dick."

Mason was confused. "What's scale?"

"Minimum guaranteed wage for union actors."

"But why didn't he just wait till David Paul was over it, and then start hiring him again?"

Will nodded. "Right? But it turns out that Jack Simon lost interest in acting, once the guest spots in *Columbo* dried up. He moved to Palm Springs and lived a basically simple life. Simple in the sense of uniform, rather than uncomplicated."

Julia smiled. "What stories you could tell, huh, Lorre?" He wagged his tail, hearing his name, and gazed up at her with an expression of deep and liquid love. He'd been happy for a long time, then his man went away and he was sad and hungry for a week, and now he was happy and full again. It reaffirmed his faith in the universe, and he was grateful.

"I still don't get it," Mason persisted. She turned to Julia. "Is there anything about it in the letters we found?"

"I haven't read them all, but not so far."

"Why keep paying him so long? It can't have been blackmail; they were friends. Right?"

Will nodded. "Yes, plus it would be the mellowest blackmail scheme I've ever heard of: Pay me a small but slowly increasing amount for decades, I'll move to another town and never come near you again." He sighed. "I'll keep digging, but it would have been much easier if Jack Simon were alive to ask."

"Which brings us to the other big question, which is whether or not he killed himself. Mason?" Julia looked over at her assistant, who was working on another donut. "You eat like a teenage boy."

"I have the metabolism of a teenage boy, too," Mason replied, licking her fingers. "Maybe I spend my free time masturbating and playing video games."

"Regardless of that horrible image, do you think Jack Simon killed himself or not?"

"Not." Mason's tone was firm. "We spoke to nearly a dozen of his friends, and they were unanimous. There was no reason for him to do so. He was happy as a clam."

"Was the gun his?" Will asked.

Mason nodded. "Yes, registered to him and used, according

to three of his current girlfriends, for shooting rattlesnakes. He was worried about his dog."

"Are they a common problem?" asked Julia, looking at Will.

Will obliged. "Rattlesnakes are native to the Coachella Valley, and the general Palm Springs, Palm Desert area. The Southern Pacific rattlesnake is the most common, obviously, but red and western diamondbacks can be found, along with the sidewinder, the southwestern speckled, and even the Mojave green rattlesnake." There was the usual respectful pause, then he opened his mouth to continue. "Of course, the bites are rarely fatal to humans, if prompt medical attention is sought, but to a small dog it would be certain and painful death. To be fair, scorpions are a great deal more common, and to a dog of this size, a scorpion bite could easily be fatal. But the best weapon against a scorpion is a stout pair of boots." He blushed. "For a human, that is; the dog might have trouble with boots." He hesitated. "And he would need two pairs."

Mason turned to Julia. "It's not even so much that he knows all this stuff, it's that he sounds like an encyclopedia entry when he says it."

Julia nodded. "He can't help it. He learns it as he reads it." She added. "Thank you as ever, Will, for knowing the answers to everything. Ignore her—she's just jealous."

"True story," said Mason. "What else have you found out?"

"Uh, on the night of Tony's murder, Jason Reed was indeed at a movie premiere, and Helen Eckenridge was volunteering at the animal shelter, so that really only leaves Cody, Christine and Jade, who spent the early part of the evening at the hospital. And Cody presumably didn't attack himself, although that's a clever way to offset suspicion. Plus whoever else we haven't thought of yet. What about Maggie Galliano?"

"They seemed to still be very close. Why would she kill him?" Mason wasn't convinced. "And, no offense, but Jade doesn't seem like a killer to me."

"Stupid people kill other people all the time, Mason."

"True." Mason turned to Ben. "Speaking of which, do *you* know where Becky is?"

Julia answered for him. "No, nobody knows where she is but me, and you need to stop being so judgmental. Becky's actually a smart cookie, she's safe, and that's all you need to know. The fewer people who know where she is, the safer she is."

Mason was still looking at Ben. "Does your grandmother know she's gone? What if she calls some of her fellow witches and casts a finding spell or something?"

Ben shook his head. "She doesn't know yet. I spoke to her yesterday and told her Becky was with her lawyer." He shrugged. "I don't know if she's reached out to the local coven yet. I'm trying to persuade her to just go home and wait, but she's not going for it yet." He laughed. "I talked to Becky the night Grandma arrived, and she was losing her mind. She thinks Grandma had something to do with Sam's death."

"Why is that such a crazy notion? Your grandma isn't exactly overflowing with the milk of human kindness."

"True, but she's not a murderer. She wasn't even in Los Angeles."

The door to the office opened and Archie walked in. There was only a little bit of room left on the sofa, so Mason promptly stood and indicated Archie should take her seat. There was an awkward little medley of hand gestures, which everyone watched with interest. Mason opened with a simple upturned palm, "go ahead, take the spot" gesture. Archie countered with a double palms up, headshake combination move. Mason followed up with a contracted eyebrow, slightly firmer open palm gesture, which Archie met and trumped with a definite frown plus closed eyes and one palm up, shaken, which several in the crowd felt was throwing in his cards too early. Mason sidestepped and simply pointed, with emphasis, a ballsy show of force that could have backfired, had Archie not suddenly realized everyone was watching them, got embarrassed and sat. Mason, trying not to gloat, folded up like origami and sat on the floor.

There was a short silence.

Then Julia said, "Well, now that the whole team is here, and Archie and Mason have performed their strange little courtship dance, maybe we can recap where we are." She turned to Will. "Are you ready?"

"Yes," said Will. "I've made a PowerPoint."

"Of course you have," replied Julia. "And we love you for it. The floor is yours."

34

WILL CLEARED HIS throat.

"Things are starting to feel a little complicated." He coughed. "I kept the presentation simple, no big transition effects or anything, but it gets the job done." He got to his feet, tugged up his pants and stepped to the front of the room. "Mason, can you get the lights?"

Mason complied and, sitting back down, realized she'd misjudged and landed really close to Archie's knees. She was a full-grown, kick-ass woman, but this lawyer made her feel like she was back in middle school, trying to negotiate the suddenly fraught physical space between teenagers. Luckily, the lights were off.

Will had produced a laser pointer and started the presentation.

"The first event was Tony Eckenridge's death."

A slide came up showing crime scene photos of Tony's body in the pool, then Will clicked to the next slide, the coroner's report. "Gunshot wound to the head, death instantaneous, no water in his lungs, this we all know."

He clicked on again. "The first suspect was Julia." He

brought up a slide with Julia's mug shots from her original arrest, then clicked on to another, slightly more recent mug shot, then on again to another.

"Very funny," said Julia, dryly.

"Jeez, how many times have you been arrested?" Mason asked.

"I've lost count, and they've stopped doing it so much lately. In the nineties it was a regular occurrence. But eventually they lost the will to fight." Then, more quietly, "And I had long stretches of sobriety and was a model citizen, at least externally."

Will continued. "Other suspects include, but are not limited to, Helen Eckenridge, Tony's wife"—he had photos—"Christine Greenfield, his partner; Jade Solomon, although saving Mason does move her off the list slightly; Jason Reed; and Cody Malone, Tony's assistant."

"Why Cody?" Mason said. "He loved Tony. And what, he bashed himself over the head after killing the fish and ransacking his own office?"

"I see your point, but he did benefit from Tony's death." Will kept clicking. "And then anyone and everyone he ever irritated, beat in a deal, cut out of a picture, passed over for promotion, etc., etc."

"That's a long list." Julia sighed. "Did we check everyone's alibi?"

"Well, not everyone he ever cheesed off, but anyone close to him," said Will. "Helen was supposedly at the dog shelter, and I got a confirmation on the phone." He hesitated. "I wasn't able to go in person. I have allergies."

"To dogs?" Julia seemed surprised. "That's news to me."

"No, to shelters. They make me break out in tears."

Julia seemed like she was about to roll her eyes, but she softened. "Fine, Mason, go check it in person. I don't want to miss something."

Mason nodded.

Will continued. "Next, chronologically, Jack Simon was killed. Or died. I'll get to him in a minute. I put him after because we don't know for sure it's even related."

"It'd be pretty weird if it wasn't, but weird happens all the time around here," said Julia.

Will nodded. "You're not wrong, but let's stick with the presentation. Julia got attacked outside Galliano's, someone broke into this house, and someone ransacked the production offices, although yes, probably not Cody. That all happened in one night, so either we have a very busy bee on our hands or more than one perpetrator."

"Don't forget a load of fish were killed," Mason added.

"Yes." Will clicked and a slide of tropical fish came up. Of course.

"Then Mason got attacked, and the attacker made it clear that he wanted Julia to stop investigating Tony's murder." He brought up a short video of Mason in the hospital, professing undying love for Claudia's baked goods.

"Where did that come from?" Mason was pissed.

"Oh my God, that's adorable," Archie said, "in a beaten-up kind of way." He was clearly still smarting over losing the seat argument.

"And wait," added Mason, "aren't you forgetting the murder at Galliano's?"

Will looked at her. "I have a separate PowerPoint for that case."

"But what if they're not separate? Tony was married to

Maggie Galliano, remember? He spent plenty of time there. Maybe they are connected."

"And it just happens that we have a personal connection to the accused in that case? Isn't that a bit of a coincidence?" Archie wasn't convinced.

Mason shrugged. "We have a connection to all of it, right? Julia knew, or knows, everyone involved in both of the cases. Maybe she's the missing link." She grinned, her teeth glinting in the dark. "Maybe it was really her that killed Tony."

"You credit me with more energy than I have." Julia looked thoughtful. "To be fair, I have motive in that I inherited a studio, means in that there was a gun found on my property, and opportunity insofar as Tony was right there standing next to the pool." For a second, she got a faraway expression on her face. "Shit, for a moment there I got a flash of memory, but it's gone again." She shrugged. "Damn that inebriated hypothalamus. Back to Jack Simon."

"Wait, you're getting ahead of my presentation. I have more slides." Will was getting flustered. "And Inebriated Hypothalamus is another great band name."

Archie spoke. "Maybe Mason's right. When was the last time Tony was at Galliano's, before he was killed?"

"A while ago, Maggie said," Mason remembered.

"But maybe he left something there, or told Maggie something important, or maybe Sam overheard something she shouldn't have." Archie was clearly warming to this idea. "I think you guys should go back and talk to Maggie again."

Will plowed on.

"Backing up in the timeline to the day of Tony's funeral, Jack Simon apparently killed himself, totally out of the blue and out of character, according to his friends." He pulled up

the coroner's report. "Mr. Simon, and this part is more in character, was pretty drunk when he shot himself, in the chest, in
a sand trap. Squeamish people, look away." He brought up the
photos of the suicide scene, and suddenly went still. "Wait a
second . . ."

"What is it?" Julia was looking at Will, rather than the
picture.

"Where are his footprints?"

They all looked at the picture. Jack Simon was lying essentially in the middle of the sand trap, wearing cutoff jeans and
a polo shirt, barefoot like the loving flower child he was. He
looked very peaceful, and only the gun and the dark stain in
the sand indicated he was doing anything other than sleeping
off a rough night.

"There are footprints all over the place." Mason was confused.

"Yes, but they are all shoes. Where are his prints? He had
to walk out there, right?"

Will zoomed in on the photo and slowly went over it, inch
by inch. "Look, here are the prints of golf shoes, which are presumably from the groundsman who found him, and there are
several pairs of regulation boots, which are the police clomp-
ing around, but there aren't any barefoot prints at all."

"Maybe they got messed up with all the people walking
around."

"All of them?" Will zoomed in on the area around Jack Simon's feet, and cried out in glee. "Not a single one, but here's
a drag mark, half hidden by his legs. He didn't walk out; he
was dragged. And then whoever dragged him raked the sand
everywhere except right around the body. They assumed there
would be plenty of footprints, and they were right, but they

forgot nobody else would be barefoot." He pulled back out of the shot, and then paused again.

Will swallowed. "Look . . . there *was* someone else there, see?" There were other prints in the sand, dozens of them, circling away, returning, looping in on themselves. He tracked the prints over to the body, where they ended in a flattened patch near the head. "Someone waited with him quite a while, didn't they?" He reached over and scratched Lorre's head, as they all took in the clear evidence that Jack Simon's dog, at least, hadn't left him to die alone.

35

~~~

IF AN ALIEN landed in Los Angeles, not that anyone would notice, they might come away thinking dogs ruled the city. Firstly, because there are so damn many of them. Walk down any street and you'll see dozens. People take them everywhere: to work, to cafés, to dinner, to dates, you name it, dogs welcome. They would also notice that the dogs are carried, worshiped, catered to. Many restaurants have water and even food dishes outside, and people lovingly pick up their poop, seal it in specially designed bags and place it carefully where it will be safe. They might be misreading that last part, but they are aliens, after all.

Despite all that, the Los Angeles Dog and Cat Shelter is always full. People throw away dogs all the time, and because the city leans toward no-kill solutions to its pet problem, there is a steady business taking small dogs from LA and transporting them to shelters all over the country, where small dogs are at a premium and can be found homes. It's a cottage industry.

Mason didn't love the shelter. There was a sense of panic and despair that permeated everything, layered under the smell of disinfectant and cat litter. As it was a Sunday, there were plenty of people hovering around, presumably hoping to find the dog or cat that would complete their lives. Mason thought about it for a moment, then went into the dog side, knowing damn well that she'd walk out with a cat if she went in the other door. As if Phil wasn't already mad enough.

She approached the desk where a woman was frowning at a computer screen.

"Hi, I'm . . ."

The woman held up a hand. Her sweatshirt said "Dog Fur Is My Glitter" and she wore a pin that said "Dog Whisperer" and a baseball hat that said "Who rescued who?" but her affect said if Mason interrupted her vital work she would eviscerate her with a dog toy and give less than zero fucks about it. Mason was familiar with the type and closed her mouth. She could wait.

Eventually, the woman sighed and hit the enter key with enough force to drive it down through the desk, and looked up at Mason. Her graying hair framed her face under the baseball hat and made Mason think of an Airedale. Context is everything.

"Surrendering an animal?"

Mason shook her head.

"Adopting?"

Mason shook her head again.

"Selling something?"

Third shake's the charm.

"Nope, I'm looking for someone who can confirm Helen Eckenridge was volunteering here the night of the first."

The woman deepened her frown. "Who's asking?"

"I am."

"And you are?"

"Natasha Mason. I'm investigating a crime."

"Are you?" If you'd happened to flip open a dictionary to "skeptical," there would have been a big fat picture of this woman. "Are you the police?"

"I am not."

"Are you from the city? A licensed investigator? A friend of hers?"

"None of those. Just someone asking a question."

"How do I know you're not a crazy stalker?"

Mason was forced to admit the logic of this. "You don't. I'm not trying to get her personal information. I just want to check that she was here when she claims to have been here. It was two weeks ago tomorrow night."

"Sorry, volunteer information is personal and private."

"Why?"

"Because."

Mason thought for a moment. "I only need confirmation. I don't need to know what she did while she was here. I just need to know if she was, in fact, here."

"You'll have to ask her."

"I did. She said she was. I'm just . . . confirming it."

"Can't help you."

Mason decided to accept this as fact. "Can I look at the dogs?"

"Sure." If the woman was surprised by this change of tack, she didn't show it. She pointed. "Through that door. Small dogs to the left, big dogs to the right." She looked back at her computer, and Mason realized she had just ceased to exist. There were dogs to be saved. People could go fuck themselves, and she could go first.

She went through the door and turned right.

~~~~

THE BIG DOGS were mostly pit bulls, sadly. Mason wandered the cages, smiling at the friendly, grinning, largely harmless and mostly confused dogs. They knew they were good boys and girls, they weren't sure why they were here, but if anybody wanted to throw a ball or chase a stick they were totally down. Also down for just sitting and grinning, if that was what you wanted. Basically down for anything, because they were dogs, and we don't deserve them.

In one corner she found a young woman lifting fifty-pound bags of dog food and offered to help.

"Do you volunteer here a lot?" she asked, as she effortlessly threw the sacks of dog food into a smaller room. It was obviously the main storage room; medications and veterinary equipment lined the walls.

"Yeah," said the woman, somewhat shyly. "I like dogs better than people." She'd been happy to accept the help and was secretly a little crushed out on this hip-looking chick who could lob a fifty-pound bag of food as easily as she chucked a bag of dog treats.

"I get that," said Mason. "I'm partial to cats myself."

"Oh, I like cats, too," said the woman. "I have four."

"That's a nice round number."

The woman laughed. "They're nice round cats."

Mason said, "My friend volunteers here, too. You might know her? Helen?"

The woman nodded. "I know Helen! She's always here on Wednesdays. I do Mondays but also Tuesdays and Wednesdays. Sometimes Fridays. And Sundays sometimes, like today."

Mason laughed. "So, most every night, then?"

"Yeah." The woman was somewhat rueful. "I don't have much of a life outside, to be honest. I'm happiest in here." She watched as Mason finished unloading the last of the dog food. "Helen likes it, too. She was here three times the other week. Normally, she just does Wednesdays, but we were both here that Sunday and part of Monday, too. In the evening."

"Oh yeah? Week before last?"

"Yeah. We were taking inventory, I remember. I think that's why she came in; we needed all hands on deck. We counted every last bag of food, every medical supply, every blanket and towel. We finished up on the Monday evening after the shelter was closed, and she was there, too."

"Wow, that's a lot," said Mason. "You must have been here all night."

The woman shrugged. "I was; other people came and went."

"And Helen?"

"I didn't see her leave," said the woman, frowning a little at Mason. "She was doing this wing and I was on the other side. The cat side."

"What about last Saturday. Were you here then?"

"Yeah. Didn't see Helen, though." The girl looked at Mason for a moment, and Mason worried she was getting suspicious. But then she said, "I don't suppose you feel like helping me move some cat litter, do you? We just got a delivery and there are two dozen fifty-pound bags of that, too."

"I would be thrilled," said Mason. "Upper body done for the day, right?"

The woman nodded, and turned to lead the way to the loading dock. With all this help, she was going to have time to spend in the kitten room. Score.

~~~~

LATER, DRIVING HOME, Mason called Will.

"Helen was at the animal shelter the day before Tony was killed, doing inventory," she said. "And at least briefly on the night he was killed. However, she wasn't there the night of Tony's funeral, so I suppose she could have driven to Palm Springs and killed Jack Simon, although I have no idea why she would. I have a witness for the night of Tony's murder, but she can't confirm what time Helen left."

"Wait, you got that harridan at the front desk to confirm it? She wasn't interested in helping me at all. I think I had two legs too few."

Mason laughed. "I had to go at it another way. She wasn't interested in me, either. Too hairless." She added, "It was unusual for Helen to be there so much, though. She's normally just there on Wednesdays. Maybe she just needed some animal companionship, and they were doing inventory, like I said. The witness said everybody who volunteers was basically there for that."

Will made a noise. "Did we ever find out where Christine was that night, the night Tony was killed?"

"Yeah, she was at Cedars, with Jade Solomon and Cody."

"All night?"

"Most of it. We don't have eyes on Christine the whole time, though. Cody and Jade alibi each other, but Christine was elsewhere in the hospital. They left together, though. We have a TMZ photo. None of them were allowed to use their phones." Mason slowed for a red light. "Which is presumably why Tony left Christine a voicemail message, rather than actually speaking to her. She says he told her Julia had agreed to

be in *The Codex*. She said it at the funeral. We heard the message." She thought for a moment. "What about the night of the
funeral?"

"Well, Jason Reed and Christine were at the funeral after
party..."

"There was a funeral after party?" Mason rolled her eyes.
"What about Helen? Jade?"

"Jade was there. Helen I'm not sure. Cody was not there; he
said he went back to the studio to work, and that was before
he even knew he was inheriting the studio. I guess that work
ethic is why Tony left it to him." He paused. "Hey, are you going to Cinespia to see *The Codex*? Just cause Julia's not going
doesn't mean we can't."

"Good point. You going to dress up?"

"Yeah," he replied, and Mason could hear the grin in his
voice. "I'm wearing the silver catsuit."

"That'll look nice," said Mason. "And they can bury you in
it once Julia tears your head off."

"You gonna dress up?"

"Not in a million years."

Will laughed. "Hang out with Julia long enough, you'll find
yourself in costume before you know it. Good night, Mason."

"Good night, Will."

36

~~~

MASON WAS STARTING to realize that when Claudia showed up at the office door without a tray, she rarely brought anything but trouble.

It was four days after the Palm Springs trip, and Mason found herself a little scratchy with her boss, who also had her nails out. Nothing had happened on the cases, no new information, no new clues, no nothing. Julia was clearly frustrated and Mason was getting antsy. They'd been spitting at each other on and off all morning, so when Claudia opened the door, both of them were privately relieved that something had come along to break up the slow-motion fight they were having.

"You have company," Claudia said. "I put them in the front room. I'll get coffee."

"What kind of company?" asked Julia.

"Extensive." Claudia looked vexed. Clearly, there was something in the air. "Helen Eckenridge, Jade Solomon, Christine Greenfield, Patty Menninger and Jason Reed."

Julia's expression struggled to land on either horror or amazement. "All of them? Like, together?"

Claudia nodded. "They came in three cars, in convoy."

Mason stood up and shook out her jeans. "Do you want me to go and see what they want? I could just turn a hose on them."

Julia shook her head. "No, I can handle it. Come and take notes."

But it turned out they weren't there to answer questions. They were there to ask one.

"No," said Julia, firmly. "Thank you, but no."

Jade looked the most obviously crestfallen. She frowned, blindingly pretty. "But it would be so much fun. We could both wear the silver catsuit and stand next to each other and it would be like before and after!"

Mason flinched and took her hands out of her pockets. Silence fell like a cleaver.

"Before and after?" Julia's voice was cool. "Like, the old and the new? The traditional and the modern? The classic and the improvement?"

Jade blinked like a doe marveling at oncoming headlights. "Well, sure, but I was thinking more the peerless original and the upstart who dares to touch her hem. The Oscar winner and the amateur. The timeless beauty and the flavor of the month." She grinned, losing some of her ingenue innocence. "The lioness and the alley cat." She literally looked at the ground, exposing the back of her neck for the bite.

Mason had been watching Julia's face for signs of snarling, so she had a front row seat for the internal conflict war. Amusement won the fight.

"Nicely put," said Julia. She looked at Jade properly for the first time, a searching evaluation. "You're very lovely, and you did excellent work in *Prosecco Summer.*"

Jade squeaked and went red. Genuinely red. "You saw that?"

Julia nodded. "It was not a good film. But you were good in it."

Claudia walked in with her tray, and Patty Menninger looked it over thoughtfully.

"Fresh fruit," she said. "Is it local?"

Claudia nodded. "Extremely. Back garden."

"Organic?"

Another nod.

"And washed in filtered water?"

Claudia's left eyelid trembled, ever so slightly. She was about to tell a whopper.

"Yes." Beat. "From Iceland."

Patty looked relieved, then concerned. "Water from Iceland? By air?" Her hand hovered above the fruit.

Claudia's body language was giving Girl Scout energy. "No, native artisans responsibly farm ice in the fjords, then tow giant blocks behind a ship running on biodiesel. The ice is packaged in hemp, to protect it from becoming polluted on the journey, and the hemp is then recycled. Gratefully."

"Super," said Patty, choosing a strawberry.

Christine coughed. "They're playing *The Codex* this weekend at Cinespia. The studio is covering the cost of tickets for the first five hundred attendees, sponsoring the food trucks, the DJ, everything. The remake is going to be the tentpole movie of the new Repercussion. We want to start promoting now and not stop until the movie opens." She smiled, transforming again in front of their eyes. "You being there would be an enormous coup. It would make it really special."

Patty chimed in, "And the museum is underwriting a set

of custom picnic blankets to be handed out as souvenirs. We're going to have a *Codex* exhibition timed to the release of the new movie. It's really going to be quite a big deal, Julia. Please play well with others."

Julia frowned at Patty and then looked at Mason. "What do you think?"

Mason was surprised. "Does it matter what I think?"

Julia nodded. "Yes."

Mason decided to go with the truth. "I think you're an icon for the kind of people who go to Cinespia." The outdoor movie series ran every summer, playing classics old and new under the stars in the Hollywood Forever Cemetery. "I think people will be thrilled to see you, I think the movie will sell out, I think Jade will do her best to look good alongside you, and I think it'll be a fun night." She paused. "Everyone will be there. The whole team can come with you."

Julia looked at her. "Well, that makes it slightly less fun."

Helen spoke up. "Hard to show a streaming series under the stars, huh, Jason?"

Jason made a face, but kept his tone neutral. "I guess that would depend on how many episodes we sold, Helen."

Julia raised an eyebrow, but carried on. "Do I have to say anything?"

Christine shook her head. "Not unless you want to."

"I want to say something about Bella."

If Christine was surprised, she didn't show it. "Of course."

"Won't that be a bit of a bummer?" asked Helen. "Tony always said it was just an accident."

The door opened again and a young woman came in. Christine looked over. "I thought you were waiting outside?"

"It got very hot," said the young woman. She looked like

every other young female executive assistant in Hollywood—overqualified. She shook back her sleeves and consulted her phone. "You have a four p.m. at the Chateau."

Christine nodded. "Everyone, this is Chelsea, my new assistant. She'll be helping Helen coordinate the Cinespia evening." She looked at the young woman. "We're very close to the Chateau here," she said, "but we should get going." She looked at Julia. "So . . . will you do it?"

Julia nodded. "I will. Not sure why I will, because I've been determined not to, but I will. It's probably crazy, but why not." She laughed. "Larry will be insufferable."

Jade jumped up and down and squealed. She was alone in this, but she didn't care. "Oh, this is thrilling. I remember watching your movies when I got home from middle school."

"Do you?" said Julia, dryly.

"Alright," said Jason, getting up and herding his leading lady toward the door. "Let's get going. I have a meeting."

Everyone was on their feet and moving. Mason was watching the assistant, Chelsea, who was eyeing Jade Solomon as if she'd never seen a movie star that close before—and maybe she hadn't—so she missed seeing exactly what happened, but suddenly Helen's voice was raised.

"It's not as simple as that, Jason. You're welcome to bring on whatever writers you need, but Tony's will makes it very clear: I get adaptation and original story credit regardless."

"I'm not suggesting you shouldn't. I merely said I thought a new set of eyes might liven up the action a bit . . ."

Christine kept the group moving, though, and just as Mason realized Helen and Jason were both genuinely angry and spoiling for a fight, they were through the door and gone. She looked back at Julia and realized she'd left the room. She tracked her down in the office, where she was standing by her desk, looking uncharacteristically aimless.

Mason closed the office door. "I cannot believe you said yes to Cinespia."

Julia shrugged. "You and me both. To start with, I thought it would be useful to see all the suspects together in one place . . . then that little actress surprised me."

"Yeah . . . Jason said she was no rocket scientist but put her in a role and she really shines."

"Then he probably wrote that speech for her. Or Helen did. Some actresses bring their own brains to work; others borrow other people's. Both ways work."

"Do you think Tony's death is related to *The Codex*?"

Julia shrugged. "Maybe. I find it hard to believe anyone would kill over an old movie, but everything points to it being connected to the studio."

Mason saw her lift the packet of letters from Tony to Jack Simon and hesitate. Flip through one or two, nearly pull them out of the envelopes, then put them back in the pile.

"Do you think those are important?"

There was a long silence, then Julia sighed. "I don't know. They span many years, and it's clear the two of them were good friends. The last letter, which was sent a few weeks before he died, mentions that he's sorry B and Jack were fighting about Jack coming back to LA. I guess for the movie? That's all he says, and we don't have Jack's letters back, so I have no idea who B is or why she was upset or what Jack decided to do. We need to find B. I think we need to go back to Palm Springs." She put the packet of letters in a drawer, and closed it. "I've said it before: Tony had this way of making everyone feel special. It was only once you realized he did it to everyone that you realized it didn't mean very much."

Then she turned to Mason and frowned. "I never thought I'd hear myself say this, but I think I need a meeting. I'm cross, and it's everyone's fault but mine."

"A meeting's always a good idea," said Mason, opening the meeting app on her phone to find the next available time. She flicked the screen. "There's one on Sunset in forty minutes. You can get your court card signed." She glanced over at Julia, who was still looking at the drawer she had just closed. "You OK?"

Julia nodded and turned to grab a jacket. "Yes. I'm fine. Just old thoughts in an old head. It'll pass." She tugged on the jacket and headed to the door. "I'm letting ghosts get in my way. Let's go."

37

DESPITE THE MEETING, Julia continued to be silent and thoughtful as they headed down the freeway toward Palm Springs. As they passed the wind turbines again, Mason tried to engage her in conversation.

"Did you spend a lot of time in Palm Springs when you were younger?"

Julia nodded. "There was a time when Jonathan and I were here a lot. We had a house here; everybody did. It seemed very far away from Los Angeles, while having the advantage of not being literally all that far away. Two or three hours is just long enough to unwind from on-set antics, studio politics, etc." She laughed. "And long enough for the drugs to kick in or wear off, whichever you need."

Mason grinned. "Or for the first lot to wear off and the second lot to kick in."

"Exactly." Julia shrugged. "Makes me wish we hadn't sold the house, but I sold it while I was in jail and wasn't sure I was even going to come back to Los Angeles once I was done."

Mason shot her a look. "But you did."

"I did. Because my life had always been there, my friends

were all there, and of course my enemies. I really thought I was going to come out and wreak revenge on Tony and everyone else who hadn't helped me when I needed them. But by the time I was out, I was kind of over it." She shrugged. "I was in prison for a little over fifteen years, and that's a long time to nurse a grudge. I don't have the stamina for it. Besides, I needed all the grit I had to persuade the California Bar Association that I was fit to be admitted. They let ex-cons become lawyers, but they're sticky as fuck about it. It took several years, but they finally got tired of my not getting tired, I guess."

"Plus you didn't do it."

"According to the law I did, I just also did the time the crime required, and got parole before my sentence was up. I maintained my innocence, but a lot of people do."

There was silence for a few minutes while Mason tried to decide how to ask Julia for more information without upsetting her. But Julia took it out of her hands.

"You know, going to prison for something you didn't do is pretty much one of the worst things I can imagine. It was terrifying, being arrested. I was working that day, on another movie for Repercussion. They came and took me from set, did you know that? Tony was there. Casper was even there, visiting. Jonathan had gone missing for a couple of days, which wasn't itself all that unusual, but I knew something was wrong. Someone always knew where he was, or heard he was partying somewhere, or with some girl, or whatever, but that time no one knew where he was and no one saw him anywhere. I'd ignored it for the first day, but after three days I reported it to the police and started hunting in earnest. I'd had to go to work, I almost welcomed the distraction, but I was having a hard time focusing, and Tony was actually, literally in the middle of yelling at me when the cops showed up. They'd found Jonathan's body on the hillside under the house. He'd been close to home all along." She looked out of the window, and sighed. "They took me to the morgue to identify his body, and something had eaten his ear; I remember that very clearly."

Mason swallowed. "Well, it would kind of stick out."

Julia laughed dryly. "Insofar as it was no longer sticking out? Sure."

Silence again, for a moment.

"I was beside myself. We'd been fighting a lot, and he was seeing someone on the side, and so was I. It was par for the course, though; neither one of us had any intention of leaving the other. It was just the way we lived, back then. So when the cops came back a few days later and arrested me, I couldn't get it through their heads that just because I was an unfaithful wife, it didn't mean I was a murderous one. They assumed I was jealous, probably drunk, and enraged, and had pushed him off the deck in a blackout. That was their case."

"That's what killed him, the fall from the deck?"

"That was the assumption. His neck was broken, and forensics weren't as advanced then as they are now, not by a long shot. I got a little crabby with them. There were plenty of witnesses to the very public fights we tended to have, and no other suspects. It wasn't a long trial, but it was as public as the fights had been."

"And you lost."

"In many senses. I lost the case, I lost faith in the system, I lost friends, my career was over, my life ended as I knew it . . . I was completely powerless, and when I got out I promised myself I would do whatever I could to help anyone else avoid the same experience. I didn't kill Tony, Becky didn't kill Sam, and neither of us are going to jail." She looked out at the turbines, spinning lazily far above them. "I always worry that birds get killed by those things all the time."

"You would think they would be able to avoid them. They're pretty unmissable."

"Sometimes you can see things coming but still can't avoid them."

Mason didn't think Julia was talking about the turbines anymore.

38

~~~~

EDDIE'S WAS BUSY, but no prettier in the early evening than it had been in the morning. Mason saw a few familiar faces, but no one who looked like they wanted to talk. Julia marched in and went over to the bar, hailing the bartender as if she were a regular. Which in some ways she was; a bar is a bar is a bar, to an alcoholic.

"Hi there," she said to the man working the counter. "Can I get two Cokes with a load of limes in one of them, please?"

"One lime slice is free; more than that will cost you."

"You're kidding," said Mason, raising her eyebrows. "This is Southern California. Limes are literally growing everywhere..."

The guy shrugged. "So go pick one."

"That's fine, Mason," said Julia, apparently not willing to fight over citrus slices. "The man has a business to run."

"He's not leaning into customer service," Mason said angrily, but Julia shook her head.

"It's not a big deal. Happy to pay for extra limes." She waved her hand conciliatorily, and after a moment the man put down two small Cokes, one of them with three whole slices of lime.

"Thank you," said Julia, taking a sip. "Delicious."

Mason turned her back on the bar, leaning there while she surveyed the room. This was her kind of place: dark, smoky, the music loud, the patrons already drunk and possibly spoiling for a fight. She saw one of Jack Simon's "girlfriends" sitting on her own and nudged Julia.

"Should we go talk to her?"

Julia shook her head. "No. I'm not sure Jack's girlfriends all knew about one another; someone more neutral would be better." She smiled and caught the bartender's eye. "Hey there, can I ask you some questions?"

The man finished serving a customer and came over reluctantly. "Is it about limes?"

Julia laughed. "No, I think we took care of that already. I wanted to ask you about Jack Simon."

The man looked at her distrustfully, then suddenly his face changed.

"You're Julia Mann." He paused. "The actress."

"Well, I'm retired now, but yes, I used to be an actress."

"You were a friend of Jack's. He talked about you sometimes." He cracked a smile, looking Julia up and down.

"We knew each other, yes. I hadn't seen him for a very long time, though, and I was sad to hear about his death."

"Yeah," said the guy, "I lost quite a customer."

"I bet he got all the limes he wanted," muttered Mason.

"He did," said the bartender, ignoring her sarcasm. "He was a serious regular, came in several nights a week for decades."

"Were you surprised by his death?"

"No," replied the man shortly. "Jack liked to play the field, didn't care if he trod on a few toes. He was a great guy, don't get me wrong, give you the shirt off his back, but there were more than a few husbands who might have shot him if he hadn't done it himself." He made a face. "Although I don't think he did that, either. He was going back to Los Angeles to be in a movie. He was looking forward to it."

"Do you know B? A regular girlfriend?"

The man's face closed down. "I don't know anything about that."

Julia tried again. "She was someone he must have talked about. They were together for years. Not exclusively, apparently, but very much together."

The man noticed a customer farther up the bar and turned to go. Then he turned back and leaned in. "You're barking up the wrong tree, lady."

"You don't think B had anything to do with his death?"

He laughed, rudely. "No, I don't know about that. But your mistake is in thinking B was a woman. I think B was a guy. Like I said, Jack liked to play the field. *Both* sides."

AFTER THAT, THE bartender refused to say any more, and Julia got a look on her face Mason was starting to be familiar with. Winnie the Pooh would probably call it *a thinking face*, but Mason saw it more as a plotting expression.

They sat down at the table next to the ex-girlfriend, and in a few moments she leaned over.

"Hey . . . are you that actress?"

Julia smiled at her. "I'm AN actress, but there are lots of us."

"Yeah, but you're the one who knew Jack, right? Julia Mann. You went to prison. And won an Oscar."

"Not in that order, but yes to both. We were here hoping to find out some more information about Jack, actually. Can we ask you some questions?" Mason was impressed at how easily Julia befriended people, when she was normally so prickly. She was realizing more and more that Julia could be many people in the course of a day.

The woman shrugged. She was maybe in her mid to late fifties, and cute in a well-preserved, still-takes-care-of-her-skin kind of way. Healthy, despite her current location and clearly regular state of inebriation. "Sure. I was just sitting here thinking about him, actually. He was a lot of fun. I miss him."

Mason sat back a little to let Julia take the lead.

"This might be a delicate question, but were you aware that Jack had, um, many friends? Romantically speaking, I mean."

"Sure," replied the woman, good-naturedly. "Jack was many things, but dishonest wasn't one of them. He didn't believe in monogamy, said it stifled the natural energy of the universe." She laughed. "I think it just stifled him, to be blunt. We hung out here a lot, hooked up occasionally if the mood struck us, but it was never much more than that. He had a serious relationship he always went home to, you know what I mean?"

"Yes, so we've gathered. What do you know about it?"

"It was with a guy, I know that. Someone he'd known up in Los Angeles, many years ago."

"Whose name began with B?"

The woman made a face. "That rings a bell, but I don't know for sure. He didn't talk that much about it. He maybe only mentioned it once or twice to me."

"And it didn't bother you?" Mason asked.

"Not at all." The woman was philosophical. "At my age, you realize living the life other people expect you to is a waste of time. Jack lived what he believed in; it was pretty freeing. I've been married three times. Commitment can be a bit of a buzz-kill, if you know what I mean. The idea that you can meet someone in your twenties, get married, have kids and forty years later still feel the same way about them is pretty far-fetched. Jack loved this guy, though, truly. I'm sure he's bro-kenhearted."

"And you think this guy was in Los Angeles?" Julia sounded a little disappointed. Another dead end.

Surprisingly, the woman shook her head. "Oh no, he's here. He belongs to the same club Jack does. They saw each other all the time. I don't think it's acknowledged there, though. One time Jack made a joke about it being an open secret that was more secret than open, although I wasn't really sure what he meant. You could ask around. Maybe someone there knew more than he thought."

She looked into her empty glass and then up at Julia, hope-fully. "One for the road?"

Julia motioned to Mason. "Not for us, but we'll happily get one for you. What are you drinking?"

"Vodka tonic," replied Jack's sad ex-girlfriend. "Jack's fa-vorite."

Mason got to her feet. "I'll see if they can spare some extra lime."

ONCE THEY WERE back outside the bar, Julia was all business.

"I have a sneaking suspicion Robert might have known

more than he was letting on," she said. "Let's go back and see if we can talk to him again. He was pretty familiar with the house for someone who 'barely exchanged more than twenty words' with Jack."

But when they got to the club, they were told Robert was out and had been out all day. Julia sat down at the bar and ordered a soda water, and waited until the attendant was out of earshot.

"Alright, go commandeer a golf cart. We're going back to the house."

"What?"

"You heard me. Steal a golf cart. How hard can it be? I'm sure loads of them are just sitting there with the keys still in them. Who expects grand theft auto at a country club?"

Mason shook her head. "I hate to burst your bubble, but I've never driven a golf cart in my life, and I'm not starting under pressure."

Julia gave her a withering look. "You give off this ball-busting attitude, but actually you can't fight and you're too chicken to steal what is essentially a motorized shopping cart. Fine. I'll do it."

And she got up and walked out of the bar.

39

~~~~

A ROW OF golf carts stood outside the clubhouse, several of them complete with keys, as predicted. A trusting lot, here at the country club. Julia Mann smiled regally at everyone she passed, climbed into the first one and deftly reversed it out of the rank.

"Excuse me . . ." called a querulous voice. "I believe you've taken my cart by mistake." An old man stood nearby with his wife, color suffusing his face. "Easily done, of course."

"Oh, I don't think so," called back Julia. "Come on, Mason."

"No, I'm pretty sure . . ." replied the man's wife, less uncertainly. "Francis, call the attendant."

"Don't bother, Francis," said Mason, who suddenly realized Julia was leaving without her. "We'll bring it right back." She started to sprint after the golf cart, which was moving away more rapidly than she had anticipated.

"Francis!" said the wife, moving toward another cart. "Don't just stand there. After her!"

"How, my dear?"

"We'll take the Abernathys' cart. Come on."

Mason doubled her speed and flung herself on the back of the moving cart.

"Floor it," she yelled. "The old folks are in hot pursuit."

Julia looked over her shoulder. "Unfortunate that I picked theirs right in front of them." She rattled across the bridge. "Hold on, Mason, we'll lose them on the uphill."

But the hill made the cart slow down, and the old couple started gaining on them. Judging by the half smile on the old guy's face, this was the highlight of his week, possibly longer.

"Get off and run, Mason," said Julia calmly. "Your weight is slowing us down."

"Are you kidding?"

"Not in the slightest. Jump off and prevent them from continuing this ridiculous pursuit. Tell them I'll be right back. Charm them. Threaten them. Improvise!"

They could hear the old lady urging Francis to put his pedal to the metal. Literally.

Mason slid off the back of the cart, stumbling and nearly dislocating her ankle in the process, and started running toward the old couple, doing her best to look insane. She waved her arms in the air, made a horrible face and started roaring. She wasn't sure where any of this came from; she was just improvising, as instructed.

Amazingly, it worked. Francis hit the brakes, nearly flinging his wife ass over teakettle over the front. Then, proving he was made of sterner stuff than your average octogenarian, he threw the cart into reverse and began whizzing backward down the hill, the high-pitched keening of his wife competing with the whine of the engine under pressure. It's conceivable they hit fourteen miles an hour, but sadly, no one was there from Guinness World Records to adjudicate. They hit the bridge at top speed and clattered backward into the darkness.

Mason, having achieved her goal, turned back and started running up the hill. When she got to the top, Julia was no-where in sight, and it was with a great deal of cursing that Mason made her way to Jack Simon's house.

When she got there, she was surprised to see that the lights were on, and the golf cart was parked neatly outside. She started around the back of the house and came across her boss, pressed up against the wall. Julia held her finger to her lips and then pointed around the edge of the house. Music was playing on the outdoor speakers.

"*Codex* soundtrack . . ." said Julia. "I'm really starting to re-gret having anything to do with that film, not going to lie."

"You won an Oscar."

"Big fucking deal. Bella died, Jonathan died, Jack got black-balled, who knows whether Tony's death is connected. It seems like a high price to pay for ninety minutes of action and suspense." She paused. "I don't even think it was Jonathan's best work."

Mason didn't reply because she was still a little out of breath, but she peered around the corner of the building.

Robert was sitting in the hot tub. A nearly empty bottle of tequila sat on the edge, a small pile of lime wedges next to it. Mason spontaneously thought of the uptight barman at Ed-die's, and wondered at her inability to stay focused on what was important, which in this case was the gun that sat along-side the limes.

She made a noise and Robert immediately looked up and saw her, reaching for the gun and swinging it in her direction.

Mason ducked back behind the house. "Shit, he spotted me."

"Nice," said Julia, dryly. "You're a fucking ninja."

"You left me alone on the golf course, fighting for our freedom."

"You were scaring old people. It's probably what you live for." Julia was keeping her voice low, but still managing to give it a lot of emphasis.

"I know you're there . . ." called Robert. "You might as well show yourself. I'm not killing anyone tonight. Well, not including myself." He laughed, although it was a pretty feeble effort.

Julia straightened up.

"Don't even think about it," said Mason. "His use of 'tonight' suggests . . ."

But it was too late. Julia had already stepped out into the open.

The floodlights lit her long skirt as she walked, and as she approached the edge of the hot tub they illuminated her face.

The man in the tub made a noise.

"Julia Mann . . . ?"

"None other," she replied, reaching a sun lounger and plonking herself down as if she did this kind of thing every day. "I was a friend of Jack's." She paused. "And so were you, weren't you, Robert?"

The hand holding the gun wavered, then gently replaced it on the edge of the tub. Robert passed his wet hand across his face and nodded.

"I was. I was his best friend. His lover, for over thirty years. Not exclusively . . ." He made a motion with his head, a remembered denial, a pain. "Jack liked to be free, never pretended otherwise. So did I, to start with. We met in the city, when he was filming *The Codex* . . ." He gestured in the air, as if to touch the music. "An incredible film. You were amazing."

ONE DEATH AT A TIME

"Thank you," said Julia. She looked over her shoulder. "You can come out of hiding, Mason." She turned back to Robert. "He was going to leave you?"

Robert nodded. "They were remaking *The Codex*; they offered him a role. For so long he'd told me he didn't miss it, the whole life of a Hollywood actor, the parties, the friends who aren't friends, the drugs . . . We lived a quiet, private life down here. No one at the club knew about us. He would come in for dinner every night, play that we barely knew each other; it had started out as fun and became a habit. I'd come over a few nights a week, when he wasn't out with his other . . . connections. It was a small world we lived in, just the two of us." He looked up at Julia. "We did the crossword. We watched movies. He told stories and I listened." He sobbed, under his breath. "He was my whole world, had been since the day I met him."

Mason had approached but stopped a little way off. She kept her eyes on the gun where it lay in a small puddle, very much within reach. She wondered how long it would take the ambulance to get here if he shot Julia, or herself. They'd passed a hospital on the way. It might be close enough . . . They might get lucky.

"Why did you kill him?"

"I didn't mean to." There was a very long silence as Robert gazed down into the water. He was naked, Mason noticed, the lights of the hot tub making his thin legs look like ribbons in the water. She looked back at the gun, smelling the tequila, wondering how drunk he was, how true his aim might be.

"What happened?" asked Julia, softly.

"Why are you here?" he asked, instead of answering the question. "You are here, right? I'm not hallucinating a movie star?"

Julia shook her head, her voice soft. "No, I'm really here. He wrote about you, you know, to Tony Eckenridge. He called you his boo, used your initial . . . Did he call you Bobby?"

Robert nodded. "He was the only one."

"Did you know Tony?"

Robert nodded. "When we were first together, and later, more recently. Tony came down maybe once a year, hung out and reminisced." He looked up at her. "He talked about you a lot. He really cared about you. He worried about you."

Julia's mouth twisted. "No need."

Robert tipped his head to one side. "We worry about the ones we love, whether we need to or not." He shrugged. "I was worried that night. I was afraid of losing him. That he would go back to the city to do the film and then get all caught up in it, in the madness. He just laughed, said he hadn't loved it then and didn't think he'd love it now, but I saw his face. He was excited."

"What happened?" Julia asked again.

"We'd been drinking, of course. Smoking a little weed, watching an old movie."

"What movie?"

He smiled at the memory, the lights of the hot tub casting his eyes into shadow. "*Passport to Pimlico*. Classic Ealing comedy, one of my favorites."

"Then what?"

"Then the stupid dog started barking outside and Jack saw a scorpion on the side of the pool. He got his gun and went out to *battle the arachnids*, as he always called it. I followed him, kept asking him about his plans, if he was going to rent a place up there or go up and down, stuff like that. He accused me of being jealous before the fact, reminded me that we weren't married, that he had always been very clear that he didn't believe fidelity was healthy or even possible." He faltered, and looked at Mason. "He was a star when we met, you know. He was going places. Everywhere we went, people would just gravitate to him; he had so much energy, so much charm. And he was just beautiful. The most beautiful man I'd ever seen. And he chose me, just regular me. My own private star, performances every night in the beginning, Oscar-worthy." He poured himself another shot, his hand steady where his voice was not. "Not so much lately, of course. Thirty years is a long time, even in the life of a celestial being." He grimaced, and did the shot, reaching for a wedge of lime automatically. He threw it in the pool after sucking it, the fruit slicing through the air and splashing down, bobbing to the surface and floating. "He was only human, in the end."

"What went wrong?" asked Mason.

"Jack was waving the gun around and firing recklessly. He nearly shot the dog. I went to take it from him and he insisted he was fine . . . I had my hand on it, we struggled . . . it went off." He looked at the women. "Have you ever done anything terribly wrong, but you just couldn't help yourself?"

"I've rarely done anything else," replied Mason, honestly.

He nodded, then continued. "I panicked, dragged him onto the golf course and into the sand trap. Put him there, raked away my footprints, came back and washed the blood off the tile. I was very calm by then, did what needed to be done." He shrugged again. "I've waited for the police to come get me, but I guess they're not coming. Nobody seemed to question it, not until you."

He reached for the gun again, picked it up, pointed it at Julia.

"It seems totally reasonable that an actress is the one who caught me out. You can tell when someone else is playing pretend. That was you, that old lady?" He pointed the gun at Mason, briefly. "I didn't think she was your granddaughter, but I didn't realize you weren't who you said you were. But then again, who is?" He sighed. "And now you're going to call the cops and they're going to arrest me because I'm too tired to lie about it anymore. I'll be in prison for the rest of my life, just another old man who did a terrible thing and has nothing to show for his life but memories. No more stars, no more stories, no more Jack."

"There'll still be movies and crosswords," said Julia. "Prison isn't as bad as you imagine."

"You underestimate my imagination," he replied.

Then he turned the gun against his temple and blew his own brains out.

THE POLICE TOOK longer than you might think, seeing as they had two eyewitnesses to a suicide and were called instantaneously to the scene, but such is life. Mason started to explain that Robert had also confessed to another "suicide" they had on their books, but Julia gave her a look that caused her to subside immediately. In the scurry and tape of the crime scene, no one seemed willing to press her.

"It doesn't matter," Julia said, drawing Mason to one side. "Why complicate matters? We know what happened. Jack had no surviving relatives. Just let it lie."

Mason wasn't convinced. "But what if they reopen the case now that Robert has killed himself at the scene of a previous crime?"

"Why would they? As far as they're concerned, a broken-hearted man just killed himself after the suicide of his long-time lover. Which is essentially the truth, if not the complete truth. I'm all for justice being served, Mason, but in this case it's already been served."

Mason frowned, but let it go. She'd found the experience deeply shocking, and wanted to go home, see her cat and drink a liter of vodka, in that order. She knew she was going to do the first two, and hoped against hope she'd make it to a meeting before she did the third.

"Honestly," said Julia, tugging her wrap more securely around her, "it's all very sad, and I'm starting to believe in the *Codex* Curse myself."

"How is this to do with the curse?" Mason frowned. She didn't see any connection at all between this case and the other two murders, but maybe she was missing something.

"If Jack hadn't agreed to be in the remake, he'd still be alive, and so would Robert."

"So the new *Codex* is as cursed as the original? That's a stretch."

"Is it? I'm just seeing dead bodies."

Julia's phone rang. It was Claudia.

"When can you get back?" She sounded stressed. "Things are going on here I don't like. I had to throw a photographer out of the house earlier, and Will is refusing to eat because he's digging even harder into Galliano's now. Lorre is the only one who's bringing me any joy."

Julia outlined the situation, then paused. "Wait . . . why is Will digging even harder into Galliano's?"

Claudia made an exasperated noise. "Didn't he call you? I should have known; he's reached the muttering stage of his research. You know what he's like. He was supposed to call you an hour ago."

Julia shook her head. "We've been kind of busy, what with the cops and all. What happened?"

"Maggie Galliano got attacked. She's in the hospital. They're not sure if she'll make it."

Julia looked at Mason, who had overheard the conversation and was reaching for the car keys.

"Tell Will to eat something and keep digging. We'll be home in two hours, assuming Mason speeds as much as I want her to." She hung up and turned to Mason. "And no one's still angry about the golf cart thing." She paused. "Let's creep across the golf course and avoid the clubhouse. Better safe than sorry."

"An unusual choice for you."

"Yes," replied Julia, "but we're in a hurry."

40

~~~~

HOWEVER FAST MASON drove, she couldn't control the relentlessness of time, and in the end they didn't get back into LA until the wee hours of Thursday morning. Julia made the executive decision to go home, shower, change, do her hair, put on a full face of makeup and a new suit (mid-'80s Calvin Klein, big shoulders) and then felt justified when a crowd of paparazzi outside the hospital took her picture for a fat five minutes. Mason, who had showered and put on clean jeans, managed to stay out of the frame. It wasn't even eight a.m., she'd only had one coffee, and she was barely functional.

She and Julia rode up in the elevator, silently, and Mason slumped against the wall.

"I'm forty-plus years older than you. How come I have so much more energy?" asked Julia, disdainfully.

"I don't know," replied Mason. "Vitriol has more calories than I thought?"

Maggie looked pale against the pillow, but Danny Agosti's face was the color of blood. Presumably his own.

"I told you something like this was going to happen," he

spat at Julia as she and Mason came into the room. "I knew your poking around was going to cause trouble."

"To be fair," said Julia calmly, leaning down to kiss Maggie on the cheek, "you didn't anticipate this precise outcome. You were worried about your reputation, not your physical safety." She looked him up and down. "And you appear to be in fine fettle, so I'm not quite sure why you're so bent out of shape." She didn't mention the crowd of reporters outside the hospital, but presumably he'd seen them, too.

He was curt. "Because Maggie could have been killed."

"Don't be so stupid," said Maggie. "The guy didn't want to kill me. He wanted the will, whatever will it was he thinks I have. Which I don't." Maggie was clearly furious. "It's total bullshit, Julia. I was coming in the back, which I don't always do, often I'll come in the front, but today I went in the back and this guy . . ."

"You're sure it was a guy?"

"Yes, I know the feeling of a man's hands—let's face it, and a woman's—and this was a guy. Anyway, this guy steps out of fucking nowhere, puts his arm around my neck and says, *Where is it? Where's the will?*"

"The will?" Julia was frowning.

"Yes," Maggie spluttered. "As if I know. The only recently dead person I know is Tony, and of course Sam, and if either of them gave me a will to hold on to, it's fucking news to me."

"It seems more likely Tony would have left you a will. Sam was kind of young to be estate planning, no?"

"I agree." Maggie was still mad, but her eyes were gleaming. "But I didn't see Tony in his last few days. I was out of town at a burlesque convention."

"There are conventions?" Mason was incredulous.

Danny Agosti answered her. "Look, it's not the movie industry, but it's still a significant art form and a multimillion-dollar business." He shrugged. "When a murder on the premises isn't ruining things."

Mason looked at him. "You're really very money-focused, aren't you?"

"I'm a businessman."

Maggie was still steamed. "Plus, if he wanted to give me a will, he would have just called me. Why would he give me one anyway? He had a lawyer. Damn, he probably had more than one. And he left a will; it's not like he died without one. It doesn't make any sense. Which I told the guy."

"You told him?" Julia's mouth was twitching. "What did you say?"

"Well, once he'd taken his arm from around my neck, which was making it hard to breathe, let alone speak, I assured him I had no idea what he was talking about, had no will to offer him, mine or anyone else's, and then told him that if he didn't fuck off immediately I was going to call the bouncers and they would tear his nuts off."

Mason grinned. "And did that work?"

Maggie smiled at her. "Yes, he seemed very taken aback. He ran off. I don't think his heart was really in it. However, when he let me go, I stepped back, tripped over my own damn feet and fell against the wall. Gave myself a concussion. It's a little bit embarrassing, but what can you do?" She looked at Danny. "It isn't Julia's fault at all. There's no point getting mad at her." She patted his hand. "Just relax. I'll be back at work tomorrow." She paused. "Who's on tonight, anyway?"

"The Great Jacqueline and Barbra Thighsand."

Maggie laughed. "Fantastic drag name, gets me every

time. And Jackie will keep the masses entertained. Brian's on the floor?"

Danny nodded. "It's all in hand. Don't even think about it."

"Can we talk about the will some more?" asked Julia. "If someone thinks you have it, presumably someone thinks there's another will. If you don't have it, where is it, and more importantly, what's in it? What might Tony have done differently?"

"Left everything to the museum, for a start," said Mason. "That seemed to be something people were surprised by, something they thought he'd done."

"Maybe he gave it to you, Julia?" Maggie said, carefully tilting her head to one side. "Ouch, that was a bad idea. Maybe he gave it to you the night he was killed and you just don't remember?"

"He gave me that film and that was all." Julia paused. "I think." She frowned. "I vaguely remember a longish conversation, but I really . . ." She tailed off. "I remember him talking about Jonathan, but I don't remember what he said." She shrugged. "Sorry."

"Where were you?" asked Danny Agosti. "I tried calling you but it just went to voicemail."

"We were in Palm Springs." Julia looked at Maggie. "Did you know Jack Simon?"

"Of course," replied Maggie, "back in the day. Not so much lately. He and his boyfriend moved to the desert a million years ago."

"You knew his boyfriend?"

"Robert? Yes, I knew everyone back then. He was an actor, too, but not as successful as Jack. Jack always came first."

"He killed him."

"Robert killed Jack?" Maggie looked shocked, but then made a face. "It's surprising, but not as surprising as you might think. Being eclipsed gets old, and eventually gets enraging. Don't you think?"

"I don't know," said Julia, airily. "No one's ever come close."

41

~-~-~

LATER THAT MORNING, Julia called a council of war. That's not what she called it; she merely opened the kitchen door, glared at Will, Ben and Mason and said, "Office, now," but once they were there it was clearly a council of war.

"I've been thinking," Julia announced. "And I have questions."

Will nodded. "I am ready for your questions."

Ben said, "I doubt I'll have anything to contribute, but I'll try."

Mason said, "I'm barely alive. I've only had two cups of coffee. Don't try me." She'd finally gotten two hours of sleep after the hospital and woken up from a nightmare of trying to stuff Robert's brains back into his skull while Julia rode a bicycle naked around the pool. It hadn't been a restful dream. She needed more coffee. She needed a meeting. She wanted three Adderall and a shot of tequila.

Julia paced back and forth in front of the sofa.

"Firstly, we now know Jack Simon's death was not connected to Tony's."

Will nodded. "Insofar as he was killed by his boyfriend in a momentary lapse of control."

"Right."

"Unless Tony was also killed in a momentary lapse of control."

Julia paused. "It doesn't feel spontaneous like that. Someone had to follow him here, take a position where they couldn't be seen, shoot him and get away."

"Yes," said Will. "It's a plan, but not a fantastic plan. Why here? They couldn't know you would be drunk; you could have been sharp as a tack and spotted them." He lifted his shirt and scratched his stomach, comfortably. "There are so many other places they could have done it."

"Maybe they planned to kill me, too," said Julia. "Maybe Claudia's return threw them off."

"Why would they kill you?"

"Beats me," said Julia.

"Doesn't beat me," muttered Mason, still wishing she had a third cup of coffee. As if by magic, the door opened and Claudia appeared with a fresh pot and warm beignets.

"You didn't give them a chance to finish breakfast," she said sourly, putting the tray down. She left, Lorre following her out. He was no fool, plus he didn't think he was adding much to the conversation.

"How did they get away?" asked Ben. He was still looking worried, and Mason had realized this was his standard expression. He had Resting Anxious Face.

Julia said, "Presumably between me running off with the car and the cops arriving. Claudia was inside the house calling for help and I was halfway down the hill. Clear path. Assuming, that is, that they didn't just leave after they shot Tony, because I was too drunk to notice."

Ben nodded.

"And what about this business of a will? That feels somewhat random. Tony had a will in place. Why would he write a new one?"

"Presumably because he changed his mind about something. Maybe he didn't want to leave me the studio after all, on account of realizing I wouldn't . . ." Julia paused, her finger held up. "Wait . . . something's coming back to me. We did talk about the studio . . ." She frowned. "Nope, it's gone again."

"But the assailant asked Maggie for it, so they assumed it's at the club. Why would it be there?"

"Because Tony trusted Maggie to keep his secrets. Maybe he didn't want it publicly known that he'd changed his mind. Thus not using his regular lawyer?"

"Although Cody did say Tony wanted to talk to his lawyer before he died."

Julia looked at Mason. "Let's you and me go to the club and snoop about."

"Does it have to be today? I'm not . . ."

"Yes. We can't go in the evenings; it's open and way too busy. No time like the present."

"Does it have to be me? Take Will."

"No, you're my assistant. I want you to assist."

"Wait," said Will. "Are you thinking Sam's death is connected, too, now?"

"No, I'm not sure about anything. But let's get down there and check it out. Just because Maggie doesn't know she has it, it doesn't mean she doesn't have it." There was a pause. Then

Julia added, "That sentence didn't even make sense to me. Sorry. Let's go look—it won't hurt."

But that's where she was wrong.

DANNY AGOSTI WAS not happy to see them.

"Why are you here?" he asked, facing them across Maggie's desk. Her office had been a surprise to Mason. It was like every back office she'd ever been in; very little about it suggested glamor or burlesque in any way. Office supply catalogs and papers were piled on the desk, last year's calendar (naked cowboys, for what it's worth) still hung on the wall, a small bookcase held a dictionary, a few copies of *Variety*, and various other books. Apart from a rhinestone bra dangling over a chair, it could have been anyone's office.

Mason was turning slowly, looking over every inch of the room. Something was itching at the corner of her mind, but she couldn't bring it to the surface. She kept looking, hoping it would come to her.

"Maybe Sam was killed because she knew or saw something," suggested Julia. "Did she have a locker?"

"Yes," said Agosti, reaching in a desk drawer for a set of keys. "I want this sorted out as much as you do. Let's go."

Sam's locker had been searched by the police, and there wasn't much there. A few clothes, a copy of *Save the Cat!* (a screenwriting classic), some photos of her and Becky. Julia was disappointed.

"What about Becky's locker?" asked Mason suddenly. "They were together a lot. Maybe . . ."

Becky's locker was a crowded clusterfuck of underwear,

makeup, tangled headphones and loose dollar bills. Mason opened the door and stepped back as a load of things fell to the ground. She guessed the police had searched it, too, but hadn't bothered to organize it afterward.

"Why does this not surprise me?" she asked no one in particular. She bent to pick everything up and managed to clonk her head really hard on the open locker door as she stood up.

Ouch. Fuck. She reached up and felt a goose egg already rising on the crown of her head. Great, now she was going to have a headache to add to her litany of complaints.

But something had joggled loose. Something she'd seen. Something she remembered.

"Wait here," she gasped, and turned and ran out of the room.

"I DON'T UNDERSTAND how you knew where it was." Will was staring at Mason, who was still flushed with triumph.

"She's smarter than she looks," said Julia, taking off her coat and putting it on the office sofa. She reached out and gave him the will. "Apparently, she saw the hollow book in *The Codex* and recognized it on the shelf in Maggie's office."

Mason nodded. "Right, in the movie there's a gun in it, but I saw it on the shelf and it just didn't fit with everything else, too ornate. It took me a while to realize where I'd seen it before." She grinned. "And a clonk on the head with the sharp edge of a locker door, but whatever."

"Tony had lots of props at the office and at his house, so he must have put it there himself at some point while Maggie was away. It was witnessed by Sam and Becky, who apparently didn't realize its importance. Next time I see her I'm going to smack her." Julia was exasperated.

Will shrugged. "Pointless." He took the document from Julia and scanned it. "This doesn't make any sense. It's dated the day before he was killed, but the changes aren't . . . He leaves the studio to Christine and Cody, except for ten percent he leaves to the Entertainment Community Fund in Jonathan's name." He looked at Julia. "You don't remember him discussing this with you?"

"Actually, yes, I do. Once I read it, that part came back. I think originally he'd wanted to leave me part of the studio to make up for Jonathan's losing it. But he knew I wouldn't want to run the studio, and he was right. And there's one other difference: He gives Christine the controlling share, forty-six percent to Cody's forty-four . . . and that, along with the rights to the *complete* movie back catalog, without *The Codex* carved out, means it's her studio."

"Is that enough to kill for?"

Julia shook her head. "That's the part that confuses me. I mean yes, sure, having ultimate control might be worth killing for, but Christine really didn't seem that upset about the way the older will did it. If anything, she seemed amused by it." She turned to Mason. "Right? I mean, she must have discussed it with him at some point. She seemed to think he was leaving the whole thing to her, but when the will didn't reflect that she rolled with it."

Mason nodded and shrugged. "That's how it seemed to me, but who knows with her."

"He also left everything in his memorabilia collection to the museum, everything, just as Patty said he'd promised. And Helen gets the properties and the money, just the same.

He gives the ten percent of the burlesque club back to Maggie—that's different."

"We're missing something," said Will. "We must be. The will is important, but it doesn't completely prove Christine killed Tony. It just gives her a motive."

Julia was gazing at the ceiling. "I have an idea."

She looked at her colleagues.

"But you're probably not going to like it."

42

~~~~

THE HOLLYWOOD FOREVER Cemetery is one of the oldest cemeteries in California, and sits across the road from Paramount Studios. Presumably, if you drop dead on set, they'll just wheel you across. Dead movie stars continue to draw attention, which is doubtless satisfying for them, and as Mason leaned against the mausoleum for both Douglas Fairbanks AND Douglas Fairbanks, Jr., she watched a steady stream of moviegoers pause to pay their respects. She looked at the inscription, *Good night, sweet prince, And flights of angels sing thee to thy rest*, and wondered if either of these dudes were getting any rest, what with all the foot traffic.

Julia was on the other side of the cemetery, "backstage" near the big screen. A podium was set up in front of it, and Jason was going to introduce Julia, Jade and the movie, in that order. Mason was watching the door, so to speak, with Will, Archie and Ben scattered across the cemetery, each tasked with keeping an eye on a different suspect. Will was watching Jade Solomon (he'd been very quick to volunteer for that job), and Archie was keeping an eye on Jason Reed. Ben had tabs on Helen.

"What about Christine?" Mason had asked. "Isn't she the main event? Who's watching her?"

Julia had shrugged. "I'm going to be right next to her, and she's not very fast-moving." As she'd slid into the original catsuit from the movie, the ex-actress had tried—and failed—to conceal her satisfaction at still fitting into it. She'd muttered that if Jade Solomon had the balls to show up in the same outfit she was going to stab her with something. Sadly for her, the catsuit was iconic enough that Mason had seen maybe two dozen people wearing it, male and female. Dressing up for the summer movie showings was traditional; she'd also seen plenty of guys in the classic white linen suit David Paul wore, and even a few dressed in the tangerine bikini Julia wore in the opening title sequence. Claudia was waiting nearby to take Julia home once she'd finished speaking. The scene was set, and Mason could feel a buzz of excitement from her boss and the assembled team. Hopefully, something would happen, but she wasn't sure what that might look like. She was glad she'd made a meeting that afternoon, and spent time talking with her sponsor. She felt ready, and even, she was forced to admit, pretty animated herself. She still had a lump under her hair, but she could live with it.

It was the golden hour, when Los Angeles gets gilded by nature herself. People with blankets and baskets had been lining up for a while, waiting for the doors to open so they could politely but efficiently compete for the best spots. Food trucks and souvenir stalls lined the pathways, and the smell of tacos and pot hung over the patchwork of people and picnics.

Her phone buzzed with a text. Archie. I've got Jason in my sights. I can also see Christine right now and she looks angry, which doesn't mean she is, so no change there. Her new assistant looks worried, so no change there, either.

Mason thumbs-upped.

Next to the Fairbanks mausoleum was a shallow reflecting pool, long and narrow, very beautiful, but also a breeding ground for mosquitoes that were making life difficult for Mason. As the sun went down, the shadows of nearby cypress trees lengthened and stretched across, sectioning the reflections of passing moviegoers like figures on a zoetrope, which was at least consistent with the theme.

Another buzz. Ben. (eyes emoji) Helen and (multiple dog emojis). She's tied them up to the little statue of Toto. Why does that seem appropriate?

Mason thumbs-upped again.

Will's turn. I see Jade. Not wearing the catsuit, so she may live the night. He attached a picture of Jade, who had gone for the bikini, with a long crochet coat she was already wrapping herself in. This is the trouble with building a city in the desert and then irrigating the shit out of it, thought Mason. Everyone forgets that the minute the sun goes down, the heat goes with it.

Julia: Take me off this fucking group chat. Jesus Christ, if my phone doesn't stop tinging every two seconds I'm going to drop it on the floor and stomp it.

Mason grinned.

Archie sent a screen grab of how to turn off notifications, to which Julia merely responded with a middle-finger emoji.

Claudia checked in. Parked on a side street just off Larchmont Boulevard. Going to get coffee and check out the bookstore. Let me know when you're ready for pickup.

The crackling of an audio system, then an unknown voice

started talking. Mason stretched a little and leaned back against the marble.

"Good evening, everyone. Welcome to the summer showing of *The Codex*, always a sold-out choice, and good to see so many people embracing the catsuit this evening." There was good-natured applause, and Mason felt Julia's eyes rolling even if she couldn't see it.

"We're lucky to be joined this evening by Julia Mann, original star and national treasure"—Mason giggled, glad she couldn't see Julia's reaction to that—"and Jason Reed and Jade Solomon, the director and star of the upcoming remake, which—I can confirm here and now—will begin shooting in the spring, right here in Los Angeles."

The crowd seemed to find this delightful. Whooping and cheering erupted.

Mason pushed herself upright and started to move around the mausoleum, wanting to see Julia having her moment. There she was, the movie's title sequence playing on a loop behind her. She looked amazing. Mason hadn't ever seen her smile as broadly as she did for her fans, who were reacting to her appearance as if this was the one moment their lives had been building toward. Julia reached for the microphone, consummate professional that she was.

"Hi, everyone. Long time no see."

Roar of the crowd. Even broader smile.

"Making this movie was some of the best fun of my life, and also some of my darkest days. Bella Horton died accidentally on set, and I want to make sure we never forget her name. I'll say it one more time: Bella Horton. If she hadn't died, she would have been in her sixties now, and probably as pissed about it as I am."

Laughter.

"There's a sequence in the movie where I apparently ride a horse down the steepest part of Mount Hollywood, just below the Griffith Observatory. You'll be shocked to hear that wasn't me. But it was her. She was the most fearless and wonderful woman, and this movie is a tribute to her." She paused. "And speaking of fearless acts, it's just been announced that Tony Eckenridge left a new will that leaves his entire studio and creative assets—including *The Codex*—to his assistant, Cody Malone, so one of the oldest studios in Los Angeles will be run by one of the youngest studio heads ever. Tony loved to take chances, and I'm sure he's looking down on us now, hugely amused." She grinned and waved at the crowd. "Enjoy the film!"

There was big applause from the crowd, but Mason could see Christine's mouth moving. Jason was turning to Julia with a frown on his face.

Things were about to get heated. The only question was what Christine was going to do with this revelation. Would she blow her top and somehow trip herself up, or would she stay as in control as . . .

Suddenly, a sound split the air, making Mason duck involuntarily.

Then another. And another.

Gunfire.

AFTER THE FIRST shot, everyone froze. These days, everyone's quick to assume an active shooter and quicker to realize they didn't make a good plan for this moment. The crowd was broadly split—those that were still saying *Was that a shot?* and the rest saying nothing as they got to their feet and started sprinting for the exit. By the time the echoes of the second shot had died away, the entire mass of people filling the lawn was on the move, the sound of screams and breaking glass rising up like smoke. The movie titles played across people's bodies as they ran, images jumping from shirt to shirt. It was pandemonium, run through with panic, like a river filled with sharp objects.

Mason headed to where she'd last seen Julia but kept getting knocked sideways by the freaked-out crowd. A third shot . . . She stopped and tried desperately to work out where they were coming from. There was so much noise now, the music of the movie, the screams of the crowd, barking of dogs, distant sirens. The bullets were loud and clear, echoes bouncing off the surrounding hills. There was something weird about it, but in all the noise and chaos, Mason couldn't put her finger on it.

She kept trying to make it to the stage. Julia had been *right there*. Suddenly, she saw Christine's assistant Chelsea, crouched under a shrub, her legs folded like a clothes rack.

"Mason! Over here."

Mason tacked through the fleeing crowd. The sirens were getting closer, police and fire. There had been plenty of police here anyway, and suddenly Mason noticed SWAT team members arriving, too.

A fourth shot. People around her were tripping and falling, gathering themselves up and launching themselves forward, heedless. Again, something poked Mason in the brain; something was wrong, or right, about the bullet noises. It wasn't an AK47 or something like that, or there would have been a steady stream of sound. This seemed like a rifle or pistol or something more manual. And the shots were so regular . . . What did it say about the world that Mason was grateful it wasn't an automatic weapon?

She reached Chelsea and crouched down. Chelsea was really under the shrub; it was actually an impressive amount of coverage for a no-warning situation. "Have you seen Julia?"

Chelsea shook her head. "She was right next to me, but when the shooting began she started running." Chelsea pointed back the way Mason had come. "Mason, I lost Christine, but I had eyes on her when the shooting started, so it wasn't her."

Mason slowly turned and looked at Chelsea. "Wait, what . . ."

"Whoops, sorry . . ." Chelsea reached up and pulled off her hair. "I forgot you didn't know."

Becky Sharp.

"Julia suggested I hide in plain sight. That way we could keep an eye on Christine and I could avoid my grandmother." She grinned. "I told you I was a good actress."

Mason just stared. This whole evening was proving challenging. "Alright, we can talk about this later. Where's Jason? Or Helen? I can't see anyone in all this chaos."

Becky shook her head. "No idea. Why haven't they stopped the shooter yet?"

"No idea. But stay here, and stay down."

Becky nodded, strangely calm. "Of course. This isn't my first crowd scene."

Mason stared at her and suddenly realized something. Shots, yes. Panic, yes. But as she stood, turned, and scanned the lawn, she realized what she wasn't hearing and seeing.

No one was down.

No one was wounded.

No ricochet.

No sound of impact.

The sound of each shot was loud and clear, the reverberations even, no distortion. They weren't shooting at anyone. Or anything. They were shooting into the air, like every starter pistol Mason had ever heard. They weren't trying to kill anyone. They were creating panic. Creating a crowd scene.

And like every time she'd ever heard a starter pistol before, Mason started running.

AS SHE CROSSED the lawn at a steady clip, Mason spotted the rest of the team also making their way to the Fairbanks grave, as planned.

But no Julia.

She got to the grave and looked around wildly. Archie was next. Then Ben. And finally Will, out of breath and the most panicked of all.

"I lost her," he said, bending to catch his breath. "She was right there, she was right fucking there, and then the shooting started and she was gone."

"Who?"

"Jade . . ."

Mason's phone had been ringing and ringing, and finally she looked at the screen. Claudia.

She crouched down by the grave, the white marble providing some cover.

"What the ever-loving fuck is going on over there?" Claudia sounded angry. "Julia's on the move, but the rest of you seem to be standing still."

"What do you mean Julia's on the move?"

"I have her location on my phone. Come here. I'm on Van Ness, two blocks down. Hurry up!"

Mason hung up. "Claudia's down the street. Let's go."

Will and Ben shook their heads. "No room in the Shelby. We'll meet you back at the house." Archie nodded, too. "We're right behind you. Run, Mason."

And yet again, Mason started running.

43

~ ~ ~

FLYING DOWN VAN Ness, surrounded by people also moving as fast as they could, Mason took to the street. Down the center, dodging cops and firemen running in the other direction, searching for Claudia. There. Pulled to one side, engine running, passenger door already open and slightly ajar.

"Hit it." She dropped into the passenger seat, and then lifted her ass to remove the phone she'd just sat on.

Claudia pulled away, moving slowly through the crowd, dodging around emergency services, getting to Melrose and turning right. It was chaos.

"What happened?" Claudia was tight as a drum. Mason could feel her tension filling the car.

"Someone started shooting, but honestly, I think they were just shooting into the air. No one seemed to get hit. The sound was . . ." Mason shook her head. "I think it was to cause a distraction, to make everyone panic." She looked at Claudia. "How do you know Julia's on the move?"

Claudia tipped her head. "Snap Maps. I started doing it

when she picked up booze again, just to make sure I could find her if she got too drunk to remember I existed."

Mason looked at the phone. "You have Snapchat?"

Claudia overtook on the wrong side of the street and narrowly avoided a bus. "Sure. I can add you if you like. I have all the rest of the team, too. See?"

Three police cars and another fire engine passed them as Claudia pulled over impatiently.

Mason frowned. "Julia's heading home. Why? Who is she with?" She noticed Archie, Will and Ben were also all on the move, though they weren't as close behind them as she would have liked. "How is she so far ahead of us? And why is her Bitmoji so incredibly accurate?"

Claudia shook her head. "She started moving as soon as the shooting began. That wasn't the plan, obviously, so I called her, she didn't answer, and then suddenly there were sirens and panic and I stopped calling and got as close as I could." She sped up, nipping in and out of traffic, steady but fast. "I perfected her Bitmoji one day when I was bored. Thanks for noticing. Where is she now?"

Mason looked at the Snap Map, at the tiny, well-dressed, cross-looking Julia. "She's just below Sunset . . . She's definitely heading home." She felt nauseous, worried. "We were all there. How did we lose her?"

Claudia shrugged. "If Julia wants to get lost, there's nothing you can do. Maybe she just had enough and left." But there was a tremble in her voice. "But why wouldn't she call me to drive her home? We had a plan."

A cop car sped past heading back toward the cemetery. Mason went online and checked social media. Live reports said the shooting was ongoing, warned people to stay away. But nothing else.

"What the actual fuck is going on?" Mason was confused. "Did you try calling her again?"

Claudia nodded. "Several times, but go ahead."

They'd reached Crescent Heights, and Claudia turned right, heading up toward the canyon. Traffic was heavy: Saturday night at nine, warm summer night, the city was alive and on the move.

"Straight to voicemail." Mason hung up. "Should I call the cops?"

"Why? Because she Ubered home?"

"Claudia . . . she didn't Uber home. Something's wrong."

Claudia said nothing, but her face tightened.

Mason texted Archie, although she could see his Bitmoji and Will's were together, and presumably they had Ben with them.

When did you lose sight of Julia?

They'd finally reached the top of Crescent Heights, the long north-heading road that winds up through Hollywood and ends at Laurel Canyon. Waiting at the light, Claudia held the car with the clutch, balanced and ready to go. As the light changed, she hit the gas, and by the time they'd crossed Sunset, she was doing eighty.

"She's home," said Mason, watching the little Bitmoji. "Maybe she's alone."

"Maybe," replied Claudia, watching the road.

Mason's phone pinged. Will had replied. Archie's driving. He says she waved at the crowd, she hugged Jason and Jade, then she stepped off the stage and he didn't see her again. He's sorry. Sad-face emoji.

Mason typed, She's home now, but I don't like it. See you there.

Right behind you.

Mason held on to the door handle as Claudia shot up and around the curves of the canyon. She hit the drive to the house at nearly a hundred, passing the gateposts in a cloud of dust that sparkled in the headlights. It seemed like the sun was still setting up here, the darkness not complete, orange and yellow in the sky.

"What . . ." Mason sat up in her seat as they got closer. "What's that?"

"Fuck," said Claudia. "Call 911, Mason, call now."

The house was on fire.

MASON HIT THE front door at a full run, discovering as she did so that the fucking thing was locked. Picking herself up, she turned and found Claudia fumbling in her pocket for the keys.

No dice.

"Dead bolt," said Claudia, heading around to the side at a sprint. She had her phone in her hand, and Mason could hear the emergency services operator asking for the address. Claudia started shouting it as she and Mason got to the back door and found that locked and bolted, too.

"Mason, look!"

Phil the cat was outside in the garden, blown up to twice his size and not happy about any of this bullshit, no sir. Claudia went to grab him, but he took off.

"Leave him," said Mason. "He's a tough cookie. He'll find a place to wait it out."

Lorre was the next to appear, barking hysterically and running back and forth. This new place wasn't working out as well as he had hoped, *not at all*.

They ran around to the front again, the dog at their heels, and Mason started to hear sirens in the distance. She also saw Will's car coming down the drive. The fire was in the living room wing, and when Mason picked up the biggest rock she could find and went to throw it through the window, Claudia stopped her. "No . . . you'll just feed the fire. We can get in through the utility room."

"The what?"

"Under the house . . ." Claudia scrambled down the hill by the pool deck and Mason followed. "Look . . ."

Under the cantilevered part of the house was a basement Mason hadn't even known existed. No door, but a window, and a rock and desperation got it broken. Mason smashed away all the glass. She took off her jacket and laid it over the frame, lifting herself up and in. "Go back to the front door. I'll come open it."

Claudia looked up at her. "Mason. Just find Julia. The fire service will be here any minute. They'll take care of the door."

Mason nodded and dropped to the floor. She looked around quickly, washing machine, dryer, the boiler . . . and a door to stairs leading up to the kitchen.

The kitchen was eerily quiet, and when Mason flicked the light switch nothing happened. No power.

There wasn't much smoke in the kitchen, but when she opened the door to the hallway it hit her like a fist. She turned back, closing the door, and wet a couple of dish towels, putting one over her mouth and nose. Back into the hallway, everything dark as hell, the smoke building, the heat from the fire palpable. Every minute, every second counted.

Mason started calling Julia, keeping as low as she could as she reached the door to the living room. Putting her hand on it, feeling the heat, knowing she should turn back, but unable to. Taking a deep a breath, she opened the door.

Everything in the room was on fire. The egg chair. The sofa. The coffee table. All blazing. As Mason opened the door, the change of air pressure caused everything to flare up, and she could only stand in the doorway for a few seconds before the heat pushed her back. But it was enough time to know Julia wasn't there.

As she started to close the door, there was a terrifying cracking sound and the glass wall at the front of the house shattered into a million pieces. The fire exulted and doubled as the oxygen poured in. The whole room became a flame, and Mason slammed the door and started running blindly to the office.

She could hear sirens now, getting closer, could hear pounding on the front door.

She touched the office door. Cool. No fire here. She opened the door and stepped inside.

Two steps in, she stopped dead and slowly raised her hands, dropping the wet towel.

Julia, unconscious on the sofa. Jade, the same, on the floor. Helen Eckenridge, standing in the middle of the room, pointing a gun at Julia's head.

"She won't feel it," said Helen. "But if you take another step, I'm going to shoot your boss, then you, then the little idiot. Totally your call."

Mason felt her blood run cold as she read the remorseless madness on Helen's face. Sirens so close now. On the driveway, if not actually in front of the house. Would they get here in time?

"There are going to be firemen here any minute, Helen. Whatever this is, you kind of screwed it up."

Helen laughed. "It's so typical. Every fucking time. I get so close and then it all goes to shit." The gun wavered in her hand, and for a second she pointed it at her own head, the muzzle tight against her temple. "I had so much to offer, so many ideas, so much talent, and it was all pointless."

The smoke was filtering under the door in cloudy billows as Mason started moving, and the gun immediately moved, too, back to pointing at Julia's head, then Jade's, then back to Julia. Mason grew still. She hadn't had a boss or a sponsee shot out from under her yet, and today was not going to be that day.

Helen kept talking. "From the minute I met Tony, he told me he was going to help me, going to build my career. But instead we would just talk and talk, and he would take my ideas and use them, and even after the Oscar, he never wanted me to compete with him. I wanted it so much, and he kept promising. The next feature. The next one."

Mason nodded. "Frustrating. Let's go outside, Helen. I want to hear it, but let's talk outside. It's going to get very hot in here."

Helen shook her head. "No. Listen. I did a feature for another studio, and he was so angry . . . he got involved and it went badly and everyone blamed me. I didn't get another chance for a very long time." She frowned, waving the gun. "Do you know if a male director messes up they just chalk it up as experience and he gets another chance? ... When a female director messes up she goes into movie jail for-fucking-ever."

"That's what this is about? Your career?" Mason couldn't help sounding incredulous. "You killed Tony over movies?" She could feel her throat tightening.

"You don't get it." Helen coughed. On the sofa, Julia stirred and started to turn over. "I had so many ideas. Wrote so many scripts. Tried so fucking hard. And he was all promises, *you can do the next one*, all the meetings where everyone smiled and said great, fantastic, incredible ... then nothing. Or where some studio executive suggested a little more personal treatment might get the project rolling . . ." She waved the gun again. Mason risked another glance at Julia; she was still so very quiet.

"I get nowhere, while male directors younger than me and dumb as bricks get projects and opportunities I should have had ... then Me Too happened and suddenly everyone wants female directors but not me because I'm too old . . . not relevant ... not current." She laughed. "Then, finally, *finally* Tony agrees to remake *Codex*, my movie, the movie I wrote when he was too busy getting high, when I was young enough but still, sadly, too fucking female"—Helen laughed—"and then we have lunch and he tells me Jason Reed wants another writer. Someone more ..." She choked up, unable to finish her sentence. The smoke was getting thicker. Mason could hear axes on the front door.

But the gun never wavered. Julia wasn't moving.

Mason frowned. "He wasn't leaving you the rights?"

"No. Because it was better for the studio. He looks at me over his damn Waldorf salad and says he's going to leave the studio to Christine and the kid and the rights to *Codex* with it. Easier, he says, simpler. The studio will control it all. Then he has the balls to smile at me and remind me the more successful the movie is, the better it is for me. Money wise. Like I give a shit about the money. He said he was going to meet with his lawyer soon, change his will."

Mason could hear the hiss and rush of water under pressure. The sound of glass contracting and breaking.

Helen was oblivious. "Do you know what it's like to have a dream and get it stepped on, over and over and over again? Executives wanting to touch my tits, openly asking for blow jobs because no one ever said no to them . . ." She stopped and tried to take a breath. "The things I did. The things they did to me. They promised and never delivered. And then Tony took away the one thing I thought was certain. And I was done with broken promises."

She shrugged. "I had to stop him and it had to be quick. I went to the shelter and got fentanyl. I was going to poison him . . . but then I saw him leaving his house, and I followed him here and I suddenly had this brilliant idea—the curse." She looked, wide-eyed, at Mason. "Good directors control, great directors *improvise*, they make the most of serendipity, a change in the light, an unexpected opportunity. Once I saw him and Julia together, I realized I could stir up the curse, make publicity for the film, nothing better than free advertising . . . he taught me that. I had some of his props in the car, taking them to the museum, including the rifle. I learned to shoot when I was a stuntwoman. I got him on the first try.

"I used another for tonight's little party, set up a nice little rig, with a timer, shots in the air. No one gets hurt, but oh, so much press . . . But then Julia said it was all going to Cody, to the fucking sandwich delivery boy, and I lost it. I pulled a gun on Julia once the movie started and was going to kill her then and there, but Jade, of all people, stepped up to protect her and I had to take them both. What better ending to the whole thing than both stars dying at once, in a highly cinematic house fire? People will be watching this place burn from everywhere in the city. You can see it from Downtown to Hollywood . . ." She started to laugh and cry at the same time, the gun veering from Julia, to Jade, to her own head. "The footage is going to be incredible."

Mason suddenly noticed Julia was moving. Her head still down, but her hand inching toward . . . the remote.

"Helen," she said, keeping the woman's attention on her, the gun still pointing at Julia, "men suck. The movie business sucks. They both suck much harder if you're a woman, I get that. But right now we should put down the gun and go out . . ."

In one fluid movement, Julia sat up, took aim and threw the remote. As it hit Helen precisely in the nose, Mason leapt forward and tackled the woman to the ground, the gun skittering across the floor. As she lay there, she wondered for the twentieth time how much practice Julia had had throwing the remote, and then was just grateful for it.

The doors flew open and two firemen burst in.

"Hello, boys," said Julia, standing up in her leather catsuit, weaving a little and holding her head. "I don't suppose either of you brought any scotch, did you? I could really use a fucking drink."

44

~~~~

JULIA, MASON, ARCHIE and Will were sitting around the pool, watching the firemen break down the remaining hot spots, kicking over the traces of the living room. It was mid-morning the following day, and only a small team of firemen remained, presumably those who'd pissed off someone else and got the sticky end of the cleanup jobs. Because the house was in wings, they'd been able to save the office, the kitchen and the guest quarters without much trouble. But the living room was toast. Burnt toast. The curved frame of the egg chair poked up from a pile of ash, the corner of a picture frame here, a fragment of charred cushion there. Julia hadn't really reacted yet, but it had to hurt.

The cops had shown up shortly after the firemen, taking Helen into custody and trying pretty hard to take Mason along with her. Come answer questions, they said; it won't take long, they said . . . but Mason climbed into the ambulance with Jade and Julia and that was that.

Now, as the sun rose with little enthusiasm and even less fanfare, it gilded the edges of the tray Claudia was carrying across the pool deck.

"How is that even possible?" Will rose to take the tray from her. "There's no power, you can't cook, everything smells of smoke, you're not even supposed to go into the house . . ."

Claudia grinned at him. "I went out for it. I just popped into the kitchen for the plates and things . . . I've walked through hazard tape before." She put down the tray and everyone helped themselves. Coffee. Croissants. Breakfast burritos with Tater Tots.

For a while, the team munched in silence.

Julia was wrapped in a blanket, half curled on a lounger, regarding her house with an unreadable expression.

Then she spoke. "Alright. I think I finally have it straight. That whack on the head seems to have jogged my amygdala—is that the part you mentioned, Will? I can remember the night Tony came over now."

"No, the hippocampus. The amygdala is also a fascinating part of the brain: It's very small, but totally essential for emotional processing . . ."

"Sure, that's great. Moving on. I woke up after the knock on the block with a pretty clear recall of the evening with Tony, at least the early parts of the conversation. He wanted to apologize for not bringing up the tense relationship between Mikey Agosti and Jonathan at the trial, and explained that Agosti had assured him that if he told the cops anything at all that suggested a connection between the Mob and Jonathan's death, they would destroy the studio. Tony wanted me to see the film, I think, so I could see what I hadn't known about at the time, but I'm not sure how helpful it was . . . It doesn't prove anything; it's just suggestive." She sighed. "I think the Mob also threatened Tony personally, but he glossed over that piece. He said he should have stepped up, and could have done so recently, too, once Mikey died, but by then I'd already done the time and he wasn't sure I even gave a shit. He was right about that—I didn't—but his doctors had given him months to live, and he was determined to deliver the film to the cops along with a statement about everything Mikey had done and said back then. I started to panic, thinking about the case opening up again, another potential trial, more exposure . . ." She sighed. "So I drank. It was a stupid reason to pick up, but it's the reason my disease presented me with and I ran with it."

"Remember," said Mason, sagely, "the disease wants you dead, but it'll settle for maimed."

"Again, your love of the clichés of the program is a mixture of endearing and horrifying. Let's keep going." Julia stared off into space for a moment. "And once I was drinking, Tony pressed home his advantage and got me to agree to be in the *Codex* remake, too. I remember him calling Christine in triumph. I thought it was hilarious. He also explained he was taking the rights back from Helen because she was worrying him."

"In what way?"

"In a way that suggested she was obsessive and insane about it, presumably, which was borne out by the fact that she killed him over that very thing not an hour later. No one ever said Tony wasn't a good judge of character."

"Good point," conceded Mason.

"I still have questions," said Will. "Why did Helen kill Sam? She did kill Sam, right?"

"Yes." Julia sighed. "Tony must have gone over to Galliano's after the board meeting, drawn up a new will and had Sam and Becky witness it. It was one of his safest places, right? He knew Maggie would keep the will safe for him, and he left it in the book as one of his funny gestures. But Sam was ambitious and she knew what losing creative rights would do to Helen. Becky said she always had a plan, and in this case Sam went to Helen and said she would destroy the new will, no worries, she just wanted a chance to break in. And Helen said yes, she knew what it was like not to get a break, that she'd come over to discuss it . . . and she killed her. She didn't know Becky was passed out behind the bar, or we'd have lost Becky, too."

"So it was Helen who broke in here? Looking for the will?"

"Yes. When she couldn't find it at the club, she thought maybe he'd given it to me."

Mason was confused. "How do you know all this?"

Julia smiled. "I asked her on the drive away from Cinespia, and she was only too happy to explain. In detail. Directors love to explain how they did things. They're like Bond villains that way."

"And the attack on Cody?"

"Helen was already on the lot, signed in to work on another project, sitting in a writer's room all day and into the night. Maybe she thought she'd get the job of director if someone else had to run the project. She was closer to Christine; maybe she thought she'd be persuadable. She stopped by the offices, walloped poor Cody—who she hated because he'd gotten chances and opportunities she never had—and then tossed a load of innocent fish around."

"Yeah, I thought she was such an animal lover."

Julia laughed. "Oh, she is. She let Phil and Lorre out before she torched the house, didn't she? But she's also a director. Did you notice how quickly the media grabbed that fact and ran with it? Ten thousand dollars' worth of tropical fish . . . a little grace note, a little detail, the kind of thing that provides a lovely hook for continued coverage." She sighed and picked a Tater Tot out of her burrito and ate it. "No one ever said Helen didn't have talent; she just didn't get an opportunity. Thwarted passion, frustrated desire . . . these aren't things women only feel for romantic partners, though the movies would have you think so. Remember that woman who wore adult diapers so she could drive cross-country to kill her lover's wife? That makes sense to us, right? We're used to that idea. But a woman who wants to succeed artistically, professionally? Of course a man has a drive for power, has ambition. But we limit women's motivations along with their agency. It's fucked up. Helen loved her work, loved it deeply, and when she couldn't express it, she slowly went mad. Tony taking the rights was the last straw, and when he told her at their final lunch, she decided she had to kill him before he had a chance to change his will. She just didn't realize he would do it so quickly."

"What about the attack on you? Or me? Or Maggie?"

"She hired actors for me and Maggie. She told them she was filming live auditions for the *Codex* remake, that there would be hidden cameras. I imagine they were both quite confused by the responses they got, but actors learn to improvise, too, so I guess they just went with it."

Mason remembered the headshots on Helen's kitchen counter, and the guy who'd said he was living the dream. "And the attack on me?" Mason felt her jaw gently. "It still hurts."

"Yeah, that was actually Helen. Ex-stuntwoman, remember? She wanted us to stop poking around, because she needed to find the will before we did. And it was all grist to the media mill; the press leapt on it immediately, right?"

"Why did she kidnap you and Jade?"

"Because when I announced that everything was going to Cody, she flipped the fuck out. She never saw the new will. She didn't know it wasn't true. And when she pulled a gun on me, little Jade saw her and intervened." Julia grinned. "I have to hand it to her, she's got balls of steel. Or a complete disregard for her own life."

"And Helen explained all this to you?"

Julia nodded. "She was full of chatter last night, chatter and an unhealthy level of obsession. But she's being quiet now, on her lawyer's advice."

Silence.

Mason said, "Julia, who's her lawyer?"

"Well, for now it's me." She looked out over the city. "I have a lot of sympathy for Helen, I'm not going to lie. Hollywood is an evil pit of venom and bile for women, and for women of her age it's particularly acidic. Tony dug his own grave with her. I wanted to kill him myself, dozens of times."

Mason shook her head. "I don't understand you at all."

"I should hope not. Well above your pay grade."

Her phone rang and she put it on speaker.

"Baby!" It was Larry. "I heard you got your tootsies singed—the press is going insane! Helen lost her mind! Jade is a hero! You're an icon! The phone's been ringing off the hook and I've gotten five offers already this morning . . ."

Julia hung up.

A car trundled up the driveway, and Becky and Ben got out of it, along with their grandmother.

Julia muttered, "Well, will you look at that? Witch shows up late for the burning." She raised her voice. "Mrs. Jones, how nice of you to come and check out my ash."

Ben laughed. "We're actually just here to say thanks and grab our stuff."

Grandma said, "I saw in the paper they arrested someone for the murder of that stripper, so I'll be taking these two back to Oregon."

Ben smiled and shook his head. "I'm coming home, Grandma, but Becky's going to stay here and go to school."

"To learn what? Advanced stripping and messing up?"

Julia put down her coffee cup and stretched under her blanket. "Listen up, you old crone. Until last night, Becky thought you killed her girlfriend. That's not something you should be proud of, that she thinks you're capable of that."

Anna Jones turned to her granddaughter. "You did? Why?"

Becky kept her face down. "Because you were there, Grandma."

Ben was shocked. "You were? She was? How?"

There was a little pause, then Anna sighed. "It's true. I went there. I showed up at that club, or whatever you call it, after it had closed. She was there, with that girl." She turned to Ben. "She texted you. I saw it on your phone months ago. She said what she was doing, where she was doing it. I prayed for her, but then I remembered that faith without works is dead, so I decided to come and get her." She had the decency to look ashamed. "I told you I was at Bible Study and I drove down."

Ben was shocked. "Grandma, you lied?"

Mason thought about Larissa . . . not *blond* hair under the neon lights . . . *gray* hair.

Anna got defensive. "I waited until all the people had gone, but I never saw Becky come out. So I went in. Into the lion's den, like Daniel, hoping to persuade her to give up her wicked ways. But it was worse than I thought: She'd become a deviant."

Becky made a noise, but said nothing.

"Neither of them would listen to reason, or to the Scripture. Eventually, Becky went to get yet another drink from behind the bar and passed out on the floor. It was degenerate. And then that girl had the nerve to say she loved Becky, and things were going to get better for them, that she was going to have a real job soon. I told her she was going to burn in hell and left. I prayed all night for both of them, as I drove back to Oregon, and God took care of it, because the next day I saw that she had been killed." She shrugged. "The wages of sin are death."

Becky spoke, her voice sad. "I guess I was passed out behind the bar for quite a bit, because when I woke up Sam was dead, the barman had called the cops, and I decided not to mention Grandma to anyone. Helen must have come while I was unconscious and hadn't seen me because I was behind the bar. No one else had seen Grandma, and I didn't think I would get convicted of a crime I didn't commit."

Julia growled, "It has happened."

Becky looked at her. "I know that now."

Mason was still a little ticked at Becky. "How come you didn't mention the will? You witnessed it. You must have read it." Even as she said it she realized how dumb she sounded.

"I didn't read it. Was that what that was? Sam just said we were going to go on vacation. To Cabo." Becky looked disconsolate. "I've never been to Cabo."

Ben reached over and took her hand. "We can go to Cabo sometime, Becky. I'm going back to work, but we'll keep in touch this time, right?"

Becky nodded. "Yeah, I promise."

Julia said, "You can stay here until you're sorted out, of course. It's going to take a week or more for the smell of smoke to dissipate, but we'll get there."

"Thank you, Mrs. Mann."

"Call me Julia. You can have Mason's room."

Mason felt a little stab, but said smoothly, "Yeah, I'll be taking my cat and going home today."

"No, you won't." Julia was surprised. "You're moving into one of the guesthouses." She turned to Claudia. "It's ready, right?"

Claudia shook her head. "Not even close. You only told me to sort it out a couple of days ago, the fucking house got torched last night—what do you think I am, a miracle worker?"

"Yes."

Claudia sniffed. "Well, you're wrong. Besides, I thought she might like to pick her own colors."

Mason was incredulous. "Hey, I'm sitting right here, and there is no way I am moving in. I appreciate your hospitality, and I'm not denying the appeal of eating Claudia's cooking every day, but I like my apartment, and boundaries are important."

"Sure, but I want you inside my physical boundary. Besides, I need you; this whole debacle has been great for business. We have three client meetings lined up for next week." Julia waved her hand at the house. "And look at this mess. I need help."

"No." Mason was getting irritated. "I am a grown-ass woman and I choose what I do. I got the shit beaten out of me, I took part in a car chase, I watched a man shoot his head off and I nearly got killed. I don't want this job."

Julia got to her feet and shook out her blanket. She turned and stared at Mason, folding her arms. "Look, instead of sullenly wandering around waiting for that haircut to come back into fashion, you'll spend every day saving terrified, helpless people from perfidious inequity."

Mason stood up, too, to even the playing field. "You can use whatever fifty-cent words you want to, Julia, but I'm not doing it."

Julia thought for a moment. "You can go back to school and finish your law degree. Then you can become a private investigator. I'll pay the tuition."

Mason frowned. "I'll think about it."

"You can see Archie all the time."

Everyone turned and looked at Archie, who looked surprised and a little bit pleased.

Mason blushed. "I said I'll think about it."

Julia shook her head. "Don't. It'll just confuse you. Besides, I'll treble your salary, let you live rent free in my guesthouse and make every day a fun-filled cavalcade of danger and opportunity."

"I'll help," said Will.

"I'll feed you," added Claudia.

"And besides," added Julia, "I like you. Despite your truculent attitude and reactionary lack of fashion sense, you're bold, smart and funny. You make me want to laugh. Not out loud, obviously, but inwardly. Which is more than most people. You saved my life, and you keep me focused on staying sober, which is like saving my life, each and every day. I think you'll add enormously to our team. Please say yes."

Mason stared at her. Actually, everyone stared at her.

"Well, if you put it that way." Mason suddenly changed her

mind, in the way she so often lived to regret. "Why not. I'll try it." She turned away, to hide the tears that had suddenly started tickling her eyelids. She realized she liked Julia, too—liked all of them in fact—and had felt more useful and engaged in the last two weeks than in the last two years. No need to let them see that, though. Tough cookie, all the way.

"That's my girl," said Julia, rewrapping herself in the blanket. "And I mean that literally."

Epilogue

~~~

A WEEK LATER, Claudia and Mason were standing in the guesthouse, which was set a little up the hill behind the main house. Mason privately thought it was maybe the nicest house she'd ever been in, guest or otherwise, but she did her best to maintain her cool. No one was fooled, but it didn't matter.

Downstairs was one big open room, with a fireplace at one end, and a small kitchen at the other. One wall had French doors that opened onto a narrow patio and the path down to the main house. Upstairs were two bedrooms and a bathroom bigger than Mason's old apartment. A claw-foot bathtub was big enough for her to float in, or would be once they'd finished cleaning up and repainting. Mason insisted on doing the work herself, and despite Julia sulking about it for two days, eventually she'd won that argument.

Now she was scrubbing the kitchen floor, as she and Claudia discussed where to put in a cat door for Phil. The cat in question was sitting on the spiral staircase that led upstairs, which he thought was a structure specifically created for him.

Suddenly, they heard Julia's dulcet tones from somewhere

outside. "Where the fuck is everyone? Why is no one here when I need them? You're all fired!"

Sighing, Mason tossed her brush in the bucket of warm soapy water, and they headed out to see what the songbird wanted. Down the hill, Mason could see laborers starting work on the reframing of the living room wing, the architect standing there clutching her hair. It was going to take a while, but it was happening.

Julia was standing on the path, a red filing box in her arms, a letter in her hand. She was as furious as Mason had ever seen her, and the younger woman stopped a safe distance away. Claudia had more experience, and just kept walking.

"What's up?"

Julia waved the letter. "This just came from Patty! It was supposed to come to me but went to the museum instead. Read this shit! Even dead that bastard annoys the crap out of me. Pull the car around, Mason. We're going to dig him up and stomp on his decomposing nuts. I mean it. Any car will do. We'll have to stop for a shovel, but we're doing it."

Claudia calmly took the note and read it out loud:

"*Dear Julia*," it began, "*If you're reading this, then I'm dead already, which is something I've always wanted to say. I'm heading to your place now to give you some film that might help you find out who really killed Jonathan. I also want to explain in person why I'm not leaving you any of the studio. I'm scared you'll donate it to a home for old donkeys or something. That would be like you. This letter is in case you refuse to see me, which would also be like you. In this box you'll find documents that I hope you'll use to clear up Jonathan's death. I was too much of a coward to give them to the lawyers back then, too scared to lose everything both he and I had worked for. Too scared, also, of the people I think killed him. You'll see in the video—Mikey Agosti was an investor in the studio and had a lot of power. I don't think he killed Jonathan himself, but I suspect the two men in the film with him were somehow involved. I don't know for sure, but I know the police didn't look as hard as maybe they should have. Their names were Don and Lucio, but I never knew their last names. They're still out there, and they still don't want to pay for what they did. But now I'm too dead for them to kill, and you're too tough for fear, always have been. Go talk to Jack Simon, in Palm Springs. He might have more information you can use to clear your name. I love you. I always have. Yours, Tony."*

Claudia looked up and made a face at Julia. "You want to clear your name?"

"No! I already went to jail. They can't give me back the time! I'm burning it all!" Julia was spitting mad. "It's all over and done with, I couldn't give less of a flying dog's fuck about it." She turned and stomped away. "Go get the car. I'm not kidding. I'll dig him up myself if I have to. Cocksucker!" She disappeared into the house, still cursing.

Mason opened the document box. She could see diaries, photos, letters. She looked at Claudia, who looked worried.

"Burn it, Mason. No good can come of it. It's just ghost stories."

Mason shook her head. "We'll see."

Julia appeared again, wearing a pale pink coat that was wholly inappropriate for digging in the mud. Mason sighed and turned back to the guesthouse. "I'd better go put on my boots," she said, "and find a shovel."

Acknowledgments

This book was over a decade in creation, and it's with enormous relief that I can now thank the many people who made it possible. To Shana Eddy and Jason Reed, who were the earliest supporters of these characters, thanks for your patience and steadfast confidence. To my editor, Kate Seaver, thanks for putting up with all my pressure to let Mason and Mann come out before they were ready, and to my agent, Alexandra Machinist, thanks for encouraging me to let them out when the time was right. To Semi Chellas, thanks for weeks of work helping me fine-tune the plot and making it soooo much better than I could have alone; I will never be able to thank you enough. And finally, to my mother, herself a mystery writer, who brought me up on Nero Wolfe and Miss Marple and made me the mystery lover I still am. It all started with you, and I love you so much.

ONE DEATH AT A TIME

Abbi Waxman

Discussion Questions

1. When Natasha Mason and Julia Mann first meet, Mason feels drawn to Julia, despite her prickliness. What do you think Mason recognizes in Julia that makes her feel that way?

2. Julia's office is very important to her, containing everything she needs to do her work—what impact does physical space have on your own work and life? How important is it to have "a room of your own"?

3. Claudia, Julia's housekeeper, is clearly very fond of Julia, but they have a somewhat prickly relationship. Discuss the relationship between the two women, and the different ways they have for showing love for each other. Is their dynamic similar to any relationships in your life?

4. When we meet Will Maier, he is clearly a man with a wide range of passions and interests. How do his intense curiosity and slightly quirky intelligence help Mason and Julia?

5. The police decide to arrest Julia because she has means, motive and opportunity, which makes sense. But how much does her previous conviction for murder play into their thinking, and how does prejudice make it difficult for people to overcome their past?

6. When Mason and Julia visit Galliano's, Mason is surprised by Maggie Galliano. In what ways does Maggie go against traditional stereotypes of women working in a burlesque club?

7. In what ways does the movie business discriminate against women, and in what ways does it perpetuate stereotypes that make it difficult for women to compete professionally?

8. Los Angeles itself plays a big role in the novel. Mason and Julia have very different relationships to the city. In what ways are those expressed in the book?

9. When Mason and Julia travel to Palm Springs, we see how Julia's acting ability can be helpful in solving problems. What role does "pretending" play in the novel?

10. Sobriety is important for both Mason and Julia, although they are at different points in their recovery journey. How does active participation in a twelve-step program impact the way they go about their work?

Photo by Leanna Creel

ABBI WAXMAN, the *USA Today* bestselling author of *One Death at a Time, Christa Comes Out of Her Shell, Adult Assembly Required, I Was Told It Would Get Easier, The Bookish Life of Nina Hill, Other People's Houses,* and *The Garden of Small Beginnings,* is a chocolate-loving, dog-loving woman who lies down as much as possible. She worked in advertising for many years, which is how she learned to write fiction. She lives in Los Angeles, California, with her three children, three dogs, and three cats.

Ready to find
your next great read?

Let us help.

Visit prh.com/nextread

Penguin
Random
House